The

Rogue River

Incident

Case XI

Book I

Mike Walters

The Rogue River Incident is
a new edition of the Outlaw River Wilde
originally published in March 2015. There
is a new cover, title, prologue, and various
changes and edits throughout the novel.
Thanks for reading.

Self Reliant Press

Self Reliant Press

Featuring Indie Authors

When you finish this novel, please take a moment and write a review on Amazon, Goodreads, Kobo, iBooks, Nook, or the platform on which you purchased it. An independent author's best friend is a thoughtful review.

For my talented son, Alexander,
whose empathetic and kind spirit
inspires me every day to be
a better human being.

Prologue

May 24, 1949

NICAP[1]

During the afternoon of May 24, 1950 (sic), five people, three men and two women, were fishing in a boat near the mouth of Oregon's Rogue River At about 5:00 P.M., they were scanning the river with 8x Navy binoculars looking for signs of jumping fish, when they first noticed a strange circular object approaching from the northeast. They watched it for about two-and-a-half minutes as it hovered east of them before it departed at high speed in a southward direction. The sky was clear, and the afternoon sun was at their backs. To the naked eye, it appeared shiny and shaped like a coin with the flat surface parallel to the ground. At its closest it seemed to be only a couple of miles away and about a mile high. They heard no noise.

Two of the witnesses, a draftsman and a wind-tunnel mechanic, were employees of the Ames Research Laboratory at Moffett Field, south of San Francisco. * These two men shared the binoculars and had about a minute to look at the object. What the men observed was circular and thin relative to its diameter, with a shape like that of a pancake, and with some sort of vertical fin on the upper surface at the trailing edge. They could see no wings, no antenna, no lights, no propellers, and no jet engines. According to the AFOSI report: they saw it speed off in a southeasterly direction, "accelerating to the approximate speed of a jet plane" in a few seconds without making any noise. About three weeks later the Ames employees reported their sighting to the security office at Moffett Field. The security office then requested that AFOSI agents investigate the sighting. They determined the witnesses to be credible and could not explain the incident.

Fast forward to today---It's Happening Again. What follows in Case XI is a retelling of present-day events by Rogue River residents.

7

Chapter 1

The Sounds of the Pacific

Mitch Wilde pedaled the river trail intent on keeping his heart rate up. Looking down at his feet in their push and pull rhythmic rotation he admired his calves with their sinewy muscles as they reflexively responded to his brain's command. Raising his head, his eyes focused on the path ahead, ignoring the acidic throat and burning sensation in his lungs. Control your breathing, relax, Mitch's brain reminded him as he rode harder than normal this morning. Today his legs intertwined with the carbon-framed bike like it was an extension of his body. Ironic, since the first mile, he'd wanted to turn back and go home at least half a dozen times. Escaping the garage his legs felt slug-like, unwilling to respond. Mitch knew they always took about a mile to loosen up, so he kept rolling.

Glancing at his cell phone in the handlebar cradle, Mitch slowed his pace. The fitness app showed almost nine miles. One more to go. This location on the river trail was one of his favorite spots with its serene views. The trail, packed firm for a smooth ride, held a slight downward grade, a little wider than the rest of the path. Mitch placed an index finger on each brake lever in anticipation for the sharp bend in the path ahead. He couldn't afford a serious wreck, knowing his body wouldn't heal very fast as he approached age fifty.

Irritated with the way his helmet sat on his head, he slowed, reaching up – a mistake. He should have just stopped. Off to the right, his brain registered something as it flashed in front of him, tore the fabric of his shirt, stinging his shoulder. It distracted Mitch for a nanosecond as his front tire caught a tree root and then stuck in a small rut in the compacted clay soil. He broke one of his biking rules—pulling solely on the left brake lever, which controlled the front brakes. The front wheel locked for a fraction of a second. An eternity in bicycle time.

"Shit", Wilde blurted, mentally preparing for a wreck. All he could do now, try to minimize the impending fall. The whole incident lasted seconds at most but played like a slow-motion movie in his mind. Wrecking more than a few times over the years taught him the art of the fall. He'd developed more deliberate and attentive riding. Not attentive enough this time, however. What in the world flew by him?

Landing on his right side with the bike on top, Mitch lay on the ground laughing in relief that he hadn't been hurt. Breaking his right foot free of the pedal attached to the shoe cleat, he pushed the bike off and sat upright as he brushed off his right side, checked the phone for damage, found none, and paused the tracking app.

Pissed he wrecked, but not too much, realizing something had hit him. But what? Investigating his condition, he heard an unusual noise across the river. It sounded like a horse. Odd, since he'd never seen a horse on this part of the trail. Mitch peered through the bushes.

There, across the river downstream on the opposite bank, was a horse. Next to it stood a large figure. The unknown river visitor was too far away to tell much, but it appeared to be a man who stared directly at him. Mitch turned and looked over his shoulder feeling a presence behind him. Nothing but empty woods and an occasional varmint. Mitch took his cell phone and turned on the camera app. He positioned the cell phone, but even with the pinch zoom maxed out, the bodies were too small. Frustrated, he turned off the app and watched the riverbank's stranger another couple of minutes. At least now, he could tell it was a man with the horse. The duo left the river shore, retreating into the woods.

Mitch plopped his ass back down on the hard, cold soil. Resting his head against a tree, swallowing hard, he wished the water bottle in the bicycle cage were closer. Looking across the river again, he saw nothing but an empty bank and meadow. With no easy way across the river and so no way to investigate, hell, did he even want to he sighed? Wiping the sweat from his forehead with the back of his hand, he shook his wrist and reached for the bike. As he placed the cell phone in its cradle, a low thud and a sting followed a loud whoosh near his left shoulder. Spinning toward the tree, he looked across the river, seeing nothing in either place.

Mitch touched his shoulder and found a small tear in his shirt. His mind replayed the morning's ride: no recollection of hitting a twig or branch, and the shoulder didn't hit the ground during the crash. His shoulder stung from a slight cut with minimal bleeding. Mitch often came home nicked up. His shins wore small scars that, like rings inside a tree trunk, showed the number of years he'd been riding. Right now, he was more upset about his favorite jersey, now with a hole. He'd take care of it at home—including getting out the small blood smear. Mitch readjusted the twins underneath his bike shorts, pushed his sunglasses into place, threw his left leg over the saddle, and clipped his foot into the pedal. Taking a quick swig of water, he spit it out to rinse his mouth. He followed with a bigger drink, swallowed, then replaced the bottle in its cage. Prior to pushing off, Mitch looked around, again sensing something among the evergreens.

High up in a tree, an unmistakable Black-headed grosbeack landed on a shimmering arrow lodged deep in the bark. The energetic little bird sang, and Mitch smiled as the feathered creature twitched. The arrow had a brilliant sheen in the sunlight; the fletching seemed to flutter with the breeze. He glanced back across the river. Still nothing.

Mitch returned his gaze to the arrow; the cinnamon, black, and white bird, singing with the joy of a new day, flew away. Watching, mesmerized by the surreal reflection off the surface, the arrow seemed to dissolve into the tree leaving a small glowing trace of liquid trickling down the dark brown bark. The damn thing disappeared as if the wind had washed away its existence as the breeze whistled, flexing its power high through the tips of the evergreens. The unstoppable force plowed its way through the tops of the pines mimicking the sounds of the ocean. Mitch never got tired of that sound. The ocean in the trees, he always told Mabey.

Rubbing his eyes, not believing what message they sent to his brain, Mitch touched the tear in his shirt, glanced again at the tree where he was sure he'd seen an arrow, and then glanced back across the river one more time. Nothing but an empty bank corralling the flowing water of the

Rogue River.

Straightening his handlebars, Mitch looked a final time at the empty tree chuckling at how the mind can play tricks. Pushing off with his right foot he pedaled back down the path. Regaining his rhythm, he pressed resume on his smartphone. Seconds later, the exercise app reported he had passed the nine-mile mark. Slowing his pace, as usual, he would give his body the last mile to cool. Not necessary this morning after the unplanned stop, he slowed anyway out of habit. Mitch checked his watch making sure he had time to mow the lawn and shower before the annual barbecue he and his wife Mabey were putting on later in the day.

Picking up a little speed, he vaulted off the dirt-packed trail, and landed the 29-inch wheels on the pavement. A hundred yards or so and he was home. Nodding to his neighbor, Jasper, he cruised past wondering if there was enough gasoline in the mower.

Mitch wondered if he should call Mabey and tell her what he'd seen. For now, he figured to hold on to this little incident—at least until he had a better idea of what he saw. Laughing to himself, an awkward nervousness to the strange sound his throat emitted, he couldn't help but think that a dissolving arrow had grazed him.

Coasting to the front of the garage, Mitch whispered to himself, "Yeah, right?"

Chapter 2

For God's Sake, Don't Run

Mitch touched his right shoulder trying to process how there was no cut, scrape, or even a scratch where his jersey was torn and bloody. He grappled with the bird's arrow perch and the fact that it had disappeared. Mitch didn't want to believe that an arrow had clipped his shoulder and then a few seconds later vanished. It made absolutely no sense, except it had happened, and he saw it. He wanted to tell Mabey, but there wouldn't be time with all the guests coming for the barbecue get-together. Mitch ran a calloused hand down the handle of the rake and got back to the cleanup of the freshly mowed yard.

A movement to his right made Mitch stop raking. Old Man Jasper was on his roof adjusting another space-age antenna. The man had a weather-beaten face and silvery hair that gave the sign of advanced age. In contrast, his clear, alert eyes made pinpointing the number of birthdays a challenge. One of these days, Mitch wanted to ask Jasper just how old he was, but his eccentric neighbor kept to himself. Most in town respected his want for privacy—at least those who understood Rogue River and her residents.

The small town, nestled in the Oregon's Rogue River Valley, hugged the banks of a wild and scenic river by the same name. The fast-moving water crashed against the polished boulders and banks guarding the town.

The town's residents loved visitors and the tourist-spent money, and when the tourist's pockets were empty, the townspeople loved them even more when they left. In this river community of 1800—mostly farmers, ranchers, loggers, hunters, and commuters—most people knew their neighbors; many participated in the Fourth of July parade or at least watched each year, and few residents locked their doors at night.

Rogue River folk cherished their privacy, and most respected the simple fact that Jasper prized his alone time more than most. He had a habit of ducking inside if someone came down the dead-end street he shared with the Wildes and the Jensons.

Mitch realized a while back that he and his significant other Mabey were exceptions. Jasper had grown to trust them. They didn't hang out and never extended a dinner invite; both parties were comfortable with this arrangement. A few lengthy talks in the cul-de-sac over the years were the basis for their polite relationship. Even through Jasper's cantankerous looks and intermittently moody disposition, Mitch had grown fond of him.

Jasper gave an excited wave, so Mitch dropped his rake and hurried over to his neighbors. He welcomed the distraction; the fresh smelling grass turned his stomach. Jasper's ladder lay on the ground between the hedgerow and the house.

Picking the ladder up, he repositioned it. Mitch watched as Jasper took caution in lowering himself. At the bottom, the old man looked around the neighborhood while grabbing Mitch's arm above the wrist. Jasper's eyes were more clear than normal, if that were even possible. Mitch would never share what popped into his mind initially—that the old guy had a damn firm grip for his advanced age.

"Don't pay attention to what you see, Wilde. Do not stare them in the eyes, and for God's sake, don't run. They won't hurt you if you don't stare right at them or run. Trust me on this, photo jock. Do not take their picture! My gut tells me if they catch you taking their photo, it won't be good. I've developed a keen sense ever since my rodeo days."

"Rodeo days? Um, okay." Mitch scanned his mental faculties trying to decide if he cared enough to ask for an explanation. He shifted his gaze across the street toward his front yard, knowing Mabey would be home soon and that his yard wouldn't rake itself. Grass odor be damned; Mitch was surprised at himself as a question he would never ask popped into his head: 'How the hell did that ladder fall?'

Chapter 3

Keep That Lid Closed

Mabey Wilde, always graceful and poised with her auburn hair and piercing blue eyes, walked past Mitch. She gave him a shoulder squeeze and a quick peck on the cheek. At nearly six-three, Mitch loved Mabey's five-foot-nine-inch frame and gorgeous legs that seemed never to end. He figured his dishwater blond hair, grey-blue eyes, and lithe frame would make for a dynamite kid if he and Mabey ever changed their minds. The thought often popped into his head but never turned into a legitimate want. It was a simple matter of wondering how their offspring would look if they did. Not a vain thought; a curiosity. Mitch gathered his wandering mind as he enjoyed the sight of Mabey's long legs in her new sexy white, two-piece swimsuit.

"Love you, babe. And, nice suit by the way," Mitch said as she headed down to the river at the back of the property.

Mabey gave Mitch one of her heart-piercing smiles. He felt his cheeks flush. He returned his attention to his neighbor and good friend Jack who sighed, laughed, and then moved the meat on the grill. Mitch chuckled, amazed at Jack's grill awareness, as he confidently flipped steaks and burgers. In typical fashion, Jack held his six-foot frame straight when around Mitch. His competitive nature made him strive to be equally tall. He fell an inch or two short, but few people seemed to notice.

Jack pushed back his dark brown hair above his hazel eyes and sighed. Sweat, drawn out by the heat of the grill, gathered in the barely noticeable crows-feet around his eyes. Mitch, for the sake of entertainment, worked at getting Jack all ramped up about the state of the homeland. "Mitch, the politicians are clueless. The entire country has leveraged itself to the hilt financially; manmade global warming is a hoax; and financial systems worldwide will eventually crash. The U.S. has become a second-class nation bordering on third-world status. Oh, we might still be thinly veiled as a super-power, but truth be known, we all realize what's going on. The politicians are content to point fingers at everyone else. They don't listen, and don't care to listen, to the citizens any more. It's a depressing fraud played to keep power and money. Makes me so damn angry, I may be the next one to go postal in D.C."

"Jack, take a breath already and finish my steak. I've been looking forward to it for a week now. Tell me, do they not 'get it' as you say, or do they simply care more about their power and getting re-elected?" Mitch laughed at how easily Jack got worked up over a few well-timed and targeted comments.

Jack grunted, flipped a couple of burgers, and moved a few to the higher rack. Mitch took a sip of beer and resumed provoking his friend. A strange sound from over the fence toward the front of the house had them frowning at each other. They turned as one toward the cul-de-sac.

Mitch frowned at the distinctive clip-clop of horse hooves and at once thought of one of his favorite movies: *Secretariat*. A line in the movie, "a tremendous machine," came to mind. He welled up inside every damn time he watched that horse thunder around the final turn. Mitch never could figure out why a horse in a movie would make him rub tears from his eyes. It was just a horse after all. Maybe it was because the animal seemed to have a soul and took pride in his accomplishments. Mitch thought he must have been an Indian with a special horse in an earlier life. Something no one knew, not even his journal.

The strange noise came again. Unfortunately, Mitch couldn't see over the fence. Mitch and Jack checked the meat grilling on the barbecue then glanced at everyone playing in the river and bustling about in the yard. It appeared no one else had heard Secretariat out front.

Jack set down the tongs, opened the vent, and then closed the lid. "Keep an eye on the meat, will you, Mitch? I forgot my BBQ sauce and

16

it's almost time to put it on the ribs. I'll check out the noise in front on the way. Old Man Jasper is doing something to his roof again. It's been almost a month since he added another short-wave radio antenna."

"No, Jasper was up there today. I helped him with a ladder. So, no way, mister, I'm going with you."

"You need to stay here and make sure flames don't kick up and burn the steaks."

"All right, but hurry."

Mitch set his beer on the grill shelf and grabbed the tongs. The Wildes' dog—a silver Labrador retriever named General—nuzzled Mitch's leg, and barked, hoping for a scrap of meat.

Mitch patted him on the head and smiled.

"Not right now, Gen, you know you can't have this; Jack would kill me, you little sneak."

Chapter 4

Put Down That Damn Monkey

Mitch focused his attention on the gate where Jack had gone. He was certain he'd heard a scream above the backyard noise. He set the tongs on the grill shelf, meat be damned, and headed toward the noise.

"You stay, General. Stay!"

He pushed to exit, but the gate was jammed. He peered through an opening gap between the boards. Someone was lying on the ground, blocking it. The person looked like Jack.

"Jack is that you?" There was no response. "Jack!"

Mitch lowered himself and pushed a shoulder firmly against the lower edge. Jack was 190 pounds, give or take. Mitch shoved all his weight against the wood. Little by little, the body moved. He got the gate open a few inches, pushed hard again, and opened it enough to squeeze through the gap.

Jack was out cold, but Mitch saw a shallow rise and fall to his chest. He knelt beside Jack. His friend lay face-up, eyes glazed. Bad enough, until Mitch saw an arrow stuck in his shoulder. An arrow, what the hell? Mitch's mind raced back to the sparrow arrow-perch in the tree on the river trail.

Jack blinked. Even though Mitch had seen him breathe, he still heaved a sigh of relief. Survival skills kicked in. "Jack don't move. Let me see if I can get this arrow out of your shoulder." Mitch acted calm though his mind was racing—odd behavior for him since he was typically cool in all situations. Both the shaft and the feathers appeared to be moving.

There was an ever-so-slight vibration and... what was that? He touched the arrow with the first two fingers of his right hand: a cold heat. His fingers felt cold, but his mind registered heat. How could that be?

A lump in his throat found its way down toward his stomach. The arrow glowed and looked as if it contained a silvery-blue liquid. Mitch experienced a sharp sting in his own shoulder where his bicycle jersey was torn earlier in the day. He shrugged it off as coincidence as he tilted Jack on his side. Probing the plaid fabric on the back of Jack's shirt to see if the tip of the arrow had gone all the way through. Mitch realized it hadn't; there was no broken skin on the back. It probably would have been good if it had. That way Mitch could break the arrow and pull the damn thing out: a recommendation he thought he'd heard The Duke or Stallone make.

A breeze brought the scent of burning meat over the fence. He grinned thinking how pissed Jack would be at him for leaving his post.

"Focus, Wilde," Mitch told himself.

He laid Jack flat on the ground. Sure enough, the arrow was still glowing, but now it was a white, turquoise, in color. Jack's pain was clear; his eyes had rolled backwards in their sockets so only the whites were showing. Mitch felt a prick in his shoulder again as if someone were pinching him hard.

"Jack, stick with me, man; we'll take care of this together, my brother."

Jack blinked once, as if saying yes, but when he seemed to relax, he suddenly went into violent convulsions. Mitch reached in his back pocket for his phone to dial 911. Nothing, he was unable to get a dial tone. No-cell-tower signal. "Shit!" Since when? He always had a signal.

Mitch frantically waved the phone as if it would miraculously pick up a signal. Still no bars. "Dammit! Come on, what the hell is going on?"

Mitch groped into Jack's back pocket. His phone was there, but the display was cracked, and there was no power. He laughed nervously. "Are you kidding me?" To his friend, he said, "Hang on, buddy, I'll get help."

Mitch stood and yelled for Mabey over the fence. A few seconds later, she raced around the house in a damp cover-up and flip-flops. General trotted at her side. She stopped beside Mitch, surprised. General came alert, sensing something was wrong.

"There you two are. Why is the barbecue smoking so badly, Mitch?

And why is Jack on the ground?" She crouched beside Mitch and wiped a bead of sweat from his brow. "What happened? Is that an arrow in Jack's shoulder?"

General sidled closer licking Jack on the cheek.

"Dammit, General, back off." Mitch pushed the dog away.

"Mabey, do you have your phone?"

"Of course, not, I've been in and out of the river Mitch. Why in the hell is there an arrow in Jack? That is an arrow, isn't it? Were you practicing with your new bow?"

"No!" Mitch barked. Taking a deep breath, he calmed himself. "Look babe, I'll explain later. Right now, we need to get medical attention. Go call on the house phone; tell them Jack's been shot with an arrow, and he appears to be dying, and fast!"

Mabey took off for the phone yelling over her shoulder, "He is dying, Mitch? Or you want me to be fast?"

She, of course, knew the answer but never wasted the chance to make a point. Mabey constantly told Mitch that words had meaning. He admitted later that this little interaction brought the point more clearly into focus. He chuckled in spite of himself.

Mitch realized he wasn't as focused as he needed to be. While checking Jack for a pulse, he thought about how Mabey took off in an amazing burst of speed wearing flip-flops and wondered how they stayed on her feet. Mitch refused to wear a shoe that wouldn't allow him to break into a run on a moment's notice. After seeing Mabey move with her flip-flops, perhaps the shoes warranted closer inspection.

Why in the hell was he worrying about flip-flops right now? He realized that damn monkey in his brain was banging cymbals again.
Mitch snapped back to the here and now, focused on his dear friend, feeling again for a pulse in his wrist. It was slight, but there definitely was one.

Mitch fired up his cranial stopwatch. Mabey would be at the phone in less than fifteen seconds, a few seconds to dial, and then five to ten minutes for the paramedics to arrive. Jack should make it: the arrow couldn't have pierced any vital organs. It was in his shoulder, for God's sake. Looking at his face, though, Mitch suddenly wasn't so sure. Jack's eyes were drawn back and listless, and the veins in his face that normally weren't visible, seemed swollen. His skin felt clammy, cooler than it should be. Hell, to Mitch, he looked dead.

Mitch tore open Jack's shirt for a better look at the damage. The skin around the arrow's shaft was red, as if it were scorched. He touched the shaft. "Ow!" He yanked his hand back. Just seconds ago, he could touch the damn thing. It was getting hotter. How could that be?

Wait, what the hell was this? The shaft was hotter, but also shrunk. Couldn't be. His mind couldn't interpret what was going on was all. Right? For a moment, he thought back to the bird on the arrow in the tree.

This damn arrow was disappearing as well—but into Jack's body.

The dog licked Jack's face. "General, sit!" He didn't need the added distraction of the dog right now. General plopped down near Jack's head, whimpering with canine concern.

Jack moaned; his head thrashing back and forth. Mitch had to do something worrying his friend was dying. Perhaps if he tried to push the arrow through the shoulder, he could extract the damn thing.

Bracing himself for the heat, he grabbed the shaft as close as he could to Jack's flesh. Before he got a grip, Jack screamed. General joined him in a similar wail. Despite the opera duo, Mitch gripped the arrow as tight as he could. The arrow, too slick, slipped through Mitch's palm shrinking yet again. It was dissolving.

"What in the hell?"

Hard as he tried to keep hold of the arrow, Jack continued making noises. Mitch's heart slowed, his nose flared at the eerie guttural sound, and stench, coming from Jack's mouth. The veins in Jack's face and forehead were blue-green now. They looked as if they were going to burst. Jack's head continued to flail. With each motion, the noise coming out of him grew louder. The veins glowed as if someone had pumped him full of luminol.

By now, most everyone who was not in the river had gathered around. Jack Junior—Jack's spitting image—crouched next to Mitch. "What's going on with Dad, Mitch?"

21

"Not sure Junior. He was shot with an arrow, but I have no idea on what's going on now. Mabey is calling the paramedics."

"Will he be okay?"

"I think so. I hope so. I have no idea, Junior. I'm sorry, but I just don't know."

No one, least of all Junior, was buying the "okay" part as Jack's high-pitched screams intensified with each breath. Mabey burst out the side door of the garage.

"I couldn't call, Mitch. There's no dial tone."

Without any warning, Jack rose into a sitting position and grabbed Mitch's wrist in a vice-like grip. He talked but all that came out of his mouth were nonsensical tones and sounds. Then, as if his energy deserted him, Jack collapsed. Junior caught him before his father's head hit the sidewalk.

"Mitch?" Junior waited until Mitch looked up. "Where is the arrow?"

A sudden dizzy spell had Mitch bracing his hand on the ground. The scene was now out of control—out of his comfort zone. He couldn't help but notice a sharp sting and throbbing from his own shoulder where earlier in the morning he was almost hit with an arrow.

Jack's arrow had disappeared. Though Mitch thought he knew where it had gone, in hopeful desperation he checked the ground to see if it had broken off and lay nearby. Staring, his eyes returned nothing but empty concrete, mulch, and dirt. He couldn't wrap his mind around what in the hell was going on. There was no reasonable, earthly explanation for what was transpiring.

"What did you say?" Junior asked.

"What?"

"You said something. It sounded like, 'It's gone'."

Mitch shrugged, puzzled. "It is gone. I tried pulling the thing out, but the damn thing kept slipping out of my hand." Mitch showed his palm—red from the shaft of the now-gone arrow. If the looks of disbelief, accusation, and guilt aimed at Mitch were any sign, the barbecue gawkers thought he was whacked.

"Are you serious?" asked Junior.

"Mitch is right. I saw the arrow," Mabey said.

Thank the gods, she could back him up. His stomach released a knot or two. Mitch tried to figure out what to do next.

"Junior, do you have your cell phone? Mine isn't working."

Junior grabbed the phone from his back pocket. He started to dial and realized he didn't have a signal. "No signal, Mitch. What the hell?"

"Run home and call then. Hurry." Junior leapt over his dad in a flurry of speed Mitch couldn't help but be impressed by.

Glancing around the crowd, Mitch yelled out. "Can anyone get a call out? Somebody call 911!"

Several people drew out phones, then everyone shook their heads in unison. Jack moaned loudly, arched his back, and collapsed into silence.

"Junior, wait!"

Junior, almost around the edge of the house and out of sight, stopped and turned, facing Mitch.

"Come and stay with your dad."

"Why, what's up? Is he okay?"

"I'll go to Jasper's; he has a short-wave radio."

Junior came back. He dropped to the ground smoothing the hair from his father's sweaty head. Mitch took off across the street. While he ran, all he could think about was a ruined steak. Again, with that damn monkey. Why in the world was he thinking about shit like flip-flops and charred meat at a time like this? Mitch's recent lack of concentration concerned him. The random useless thoughts clouded his judgment and weren't helpful to anyone. He had to put down that damn monkey.

Chapter 5

"There is no death, only a change of worlds."
Chief Seattle - The Duwamish

Never Mind

As Mitch crossed the street, an EMT vehicle screamed towards him. He waved at it to hurry up and follow him to where Jack lay. The paramedics jumped out, heading around the vehicle for their gear.

"How did you know to come here?" Mitch asked not expecting a response. "None of us has a phone signal, and the house phone has no dial tone."

Jasper must have called. Mitch would thank him later. He pushed through the crowd of elbows making room for the paramedics.

Jack looked better now; his breathing appeared more normal, and his eyes no longer rolled back in their sockets. But the motionless way he lay seemed odd. Junior had his father's head on his lap; Mitch could tell from the way he held him, how much Junior loved his dad.

The paramedics looked at the crowd. One of them asked, "What happened here, exactly?"

Knowing in advance how strange his explanation would sound, Mitch plowed on anyway. "I found him lying here, in pain with a glowing arrow in his shoulder. I tried pulling it out, but it disappeared inside his shoulder. See?"

The techs knelt and started an examination. Mitch thought Jack looked freakishly hot—sweat beads dotted his entire face—at least he wasn't dead. Mitch bolstered his story. "Look, his shirt is torn. See the mark on his shoulder?"

The paramedics looked pleadingly at the Wildes' guests, then back at him. Mitch kicked the thought out of his mind. He needed to focus, with no self-doubt. The hell with these two pimply paramedics. This shit happened and was happening right here and now.

An entry point, that five minutes ago had been round, red, and seared like meat on the grill had all but healed. Naturally, this made Mitch's explanation all the harder to believe.

Too late he realized he should have used his phone to capture a photo of the arrow in Jack's shoulder. He wasn't daft. Thankfully, Mabey had seen it. Where was she anyway?

"Why is he steaming?" the female paramedic asked. "You said there was an arrow. Where is it?"

Mabey stepped forward and said, "It dissolved and..." she shrugged in that cute way she had, "... disappeared inside him."

"As crazy as it sounds," Mitch tried again, "the thing appeared to be alive. It turned silver and slowly sucked into his body like it was alive."

The paramedics gave a couple of quiet chuckles. Then the fat male EMT asked, "How long ago did he stop breathing?"

"What!" He was in pain but breathing. Mitch didn't mention Jack's screaming, "just before you got here!"

"Halsey! Resuscitate him! We can figure out what the hell happened later," Mabey barked. Mitch realized she got the guy's name off his shirt.

She was awesome, not psychic or anything, just observant and extremely intelligent. But please don't ask her for directions anywhere. To think that in college twenty-five years ago, Mitch almost had not asked her to spend the rest of her life with him; he often thanked the stars he was the designated driver that night while he and Jack were at the bar. Asking her to dance was the smartest thing he'd ever done. He struggled to imagine where he would be in life without her.

"Please do something!" Junior shouted. "Get him breathing, will you?"

The female tech held a portable oxygen tank against Jack's face. The male tech was doing heart massages.

"Look!" Mitch exclaimed.

Jack's entire body was glowing silver. All visible veins looked as though they might burst through his skin. Both techs jumped back while Mitch bent forward. Jack's stomach, distended and reddened, was glowing.

Mitch speared Halsey with a glare. "Don't you dare let him die!" Mitch realized at that moment that he'd grown to love Jack—losing him would be devastating.

Just thinking of telling Jack's parents about this made his knees weak. 'Did everything I could, but it was just his time, folks.' That would be hard for them to swallow considering what happened to Jack's wife early last year.

The paramedics jumped into action. They were unable to find a pulse. The female tech listened with her stethoscope; the male grasped his wrist. They mumbled medical shorthand to each other and then broke out their equipment. They shocked Jack twice with the defibrillator.

Suddenly, Jack sat up, coughed a couple of times, and screamed, "*San'aaWawli an ambo!*" His eyes popped open wide. He stared at the surrounding gapers as if they were strange crazy assholes.

In the following days, Mabey and Mitch had several conversations as they tried to recreate the sounds that came from Jack's mouth. It sounded like gibberish, but both had the feeling Jack knew exactly what he was saying.

A few seconds later, looking as if nothing had happened, Jack gazed at Mitch and said loud and clear, "What happened? Where am I? Who are you? Why are you all standing around? I need water, I'm thirsty as hell."

"Dad, are you okay? I thought you were dead for sure."

Mabey ran off, returning moments later with a bottle of water from the garage fridge. While Jack guzzled the water, small wisps of steam seeped from around his eyes.

The paramedics traded puzzled expressions. Mitch wasn't sure what it meant but figured it couldn't be good. Jack asked Mabey for more water. After the fourth bottle, he appeared as if nothing had happened. His skin color was completely normal; no more steam came from around his eyes. His veins had shrunk to normal size and showed no traces of extraordinary color.

The female paramedic chimed in, "Your blood pressure is fine: 120 over 80."

Jack stood up. "Why is my shirt all torn up?" He touched the blood spots drying in the afternoon sun.

Hell, there was no appearance of trauma whatsoever to his shoulder—same as with Mitch—just a ripped shirt. A squawking voice blared over the paramedics Walkie-Talkies commanding them to respond to a situation a couple miles away. It sounded like a traffic accident.

Mitch, with resurgent assuredness, asked the paramedics, "Will you guys finish with Jack here before you think about leaving? An arrow clipped him in the shoulder, and that arrow no longer exists. Don't you find that a tad bit strange?"

The female paramedic addressed Mitch.

"Sir, I'm sorry, but we're getting hammered with calls right now. I don't think your friend needs to go to the hospital, but he should see his doctor as soon as he can. If he starts to feel lightheaded at all or strange in any way, take him to the E.R. in Medford."

With that, the two boxed up everything, walked out to their truck, whispering to each other along the way, and took off.

They did take the time to yell back as they were getting in there rig, "Make sure you get him to the doctor as soon as possible."

Mitch laughed, but he couldn't let this go without a response. "Really, Mr. and Mrs. Einstein, a doctor? Y'all think that a 'doc' could help a simple man like Jack here?" He also mumbled, "Bite me," but there were a few kids standing around, so he knew better than to let the expletives really fly.

27

"Mitch, stop it. They came to help." Mabey gave Mitch the spouse-eye. As beautiful as Mabey's eyes were, Mitch hated her spouse-eye—the angry, disapproving, you-will-pay-later look.

Mitch took a breath and gathered his thoughts before replying. "You did more for Jack with the water than they did, Mabey."

His rant accomplished nothing, and he knew it, but as the dynamic PT duo was driving away, it made him feel a touch better. On the other hand, did it? It bothered him that he allowed other people's behavior to ratchet him up. He didn't like it when Mabey pointed out the behavior to him.

Mitch turned back to Jack. He ignored the crowd gathered around them and grabbed him by the arm.

"Come on, I'm taking you to the hospital."

Jack shoved Mitch's hand away. "Who are all you people, and where am I?"

"Dad, it's me, Ace. We're next door at the Wildes' for their annual summer barbecue bash. One minute you and Mitch were talking, and the next we find you lying here with an arrow in your shoulder. You really don't remember?"

"Yeah, I remember. I'm just messing with you guys."

Jack showed a strange, wide grin – strange in the sense that, to Mitch, it seemed forced and unnatural. Mitch loved Jack's laugh and infectious smile and knew a real one from this shit. Jack started walking away as if nothing had happened saying, not really to anyone, "God, I'm hungry. Any of the barbecue left?"

"Jack don't freak us out like that!" Mitch held back what he really wanted to say, knowing that Mabey, and a few kids were still within earshot.

Jack looked at Mitch as if he saw something he didn't like. 'Freaking weird' is the way Mitch later described it to Mabey.

Mitch grabbed Mabey by the arm and whispered in her ear, "Something's wrong with Jack. We need to talk later. Jasper was right all along."

"What?" Mabey replied, because as Mitch always said, she never heard him the first time.

Tilting his head toward Junior, Mitch repeated the words letting Mabey know he didn't want to be overheard.

Mabey shot back with, "Jasper wants us to come over later?"

Exasperated, Mitch replied, "Never mind."

Chapter 6

Wilde Tales

As the hours passed, things settled down, and the arrow incident was set aside, but not forgotten, by everyone except Mitch, Mabey, and Junior. Concern radiated from their actions and mannerisms as they huddled, talking over the situation. The guests who'd bothered to get out of the river had jumped back in. Others found beers and sodas, threw the Frisbee, played volleyball, and continued as if nothing had happened. Mitch supposed since no one other than he and Mabey saw the arrow in Jack, and given the fact that Jack was moving and talking as he normally did, few showed concern. To them, it must have looked more like a person who fell after too many drinks. Hadn't the paramedics said he was okay? So that was that.

On the other hand, was it? Mitch just couldn't come to terms with not taking Jack to the hospital.

"Why didn't I video that arrow in his shoulder?" Mitch mumbled.

He stepped away from Mabey and Junior to join Jack at the grill. "Shit, Jack," he said, "all this good meat is black now. Nothing looks savable."

Jack picked up one of the charred kielbasa sausages, doused it with a little mustard, and ate it as if he were a starving lion. After a third one he asked, "Why are you staring at me? Isn't anyone else going to eat?"

"These remind me of days on the prairies in the buffalo camps. Man, that was good meat."

"What the hell! What in the world are you talking about—buffalo camps? Prairie?"

There was a lengthy two or three minutes of awkward silence.

Quiet wasn't normal between them. One thing they'd never experienced was awkwardness around each other, and neither was ever at a loss for words. They weren't your typical sports-talk-only guys. Both had IQs north of 120, and both could hold a conversation with anyone, even with a woman, Mitch liked to joke. Mitch scuffed at the ground with his feet, and Jack pretended to brush the grill. Mabey removed the overdone meat and brought out more hot dogs and hamburgers to grill. Mitch's prized steak was all but lost. He would chop it up later for the dog. Mitch and Jack glanced occasionally at each other while pretending to study the rest of the guests and their antics.

During the awkward silence, Mitch, thinking of a way to find out Jack's problem, dove right in.

"Jack, you remember that time we were at the river our senior year of high school, and you almost drowned while cliff diving?"

Jack tilted his head sideways, furrowing his brow; the skin around his eyes pinched. "What the hell are you talking about, Mitch?"

Mitch smiled. Jack's response was a good sign. The event hadn't happened; Jack hated cliff diving and swimming in the river. The last thirty years taught Mitch one thing about Jack: he was predictable. However, right now, his mannerisms were different. He slurred his words slightly, and his normally alert eyes looked cloudy. A person doesn't get shot by an arrow that dissolves inside of him, scream out in bloody pain, yell at everyone in gibberish, and then just go on as if nothing had happened. Does he? Perhaps Mitch missed that episode of the *X-Files*.

"How you feeling, bud? Come on. Let me take you to the hospital."

"Geezus, Mitch, why the hell are you fawning over me? Things getting a little boring in the bedroom with Mabey? I find that hard to believe," Jack chuckled.

"What the hell does my sex life have to do with anything right now? What, no response from the wise-cracking arrow catcher?"

Bull's-eye! Mitch thought before focusing on Jack again.

"You need to go to the hospital, you dumb ass. Uh, you do remember getting shot with an arrow, right? And no, the bedroom is great,

31

as always, asshole."

"Another one of your Wilde tales, huh Mitch?" Jack started to walk away, then stopped and turned. His eyes were familiar again.

"Look, Mitch, I'll go on Monday if it makes you feel better. If anything strange happens in the meantime, you can take me to the hospital. Right now, I'm fine."

"Strange?" Mitch said, a little incredulously. "You mean like getting shot with a dissolving arrow?"

Jack's unfamiliar eyes danced again. One thing that always impressed Mitch about Jack was his normally rock-steady gaze; his ability not to flinch and then lock onto a target made him a great archer. Jack didn't flinch now, but his eyes moved ever so slightly, and their color looked a little off. They weren't their normal deep hazel—the hazel color Mabey always made an admiring comment about.

Jack walked awkwardly toward the volleyball game. "Hey, Ace, you mind if an old man plays? I used to have a pretty wicked serve."

"Sure, Dad. Are you feeling okay? Shouldn't we take you to the hospital?"

Jack, in a very atypical reaction, yelled, "*Moo ?an dic hoslta!*"

The incident brought everyone in hearing range to a stop. In the ensuing silence, Mitch could hear the river pressing up against the rocks, searching for a way around.

"What did you say, Dad?"

Jack's eyes rolled back and danced in their sockets showing more white than Mitch had ever seen in a person's eyes. Jack laughed as if he were in another state of mind.

"I'm fine, Ace. Let your old man serve, okay?"

Chapter 7

Just Like Charlie Brown

"Hey, Mitch, sorry Dad bailed on the cleanup. He won't admit it, but he isn't feeling well."

"Don't worry about it, Junior. In fact, you should get going as well. Make sure he's okay. See if you can talk him into going to the hospital. I'm pissed at him right now, but I suppose if the tables were turned, I wouldn't want to go either."

"Big difference, though, for you, Mitch, is that Mabey wouldn't give you a choice, would she? Man, I wish my mom were here."

"Hey, what are you saying, kid? That I'm not the lord of my own manor?"

Junior chuckled, a good thing. Mitch was trying to get the kid's mind off his recently shot dad and his deceased mother.

"Mitch, if you don't mind, I'm going to catch up with Dad."

Mabey came around the corner. "Why are you still here, Junior? You should be with your father. Please see if you can get him to the hospital. Mitch and I would be happy to go with you if you want."

"I am taking off now, Mabey. Thanks again for everything, and sorry I can't stay to help."

"Don't worry about it. Call if you need anything, okay? The lord of the manor will get this mess cleaned up." Mabey displayed a smart-ass grin on her face. General barked and escorted Junior to the front gate. Mabey and Mitch went back to the cleanup.

"What happened to Debbi and Cindi, babe? They usually help with this."

"They took off, your lordship, at my command."

Mitch stood on his toes, forced his stomach forward, placed one arm behind his back, the other at his side, and did his best royal-king impression. "I doth protest. I did not give the wenches permission to leave."

Mabey laughed. "You are so full of yourself, Mitch."

Mitch loved when she laughed. He'd die happy if he could bottle her laughter and take it with him. Mabey's face took on an affectionate cast thinking of her best friend and friend's daughter who felt as though she was her and Mitch's daughter.

"The girls are opening the Shack at five a.m., so I chased them out. We can handle this. By the way, dream on, mister. I can sense what devious and demented thoughts you have going on in that thick skull of yours. How can you even think about sex after a day like today?"

Mitch mentally admitted, 'God, she is good. No way should someone be able to know me that well.'

"Oh, I don't know, because I am a man. Or rather, lord of the manor."

"Well, come on. Let's finish, get inside, and see how we're feeling. Perhaps, if you run me a bath and pour me a glass of wine, I might find the strength to please you, my lord."

"Really?"

Mitch, realizing he sounded like a desperate teen, laughed. He reflected, as he often did when they bantered, on the first time he got silly with her in college and how hard she'd laughed. It was a moment he'd never forget. It was as if Mabey's laughter filled him with joy, satisfaction, and confidence, all at the same time. The first Mabey-laugh always ended with Mitch remembering a day at Sunday school: when the youth pastor talked about 'laughter being like a medicine,' or something close. Mitch thought the Bible at least got this notion right. Smiling—at least in his mind he was smiling—Mitch went inside.

After running Mabey's bath and pouring her the requested glass of wine, Mitch knew she would be too relaxed and tired for amorous activities. He wasn't being cynical; this was what usually happened. Mitch never complained out of respect and love, but damn he wasn't an overly complicated guy. He wished Mabey could understand how much it meant to him to make love with her on a regular basis. He always felt so connected, so appreciated, and so… well, loved. For Mitch the joy came in making his wife feel good. Up to now, he wasn't sure he'd convinced Mabey of this. He always felt selfish, and the feeling made no sense. He wanted to spend more quality physical time with her. Perhaps he was abnormal, out of balance with the laws of nature.

"Shit" what was wrong with wanting to make love to his wife as often as he did. She was gorgeous, and he craved her. Besides, he always felt he would take two bullets for Mabey—or at least one—with a smile on his face.

Mitch held out hope for tonight. At the top of the stairs, he turned into their wine-colored bedroom and headed for the large bathroom with walk-in shower—two showerheads, of course—and Mabey's large soaking tub. He always called it Mabey's because he'd never been in it. Something about sitting in his own pool of filth didn't quite work for Mitch, and besides Mabey hadn't invited him. His queen liked the alone time, so he respected it. Unfortunately, he was too big to do a cannonball. Mitch closed the drain and started the hot water. Frowning for a fraction of a second, Mitch smiled, shook his head, then chuckled to himself as he thought, 'I'm just like Charlie Brown.'

Chapter 8

A Guy's Journal

The next day, Mitch closed himself in his office and started an entry in his journal.

Is this finally it? Armageddon, the end of the world, the apocalypse, Native Americans getting their revenge or the ancient Aliens coming back finally to reclaim earth?

Mitch tried to watch *Ancient Aliens* several times but the guy with the big hair made him uncomfortable. He wasn't sure why, but discomfort always reared its ugly head when the ancient astronaut expert and his Kramer-like hair made an appearance. So, he avoided the show opting for a few minutes of guilty food pleasure of any kind on the Food Network.

Focusing on the computer keys he continued the entry:

I slept in late on Sunday. Late for me, anyway. An uneventful day. Mabey and I relaxed around the house and took a walk by the river. It was pleasant as always with her. General had fun, never a surprise. I was a little preoccupied with thoughts of Jack. As the day passed, it was almost as if nothing had happened.

With Jack's not going to the hospital, the event faded from people's memories since we had nothing tangible to hang on to. What happened to Jack has me paying closer attention to regional and national events. News events are odd right now. The Native Americans in the Pacific Northwest, according to reports,

started disappearing earlier this year. The public at large didn't notice at first because most Americans have little contact with them. Much of the buzz was still about the presidential write-in candidate and all the legal challenges taking place from both the Republican and Democratic sides over the latest election. It wasn't until the casinos were affected negatively that anyone paid attention.

No one in the mainstream saw these crazy events coming, at least no one was talking about them with the media. I'm sure I could go back and find bloggers who were close to guessing, out of luck, but none had piqued anyone's interest at the time. The Mayan calendar may have been wrong about December 22, 2012, or at least the way many of the "experts" interpreted it. Nonetheless, the world, at least as we know seems to be ending. Things are a-changing. No doubt about it.

"Mitch," Mabey called from downstairs, "are you almost ready? You know we need to be there in twenty minutes, right?"

"Yes, I know. No one is ever on time to these damn things. I'll be right there." Mitch looked

around the room hoping to buy a few more minutes. "Where are my brown shoes? I can't find them."

"Down here by the door to the garage."

"Okay. Thanks, I'll be down in a minute."

Mitch turned back to the journal on his laptop. He wanted to get a few more thoughts down before a night of probable misery ensued. They were to attend a local charity auction for the Rogue River Flower Club. Mabey was a casual, but key, member. Mitch wasn't naturally a pessimistic person. He liked to face facts. These flower events were flat-out boring. They did have an open bar, though, so it wouldn't be a total loss. In addition, he was donating a twelve-pack of his home brew: Wilde Imperial Stout. His beer donations typically brought in several hundred dollars each year. Wilde's personal brew was a sought-after commodity in their small river town. Mitch focused on his journal. He needed to wrap this up:

Jack hasn't gone to the doctor yet, and I don't know how to get him there. I haven't seen him much since the incident. If anything serious was happening, Junior would get in touch with Mabey or me, so I will let it go for now.

Mitch continued writing a few more thoughts.

The internet and TV news have reported that Indian casinos all across the country are developing serious work-force problems. More and more Native Americans every day are simply not showing up to work.

People across this great land are debating the meaning of the event, like Hank Argyle, a religious-right zealot, who claimed it was "a prelude to Armageddon." He said that God, started with the Indians because they were largely "uneducated, uninformed, and blameless." Wow! Really? The one and only failed politician, Sal Bore, claimed on Wolf News "Man's rampant and prolonged raping of the earth has finally brought the end of the world. It only makes sense that nature's children, the Native Americans, are being taken to a better place: a place where no trash, no concrete jungles, and no hate or violence."

Mitch ended the night's journal entry with the following:

Isn't it fitting that Wolf News had Cocoa Puffs as the sponsor for their evening show? Okay, gotta go endure a bit of misery for my lovely wife.

Mitch liked to journal. He hadn't had the best early childhood. Yeah—who did, right? But, when he was a youngster, his grandmother taught him to write his thoughts on paper, eventually morphing onto his laptop. On his eighth birthday, Mitch's grandmother bought him a little black journal. Mitch clearly remembered her saying, "You can draw in it, write in it, do whatever you want with it". She also stressed: "It's your own private space. What you write is between you and the stars, Mitchey."

Only Grandma called him Mitchey. Fortunately, life improved as he grew into his teens and dramatically more so thereafter.

Chapter 9

Fashionably Late

Mitch put the laptop into sleep mode and went downstairs for his night of joyous fun. He reminded himself to leave the sarcasm at home as he skipped steps to find Mabey waiting in the kitchen and looking hot as ever. Mitch had never seen another woman make a pair of Levis look so good.

"Nice you could make it, Mitch. You know I cannot stand being late. Why are you always late?" Mabey walked out the kitchen door into the garage. Mitch followed, eyes locked onto her ass.

"Sorry, babe, I needed to journal before my thoughts escaped into the mindless void. Hardly anyone will show up for this thing until thirty minutes in, except all the old ladies dressed in their finest curtain dresses pretending to like each other's flowers."

"Mitch, my flowers are on display too, and those ladies are my friends."

"Yeah, but you aren't old, and you have a personality. Most of those women look for any secret opportunity to snap off a friend's flower to make their own precious flora stand out."

"Are you serious?"

Mitch opened the car door for Mabey, closed it behind her, and headed for the counter at the front of the garage. He grabbed his Wilde Stout for donation and set it in the back seat. Mitch sat in the driver's seat, buckling up before Mabey reminded him, and closed the door.

"I'm serious, and I'm right. Their flowers are the only reason they have to live. Sad, really. Mabey, if anything happens to me, promise you'll find a nice-looking woman and settle down. I don't want you spending the rest of your life trying to have the prettiest lily."

"Woman? And is 'lily' a metaphor?"

"That's right, dear: a woman. Simply isn't fair to another dude after being Mrs. Wilde; I'm just stating the obvious. The image of your being with a woman is downright enticing. It does something for my sex-starved brain. As for the lily, I hadn't thought about it, but now that you mention it…"

"God, you can be bizarre. Why on earth did I ever agree to dance with you?"

"My being bizarre is one of the many reasons you love me. And admit it that dance was the best decision we ever made."

Mitch pressed the garage door button on Mabey's visor, adjusted the rearview mirror, and then focused on the car's back-up monitor as he eased the car out of the garage. He allowed his mind to wander to the beer in the backseat. Mitch was excited tonight about people's bidding on his creation. He liked the respect he got for his beer-brewing talent; it made him feel warm and fuzzy. The new labels he'd created were impressive, and he thought they might garner a few more bucks for Mabey's flower club tonight: a majestic mountain provided the backdrop for a cool river running from the base with a regal-looking black-tail buck bounding across the waterway. He'd also designed the crest making it look like an old European Wilde family signature. The broad letters across the top said *WILDE*. At the bottom, the label read *IMPERIAL STOUT* in a crested-moon shape. Mitch believed he could sell the stuff outright, beyond a flower club silent auction.

Silence settled over the two during the uneventful ride, putting them in the Rogue River Lodge parking lot in about eighteen minutes, roughly fifteen minutes past the 5:30 start time. As they pulled up, Mabey checked her watch. "Dammit, Mitch, I hate being late. This event is important. These people count on me to help get things going."

"Look, Mabey, there's only one car in the lot," he said to prove the point he'd made at home. He realized the words coming from his mouth were bullshit, but they flowed nonetheless.

"The ladies have been able to talk behind our backs for the last ten minutes now."

In Mitch's best old-lady voice, he squawked, "What does Mabey see in Mitch? He's never on time and so laid back, thinks everything's about him. Mabey should leave his good-looking ass."

Mabey laughed as they got out of the car. Mitch felt bad for making her late, but the laughter was good. Tonight, could be stressful for her. He made a mental note not to be late to her functions anymore and to work on his empathy. The evening should be about her. His journal was nowhere near as important as his beautiful wife.

Chapter 10

You Go, Girl

As if on cue, the usual crowd arrived for the bi-annual flower show fundraiser, held late each spring and then again in the fall. The attendees consisted of the town council: seven old codgers who all had storefronts on Main Street, a good core group that any small town in America would be proud to have as business owners and council members. And everyone loved Mabey. Mitch was fond of all of them except Mayor Asshole as Mitch called him.

Mayor Jenkins, fresh off another unopposed election win, had arrived. He spotted Mabey across the room, smiled, and walked straight for her. He wrapped her in a big hug. Jenkins held it for as long as he could, typical for the grease-ball. His whole display was for show and to piss off Mitch. The mayor wouldn't do it if he knew how little Mitch cared. Mabey and he were rock-solid.

He chuckled at her ability to slip gracefully out of the mayor's shackles. Jenkins' tagalong entourage, two overweight security behemoths, also got in line for hugs from the best-looking woman in the room—hell, the whole damn town, no contest. Mabey executed a beautiful spin move and avoided both of them.

Mitch pulled Mabey aside, whispering in her ear.

"I'm going to run against Jenkins next election."

"You don't want to be mayor."

"Hell no, but it would be worth it to see the cheese-ball lose. Make him go out and get a real job like the rest of us."

"God, Mitch, you are going to be a spiteful and mean old man."

"I sure as hell hope so," Mitch smiled playfully.

He thought Jenkins a jerk at times and just an average mayor; Mitch still couldn't believe he'd won another election. Name recognition was the only explanation. Jenkins' father, who'd been mayor for twenty years or so, was a genuinely nice man and good for the community. Mitch figured everyone felt they would let Senior down if they didn't cast a vote for his son. Unfortunately, Mabey had to be nice to him. He was one of her current clients. Mabey did the song-and-dance routine for the next two hours. During that time, Mitch nursed three beers. That's right, nursed. For the pain and misery he had to endure for two-plus hours, ten beers wouldn't have been enough. Mitch mumbled to himself, "As sure as a damn donut has a hole," every one of those irritating women on the flower committee knew how many beers he drank, what the brands were, and approximately how many gulps it took for him to finish off each one.

Mitch sauntered back to his wife, pressing himself up close. "Why the hell do I dislike them so much, Mabey?"

"You're jealous; that's all," Mabey whispered.

"Jealous?"

"Mitch, come on. Yeah, they're busybodies, but the fact they profess not to like you so much pisses you off. If you stopped worrying about it and just ignored them, I bet they'd lose interest and move on to something—or someone—else."

"Go tell it on the mountain, sister," Mitch said, a little too loudly, in his best try at a less-than-masculine voice.

When more than a few heads turned and stared, he wished he hadn't said anything at all. Screw it! What did he care? He had half a mind to extend his middle finger, but he realized it wouldn't solve anything and certainly would piss off Mabey.

Anyway, she was dead-on, and Mitch knew it. He had learned by now, with continual reminders from his better half, to make a mental note when he found himself arguing and getting defensive. It was usually a red flag. Mabey forced a thin smile. As she walked away, she stopped briefly.

"Let me go say goodbye to everyone Mitch; I'll meet you by the car; and don't you dare get another beer on the way out. You can have one when you get home."

"Hey, dear, I don't plan on drinking when we get home."

"Not tonight, Mitch, I feel a headache coming on."

"Coming on? Headache, my ass", Mitch mumbled regretting the words, realizing she'd heard. He pretended not to care, but in his head he stomped his feet.

Mitch thought the female species had too much power and leveraged the hell out of it. God help a man if he said no whenever and wherever a woman's next desirous moment might come. Men generally didn't have the liberty to have a headache without setting the relationship back a decade. Mitch couldn't imagine saying no. There'd been many times—okay, a few—that he didn't feel like making sweet love either, but he'd performed as required for the sake of the relationship. It was his job to take one for the team, dammit.

Mitch moped out of the lodge heading to the car. For Mabey's sake, he made a gallant effort being nice to everyone he passed. Normally it wasn't difficult, but tonight he was tired and more than a little irritated at the Mayor and his cronies.

Mitch relaxed seeing the blackened sky's bright sparkles on Mabey as she made a graceful exit from the lodge ten minutes later. This was a full ten minutes earlier than Mitch expected she would make it. She was visibly upset as she hurried towards the car.

"Told you my head would be aching, that bastard of an ungrateful Mayor was complaining the fundraiser wouldn't bring in the money the town council was hoping it would. He said the club should, 'Do a better job of planning in the future and invite more prominent people willing to spend money,' Like we sit on our asses doing nothing. Molly, Gertrude, and Penelope just sat there with concerned looks on their faces agreeing with everything he said and told him they 'would try to do better next year.' I walked away before saying something I'd regret. Man, it's challenging having to be nice to him."

"Well, I did my part for the club. The twelve-pack of Wilde Stout brought in a whopping $275. As I expected, the Parson twins bought it.

44

Robbie loves the stuff." Mitch hoped a redirect of topic would get Mabey's mind off the Mayor.

"Yeah, thanks for that, by the way, Mitch," Mabey said with true appreciation. "Next year you should donate more."

Mitch pressed the unlock button on the key fob and handed the keys to Mabey. "Do you mind driving, babe? I had a couple of beers."

Mabey took the keys and hurried to slide in behind the wheel. Mitch got in and closed his door. Mabey slammed hers, started the car, and accelerated out of the parking lot. One of the flower club women— from the way she was wobbling that overweight frame of hers, Mitch thought it was Penelope—ran out waving a piece of paper.

Mitch was sure Mabey saw her, but she sped away anyway. Mitch peered back over his shoulder. Poor old Penelope appeared as though Jason Voorhees had sawed her dog in half. Mitch got a good chuckle out of that.

"Damn, I wish I could have gotten a picture of her face."

"Drop it, Mitch. I'm not in the mood to defend anyone."

"You go, girl!"

Chapter 11

Just Dreaming

Silence held the air for a minute or two before Mitch spoke to Mabey. He'd given her time to cool off. "With another depressing flower club event behind you, why not go home and make love to your dashing husband?"

There was a loud screech. The braking force hurled Mitch forward, causing him to slam his head into the dashboard. Mabey's knuckles were white on the steering wheel. They'd stopped in the middle of the road.

Mitch grabbed his forehead. "Shit," he groaned, "what the hell? Never mind, it was a hopeful request. That's all."

"Mitch, you okay?" she whispered, "I'm sorry. Sit back slowly and look straight ahead."

"Dammit Mabey, what the hell?"

Under her breath, she said, "Please stop talking. Tell me you see this."

Mitch stabilized himself, placing his right hand on the dash and his left on his forehead. He probably had a Ford logo tattoo pressed into the skin. "Your damn dashboard hurt, Mabey. I need to remember to seat-belt up when you drive."

"Look already, Mitch."

Sitting back, Mitch turned his stare through the windshield and felt his mouth drop open. "Holy shit! What the..." Mitch popped open the glove box.

"There isn't a camera in there; you know that. Can't you just use your phone?" Mabey stated in a direct but cautious voice.

"Dammit!" Mitch fumbled for his cell phone. Typically, he used the cell phone camera only as a last resort. This qualified as a last resort.

"Mitch, I don't get the impression it wants to be photographed."

"Well, too damn bad. Dammit! I can never find the camera app."

"It's the icon in the lower right, Ansel."

"Nice one, dear. Okay, come on, get going," Mitch talked to his phone as if it would respond more quickly.

"Mitch, he's staring right at us. What do you think he wants?"

"How the hell do I know? Perhaps he's just pissed because we almost ruined his midnight ride."

"Shut up, Mitch, and take the photo already."

"Roll down my window for me, please, babe."

Mabey pulled the switch to lower the passenger window and Mitch eased the cell phone out the window, his finger hovering above the icon on the screen. Without taking his eye off the intended subject, he pressed the button as the two sat in silent disbelief.

Neither had any idea what to do. Mabey hesitantly, and still whispering, broke the silence. "Did you get the shot?

"I'm using a phone, so who the hell knows. Let's check." Mitch talked out loud hoping it would help him process the event.

"Gallery, C, D, E, F, G for Gallery, Camera Images! Great, a nice image of the damn road: how the hell is that possible? I hate these phone cameras. Shit!"

"What do we do?" Mabey asked.

"What I do is buy another camera and put it in your glove-box. I should know better. I can't believe it! What a shot that would have been."

"No Mitch, I mean should we call anybody?"

"And tell them what? That we just saw Sitting Bull in full battle dress on Gandalf's white stallion, Shadowfax?"

Mitch had never expected to use that horse's name in a sentence and have it make sense. His man-brain, bruised and rattled from the dashboard beating, registered a small piece of satisfaction. "You know, Sheriff Gunther and his staff will laugh their asses off. He'll insist we

47

drank too much at the auction and make us the butt of every lame joke at the Coffee Shack for months. Guaranteed!"

"We have to do something."

"You're right. We go home, have a few healthy drinks, great sex, and call it a night. When we wake up in the morning—if we wake up in the morning—perhaps neither of us will remember anything."

"Oh really, Mr. Wilde? Why am I not surprised you'd be thinking about sex at a time like this? Regardless, I wouldn't be good company."

"Bullshit. You are always good company."

"Flattery will get you nowhere tonight, mister." Mabey smiled.

Mitch grinned while buckling up.

"Perhaps we'll see other warriors on the road. One person I will tell is Jasper. I know that old guy will believe me. He may even know what it was."

"Seriously, Mitch?"

"Yes, seriously."

Mitch recounted what Jasper had said a couple weeks ago about their not wanting their photos taken. Mitch was a consummate professional photographer; even on a hated cell phone camera, he did not miss shots. They may not always come out as he wanted, but he got them. The supposed continuous exposure setting on the cell phone made no difference. Mitch took four rapid shots, and all were blank.

Mitch decided he would finally put a camera in Mabey's glove box for the future. Trying to capture an important image on a cell phone could be frustrating. Perhaps if he forced himself to use it more? No, he needed a real camera. If the damn warrior hadn't disappeared like a popped balloon, perhaps he'd have gotten the photo. The more he thought about it, Mitch wasn't even sure he'd have gotten the shot with a camera.

"Where the hell did it go?" he asked.

"Not sure, but it couldn't have just disappeared; could it?"

Mitch didn't reply.

"Mitch?"

"Jasper will have salient thoughts about our breaking-news-at-eleven story. I wonder if this has anything to do with the reports about missing Indians."

"Why Jasper?"

"Do you remember when I told you his ladder fell, and I helped him?"

"Yes."

"He said not to stare them in the eye or take their pictures. It didn't register until now. I'm certain our roadblock was his reference point. The last time I was out on my bike, I saw a man and a horse on the opposite side of the river, and I swear, Mabey, an arrow clipped my shoulder."

"And you didn't tell me? What the hell, Mitch, let me see your shoulder?"

Mabey steadied the steering wheel with her left hand as Mitch pulled the collar back on his shirt. He did his best to reveal a normal looking patch of skin on his shoulder.

"I didn't want to make a big deal out of it. It was so strange. I thought I saw the arrow in the tree, and a bird landed on it, but then the arrow disappeared. In addition, my shoulder healed as if nothing had happened. I wonder if it was the same type of arrow that nailed Jack."

Mabey touched his shoulder gently rubbing her right hand across the surface of his skin. She felt nothing.

Mitch straightened his shirt and leaned over kissing Mabey on the cheek.

"Geezus, Mitch, what's going on? This is so weird."

Mitch didn't comment. He was wrestling with his mind as it tried to figure out how he could make love to his wife tonight. He was relatively certain Mabey's thoughts were going in a different direction. Mitch figured her Venusian brain was not thinking about sex.

"Damn male Martian libido," he mumbled.

"What?"

"Nothing, babe, just dreaming."

The rest of the drive home the only thing Mitch heard was the pavement crunching from the tires' contact with the road.

Chapter 12

A Boxer's Nose

Fifteen minutes later, the Wildes pulled into their garage. They entered the house through the garage, and Mitch went straight to the patio door off the kitchen to let General inside. General did his normal excited dance routine trying to get attention, but neither Mitch nor Mabey paid serious notice. Mabey went for the wine rack, steadying herself on the counter before pouring a rather large glass of Pinot Grigio. She took a long drink and then poured Mitch a glass of Jameson's on the rocks.

Now in better lighting, Mitch couldn't help but notice the paleness of Mabey's skin and felt a tinge of love and sadness seeing her tremble.

"Mitch, with what happened on the road, my love tank is on empty tonight. Don't get pissed."

"Thank the gods because my head is still ringing. I don't want to be worried about the pain in my head and thinking of Sitting Bull while I'm trying to please you." Mitch worked a little harder than normal to get Mabey to relax. Her continued reaction to the sighting had him concerned. Mabey smiled. "How long have you been waiting to say that?"

"What? Thinking of Sitting Bull?"

"No, that your head aches."

Mitch chuckled. "Shit, I guess I did just say that. Well, your braking skills did jam my head into the dashboard."

"You should wear your seatbelt, mister."

"Well, okay, Danica. The damn seatbelts in your car cut into my shoulder. I sure as hell will wear them from now on, though, no matter how uncomfortable they are."

Mabey touched the side of Mitch's head, rubbing his temple with her fingertips. She gently kissed him on the cheek. "I'm going to take a shower and go to bed. I have a couple of mid-morning training sessions tomorrow, and I want to get in early and work out myself."

"Okay, babe, I'll take General for a short walk and then jot a few things in my journal. I'll be back in twenty minutes and in bed within forty-five. My phone is on if you need me for anything. Anything at all, dear," Mitch said with a big grin.

Mabey looked back over her shoulder as she headed up the stairs with her wine. "You're going to write about what happened tonight?"

In his best smart-ass tone, Mitch shot back, "What, Penelope running out from the lodge yelling your name while we sped away? Hell, yeah!"

"No, Mitch, I mean… Oh, never mind, you asshole. Very funny."

Mitch looked at his cell phone again searching for the photo of the Native American apparition. He thought briefly that perhaps the damn image was hidden deep in the bowels of the phone though in his heart he knew better. Two minutes later with no success, he put his phone in his rear pocket, downed the last of his whiskey, and set the glass on the counter. He grabbed General's leash off the coat rack by the door, clipped it to his collar, and the two walked into the garage. General bounced up and down, excited in anticipation.

"We're going to the shed first, Bud, so be patient."

The two went through the yard to the shed. Mitch placed the leash in General's mouth, freeing his hands to open one of his two, gun safes. The other was in their bedroom. A person can't be too prepared. If anything treacherous happened in the house and Mabey or he had to get out quickly, they'd go to the shed for the backup guns.

As Mitch spun the dial to open the safe, General paced and shook his body like a licorice whip, still holding onto the leash. Mitch patted General on the head. "Good boy, just another few seconds", and then grabbed his Berretta 92FS from the safe and a shoulder holster off the wall, placing the gun inside its resting spot. Sliding on his windbreaker over the holster, he took the leash from General. "Okay, let's go, boy."

They left the shed for a quick head-clearing stroll. Normally Mitch didn't take a gun with him on their walks. But tonight, Badass Geronimo had him on edge.

"Come on, boy; I want you to leave your special Labrador fertilizer on Jack's lawn."

General barked and tugged at the leash. He was ninety-five pounds of pure lab muscle. If he chose to take off, there wouldn't be a damn thing Mitch could do to stop him. Mitch's plan was to yell, "General, come here, boy!" and then switch over to, "Well, enjoy yourself then, dammit. Be home by suppertime."

General crapped on Jack's yard, Mitch made told himself he'd scoop it up tomorrow knowing he would forget. Fifteen minutes later he and the dog returned home. Mitch released the clasp on the leash; the dog went for his food bowl. Mitch returned to the shed to lock the gun away. After closing the safe, he shut off the lights and called General, giving him a couple of pats on the back before he went inside.

"You bark extra loud tonight, Bud, if you need me for anything, okay? Good boy, that's a good boy."

Mitch looked around, half expecting to see another warrior on horseback, this one leaping over the fence. He shook off the chill that had crept up his spine as he entered his home.

Mabey was already asleep. What they'd seen had really freaked her out. He had to admit he was on edge as well, but he didn't feel threatened. He was confused and curious. Mitch would make a point to see Jasper tomorrow. He wanted to go now, but it was too late. He opened their bedroom safe and left the door open for quicker access. Mabey's S&W .38 was missing. He scanned the room and was surprised
to see it on her nightstand—confirmation that she was spooked.

Mitch brushed his teeth and washed his face with astringent. He placed a little benzoyl peroxide on his nose in hopes of minimizing the effects of old-man nose. He always told Mabey, "I'll spend every last dime we have on plastic surgery to keep that from happening. I heard it's exacerbated by heavy gin consumption."

"Yes, Mitch, I'm fully aware of your insane reason for drinking

Irish whiskey. And, no, I've never seen an Irishman with a big lumpy nose. Guinness and whiskey, I get it already. You know how many times you've told me that?"

Mitch chuckled. She was so special. After changing into gym shorts and t-shirt, he walked down the hall to his office where he woke up his laptop. The journaling software popped up, ready. Rubbing his still-sore Ford-Motor-Company-logo forehead, Mitch decided he needed to record tonight's events quickly while they were still fresh.

Mitch pressed the following letters on the keyboard:

Tonight, Mabey and I saw something incredible...

Chapter 13

A Gentle Touch

Thirty minutes later, and twenty more than he wanted, Mitch turned off the laptop. He went to the bedroom and checked on Mabey. She was in a deep sleep, which comforted him. His mind raced thinking of what Jasper had shared during his rooftop escapade. At the time, Mitch had thought the warnings were nothing more than the ramblings of an old man. Now he wasn't so sure. He thought about Jasper's invitation, and his acceptance, during the recent encounter.

"I have a few things to show you. You should know what's going on in the world. Just knock on my side garage door."

Mitch pulled back the covers on his side of the bed, sliding in next to a very warm Mabey. Laying there listening to the calming, rhythmic sound of her breathing he wondered what Jasper might reveal tomorrow and what the old guy would think of the sighting. His insight might be valuable since Mitch had no clue what to make of it.

He gave Mabey a gentle touch on her shoulder, so she would know he was in bed. She mumbled but Mitch couldn't make out the words as she repositioned herself closer to him. Mitch basked in her warmth and closed his eyes wishing for quick sleep.

Chapter 14

Whatever

In what seemed like minutes later, Mitch rolled over, viewing the clock—5:31. He got out of bed and put on sweatpants and a clean long-sleeve t-shirt. He grabbed his sneakers from the floor and prepped for his morning stroll with General. Certain mornings, exercise was on the bike but General liked jogging better and Mitch wanted to oblige his canine friend today.

Mabey left for work early on Mondays and got home late. Today was no exception. Mitch recognized the sounds coming from their shower. He hurried his pace downstairs because he wanted to get back from the walk before she left. They needed to talk. Neither of them ignored shit, buried their heads, or tried pretending things away. It was a pact they'd made before they married. Until now, full disclosure had worked very well.

No luck that last night's viewing of the Indian warrior on horseback was a dream. His feet, contacting the earth, stride after stride, kept him grounded and centered, something he wanted this morning. Mitch decided he'd drop in on Jasper tonight and share his tales. There'd be plenty to discuss.

Mitch grabbed the leash and got General off the back porch. The two headed out the side gate next to the garage.

Jasper stood in his driveway drinking a cup of coffee. Mitch and General jogged over to say hello. He wasn't happy, which was clear to Mitch from the whimpering and leash tugging.

"Morning, neighbor," Mitch said. "I'll take you up on your offer and head over later today."

"I wondered if you'd come at all."

"Sorry, I always spend Sundays with Mabey."

"What did you want to talk to me about, flowers? I don't think so, floral king."

"No, not about flowers. Damn, Jasper, lighten up; should I come or not?"

"Not sure about tonight. We'll miss Monday night soccer," Jasper said with a smart-ass grin on his face. He chuckled. "How about six, Wilde?"

"Funny, I almost believed you for a second."

Mitch grabbed General's leash a little tighter and gave it a tug. A wasted motion, he realized, as General was more than ready. The two continued their jaunt toward the river trail. Looking back, Mitch called over his shoulder, "Okay, Jasper, see you at six."

Mitch couldn't figure out if Jasper was bitter, senile, or plain old angry. Perhaps a little of each? Right on cue, Mitch's ears picked up one last comment from Jasper.

"Yeah, Wilde, whatever."

Chapter 15

Bacon and Eggs

Thirty minutes later, General and Mitch arrived back at the house. Mitch put General in the backyard, fed him, and then found Mabey in the kitchen making coffee.

"Hey, babe, you and General have a nice ride?"

"We jogged instead. I thought if we ran, I could think better. You know all that staying connected shit?"

Mabey laughed. "Did it work?"

"Oh, hell, I don't know. The exercise was good for sure. General had a great time as always. I saw Jasper, and he invited me over to chat. Remember, I told you yesterday he has something he wants to show me in his garage?"

"Oh yeah, that's right; are you going?"

"I told him I would come about six."

"I have my typical Monday. Not sure when I'll be home, definitely by nine, though. I'll call if I'll be later than that."

Mitch gave Mabey a kiss on the back of her neck rubbing the small of her back. She started a playful purr.

"Okay, babe, I'm making coffee with bacon and eggs. Want any?"

"No. Thanks, though. I'm heading up to finish getting ready."

"Okay, say bye before you leave."

Mabey left the kitchen, and Mitch flipped the countertop TV to the news. He grabbed a frying pan, eggs and bacon, and frozen hash browns. On TV, a news promo was just finishing.

"And finally, the missing Indians in the Pacific Northwest continue to stump

everyone. Tune in tonight at five for the latest information."

Mitch briefly turned to the TV, but it was too late to see anything. He walked to the sliding door and let General in. "Come on, boy. How about a little people food?"

Chapter 16

Plenty of Time

Mitch did his best to kill time, but he still had a couple hours before he needed to be at Jasper's. Frustrated at the crawling clock, he decided to check on his latest batch of beer. First, he'd pull his Jeep, aptly named 'Black Steel' into the garage. The neighborhood was safe, but Mitch didn't like to leave the Jeep out at night.

Closing garage door, Mitch headed to the shed, built shortly after he and Mabey bought the place; it worked well for beer brewing. The shed had the brew area, dartboard, and a small refrigerator stocked with adult beverages and water. Bicycles hung from the rafters above a mower and in front of several grass-covered garden utensils, a well-placed wood stove, and a window-mounted air conditioner. If he and Mabey had to make do without the house for any reason, they could manage in the shed for a short time, no matter the season.

"A hotel would be better," Mabey would say.

Mitch grabbed for a buzzing phone in his back pocket and saw Mabey was calling. "Hello, this is Mitch. Can I help you?"

"Mitch is that you?"

"Yes, it is. Can I help you?"

"Can you talk?"

"Sure, just bustin' on you. What's up, honey? How many steroid-heads asked you on a date today?"

"No BS, Mitch. I'm not in the mood. Can you pick me up at seven-thirty? Michelle borrowed my car. She has a hot date, and the guy doesn't drive."

"Again? How hot can the date be if he doesn't have his own car?

When will she ever stop dating freeloaders? She'd better bring your car back with gas in it this time."

"Mitch, I need to go. Will you pick me up?"

"Yeah, I'll be there, but you're cutting into my man-time with Old Man Jasper.

"Is that it, Mitch?"

Mitch heard the irritation in Mabey's tone. "Yes, babe, I'll be out front of the club at seven-thirty. Medford Health correct?"

"Yes, and thanks; see you then." Mabey hung up before he had a chance to say bye. He ended the call on his phone.

Even though they'd gone to high school together, Mitch had seen Mabey for the first time at Portland State—in one of PSU's fitness centers. She got her degree in physical therapy, and he was a photo science major. Over the next weeks, to meet her, he worked out at the fitness center whenever he could, but she never showed. Mitch got his opportunity one night at a dive-bar where the college kids hung out.

Mitch shook himself alert. Capped a bottle of stout and placed it in the fridge. He cleaned up while thinking about Mabey and their current state of affairs. She'd worked as an independent physical trainer for the past three years at various clubs around Medford and Grants Pass. It was a good career. She made her own schedule; the clubs and the clients paid her directly, and she enjoyed what she did.

General barked, shaking frantically back and forth, as he did when he wanted attention. Mitch knelt, grabbed General's head, and let the dog lick his face, then wiped his face. One last check at the beer counter, he was satisfied with the clean-up. He tucked a four-pack of his Wilde Imperial Stout under his arm for Jasper, encouraged General out of the shed, and closed the door. Mitch had worked hard to perfect his beer-brewing process. Not yet fully confident in his beer, he thought he should also pick up a four-pack of Guinness. Mitch hoped the old guy would like his dark beer—an imperial stout knock-off recipe he'd picked up at his favorite beer craft shop. He still had time to kill, so he threw General's leash in the backseat of Black Steel. He never really could explain the Jeep-naming to Mabey, who found it a little odd. She often ribbed Mitch about it.

He countered with, "And I can name something else, if you would prefer." At which point Mabey always hit him on the shoulder and smiled. "You'd better not, Mitch Wilde. Besides, you know I own that, anyway." Mitch started to tell the dog to get in, but General knew what the leash meant and already jumped in the passenger's seat. "Want to go for a ride, you knucklehead?"

The five-year-old lab loved going if he got shotgun. Mabey was certain General resented her when she went with them.

Thirty minutes later, Mitch and General were pulling back into the driveway from the beer run; the two Jacks, as Mitch called them, were backing out of their driveway. Mitch brought Black Steel to a stop outside the garage, undid General's harness from the seatbelt, and waved at Jack to stop.

"General, heel, boy!"

General jumped out and stayed stride for stride with Mitch who approached Jack's window.

"What's up, Mitch?"

"I realize you have a game, Junior, so I won't keep you guys long. Old Man Jasper asked me over to his place this evening. I wanted to let someone besides Mabey know. He says he has something he wants to show me. Don't ask me what because he didn't explain. The old guy made it sound like the world was going to end, or get seriously messed up, and he wanted someone else to know."

"Damn, that sounds like a real exciting evening, Mitch."

Jack could be almost as big a smart-ass as Mitch. It occasionally pissed Mitch off, but he relished the fact that there was someone else, besides Mabey, who thought as he did.

"Why are you telling me?"

"In case I end up missing. And, it must have something to do with your getting shot by that arrow."

"It's only Old Man Jasper. The guy's harmless."

Jack squirmed a little in his seat, and Junior's eyes flickered.

"Yeah, Jack... well; just don't say I didn't tell you."

"Whatever, Wilde," Jack retorted.

Mitch doubted his friend's loyalty right now. Not really, but hell, if it was important for him, it should be important for his bud.

"Final game of the home stand against the Newtown River Rats tonight, Junior?"

"Yeah, Mitch, Giants superstar Jake Housebender is on the roster tonight rehabbing his shoulder. I'm starting, so it should be fun throwing BBs at him."

"Okay, have fun and good luck. Tomorrow I'll fill you in on what Jasper has going on, Jack."

"Sounds good, Mitch."

Mitch and General stepped back from the F150.

"Junior, don't be afraid to keep Housebender off the plate," Mitch shouted.

"Throw chin music at him for me, will you? I expect a full report tomorrow and I want to see you on SportsCenter at eleven."

Junior laughed. "You got it, Mitch. I will personally put your name on one of my fastballs."

"Dang, Junior, I'm sorry. I should be going."

"Don't worry about it, Mitch, next game. Housebender will probably jack a couple out of the park off me. I would rather you didn't see that."

Mitch laughed. "Well, kid, wish I could be there. Good luck, okay?"

Mitch went back to his driveway and eased the Jeep into the garage. "Come on, boy. Let's go put the beer in the refrigerator until it's time to go."

Woof, woof!

"What's that, boy? No, I'm sorry, but you must stay in the yard. I don't think Jasper would like you in his garage. Perhaps next time though. Good boy, that's a good boy."

Mitch rubbed General on the head as they walked to the shed. Checking his watch, he decided to get the beer in the refrigerator then shoot a few arrows since he had more than enough time.

Chapter 17

Reminiscing

Mitch replaced the worn-out target on its base and resumed shooting, reflecting on his first meeting with Jasper. One day Mitch was doing yard work, and Jasper came over and struck up a conversation. It started out with typical neighbor banter and quickly transitioned into the day's being his ex-wife's birthday. It was as if he launched information about his first wife.

"The bitch's birthday," were Jasper's exact words. Jasper's floodgates then opened.

"Listen, pretty boy, I've lived here since the development was built almost thirty years ago. I married my high school sweetheart in Klamath Falls two weeks after graduation. Right after that, I started working for one of the larger logging companies in town."

"No shit," Mitch said, afraid not to engage. He wasn't sure if indifference would have mattered, though, as Jasper seemed to be staring through him, as if he were in a different place altogether.

"Two months into a logging gig, I had my pelvis crushed when a massive pine tree fell the wrong way. We scrambled like hell, but the forest was evidently pissed and did what it could to ensnare us. I got tangled in thick underbrush and couldn't free myself. To this day, I hate pine furniture."

"How the heck are you able to walk?"

"Sheer spite and determination. The crew got me to the helicopter, the emergency crew flew me to the hospital within an hour, and the doctors went to work. They told my foreman, Mr. Newman, that I'd never walk again. I made up my mind to prove the fancy doctors wrong. I wasn't one of those pansies that up and quit. I'm a fighter, Wilde. Only thing I've ever walked away from was my marriage. Eighteen months later, I was walking. With pain and effort, but I was walking. I still get shudders that reverberate through my whole body. They rock me to the core."

Jasper's eyes glazed a bit, as if he lost a moment in time, and a tear hung on the edge of his eye.

"There was one right there," he proclaimed. "One of the mild ones; sometimes I black out."

"No shit," Mitch blurted.

"Anyway, during my rehab, my wife left me for a goddamned rodeo clown. I knew something was up when she didn't even bother coming to the hospital."

"Did you say rodeo clown?"

"Yeah Wilde, you heard me right, a rodeo clown. I never remarried. A guy can't trust a woman. She's always planning her escape, lookin' to get a better deal. Most of us are just too damn blind to notice."

"I'm not so sure," Mitch responded.

Jasper shot Mitch a look of pain and anger. Mitch shifted his weight, making it clear he was regretting his last comment.

"As I was saying, after my long rehab, I wandered around from job-to-job on farms, in the woods, and at a few lumber mills. I did whatever kept my stomach full and my mind occupied. Anyway, to make a boring story less boring, I did odd jobs around this part of the state; always loved the way it looked and felt. So, I bought a home here in Rogue River and settled down. I haven't been with a woman since. Women, you can't trust 'em, Wilde."

"Seriously?" Mitch's mind raced trying to understand how a man could go that long without sex. He didn't picture Jasper to be one to entertain himself. At least he didn't put any serious effort into the image. It made his masculine senses uncomfortable.

Mitch understood in marriage, there could be no-sex stretches of weeks depending on schedules, moods, timing, and just plain old desire, but he also knew the possibility existed, every day of his life, that he was one thoughtful comment away from feeling the soft warmth of his wife's skin next to his.

Thwack. Another arrow left Mitch's bowstring and hurtled into the target. He walked to the straw-covered circle and took his time pulling out all six arrows. Mitch turned and went back to his shooting line continuing to think about his old neighbor.

"Don't make me regret telling you any of this," Jasper had said. "You're the only person I've ever told. As my years get on, I worry less about what is seemingly supposed to matter and more about what feels right. Talking with you, Wilde, feels right."

Mitch held the bow against his chest and pulled his shoulder blades together, breathing calmly as he let an arrow fly, finding yellow.

After that, Mitch felt newfound understanding and respect for his neighbor. Jasper must have really loved and cared for his wife because she really screwed up his mind. To have the self-motivation and drive for rehabbing such an injury and the discipline to be alone for all this time: Mitch thought Jasper might be a monk in his own religion. On the other hand, he was too bitter and full of resentment. Mitch could not imagine losing Mabey to anyone, ever. In particular, a rodeo clown.

Chapter 18

See You in the Morning

Mitch loosed a final shot. Walking toward the target he counted seven out of ten in the yellow, with three finding red.. He had a lot on his mind, so he felt the three reds were forgivable today. As he headed to the shed to put the bow and arrows away, he felt the air coming off the river was particularly sweet today, and the clean water smell heightened his senses. His brain recognized the sound of the water pushing between the rocks and the wind whistling through the tops of the pines. Funny how the noise was always there, but his mind didn't always register what the ears captured.

In life, Mitch needed to be aware of what was happening around him if he was going to stay out of trouble. Mabey increasingly tired of his rants about preparation and being cognizant of surroundings and would tell him he acted like Jason Bourne. Mitch's standard reply, which always got a smile, was, "Jason Bourne was fiction. I'm real, babe."

Mitch said a quick goodbye to General in the backyard and headed for the garage. His canine friend whimpered as the door closed behind them.

Mitch located the beer, checked his pocket for his cell phone, and walked across the street to Jasper's place. The old guy was standing outside his cream-colored garage. As Mitch approached, Jasper looked at his wrist, then up at him, back at his wristwatch, and finally at Mitch as if he were timing him. Mitch quickened his pace.

"The old guy is a Svengali as well?" he mumbled.

Jasper greeted Mitch. "Good man, I can't stand it when people are late. You had thirty-three seconds to spare."

"Uh, thirty-three seconds, seriously?"

"You can tell a lot about a man who takes a time commitment seriously."

Mitch didn't know how to reply. Jasper stared back at him as if he were looking for a confrontation.

"I've been looking forward to this." Mitch added, "Here's a four-pack of my home-brewed Wilde Imperial Stout. I also brought a 4-pack of Guinness Extra Stout in case you don't like my craft."

"A four-pack? So, what are you going to drink? Aren't you thirsty?" Jasper wore a slight smile. More like a smirk really. It took Mitch a few seconds before he recognized Jasper was joking. Mitch realized just how little he knew his neighbor.

Jasper grabbed one of Mitch's brews, popped the top, and tilted his head way back, lips tight against the bottle. He continued chugging the beer as they walked towards the side of his garage.

"Damn, that is good, brew-master; I had no idea you could make this."

Mitch thought Jasper couldn't properly taste his beer-brewing excellence since he was drinking so fast.

"Don't look at me that way, Wilde, and stop being so sensitive. I said I like it. I taste a hint of coffee and slight chocolate undertones? I also believe a nut of some kind and is that cinnamon?"

"Thanks. I put serious effort into my beer, the stout in particular. You have a good beer palate Jasper. I'd like to use you for taste tests down the road, if you're up for it."

Jasper stopped about ten feet from the side entrance to his garage, finished off the beer, and set the empty bottle on a fence post.

"Any time you need me to taste a new batch, just give me a buzz. I might even come over to your place."

"Be still my beating heart. You'd come to my house, old man?"

Jasper smiled with his eyes, but turned the corners of his mouth down, trying to look stern while pointing at the empty bottle on the fence post.

"I suspect you'll want to take that empty home when you leave, right?"

"Yes, definitely, I sterilize them and reuse them."

"Okay, well, don't forget it. I don't want any trash in my yard. Hey, are you going to have one?"

"I'll leave the Wilde Imperial Stout for you. I'll have a Guinness." Mitch would have only one since he had to pick up Mabey soon. He didn't want to mention this, at least not yet. He decided to save this potentially unsettling news for a short while.

"Come on; let's do this." Jasper held the door for Mitch, almost pushing him in. Jasper followed, closing the door, locking it, and pulling down a security bar. "You can never be sure these days. Uncle Sam watches everything, and I ain't gonna make it easy. If they want to come in here, it'll be crawling over my dead body."

Why the hell did I come over here? Mitch wondered.

Jasper flipped the light switch, eliminating the darkness. Mitch couldn't find any windows. He knew that from the outside, there were three. He'd stared at Jasper's place at least a hundred times over the years, and each time, he distinctly remembered seeing windows. Mitch realized Jasper had built another wall in front of his main door.

"I know what that thick skull of yours is mulling, fancy lad. The wall, right?"

"As a matter of fact, yes."

"I built it for two reasons. Security of course and for climate control, which might not be so obvious."

"Okay, that makes sense. Garage doors certainly aren't insulated enough if at all."

"Exactly, they aren't very secure, either."

Within minutes, Mitch was more aware of what Jasper had been doing these last thirty years. "Damn, Jasper. What the hell is all this shit? Are you a member of a secret society or working for Uncle Sam in some cloak-and-dagger shit?"

"Now, if I were in a secret society, would I just up and ask you

68

over here to see all this? Uncle Sam used to be decent back in the day, but now he can kiss my ass. He doesn't care about anyone or anything of value any more. Only interested in making sure to stay as big as possible and keep the common folk busting their asses all day so he can stay fat. Once those politicians get a feel for serious power, they get addicted. Political power is worse than crack if you ask me because it messes with all our lives, not just the addict's."

Clearly, Jasper had all his wits about him. Mitch guessed he was in his seventies, and he obviously took care of himself.

"I didn't mean anything, Jasper. You'll see the more you're around me that I tend to be a smart-ass." Mitch sipped his Guinness, avoiding direct eye contact.

Jasper shot back. "That's why I like you, Wilde. You got a wit about you. I never much cared for people who don't have a sense of humor. They usually think the world begins and ends with them and are about as much fun to be around as an erudite college professor who thinks FDR's Great Society was what saved America. Goddamned horseshit— more like what started us down the road to mediocrity and government dependency. Anyhow Wilde, people without a sense of humor are boring, and they never know when to shut up. One thing I've noticed about a smart-ass is he can get in and out of conversations quickly. I like that."

"Yeah, I hear you, Jaspy," Mitch shot back, thinking that he had to get Jasper and Jack together. Watching the two of them talk politics and government would be a real event. Mitch couldn't wait to start that conversation.

"Okay, fancy-lad, follow me, and look at this. For goodness' sake, don't go running out of here wanting to change your panties. We aren't too late, but we should move quickly, and be ready. Oh, and another thing, you can't tell anyone until I know more details. If you walk out of here agreeing with me, we'll want to come up with a short list of people we can trust and bring them in as needed."

"If I walk out of here? Um, okay..." was all Mitch was able to stutter.

The old coot guided Mitch to a large four-by-ten table in the middle of the garage. He'd polished off his second stout and was working on a third. Mitch figured he should tell him the alcohol content was high, for a beer, but he had the impression the man could handle his adult beverages just fine.

"Okay, panty princess," Jasper blurted.

Mitch chuckled, realizing he may have finally met his smart-ass equivalent.

On the table were maps, old photographs, what appeared to be satellite photos, drawings and sketches, a couple of small Crater Lake photos, several old books, a tablet PC that was off, and a Twinkie. Yeah, long live the Twinkie. Mitch transitioned to an examination of the table's contents trying to decide what didn't belong.

Jasper picked up the small golden loaf of heaven, unwrapped it, polished it off in two bites, and then chased it with a large swig of stout. "Now that's good beer. Son-of-a-bitch, Wilde-man, you make good suds. I ain't gonna have to spend the night praying to the porcelain god, am I?"

"Ha! No, but you may be changing your underwear more than a few times." Mitch smiled.

"Okay, funny, fancy lad. Sit on this stool and get comfortable because it's going to take a while to step you through this."

Mitch thought it was hilarious. Jasper never called him the same name twice—at least not in a row. Mitch checked his watch, 6:10; he wanted to pick Mabey up at 7:30. He could stretch his arrival time out to 7:45 before she got worried. He could make it to the club in twenty minutes, fifteen to eighteen if Black Steel and Wilde-man flouted the law. Mitch couldn't imagine this would take more than an hour. He was wrong, and it almost caused a setback with Jasper.

Jasper pointed at the monitors on the table. Mitch put aside random thoughts, focusing on what his neighbor was saying. This wasn't hard since Jasper was very articulate, opinionated, and flat-out compelling.

"So, if you look at this, Wilde, and you're open-minded enough to step out of the batter's box, you can see that…"

Mitch checked his watch and realized time had flown by. He was going to be late picking up Mabey. He cut off the old-guy in mid-sentence.

"Jasper, I'm really sorry, but I have to go. When you first invited me over, I didn't think I would be here this long. I have to pick my wife up at the health club. She loaned her car to her sister."

"Again?" Jasper replied, which made Mitch take pause. How does he know about Michelle and her car-borrowing?

"Damn, Mitchey. This is serious. When can you come back?"

"When do you want me?"

"How about ten tomorrow morning, or will you be sleeping in because you lead such a hard life?"

"How about eight, and I'll bring coffee and donuts?"

"Forget the coffee and bring pastry. While you're at it, bring more of your Wilde stout. They'll go nicely together. And make it nine; I'm going to be up late, and I need a little extra old-man sleep."

"Seriously, Jasper, more stout?" Mitch was now officially flattered.

"Come on, Wilde. My clock is different from most people, and frankly since my wife divorced me, I have the motto of doing what I want, when I want, as long as it doesn't hurt anyone. It has served me damn well for a long time. Besides, I would think you'd be glad."

Mitch chuckled. "Well, I am, and okay I'll bring more. See you in the morning."

As Mitch walked out the door, Jasper mumbled, "I hope I didn't make a mistake."

Mitch regretted having to leave. He should have told Jasper right off. Mitch didn't usually worry about offending people. You give them the straight dope and let the chips fall: a lesson learned from his father long ago. With Jasper, though, he had an unusual aversion to disappointing him. He wasn't sure why, but he was aware enough to realize it was an issue.

Mitch grabbed the empty stout bottle off the fence and jogged home, pressing the garage door key code on his cell phone app. He always got a kick out of the phone app's opening the door, no matter how many times he did it. Mitch hopped into Black Steel and got on the road. He selected the local country radio station as it dawned on him what Jasper said while he was leaving, "I hope I didn't make a mistake."

"Shit." Mitch turned up an old country classic of Tim McGraw's. He didn't want to let Jasper down, and, like Tim, regret it the next thirty years.

Chapter 19

Penance

Mitch tried calling Mabey to inform her he was on the way. She didn't pick up. Then a text message came in.

Mitch, where are you? The wolves are on the move.

It was 7:42; he was still five long minutes away. Black Steel was hugging the corners but cornering with speed wasn't the Jeep's forte. Mitch pressed speed dial one more time, and Mabey picked up this time. "Honey, sorry. I'm almost there."

"Hurry, I turned down three ride offers already."

"I hear you, babe, and just a couple more minutes. Want to talk, or do you need both hands free to fight off the hounds?"

Mabey's response; a dial tone. Dammit, why did he not making being on time more of a priority? He hated letting her down. He pressed the accelerator a little harder. Mitch remembered Jack Junior's game and searched for it on the radio as he flew through town. He pulled into the parking lot four minutes later, and, sure enough, a meathead stood there chatting up Mabey.

She had her ball cap on with her hair pulled through the back the way Mitch loved. She was doing her best to keep her distance from potential male chatters.

Mitch chirped the tires on cornering, slammed on the brakes in front of her and the current stalker, opened the door, stood on the side step, and yelled across the top of the Jeep, "Honey, good news! The test came back, and I'm clean, too. Doc says the discoloration is from the laundry detergent."

Mabey smirked with a shit-eating grin on her face; the steroid-proud dude retreated. Mitch climbed back in, reached across the passenger's seat, and opened the door for his athletic wife.

"Dang it, Mitch, that guy is a total gossip around here and will tell everyone what you said."

"Well, good, perhaps the guys will stop asking you out now."

"The women, too?" Mabey returned.

"Dammit, I didn't think about that. Oh, well, I can still imagine it."

"Crack," the radio hissed. The announcer followed with, *"If that stays fair, it's gone."*

"Foul ball!" the radio blurted. The raised voiced of the announcer caught both of them by surprise; they both felt their bodies jump.

The Rogues were hanging on to a one-run lead. It was 2-1 in the top of the seventh. Jack Junior was still on the mound working on a three-hitter. The announcer gushed about his performance.

"Housebender is one for three with a run-scoring double and two strikeouts. No outs in the top half of the last frame. Count is two and two now as Rogue manager Jeff Collins, and catcher A.J. Costa are on their way to the mound. Jenson has thrown 84 pitches so far, walked two, and struck out nine. He looks as though he might be starting to tire; Collins will need to talk with him to find out more. Good solid performance up to this point for the youngster. If Collins leaves the kid in and Housebender ties the game, everyone will forget Jenson's outstanding outing and be talking about Housebender. ESPN will be showing it repeatedly for the next 24 hours. Single-A players rarely get on SportsCenter, and you have to know Jenson doesn't want his first appearance being related to serving up a game-tying tater to Housebender."

The announcer paused for a moment, and then added, *"We have Manager Collins miked up tonight. Let's listen in as he talks with Jenson on the mound."*

"Jack, how you feeling, and remember we're live?"

"Good, Skip. I can get Housebender and finish out the game. No problem!"

"Okay, you can walk him, and we can play for the double play and get out of here. I can also bring in Rubenstein. He's been warming up for the last five minutes, and he's ready."

"No, I got this prima donna and don't worry skip I'm not going to walk him. Rubenstein is dying to finish up for me. I am not leaving him a mess. I'm going low and outside edge on this one, as hard as I can throw, then follow it up with a fast-ball right down the middle. No signals and let's do it."

"You got it, Jenson, sounds fun."

The radio snapped and crackled a bit. "Well, it looked like Collins was going to give the young pitcher the hook, but as you heard, Jenson persuaded Collins to let him finish things out. He has thrown a whale of a game until now, but there's no way that Collins wants to let Housebender beat them. If he makes a wrong decision by leaving Jenson in, he'll have to listen to SportsCenter second-guess his decision for the next day and a half."

The reception came and went fueled by static.

"Damned AM reception, I wish they'd broadcast these games on FM," Mitch blurted, breaking the silence.

Mabey was texting on her phone, most likely to her sister.

"Jack Junior is pitching. I'm surprised you aren't at the game."

"I had the thing with Jasper and didn't want to cancel. I wish now I'd gone to the game."

"Well, I'm sure Junior understands. You can't see all of them. The way the radio announcer is talking, it sounds like a big deal with the House guy."

Mitch chuckled over Mabey's reference to the player she called House.

"Yeah, it's a big game. The visiting team has a major-leaguer, Housebender on the roster tonight. He's rehabbing his knee, getting ready to re-join the Giants in a couple of days."

Hiss, snap, hiss. No more words coming from the radio, only static.

"I don't believe it. Normally I have no problem getting the game out here. Wonder what's going on?"

"Sorry, Mitch, I'm sure Jack will tell you all about it tomorrow. I guess you'll have to talk with me now."

Mabey smiled. Mitch loved seeing the very slight crow's feet on the edges of her eyes when she smiled. She was so beautiful, and the older she got, the more beautiful she became.

Mitch re-engaged Mabey despite his irritation over losing the game reception on the radio.

"I won't see him until late in the day when he gets off work."

"What about Junior? Won't he be around?"

"No, I don't think so. His team has a road-trip coming up for the next week or so. Pretty sure they're heading out of town."

"So, why were you late? You said something about being at Jasper's place; did I hear that correctly?"

"Yes. I'm not sure where to begin. I'm a little put off with the whole experience."

"What do you mean?"

"Well, Jaspy showed me several things tonight that are disturbing, to say the least. He's either well informed, or a total nut job. Haven't made up my mind up yet. He wants me to go back over to his house at nine tomorrow morning."

"Jaspy? Well, what did he show you? Was it big and unexpectedly personal?"

"Ha ha, the pretty woman makes a funny. No, it wasn't personal, but it certainly was horrific, or will be horrific, if it happens."

"Okay, I'll bite. What are you talking about?" Mabey shot back.

"Babe, I promised I wouldn't say anything until he determined it to be okay. He even made me swear on the book *Chariot of the Gods* that I wouldn't say anything to 'that hot, out-of-your-league wife of yours.'" Mitch made up this part, hoping to deflect her questions. Why not work the angles a bit? Mitch thought his bullshit sounded good and was harmless. Mabey was hot after all.

"Out-of-your-league,' what a wise old man," Mabey responded in a monotone voice as she stared out the window, clearly somewhere else in thought.

"That I can talk about."

Mabey blew off Mitch's last statement. She either didn't care or wasn't listening. Knowing her, the way he did, the latter made the most sense.

Mabey re-engaged quickly though, surprising Mitch.

"Why haven't you taken the doors off the Jeep? It's warm enough now and will be for the rest of the summer. It's a lot more fun to ride watching the earth zoom by."

"You tell me every summer. I thought about the doors today. I'll take them off Sunday after the lake trip. I have the shoot coming up on Saturday at Crater Lake, and I don't like going up there with them off."

"You didn't tell me about this shoot. What's it for?"

"I didn't? Shit, I could have sworn I mentioned it."

"No, sir, you did not."

"Oh, it isn't anything big. Ron at the *Tribune* is doing their early summer spread on the region.

They're looking for Crater Lake, among other things, in the area. You know Ron: anytime he needs anything outdoorsy down south, he calls me. He said he was going through their archives, looking at my Crater Lake shots and didn't see anything he wanted to use. He was hoping I could come up with something new and unique. I was half-tempted to pull images out of my files, but I figured the drive might be nice. And, it gives me an excuse to try out my new lens. Why don't you go with me?"

"I wish I could; I haven't been up there since the last time you did a shoot, but I have three different training sessions, and it's too late to back out. The fitness center, not to mention the clients, get a little pissy when I cancel at all, let alone this late. You know that, Mitch."

"I'm looking forward to the alone-time. The drive will do me well, especially with what Jasper is telling me."

"About that, you never did tell me what's going on. You were too busy trying to distract me with your spot-on compliments." Mabey smiled.

Mitch reached over and squeezed her leg. "I will, babe. I'm not trying to be a jerk, but I need more time to understand everything before I talk with you about it, okay? Otherwise, I'm going to confuse you."

"Okay, but I'll want answers at some point, and soon. You understand me, Mitch?" Mabey squeezed Mitch's leg in return.

Mitch tried the radio again, still nothing but static.

Mabey rolled down her window and let the warm evening air sooth her forehead. Closing her eyes, she leaned her head back focusing on the fresh evergreen smells wafting through the Southern Oregon air.

Ten minutes later, Mitch pulled into the driveway and guided Black Steel next to the slot normally occupied by Mabey's car. She jumped out and entered the house.

Mitch closed the main garage door and followed her.

"Hey," she said, "perhaps Jasper will go with you and share more of his pent-up rage. That ought to be good for a bit of alone-time."

"In what world?"

"Come on, Mitch, I was just—"

"Actually, not a bad idea, I've been conceptualizing a style of writing I could do in conjunction with my photography. Jasper may be what I am looking for. Thanks, babe, inviting him is a good idea."

"Glad to help out, dear. Now pour me a glass of wine and run me a bath, your penance for being late, mister."

Chapter 20

I Got This

Jack Junior knocked on the Wilde's front door two hours after Mitch got home. The unexpected interruption didn't matter as Mabey's bath had evidently brought on a headache.

Mitch opened the door. His pretend-son stood there looking excited. "Hey, Mitch, hope I'm not intruding, but I have something to tell you."

"Junior, come in. What the hell happened? We had the game on the radio: you were facing Housebender, gave up the long foul ball, and when the coach was leaving the mound, the damn radio reception went out."

"You'll never guess," Junior shot back. "I got called up."

Mitch smiled in thought as the kid looked as if he forgot to take off his jock, he was hopping around so much.

"Whoa, hold on there, partner. They called you up. That's fantastic! First things first, though, Kershaw. What happened with Housebender?"

"Oh, yeah. I struck him out."

"That's it? You struck him out? No back story, no SportsCenter highlight? Give me more than that! Damn, you're just like your old man."

"Well, after Coach left the mound, I threw it high and tight as Costa knew I would right at Housebender's chest. He bailed. Funny as shit and surprised me. He picked himself up, brushed off the dirt and then looked at me as if he was going to kill me. Anyhow, full count, first base was open with no one on. So, I felt like taking a chance. No risk, no reward, right?

As soon as Housebender stepped into the box, I reared back as hard as I could and threw an 80-mile-per-hour change-up. He swung so hard and was so far out in front, I smelled a slight hint of oak in the air. Wish I had a photo of his facial expression. It was awesome."

"I figured you might throw a change-up to him. That was ballsy. If he was expecting it, he would have hit it to Seattle."

"I had nothing to lose. Most people expected him to get the best of me, anyway. No loss on my part; it was Housebender after all. Since you mentioned it, SportsCenter is playing the hell out of it. My adrenaline was pumping so hard when the next guy came up, I threw three straight fast balls and struck him out to end the game."

"What did you end up with, ten Ks?"

"No, a three-hitter with eleven. No way was I letting Al "The Dominator" Rubenstein clean-up for me and get the highlight tonight".

"Coach came out to the mound to congratulate me after the game and said management called me up to Double-A Chattanooga. Can you believe it?"

"Yeah, I do, kid. I've seen your talent. Anyway, you're too stubborn to realize you can't succeed. Just like your old man. Where is he, anyway?"

"Glad you asked. He seems more depressed than usual. Ever since Mom got hit by the garbage truck, he always gets down on game nights."

"Shit, he can't blame himself. That clueless garbage man should be in prison, or better yet, hanging from the nearest oak tree. He was texting while he was supposed to be picking up garbage cans. I still can't believe he got off without jail time."

Junior hung his head. Mitch mentally kicked himself as he realized he wasn't helping matters.

"Yep, Mitch, you're right. Can you do me a favor and keep an eye on Dad? I'm leaving first thing tomorrow morning for Chattanooga."

"Sure, Junior, and I'm sorry. I didn't mean to bring you down."

"That's okay. Don't worry about it."

"Damn, Chattanooga? That is a ways from home."

"Yeah, it's where their Double-A team is located. I told Dad I'll try hard to pitch my way up to Triple-A Albuquerque by the end of summer."

"Your dad will be fine. Just visit him if you get a break. You should be able to afford the ticket now."

Mabey entered. "Mitch! Junior, how're you doing? Oh, yeah, Mitch said you pitched tonight. How'd the game end up?"

"We won. I had a good game and got moved up to Double-A."

"That's fantastic! Your dad must be so proud!"

"Yeah, he is. He took me to Denny's after the game for a Grand Slam. It was nice. Just like old times."

Mitch slapped Junior on the back. "Don't worry about your dad. I'll keep him busy. I have several photo shoots coming up. I'll talk him into taking time off and going with me."

"Thanks, Mitch. Well, I have to go pack and rest. My flight's at seven in the morning. I have three connections to Chattanooga."

Mabey gave Junior a hug and headed upstairs. "Have fun and be careful."

"Yeah, be careful that those big old baseball player athletes on steroids don't get mad at you for striking them out. They might come after you with their hard, wooden, bats and give you an oak shampoo."

Junior chuckled.

"Mitch, you're an asshole. Very funny." Mabey went back up the stairs.

"Well, dear, at least the kid will get some action."

Mitch didn't dare look at Mabey's face, although he wished he had, to gauge her reaction at his intended jab.

Junior chuckled. Mitch patted him on the back again, this time noticing his rock-solid right shoulder. This kid would win a World Series game someday.

Junior left, and as Mitch was about to close the door, Junior put his hand out to stop it. "By the way, my dad has been going out somewhere late at night. I don't know if he's sleepwalking or what, but his pickup is always in the driveway."

"What do you mean?"

"I mean he isn't in his bedroom; he isn't in the backyard; his pickup's in the driveway, and he's gone. His cell phone is always on the nightstand. When I ask him about it, he says I must be dreaming. It's strange. The way he talks to me and looks at me is weird, too. Something just doesn't seem right. He keeps randomly saying, 'Mitch is tied to the Old Man,' whatever the hell that means."

"Tied to the Old Man? What in the world? He's probably stressed about your career. I'm sure he's okay. I'll talk with him. General and I will keep an eye on things. There isn't anything serious for you to worry about, Junior."

"Thanks, Mitch. I don't know what kind of shape I'd be in if I wasn't sure you had his back."

"You have our cell phone numbers, right?"

"Yeah, I have both yours and Mabey's."

"Good, then don't hesitate to check in whenever you feel like it. Now, get out of here and go make it to the show."

"Thanks, Mitch, I really appreciate it. I'll be in touch."

When Mitch turned around, a blanket and pillow flew over the stair rails.

"Too late, Mabey, for any try at more humor. Junior already left."

"Who said I was being funny?" The door closed—hard!

"Son of a bitch, seriously?" was all that came out of Mitch's mouth. Must have been the comment about getting action he made in front of Junior.

A few depressing moments passed.

The door opened; Mabey came out and stopped at the railing, laughing. "I got you good, Mitch. You hardly ever fall for my crap." She winked, turned, and hurried back into their bedroom.

Mitch chuckled nervously, picked up the pillow and blanket, and shuffled around the entryway, deciding what to do. He was thinking about Jack and what Junior had said. Mitch walked up the stairs, skipping every other step in anticipation. As anxious as Mitch was about what might be waiting for him, he struggled to get Jasper and Jack out of his mind.

He hesitated at the bedroom door, his thoughts racing back and forth. Quality time with Mabey was normally an easy decision. His mind, flooded with the events of the day, pushed his sexually starved libido aside, for a moment. The former finally won out; Mitch had priorities to consider. Jasper and Jack could wait until tomorrow.

Entering the room unsure of what to expect, Mitch reflexively squeezed the blanket and pillow when he saw Mabey. He knew it would hurt when his jaw hit the floor. Mitch composed himself as best he could. He couldn't, wouldn't take his eyes off his beautiful wife. Mabey stood in front of the bed dressed in what he would later pen in his journal as 'Are You Kidding Me' lingerie.

Looking back over his shoulder, Mitch winked before closing the door, saying quietly. "I got this," as if someone were watching.

Chapter 21

Technicolor Dream...

After the flesh-yoga session with Mabey, Mitch found himself physically drained. Helping Mabey achieve her desired finish was never easy and tonight; no different. There were certain buttons that had to be pushed in just the right way. It was always a workout Mitch would joke with her. Albeit the best workout a man could hope for, but it drained him. Mabey fell asleep while Mitch stroked her bare back with his fingers tips. He loved feeling her soft silky skin as he ran his hand up and down her back as the slowest, most deliberate motion he could control. Mabey, fast asleep as always left Mitch to toss and turn; his own needs left unmet. His goal; always make certain Mabey had a wonderful time, but he did need his own release every so often. Preferably with his wife and not by himself.

Thinking of Jasper and Jack, he tossed and turned while his mind continued the fruitless struggle with recent events. Unwilling to roll around in frustration any longer, and not wanting to wake Mabey, Mitch slid out of bed. Slowly, in the dark, he went down the hall to his office, sat at the desk, and turned on the desk lamp. He brought the laptop out of sleep mode watching the icon swirl and spin.

Seconds later Mitch searched through journal entries until he found what he came for, an entry he'd written years ago. He found the page he wanted—the one where he and Jack first met in school so long ago. The memory always made him smile. The bulb in Mitch's lamp made a slight crackling sound and then fizzled out. He sighed, started to get up, then decided to replace the bulb later. The clock read 1:45 as he peered out the window covered in dusty stained water droplets.

Someone moved up the street all zombie-like. Stiff and disjointed, without pattern or purpose. Mitch wondered if his apocalypse dreams were coming true. Puzzled, he jumped up and hustled downstairs to get a better look. Sure enough, the person walked like a zombie, only a little more limber, without the death part. It looked like Jack; his head was acting strange though. Mitch thought of the Sitting Bull sighting he and Mabey had the previous evening. This wasn't quite as ominous but disturbing, nonetheless.

Mitch rubbed his tired eyes and focused again. Sure enough, it was Jack. He walked straight through the front yard, stopped, looked at the pile of what Mitch guessed was one of General's signature dumps and then turned to face the Wilde house. More than a little nervous, Mitch ducked; though he had no idea why.

After a few seconds, which seemed like minutes, he stood back up to peek outside. Mitch felt his heart pulse, the hair on the back of his neck tingled, and he froze. Jack stared right at him, at least, it looked like Jack. Dammit, he wasn't sure. Mitch gathered his courage, opened the door, and whispered, "Jack. Jack are you okay?" Nothing. "Jack are you okay?" Louder this time.

The figure turned, walked to Jack's house, and paused on the front doorstep. It stopped abruptly and turned. As it turned, the distorted head morphed in a fashion to a regular human appearance. The body went from stiff and rigid to completely normal. It—Jack now—Mitch guessed, held its finger to its lips making the signal for Mitch to keep quiet. He made a slight wave of his right hand, odd to Mitch because Jack was left-handed. Jack turned and walked into the house, slamming the door.

Anyone watching Mitch would have thought he'd saw his own death. Mitch, standing with his hands by his sides and mouth open: the perfect landing strip for a bug or two as his puzzled brain transitioned to worry.

Mitch closed the door, recognizing General's barks out back. He realized his buddy had been barking the whole time. Mitch, frustrated with his own lack of attention to everything going on around him, shook his head in disgust.

He looked out the front window across the street. A light turned off at Jasper's place. Mitch headed up the stairs and crawled into bed, mentally trying to make sense out of what he'd seen. He wanted to wake Mabey, but she was comfortable, and he didn't want to scare her. She wouldn't be able to go back to sleep. He was finally tired. His little enclave of Rogue River was certainly getting strange, he thought as he pulled up the sheet.

Mitch watched Mabey release a cute little sigh, roll over, and nestle her sweet face into her pillow. Mitch desperately wanted to fall asleep too. He snuggled close to the warmth of her soft skin. His eyelids grew heavy; he thought he would wake soon and realize tonight's events were only a Technicolor dream.

Chapter 22

A Good Day

Early the next morning, Mitch took General for a quick walk around the neighborhood. Birds sang, squirrels scattered as man and dog approached, and the wind surged its way through pine tops. Breathing deeply, pulling in the clean earthy smells of the woods, Mitch could tell General was upset at the morning's faster-than-normal pace. His canine buddy had no lab smile, and lacked his normal energy, but Mitch wanted to get his day started. On their return, Mitch fed General and said goodbye to Mabey with his signature hug, heavy squeeze, and tight hold, letting her know how much he cared. Then he went to his Jeep.

As Mitch drove more slowly than usual, he halfway hoped to see the warrior chief seated on Shadowfax again. His smart half hoped he would simply forget the whole weird incident. Neither happened. Mitch turned the corner and drove toward the Coffee Shack a few minutes after eight. Checking his black sports watch, noticing he had plenty of time to get what he came for and make it to Jasper's. He didn't want to be late for several reasons.

Mitch eased Black Steel into place, stopping short of the round rails protecting the front of the establishment. They were supposed to look like the hitching posts from 150 years ago. One of these days, Mitch decided he would jump out, grab a rope, and wrap it around the post. He thought it would be funny, might even earn him a free cup of coffee.

Mitch stepped up and in through the door. Cling, cling, cling. The old steel bell hanging atop the doorframe smacked the door and announced his entrance.

There was a drawn-out, "Mitch, haven't seen you in a while.

What brings you down this morning? Coffee?"

"Hey, Debbi, how have you been? Yeah, can I get a double espresso? Also, a couple of bagels, the ones with all the salty pleasantness sprinkled on top, a couple of old-fashioned donuts, and two croissants, please?"

"Hungry this morning, are you?"

On the newspaper rack, the headline in *The Oregonian* read: "Alford Upholds Promise on Health Care." Mitch realized it was another BS article on the President and his disdain for the Constitution and the will of the masses. What really caught his eye was in the lower left. A small teaser headline for a story buried in the back pages, probably near the classifieds. "More Indians Disappear, Casinos Baffled." He picked up the paper.

"Mitch, I asked if you're hungry today."

"Huh? Oh, I'm sorry, Debbi. Late night last night. Yes, I'm hungry, but I also have a meeting with a potential client."

Mitch didn't want to tell Debbi he was meeting Jasper. He wasn't sure why, but he stuck with the cover story for now.

"Please tell Mabey I'm sorry I wasn't able to stay for the flower show. I did drop in for a few minutes; I even made a silent bid on your beer, but, apparently, I didn't win because none of the three hens called me. I tried to make it over to her to say hello, but she was pretty busy."

"You didn't miss much. I stayed hidden and avoided as much conversation as possible myself. I really don't enjoy that crowd. The Parsons won the beer, by the way. Thanks for bidding though. I'll be sure to tell Mabey."

Debbi's daughter and right-hand assistant each summer walked out of the kitchen. "Hi, Mr. Wilde, how are you today?"

"Hey, Cindi, your senior year is coming up, right?"

Cindi, a beautiful young woman, had a slight crush on Mitch. He knew it was a father-figure crush, nothing disturbing. The girl's dad had walked out years ago. Mitch had gotten along with him well enough, but they'd never really clicked. Now he thought the guy was a bastard and hoped to run into him again. Mitch always thought Cindi and Junior should date. He had brought it up a couple of times to Junior, but for some odd reason he always received a cold shoulder in return.

"So, Debbi, what's the word around town? Anything strange going on?"

"What do you mean?" Debbi said as she helped a couple of out-of-towners get coffee and pastry.

"Everyone knows the Shack is the ears of the town. If I didn't know better, I'd think you put an addictive ingredient in your coffee."

Debbi wore a large shit-eating grin on her face. "Addictive, you say? I do, Einstein—it's called caffeine. Here's your espresso. Give me a couple of minutes to box your pastry."

"Thanks. Einstein appreciates it very much."

Cling, cling, cling. This was the sixth or seventh time the noise had sounded since Mitch arrived. He turned; this time it was Rogue River's very own Sheriff Robert Gunther.

"Morning, Debbi, do you know where that Ansel Adams wannabe driving the piece-of-junk Jeep is?" He looked right at Mitch when he said it.

Debbi nervously laughed. "Now, boys, keep it civil and orderly. I've got a business to run here."

There was no love lost between Gunther and Wilde since their falling-out as high school classmates. Gunther would've been the next starting quarterback on the Rogue River High School football team. Mitch's arrival apparently ruined sports glory for the Sheriff. Notoriety as a backup was all he achieved after that. Gunther started at defensive back for a while, but he really wanted to be the quarterback.

There'd been tension between the two for a long time. The issues went way beyond who started at quarterback. Gunther was five inches shorter than Mitch; he had athletic shoulders with a given-up-on-life belly, nothing his sheriff's shirts couldn't hide though. He had a nice head of hair and brown eyes that always looked guilty. Gunther, the head lawman in town, went out of his way to make sure, when Mitch was around, that everyone knew who was in charge. Mitch usually put up with the attitude, but today he was feeling a little different, almost like a wounded animal with its back to a wall.

Mitch bit the inside of lip.

"Good morning, Sheriff Gunther. How are you doing on this fine Rogue River morning? I see as usual you have this town humming along peacefully with not a violator in sight."

This got a frown from the tightly wound sheriff and a chuckle from more than a few of the local patrons pretending to hide behind their tablets. Covering up with a tablet didn't carry the same effect of vanishing behind a newspaper. Nevertheless, he appreciated the effort.

"Well, what brings you into town so early in the morning, Wilde?"

The next cling, cling, cling indicated the entrance of Gunther's best friend and partner in Sodom—they believed it was a secret—but the whole town was aware. At least those with a modicum of observational skills understood.

"Shit," Mitch muttered.

Sheriff Gunther's face lit up. He tried to act as if he didn't care at all. "Mayor Jenkins. How are you this morning? Are you stopping in for a cup of Debbi's finest before heading over to City Hall?"

"Morning, Sheriff Gunther, good to see you. And yes, I am."

"Mitch. Here's your order. Cindi will ring you up."

Meanwhile, Jenkins and Gunther chatted each other up near the coffee bar. One good thing, Mitch realized, the Mayor's entrance pulled Gunther away from him and potential trouble.

"Thanks, Debbi; please keep me in the loop if you hear anything strange, will you? I'm trying to come up with new ideas for a photo piece, and anything out of the ordinary may prove helpful."

A lame excuse, but Mitch didn't feel that full disclosure was the best thing right now. He also knew if anyone saw anything around town, it would most likely be public information here at the Shack.

"Will do, Mitch, have a good day, and tell Mabey to stop in, will you? I want to give her something."

"It will be $12.50, Mr. Wilde. Do you need anything else?" Cindi asked.

"Did you add the paper as well?"

"Oh, no, I didn't, so make it $15.00 then: debit or credit?"

Mitch thought hardly anyone carried cash any more.

"Debit, and thanks."

Mitch punched in his pin, Cindi handed him the receipt, and he tried like hell to sneak out without making eye contact with Jenkins or Gunther.

Mitch opened the door, and Cindi said in a very loud voice, "Have a good day, Mr. Wilde! Hope to see you again soon and be careful on your bike."

Mitch wasn't sure what to make of Cindi's comment. He figured it was nothing more than immaturity on her part. He let it slide without rebuttal.

Cling, cling, cling. He was almost out of the Shack. Mitch held his breath, but sure enough, Gunther piped in.

"Get the taillight fixed on that vehicle of yours, or I will ticket you."

"What are you talking about?"

"That busted taillight. Get it fixed or get a ticket."

Mitch let the door close without further comment. He walked around to the back of Black Steel, and sure as shit, the taillight on the driver's side had a crack and a large hole in it. Without batting an eye, Mitch could bet a dozen of Debbi's finest donuts that Rogue's pride and joy, Sheriff Gunther, has red plastic residue on his oak baton.

Opening the passenger door in anger, Mitch set the pastry bag on the floor, and put his espresso in a cup holder between the seats. Shutting the door, he walked back around the Jeep looking one last time at the taillight before climbing inside.

Slamming the door, he grabbed the steering wheel with white knuckles. Mitch counted to twenty, took a deep breath, exhaled, and backed out. He wouldn't let Gunther get under his skin. He turned the music up and headed for Jasper's place repeating aloud.

"Today is going to be a good day. Today is going to be a good day. Today is GOING to be a GOOD day."

Chapter 23

Suck It Up

Mitch speculated many times with Mabey that Gunther led a sad life and had serious self-esteem issues. He couldn't wrangle why in the world the Sheriff would take a chip out of his rear taillight though. Gunther had no character and no business being a sheriff. It would cost at least $100 to replace the busted light, not to mention the time. He was so pissed he wanted to turn Black Steel around, find Gunther, and punch him in his sad face. It wouldn't be the most productive thing, but for a moment it might feel good. The mental picture of his clenched fist slamming into the side of Gunther's face was tantalizing, but Mitch had more productive things to do now. Moreover, he reminded himself, Gunther wanted him to lose his composure.

Mitch refocused. He had fifteen minutes to get to Jasper's place. He would have to save any fleeting retribution for another time. Gunther would get his eventually.

Mitch braked as he approached a four-way stop. The brake lights on the car in front reminded him of the current situation. "Shit!" He didn't want to drive all the way into Medford later today to pick up a replacement light. He had to repair the damn thing or not drive the Jeep at all. Parsons should have tape at the hardware store. If not, the small auto parts store in town should.

Mitch pulled into his driveway at 8:58. He grabbed the pastry bag and remembered Jasper said to bring more Stout. He didn't have time. Mitch wouldn't let a beer run make him late. A light jog across the street found Jasper standing by the side entrance of his garage with a slight smile on his face.

"Why're you so worried, Mr. Wilde? You're right on time."

"I look worried?" He was right, but Mitch didn't want to give him the satisfaction by acknowledging the fact.

"Yeah, your face betrays you. I'm all bark, so don't sweat it. No Stout?"

"Sorry, Jasper, I remembered too late. I got tied up at the Coffee Shack."

"Tied up? What happened?"

"Piece-of-shit Sheriff Gunther was making his usual fuss over the mayor. He made a few nasty comments intended to goad me into a confrontation, as usual, but I let it slide. Fortunately for him—and for me—I wanted to get to your place on time." Mitch added the part about the broken taillight.

"I saw your lights when you drove away this morning, and they looked okay to me."

"Exactly."

"So, what—Gunther broke it?"

"I know he did. Looks like a wood shaving in the plastic. I bet it came from his baton."

"Well, Tom Brady, you shouldn't have moved into town and beat him out for quarterback in high school. He'll never let that go. I go to all the Chieftans home games. Have for a long time. I started when you were a sophomore. You had a helluva arm, by the way. Why didn't you play in college?"

"It's a long story, perhaps someday I'll tell you."

"Well, suck it up, and get over it. Order a replacement off Amazon and fix it. You might want to get a spare while you're at it."

Jasper made his last comment with a smile. Mitch wasn't what sure to make of it. It was safe to bet, though, that he was trying to incite a reaction. Mitch didn't give him the satisfaction this time.

"All right come on in. In a few minutes, you won't remember anything about Rogue River's wonderful sheriff. I can promise you that."

Chapter 24

Little Moments of Winning

Sheriff Gunther pulled his cruiser to the curb outside Parson's Hardware Store. With a few minutes to kill before he made his rounds, which inevitably would take him to the Mayor's office for what he hoped would be a private, and very personal, consultation, Gunther listened to the radio chatter for a few minutes before placing his new shiny, black police loafers on the pavement. In typical fashion, the sleepy little river town presented no challenges for its sheriff's Bourne-like abilities.

Although the streets were more crowded than normal today, Gunther wasn't sure why. School was out, but it was still morning, so that didn't make sense. Probably more rafters than usual heading to the river and all were getting an early start. As Sheriff, he should know, but he didn't really care. He had more important things going on now.

Parsons was the only hardware store in town with the closest big-box store thirty minutes away. Gunther hoped Mitch wouldn't want to drive that far and would settle on Parsons himself.

The Sheriff adjusted his belt which held fast his holster and gun, baton and cuffs. He slammed the car door and thought the glass may have cracked. He didn't look back afraid of what his eyes may see.

"Morning, Sheriff," said a passerby on the sidewalk.

'Go to hell!' was what Gunther wanted to say. He believed in taking out most of his unresolved shit on strangers and those he perceived weaker than he. It made him feel better.

Gunther worked his way through life as if it were a first-person-shooter video game and he was the renegade. He didn't have time for niceties. Frankly, he wished everyone else were the same way too. To his surprise, he said, "Morning to you," as he headed towards the front door of the store. Gunther took his hat off an already-sweaty head. The cashier greeted him. "Welcome to Parson's Hardware, Sheriff. Can I help you find anything this fine morning?"

Jesus, this kid is pathetic; he cannot be so happy. He's working a cash register in a hardware store.' Gunther mentally tossed around the fact that everyone in the little town seemed happy but him.

"What aisle are the electrical supplies in?"

"That will be down on aisle three, sir. I believe on the left side. Perhaps a little on the right as well? What specifically are you looking for?"

Gunther figured he didn't need to respond. 'Screw the kid.' He was Sheriff; he didn't have to respond if he didn't want to. Gunther knew he was being an ass but found it difficult to stop. He wanted to get in and out without running into the owners, Robbie or Ginny. They didn't like him. Avoidance of most of the Town Council members was one of Gunther's best ways to keep his job.

A young couple, looking like vegan-earthers, clearly not locals, walked to the register. Gunther could smell them as soon as he walked in. They looked like the Pacific Crest Trail type, but why were they in Rogue River and not Ashland?

Watching out of the corner of his eye, out of nothing more than morbid curiosity, Gunther saw the hikers heft their basket on the counter.

"Hi, there, will this be all for you two today?"

Rolling his eyes at the pathetic clerk, Gunther headed to aisle three. He looked up and down and back and forth until he found what he wanted. "Here we go," Gunther said to himself, with satisfaction, as he knelt at the bottom shelf.

"Let's see, seven red rolls and four orange." He picked them up one by one dropping them into his basket, smiling the whole time, counting each one as if he were Gollum talking to his Precious. He enjoyed the way each one bounced off the bottom of the plastic crate before settling. Gunther did a quick scan around the aisle. There must be something similar that would provide a temporary fix. Seeing nothing that made sense, he hoped Wilde wouldn't find an alternative solution either.

The checkout-kid finished putting the items in the woman's bag and handed her a receipt. Gunther, giddy over the items he held, tried to step forward and pay but the woman kept talking.

"Thank you do you happen to know the best way to get up to Crater Lake? We are trying to get back to the PCT after a slight detour to an old friend's place here in town."

"I said I would get us there," her male partner blurted.

"I understand, sweetie, but let's ask just the same to make sure we aren't wasting any time."

The cashier pointed as he responded. "Uh, I think you go down the freeway and turn left at Medford. There's probably a better way, but that's the route I take. On the other hand, we could ask the Sheriff here. I'm sure he knows the best way."

Gunther of course knew a better way but stayed out of the conversation dreaming of an incarcerated Mitch Wilde, but the little shithead made his interaction all but unavoidable. Ah, what the hell. He was in a good mood now, so why not do his civic duty?

The young woman turned around and faced Gunther. He noticed her lovely smile but struggled with her pungent body odor.

"Oh, hi, Sheriff. My boyfriend and I need to get to Crater Lake, and neither of us has been there. What's the best way?"

The pungent male partner looked at the ground, refusing to make eye contact with Gunther. Gunther's law senses told him the kid had pot in his pack, making the kid nervous. The Sheriff pegged this traveler as one with a guilty conscience and no character. Gunther didn't care right now. He had a mission, and wasting time harassing a couple of out-of-town, greasy, smelly, PCT backpackers made no sense. They appeared to have no intention of hanging around Rogue River, so he saw no need to pry for information.

"Sure, young lady. Take the interstate south for one exit and get off at Silver Hill. Then, drive north on 234 until you see the Highway 62 signs for Deep Creek Lake. It's about 85 miles and beautiful." Gunther acting unusually kind, beamed over the success of the Wilde childish mission he was on. Nothing was going to deflate him.

"Thanks, Sheriff. Is there camping along the way? We are going to try and hitch but not sure if we can get a ride all the way there."

"Yeah, plenty of it. Great fishing this time of the year as well." Gunther threw this in because they both had fishing rods strapped to the sides of their packs.

"Well, thanks very much. You have a nice day, Sheriff."

"I hope the both of you have a pleasant day as well. Be careful hitching and don't play with matches." Gunther smiled and winked at the guy.

"Um, you, too, sir," the young man mumbled, his brow furrowed as he spun away from Gunther's prying eyes. The kid grabbed the arm of his partner, practically dragging her out.

The young woman said, "Ouch, not so hard. Stop worrying. It's legal, asshole."

Gunther put his basket of goods on the counter.

"Wow, that's a lot of electrical tape, Sheriff. What are you going to do with all this? I hope someone else in town doesn't need any."

Gunther normally would have told the young schmuck to mind his own business, but again he was in a particularly good mood, so he responded as if he were one of his deputies.

"I'm teaching a seminar over at the station this month on how to do emergency car repairs, on rear taillights. Easy to make a quick fix when you have ordinary colored tape."

Another shopper got in line behind the Sheriff, so the kid cut the chatter short. "Oh, that sounds cool. Want me to put this on your tab, sir?"

"No, bill it to City Hall." Gunther would classify it as training, but the nosy kid didn't need this information.

"Will do. Please sign here and have a nice day." The kid handed Gunther a copy of the freshly signed receipt and the bag of tape.

"Thanks and tell the Parsons I said hi."

Gunther took the bag, put on his sweat-stained sheriff's hat, and exited the store. He threw the bag of tape in the trashcan, making sure it wasn't easily visible, carefully folded the receipt and put it in his wallet. He made a mental note to fill out an expense report later today, so he could properly bill the taxpayers. Smiling, Gunther looked around and made a half-hearted attempt to wave at a local who passed in his pickup. Half-hearted because he never waved to anyone and felt strange doing it. Adjusting his hat, Gunther started a slight whistle and then looked both ways before he crossed the street to the auto parts store. They were sure to have taillight repair kits. And he would need to buy more tape for the training class.

Sheriff Gunther chuckled thinking of the warmth that would flood his body when he pulled Wilde over for driving with a broken taillight.

Mitch-Fucking-Wilde would head to this very auto parts store for a repair kit himself. 'Darn sorry to say, Mr. Wilde, but we are out of stock. The sheriff purchased it all for a training class.' The sheriff beamed as he could almost hear the words coming out of the cashier's mouth. Gunther knew the cash register kid would blurt out similar words.

Oh, how he cherished these little moments.

Chapter 25

They Were Timberlands

As Mitch grabbed for his ringing phone, he caught a look of disappointment in Jasper's eyes.

"Jasper let me answer this text before I come in. More than likely it's Mabey. Can you take these pastries? I'll be right behind you."

"Tell the little vixen that her sexy old neighbor says hi."

Mitch smiled and handed sexy 'old Jasper' the bag as he headed into the garage. Sure enough, it was a text from Mabey. *At the gym, done with workout, starting sessions now. Hv a great day. Luv Mabey.*

Mitch responded with *thx, at Jasper's, C U 2nite. LV WM (Wilde Man)*. He pocketed the phone, then walked inside, closing the door behind him.

"Turn off your cell phone Inspector Gadget. This is a no-cell area. If "The Man" is tracking you, I don't want him having access in here."

"Okay, no problem."

Mitch pulled the phone back out of his pocket and turned it off. Man, Jasper's garage was spotless. He hadn't noticed yesterday.

At the counter, Jasper wrestled with the bag of pastries. "Hope you got one of them bagels with the goodness seasoning."

"As a matter of fact, I did." Mitch understood 'goodness.' These were bagels with all the seasonings from the cupboard plastered all over the top. When toasted with cream cheese, they're nearly the perfect food. Unless you happen to be dairy intolerant or a glutard.

The corner of Jasper's mouth turned up as he pulled out a bagel to slice for the toaster. Mitch liked Jasper's set-up in the converted garage. There was a small microwave, a single deep-welled sink with disposal, and a twin cabinet above it. Mitch wondered how many nights Jasper had slept in here.

"How about cream cheese? The bagel is no good without cream cheese."

"Debbi must have put some in the bag." Mitch hoped so anyway, because he forgot to ask.

Jasper looked deep. "Yep, here you go. While you're waiting, walk around the table, look at everything, and be prepared to talk. You want coffee?"

"Yes, please. Black, no sugar."

"Good for you, Wilde. Coffee is meant to be consumed black. Hot at least. Nothing wrong with a little milk and sugar if iced."

Mitch chuckled, agreeing with Jasper as he headed to the table wondering what to look for. There were aerial photos, low quality but viewable, covering all the tables. A couple of monitors were embedded in the table, flush with the tabletop, and were looping videos on what appeared to be lakes, monuments, cave drawings and more from the TV show *Ancient Aliens*. One amateur video showed a mountain erupting. It seemed innocent enough, and he couldn't put his finger on the event, but something appeared strange. He made his way around, trying to take in all the information—simply too much going on to absorb everything at once.

Jasper sidled up to Mitch and handed him a cup of coffee in a black mug with a large X on the side. Underneath the X, the word *files* ran from left to right. He also handed Mitch an old-fashioned donut with a napkin. Jasper pulled up a stool and started a pointed discussion. "Yeah, Mr. Trust-No-One," in reference to Mitch's gaze at the cup.

"I liked the show myself. A lot happening. More than people realized. I heard somewhere the show's creator used inside information. The government manipulated him to release information so we all wouldn't be surprised when certain shit went down."

"Seriously?" Mitch shot back.

"Yes, too many implausible coincidences. Okay, so did you notice anything special going on here?" Jasper head-pointed at the table. Mitch took a bite of his donut and chased the pastry with a swig of black java. "Well, I didn't have a lot of time. The video of the erupting mountain did catch my attention."

"Good eye, Wilde. That is where our story will begin today. The rest will quickly fall into place. I found the video online. Looks to be from Homeland Security."

"How do you know the video is even real?"

"I spent about a year with various pieces of equipment and sophisticated software doing a lot of testing. It's real. I'm certain."

"Okay, so you have a real video of a volcano erupting. Lots of people have videos of erupting mountains."

"Watch again. Focus on the right side of the screen."

The video, about twenty seconds in length, started again. Mitch kept his eyes on the right side. Something seemed strange for sure.

"See anything?" Jasper asked.

Mitch ignored him and watched again. "Wait... yeah. What the hell? Is that something hitting the mountain?"

"Yep, sure is. The mountain is smoking and appears destined to blow; then something comes in fast and rams into the side."

"What was it?"

"That's the billion-dollar question. From what I can tell, it's an unidentified flying object."

"No shit! A UFO?"

"Yes, and don't get too jazzed. Remember, Wilde, the 'U' simply means unidentified, not necessarily Alien. People often forget that little fact. Watch this." Jasper grabbed the mouse and clicked on the video pausing so he could click through frame by frame.

"Side note Wilde you probably don't know. In 1947 in Gold Beach, five people saw a UFO hovering over the Rogue River. They reported it, the Air Force investigated and couldn't prove, or disprove, the sighting. What I have been able to glean from the information the Air Force released on Case X; the individuals were lucid and credible. So much goes on Wilde we know nothing about. There is no way little ole earth is all alone. No way. Interesting that the Rogue River appears to be a hub. All the magnetic poles perhaps?"

Jasper paused, stared up at the ceiling, and then looked directly at Mitch.

Listening with new found curiosity, thinking about the possibilities of other-world life, Mitch finished off his old-fashioned donut and the java, then stuffed the used paper towel into the cup freeing his hands. He didn't want to spill anything in Jasper's lair and knew the paper towel would soak up any remaining coffee.

"Okay, Wilde, pay close attention right here." Jasper pointed at the screen. "You see this, right? Watch the tail end while I click through one frame at a time and tell me what you see."

Jasper clicked one frame at a time, pausing for a second or two after each click.

"Stop," Mitch said to Jasper. "The back-end turns white."

"Exactly, that has to be an engine or a propulsion system. The flame you see in these two frames looks like the craft accelerated right before hitting the mountain."

"Is it St. Helens?"

"Yep and guess what year?"

"1980?"

"Yes, sirree, 1980. You must remember when the mountain blew?"

"I do. Twelve years old, but I remember it well. I was living in Klamath Falls at the time. The mountain blast covered our yard and everything we owned with ash. Pretty cool for a kid. I remember my dad getting frustrated at the time, but I didn't really understand why. Now, of course I do. The ash screwed with all the engines—the lawn mower, his tractor, the cars, everybody's lungs. What did I care about all that stuff? Hell, I was just a kid looking to miss a day of school and ride my bicycle through the stuff and make tracks."

"Well, I was contract logging up near Terrapin River at the time. Fortunately, when the mountain belched, I had the day off. Strange as shit because I'd planned a trip to Ghost Lake that day with a few of the crew."

"The same Ghost Lake next to St. Helens?"

"Yep, same one. At the last minute, I decided to head into Portland and buy new boots. Those boots saved my life."

"What happened to the guys at Ghost Lake?"

"They all lived, never made it to the banks of the lake. They stopped for breakfast on the way, and while eating, they felt the quake. One of the crew insisted the quake was a bad omen, so they left and got off the mountain. Three and a half hours later she blew."

"Damn, what type of boots did you get?"

"Shit, Wilde, you can be an insensitive prick, but I do admire your attention to detail. My kind of fella." Jasper smiled.

"So, what are you saying exactly?"

Jasper paused, took a swig of his coffee, polished off the bagel, and licked the cream cheese from the corner of his mouth.

"What am I saying? A type of aircraft or ship, under control, with an engine or engines, and accelerating, slammed into the side of Mount Saint Helens at five a.m., precisely when the earthquake happened. She erupted three and a half hours later, and one final thing, Wilde-Man, the boots, they were Timberlands."

Chapter 26

Just Ants

Mitch stretched, pushing both hands down on his thighs while arching his back. He felt constrained in his skin, wishing he could get outside himself and be a spectator. Jasper stared at Mitch as if he knew exactly what he was thinking. Mitch rotated his head, stretched his neck, and jumped back into conversation. "So, you own a video of an unidentified flying object slamming into a mountain that apparently caused a volcano to erupt?"

"No. The mountain was going to erupt anyway, but the UFO possibly intensified the blast. Perhaps that's a better way to phrase things. Or perhaps it had nothing to do with the blast at all, and it entered another dimension."

"Um, dimension? Intensifying a blast, I can comprehend, but another dimension is out of the realm of my sci-fi knowledge, old man."

"I know, I know. It's a stretch, but crazy ideas sometimes make the most sense."

"Okay, Jodie Foster, get back to the blast part and talk to me. What are you trying to say? Don't make me work so hard on this."

"Use your noggin, neighbor. Let's say, for example, the craft slamming into the mountain is Alien. What if you found this planet and created a master species – the humans – and a little population control was in order? What do you do?"

"Blow up a mountain?" Mitch almost whispered.

"Not only a mountain, Wilde, much more than a mountain.

Remember, you're constantly monitoring earth, and when you're alerted to seismic activity, extreme weather patterns, and other events, you seed them and make them worse, so you can watch the chaos."

"Few people died though during St. Helens, if I remember correctly."

"Well, bicycle-jock, depends on your idea of few. Fifty-Seven is the number."

"Dang, I didn't know it was that many." Wilde expressed genuine surprise with a head tilt and furrowed brow.

"Yep, most died from asphyxiation after the blast but died as a result none-the-less."

Jasper paused, as if in considerate thought before he continued. Wilde drew in a bit closer and concentrated.

"Perhaps Wilde, it isn't so much about human death than about control of our planet. That is, if the intention is destruction and disruption. Did you ever mess with ants as a kid?"

"Oh, yeah, all the time," Mitch replied.

"What did you do to them?"

"I burned them—or tried to burn them—with a handheld magnifying glass. I plugged several of their holes or barricaded their routes forcing them to take a different path. Poured water on them—stuff like that."

As Jasper stared at Wilde, Mitch realized quickly he wanted him to come up with his own conclusion. He rubbed the side of his face as he exercised his mind. Jasper patiently waited for a response.

"Okay, so we're the ants. We're being played with, and experimented on, by Aliens."

"Give the man a rose! Yes, Wilde, of course, I can't be 100% certain, but video documentation like this makes me even more curious. In this next clip is satellite documentation, since the 1980s, that shows in nearly every major natural disaster, a kind of vehicle or a beam of light disrupts each event, minutes or seconds before the destruction."

"Why haven't others noticed this?"

"Others have—especially at the highest level of governments and certainly talked about and debated in secret. There's a lot of internet traffic on the subject, but governments do a great job denying and obfuscating the truth. Unless you're slowing these disaster videos frame-by-frame and really looking for the penetrations, they're almost impossible to notice. Plus, video hasn't been around long enough to capture most of the disasters on earth."

"Okay, so we aren't alone. I always thought there was more out there. Too many unanswered questions in our short history."

Mitch thought about going back and re-watching all seasons of *Ancient Aliens*. He would have to get over the fear of the guy with the crazy hair that looked as if it were trying to escape the skull and head to the stars.

Mitch paused and then directed another question to Jasper. "What's this mean other than we're ants and the bullies like to play?"

"Things are deeper and more insidious than an ant hill. There will be an Alien war, or cleansing, on earth at some point. Near as I can tell, seems ready to start."

"No way!"

"Way! Probably more serious than a natural disaster or two."

"You know Wilde it isn't as if Oregon, hell the Rogue River and Crater Lake to get closer to home, haven't been without incident. Back in '49, or '50, seems to be conflicting dates, five people on the Rogue River, near Gold Beach spotted a flying saucer. The Air Force investigated concluding the people were credible and they couldn't disprove the event. It was called Case X. Google it when you have time. NICAP reported on the event. Isn't lengthy and fascinating considering what is going on now."

"Really old-man? What about Crater Lake?" Mitch asked with new found interest.

Well, also in '49 there is a strange UFO film in Crater Lake where a white object looks to be heading for one of the banks, and there have been many other incidents throughout the years where jets are scrambled out of Kingsley in Klamath Falls to pursue and investigate."

Mitch's watch indicated eleven-thirty already; his restlessness started to show. A break was in order. Besides, he needed to clear his head. He needed to get out of the overwhelming Alien research lair for a while in hopes of slowing his mind, currently spinning with information.

"Jasper, I need to walk my dog. This might be a good place to take a break if you don't mind. How about we reconvene at 1300 hours?"

"Okay. Upset Wilde's world view, huh?"

"Exactly, Yoda. Look, when I woke this morning, I didn't expect to be in a real episode of *Ancient Aliens*. Are you filming this?"

Jasper's eyes grew darker and more intent. He lowered his voice, and with an eerie tone, words escaped his mouth. "Why do you ask?"

A chill ran down his spine and made his ass recoil in fear. "Just joking, Jasper. Geez, this is getting serious."

"Well, it's no goddamned joke. I asked you over here because I thought you could handle the truth. Yes, everything that goes on in here is recorded."

"Damn! Okay, I'm leaving. I'll be back at 1300 ready to continue. There's something I would like to talk with you about. Mabey and I saw something strange; the sighting is part of the reason I'm weirded out right now."

"Here, take these, will you?" Jasper handed Mitch three empty Imperial Stout bottles. "Feel free to refill them if you're so inclined. Outstanding beer, artisan."

"Thanks, Jasper, glad you approve." Mitch went out the door, carefully closing the metal entry point behind him as if being gentle would somehow rewind the last sixty minutes so they had never existed.

Mitch decided to walk General down to the river. He needed alone time with the flowing water and his canine buddy. Mitch could think of few things more peaceful than listening to the river water tumble over the rocks, gently pushing the banks, and inviting a skipped rock or two... or even a plunge into it. He wondered if he should try to rinse away the last several days of memories in the cold water. General would love it. The thought faded fast knowing his figs would try to hide, shriveling in a cold protective retreat.

Chapter 27

Double Time

While walking across the street, Mitch pulled his cell phone out of his pocket. Stepping into his garage he set the Jasper-drained beer bottles on the bench then wiped beads of sweat from his forehead. Leaning against the counter, his head dropped in silent contemplation recalling talks with Mabey, more than once, how they were a safe distance from potential outside manipulation in Rogue River. Right now, his confidence waned. In Mitch's mind humans had evolved well, all things considered—the want for freedom being the key driving force to earth's success. As long as humans infested the earth, conflict would exist. History continued to prove this. There would always be people wanting to subjugate others. And there would always be people who refused subjugation. Mitch questioned these deeply held beliefs for the first time as he thought about real freedom. Was it all an illusion? The loss of control frightened him. What Jasper had shared, what Mabey, and he saw the other night, his magically healing shoulder, and Jack's arrow incident brought deep doubt into his mind for the first time.

A buzz against his thigh startled him. Mitch grabbed the cell phone from his pocket and confirm what he thought would be a text message from Mabey: *Mitch, my 1 p.m. canceled. Want to do lunch?* Message 2: *Mitch, where are you? Text or leave a message if you can come.*

Next, Mitch checked his voice mail. She'd also left a message at eleven, about thirty-five minutes ago. He grabbed General's leash. Already waiting, General was clearly excited and ready to go, jumping and panting.

Mitch smiled at his dog, then called Mabey's number and got her voice mail. "Hey, babe, your Wilde man here. Sorry I missed you. At Jasper's, he won't allow phones to be on. I'll tell you more tonight. I'm taking a walk-break right now with General at the river. I told Jasper I'd be back at his place at one. How about a rain check on lunch? Love you. Oh, and my phone will be off from one until three or four, but I'll power up as soon as I leave Jasper's."

Lunch breaks with Mabey were nice, but Jasper had successfully set the hook in Mitch and was reeling him in. He wanted and felt like he needed more information.

"Come on, boy, let's go play ball at the river. Such a good boy." Mitch wondered if Aliens talked to their pets. Did they even have pets? Perhaps Aliens looked at humans as pets. He found the possibility downright depressing and potentially scary. One thing Mitch was sure of, he would absolutely refuse to wear a collar. With his luck, he figured he'd be stuck with a creepy alien who had an S & M fetish.

General and Mitch walked down the road to the trailhead. His place sat on the northern banks of the Rogue River, but the trail went inland around the neighborhood, so he or Mabey couldn't simply go out the backyard and get on the trail. This was nice because the banks stayed mostly private for their house and the homes on either side. Mitch found himself counting his steps today, hardly hearing General's rhythmic pants. Mitch dropped the leash and then stepped on it so General would stay close. He rolled up the sleeves of his shirt and picked up the leash. "Come on, boy, let's go!"

On the riverbank, Mitch launched an orange tennis ball about thirty feet into the water for General, who loved going after the dang thing. But what he loved even more was dropping the ball at Mitch's feet for an anticipated return trip.

General stared up at him, looked down at the ball, then up at Mitch, and barked. Mitch realized he'd been in a trance. "Damn, boy, I'm sorry. Here you go."

Mitch chucked the orange object into the water. General did his thing, returning in little time. Two people approached on mountain bikes. One said, "Hi" as they pedaled by. Mitch thought about saying something, but words wouldn't exit his mouth. General brought the ball back, and they went a little further down the trail.

"Hey, boy, sorry I'm not into this today. I have scary shit on my mind, and I can't seem to shake it loose." General made Mitch grab the ball out of his mouth this time. "Okay, boy, come on, last time." Mitch chucked the ball. The throw went upstream. General swam out but veered off and headed away from the ball.

"General, wrong way! What the hell, bud? Get the ball!"

Barking a couple of times, an oddity for him while swimming, General continued away from the ball swimming toward what appeared to be a stick. He grabbed something, turned, and headed back. Mitch kept a close eye on his canine partner while the tennis ball found freedom. This wouldn't be the first — or last — ball lost. He hoped the environmental police weren't at the Pacific Ocean waiting for his balls to wash up on shore and lead them to arrest him for littering. Mitch kicked the ground, anxious to see what the dog found this time. He loved a happy dog and could tell by the body language that General was pleased with himself. The lab dropped the dull silver object at his feet. It was an arrow, not unusual since there was an outdoor archery range a couple miles upstream. Mitch had found an arrow or two over the years on the shoreline. This arrow seemed different at first glance. He patted General on the head and picked up the river treasure. The arrow weighed virtually nothing, an ounce or two, at the most. The arrows Mitch used for target practice usually ran around 420 grams, about fifteen ounces. Mitch flexed the shaft, curious over the appearance and apparent strength. No nicks or scrapes. This was, again, rather odd, especially after being in the water. The fletching on the end looked like a synthetic material mimicking a feather. Not odd in and of itself, but when he touched it, the feather-like material moved feeling alive. He thought of a sea anemone moving with the tides. Inside the tip was a translucent material that appeared to be liquid. The color reminded Mitch of something similar he'd seen recently. He couldn't remember where.

Mitch looked out over the river as if it would answer the questions racing through his head. The water simply flowed on, unending, returning no wisdom or knowledge. Thinking back to his bike ride when he saw the horse and rider he wondered if this arrow had any connection. There must be, but what? Questions he hoped his newly discovered friend could help answer.

Mitch felt a tingle in his recently nicked-up shoulder. "General, come on. We gotta go double time!" Mitch didn't attach the leash and took off at a fast pace toward home. He wanted to get back over to Jasper's and fast. General took the lead, setting the pace.

Chapter 28

New Taillights

Mitch put General in the backyard, then grabbed another four-pack of Wilde Stout from the garage refrigerator and headed back to Jasper's. He closed the garage door with his cell phone at 12:45. Mitch wasn't sure how Jasper responded to people's being early and he was about to find out. Across the street and down the court in less than a minute, he pressed the door buzzer; Jasper showed up within seconds and opened the door.

"Well, good to see you, Mitchey; I figured I scared you out of coming back."

"You did scare me, but at no time did I consider not returning."

Jasper looked surprised, then firmly touched Mitch's shoulder. A reassuring warmth moved through Mitch, and instantly he felt as if there were a calm clarity in the room.

"Here's more beer and do you have any food I can raid? I'm starving."

"Sandwich stuff in the fridge. Help yourself."

"Thanks. Check out this arrow General found in the river." Mitch handed Jasper the arrow and walked to the refrigerator.

"Alien technology arrow: I haven't seen one of these in a while." Jasper didn't seem surprised at all, and neither was Mitch a touch startled by Jasper's lack of surprise. If the shit ever hit the fan, this old lumberjack was exactly the guy he wanted around.

"Are you serious about the Alien technology, Jasper? It does look different and odd, but alien?"

Mitch headed towards the food. He made a sandwich with what he found: bologna, mayonnaise, and a slice of pepper jack cheese on dark rye. He grabbed one of the Guinness beers. Mitch didn't want to take away from Jasper's Wilde brew, even though he'd rather drink one of his own stouts. Guinness, no way a lesser alternative as the brewery had made the stuff for around three hundred years but it wasn't his creation. Putting his sandwich on a paper plate Mitch sat on a stool. With a full mouth, he replied to Jasper, "In a while?"

"So, you did hear me? Yeah, I found one about three weeks ago on the riverbank."

On the wall opposite the kitchen area, Jasper unlocked a cabinet and opened both doors. Inside was another arrow, among other things. The arrow looked about the same as the one General had found and the one Jack got nailed with. Jasper closed the cabinet doors, held the arrow carefully, and approached Mitch. This one carried a different color fletching. The tip had a small chip in it that had allowed whatever was inside at one time to leak out.

Jasper held out the arrow as if he wanted Mitch to take hold of it. Something about this arrow seemed more familiar than the one General just found in the river. Filing the thought away he decided he'd come back to it again soon.

"Okay, Jasper, let me finish this sandwich. I have news to share." Mitch took another bite and wiped his mouth with a paper towel. As he took a long pull of his Guinness, he prepared himself to explain about Jack being shot, himself getting a glancing blow from an arrow, and a description of what Mabey and he saw after the flower show. Mitch no longer worried about sharing this with Jasper; the old guy would take the news in stride.

Mitch also figured Jasper already knew about both incidents.

"Enjoy the food. I'm going to step inside the house for a few. I should be back in five minutes. By the way, while you were gone, I went online and ordered a taillight from Amazon. Your Jeep is a Willy's, right? The replacement was eighty-five dollars and twenty-five for overnight delivery. You can pay me later."

Jasper closed the door before Mitch, surprised by the old guy's generosity, could even say thank you. Focusing on the arrow Jasper had handed him Mitch realized what was familiar.

"Shit!" he said aloud.

The liquid solution encased in the tip looked to be the exact same color that surged through Jack's veins in what seemed like only minutes ago.

Chapter 29

What About Rodeos?

Mitch's cell phone rang. He set down his beer, threw the paper towel in the trash, and raced out the side door. Junior's name showed on the screen. "Hello, Junior, that you? Everything okay?"

"Yeah, Mitch, sorry to bother you, but I can't get hold of my dad. I need to let him know I'm stuck in Portland. I'm worried. Most of the time I'm the one not returning texts or calls."

Mitch looked down the street towards Jack's house hoping to see his friend in the yard, but the yard was as empty as the driveway. Mitch looked back towards Jasper's wondering if he had returned from inside yet.

"His car's not here. Don't worry, Junior, he's probably at work and swamped. I'll keep my eyes open for him. When he gets home, I'll tell him to give you a call. Does that sound like a plan?"

"Thanks, not sure what I would do if something happened to him."

"Nothing is going to happen. Just worry about pitching. He's fine; I'm sure."

Mitch looked inside again. He didn't want Jasper to come back and find him gone. He'd made nice progress with his neighbor. He was afraid his stepping outside might be misconstrued. He hated to do it, but he needed to end the call.

"I'm sorry, Junior, but I'm in the middle of something. Anything specific you want me to tell your dad?"

"Please tell him I'm stuck in Portland because of mechanical issues on the flight. The airline is putting all the passengers in a hotel overnight. Please don't forget."

"You bet. Take care and let me know when you get to Chattanooga. I'll bring your dad up to speed. Later, okay?"

"Thanks Mitch I really appreciate it. Bye." Mitch hung up, turned off the phone, went back into the garage, and planted himself on the stool. He took a swig from his Guinness as Jasper returned.

"You get enough to eat, Wilde?"

"Yes, thanks. Hit the spot."

"Well, don't be shy; help yourself. Twinkies and Ding Dongs are in the cabinet above the coffee machine."

"I'm watching my figure, but thanks."

"Well, for me, fried eggs, steak, drink like I want, and no fear of a Twinkie or a Ding Dong. Weigh a mere five pounds more than I did at eighteen."

"Good genes, I guess."

"Perhaps, perhaps. Moderation, staying active both mentally and physically, and trying to enjoy things day to day seem to work for me, though genes have something to do with the whole long-life thing. However, and this is key, Wilde: doing the opposite of what the naysayers say I should do always works. So, the hell with 'em!"

"What about rodeos, you enjoy those?"

Mitch let out a sigh, wondering why in the world the last statement spilled over his lips. Jasper stopped, stared straight at Mitch with a bewildered facial expression, and busted up laughing. "You are a SOB, Wilde. A goddamned certified SOB." Mitch felt relieved. Jasper's laugh came deep from the belly as the old coot understood the smart-ass intention behind the comment.

Jasper was about Wilde's height and of a similar build. Mitch last tipped the scales at 195, and he estimated Jasper to be 10 pounds lighter. Mitch figured less body mass with the older age.

"Well, I hope to look as good as you when I'm your age."

"My age? What am I, ancient? You like to pile on, don't you, Wilde?"

Mitch stared at Jasper, unsure if the old man was being serious before the two burst out in laughter.

Chapter 30

Catch

Stepping out of Jasper's garage-turned-sci-fi lair, Mitch's mind raced. Neither description had brought understanding to the room. Jasper bombarded Mitch with information, and he was doing his best to digest it. Throw in the sighting after the fundraiser, his newfound ability to heal himself, the barbecue incident, Jack's recent behavior, the arrow at the river—and he had a tangled mess.

"What the hell?" he blurted. Mitch wanted to push these thoughts aside, at least most of them, when he talked with Jack.

Jack's pickup truck was in the driveway. Mitch altered his course as he powered his phone on. Once the cell got its tower signal, buzzing alerts sounded. Several text messages appeared one after the other.

Mitch – home late, eating dinner with Michelle. Hv Fn w Jasper. Luv M.

Mitch replied, *Enjoy yourself. Txt on wy home. M*

The next text read, *Mitch, Dad called me finally, sounds okay, I guess. Gotta go. Thx, Jr*

Mitch replied to Junior, *'Good. Travel safe, your dad is fine. M.W.*

Now for the five voicemails. Mitch slowed his walk toward Jack's and played the messages. He realized he didn't want to face his friend at the moment. The thought of having more unexpected shit to deal with put him in avoidance mode. Since Junior contacted Jack, Mitch no longer felt the same need to reach out. This wasn't true, but he welcomed the avoidance of more potential stress.

First voicemail: *Mitch, it's Ron. How're the pictures on Crater Lake coming? I need them in three days if you can; we are moving up the feature a few days. Call me back, will you?* Mitch made a mental note to call or email him.

Next voicemail from Debbi: *Mitch, please call, I overheard something you may want to know about.* Mitch made another mental note.

Next voicemail: *Oh, Mitch. Sorry, this is Debbi down at the Coffee Shack.*

Voicemail number four, a stressed voice this time: *Mitch, please call. It's important I talk with you.*

Mitch thought he heard Cindi in the background say, "Mom, do something. Please, let's call the police."

Voicemail number five, the final one: *Mitch, never mind, all is good. False alarm, I guess. Stop in for tea next time, and say hi to Mabey, will you? Hope all her work as a nurse is going well.*

A nurse? Mitch contemplated. Debbi had known Mabey for at least fifteen years, and she knew damn well what she did. She knew Mitch was a coffee drinker also, not tea. Was Debbi preoccupied, nervous or sending Mitch a cryptic message? He voted for the latter.

Mitch pressed 411 on his phone. "City and state please," the recording said.

"Rogue River, Oregon," he stated clearly.

"Please state the name you are searching for."

"The Coffee Shack."

Mitch wondered why he didn't have the number on speed dial already. He would need to save it for future use.

"You have asked for the number for Caufey's Hack. If this is correct, press 1; press 2 to try again, please." Mitch pursed his lips in frustration. He wanted to reach through the phone and strangle the computer on the other end. He pressed #2, with drawn-out deliberation as if the extra pressure would have a magical effect on the voice recording on the other end. These ingrates needed to understand his level of frustration. "Coffeeeeee" semi-long pause "Ssshaaack." He tried to enunciate perfectly.

"You have asked for the number for Coffee Shack, if this is correct, press 1; press 2 to try again, please."

"Thank Odin," Mitch said out loud, as the phone voice continued, "If you would like me to dial for you, press 1 now."

Mitch pressed 1. "Connecting now, please hold."

The phone rang; after the sixth ring, Cindi picked up. "Hi, Coffee Shack, may I help you?"

"Hey, Cindi, it's Mitch. Everything okay? Your mother left me a couple of messages."

"She took off a little while ago. She said to tell you 'yes' about what you asked her about earlier today. Whatever that means. Come in for coffee in the morning, okay? Sorry, gotta go."

Click. She hung up without so much as a goodbye, thank you, or anything. "Dammit."

Mitch looked up and found himself standing at the end of Jack's driveway about ten feet from the back of the charcoal grey pickup. Jack sat inside; the engine growled. He revved the vehicle as if he planned to back right over Mitch.

"Hey, man, how're you doing? How's Junior?" Mitch hoped Jack would recognize the familiar voice over the engine noise.

Jack put the vehicle in gear and backed out of the driveway. He didn't even look at Mitch as the truck barely missed him. Jack put the F150 in Drive and moved out of the cul-de-sac as if someone's life were at stake.

For the second time in as many days, Mitch stood with an open mouth. He looked around to see how many people saw his foolish expression. Fortunately, he stood alone. His cell phone buzzed. Another text from Junior: *Mitch, talked with Dad. Said he is going to Crater Lake with you soon. Thanks! Jr.*

Mitch, recognizing the false information, didn't want to alarm Junior. Not yet anyway, so he responded with, *No problem, Junior. Later, M.W.*

In fact, several huge problems were shouting in his mind. As Mitch stood in Jack's driveway, he wondered what to do next. His best friend just blew him off as if he didn't recognize him. Mitch hadn't talked to Jack about going to Crater Lake—not recently, anyway.

The short trip from Jasper's to where Mitch stood was one of the longest walks he remembered. He lowered his chin, put the phone in his pocket, and headed for the backyard shed. Mitch rubbed his head as if it would have a positive effect on his stress level. He grabbed the hem of his shirt, pulled, stretching it toward his face and wiped the sweat he could reach. Exasperated, he walked back home. Checking his watch, he figured he had enough time to shoot a few arrows and clear his head.

Chapter 31

Are You Done?

Mitch loosed a final arrow, and as it pierced the yellow center of the target, his next action became clear. Mitch put the equipment away and grabbed General's leash. "Come on, boy, we're going to go visit Delilah." General reacted, jumping and shaking with excitement. He loved riding in the Jeep. Even better, when Mitch said Delilah's name a couple of times, he knew the time arrived to go frolic with his sister.

The sun hung on, not wanting to let go of the day, soon to bow to the moon for one more cycle. Mitch's clock showed seven-thirty, and Mabey wouldn't be home until ten. He wanted to beat her home, so she wouldn't worry. Still, Mitch left her a quick text just in case.

Mabey, heading to Debbi's for a bit. Tell you why when you get home. W.M.

Mabey responded at once, *Thx. At dinner, should be home by 10. Luv U.*

In fifteen minutes, he and General pulled up to Debbi's house as she walked out the front door. Mitch let General out of the Jeep. Mabey often brought the dog here when she and Debbi were gal palling. Cindi's dog Delilah was General's sister; they got along great and loved running around the yard together.

"Hey Mitch, sorry about my messages earlier; Cindi and I were a bit freaked out, and I didn't know what to do."

"No worries. You appear okay. You are okay, right?"

Mitch didn't want to deal with anything extreme right now, so he gently asked his questions. Mitch gave General a pat and nodded okay. The canine raced off across the yard to join Delilah.

"Yeah, and thanks, Mitch, Cindi wanted me to call the police, but after hearing Gunther talking with Jenkins earlier in the day, I wasn't so sure the idea was sound. Anyway, you know how Gunther has a propensity to make people look like idiots."

"Yes, I know exactly what you mean. What were Gunther and Jenkins talking about that made you cautious?"

"Gunther kept referring to 'the damn Indian sightings and lack of manpower to cover all the complaints.' Jenkins sat there nodding, staring out the window as if he'd seen a ghost or something. The whole thing was very strange."

"How long were they there?" Mitch asked because he couldn't think of what else to say. Instead of responding, she asked Mitch if he wanted something to drink, "something besides iced tea," she said with a smile.

"Ha. I also got the part about Mabey and her nursing. Good clues, why did you drop them?"

"A drink?" Debbi repeated.

"Sure, I'll take lemonade with a shot of tequila if you have some." Mitch had an hour before he had to go home. He knew Debbi always had lemonade on hand and that tequila wasn't a stretch.

"Okay. Grab a seat on the porch. Let's sit outside; the weather is lovely." Debbi entered the house.

Cindi exited simultaneously and spoke to her mother as they passed in the doorway. "I'm going over to Shontey's, Mom. My phone is on if you need me."

"Okay, but please come home early. Say by eleven-thirty. I'm a little worried about your being out tonight."

"Oh, Mom, I'll be fine. You know I'm only fifteen minutes away. How about midnight? Shontey wants me to help with her viral video. The college contest she entered. If she wins, she gets a partial scholarship to NYU's film school. I told you. God, you never listen to me."

"Okay, but no later than midnight. We open the Shack early tomorrow, and I need your help. And, for your information, I remember your mentioning NYU and film school. Don't be such a smart-ass."

Cindi smiled and replied to Debbi, "Yes, Mother. I'll be home by midnight. I promise."

She hugged her mom and closed the screen door.

Debbi continued into the house. As Cindi turned, she dropped her keys, which Mitch thought strange, as the motion looked deliberate. She bent to pick them up going down very slowly and lingering extra-long facing Mitch and providing him an unavoidable glimpse of a very healthy chest. She quickly raised her head, but Mitch, alertly and wisely, stared into the front yard showing no interest in her cleavage at all. She was like a daughter to Mitch, which made things like this easier for him. He was a man, after all—an unrelated young woman would hold his gaze a moment or two, like any healthy man—hell, most men for that matter. A simple matter of nature. Mitch reflected and chuckled thinking of something he heard Billy Graham say once; "It's the second look that's a sin."

Mitch always avoided a second look.

Cindi sounded disappointed. "Hi, Mitch, how are you doing? Are you going to be all right alone here with my mother?"

Now normally this might make Mitch uncomfortable, but he let the veiled comment slide. "Sounds like you and your mother had an interesting afternoon at the Shack."

"I'll say."

"Hey, has Jack Junior been in touch lately? You know he got called up to Double-A and will be pitching in Tennessee, right?"

"I know. I saw him pitch his last game. I never miss when he's starting. I'd love to go out with him sometime, but he doesn't even know I exist."

Mitch sighed, feeling better. The fog in his conscience cleared. Cindi, interested in Junior, flirted with Mitch because he was safe, and wouldn't reject her outright. However, a seventeen-year-old young woman's putting herself on the line for a local sports star, now that was ripe for potential rejection. This made sense.

"Hey, so you know, I put in a good word for you now and then with Junior, and he always blushes. Dating is the last thing on his mind right now. His career comes first. I know he likes you though. A romance with an attractive and smart lady like you can quickly derail a career."

"Really, he likes me?"

"Yes I'll tell him you were asking about him next time I see him. Could be awhile, though, since he's on his way back East."

"Thanks, and good night; you'll be at the coffee shop soon, right?"

"Yes, at least once or twice in the next week or so."

The awkwardness faded. Cindi, again her pleasant self, showed a new bounce in her step. Mitch smiled, knowing she'd be thinking about Junior all night long. The door opened; Debbi stepped out with a glass of lemonade and handed it to Mitch.

"Is everything okay? You and Cindi were talking a while."

"Yeah, we were talking about Jack Junior. You know she has a crush on him, right?"

"Seriously?"

"Really? You didn't know?"

Debbi paused, "Makes sense, I suppose. I get so busy with the Coffee Shack and being both parents, I lose sight of what goes on in her head sometimes. I need to slow down and talk with her more. It's so damn challenging with Ed not being around. Bastard."

"You ever hear from him?"

"Nothing at all and no idea where he is, what he's doing, hell… if he's even alive. Good riddance. Can you imagine walking out on your kid during her tenth birthday party and never coming back?"

"No, I can't. Frankly, it's remarkable the job you've been able to do with Cindi and how she's handled the situation."

"Thanks, Mitch. I hear a lot of whispers saying I'm too loose as a parent."

Mitch took a sip of his lemonade. "Oh, the hell with them. It is the three hens leading the charge. They complain about everyone. Those three ought to try looking in the mirror sometime."

"Dang, Mitch, did I hit a nerve?"

Mitch shook off the hot feeling in his cheeks. "Yeah, they rub me the wrong way for sure. They're constantly saying shit to Mabey in backhanded ways. My gut tells me she's getting ready to tell them off and quit the flower club."

"Well, if she does, I hope I'm there."

They both laughed and looked out over the yard at General and Delilah playing. Silence hung in the air as they searched for something to say.

"So, Debbi, what's going on? Good lemonade, by the way."

"Good. Mitch. This is going to sound a little crazy, but both Cindi and I saw the same thing. It's the reason I called you."

"My recent days are full of crazy, so try me."

"It was six-thirty. We were closing the Shack. It had been quiet, so we weren't really expecting anyone in. Anyway, we were both in back when the bell on the door rang. Cindi was mopping the floor, so I stepped out front. I didn't see anyone, so I went around the front of the counter and checked more thoroughly. I couldn't see anyone. I made sure it wasn't the wind. The restrooms were also empty."

"Does the bell ever ring randomly? Like from road vibrations or something?" Mitch asked.

"No, never. I went back and told Cindi no one was out there."

"She said, 'Yeah, Mom. Was the door closed?' Cindi stopped mopping, came over to me and said, 'We're both a little tired from the long day. I'll go check.'" I told her, 'I know the bell rang.' As she started to go out front, the bell rang again. 'I'll be right back,' she said."

"Jesus, Debbi, what'd you guys do?" Mitch asked.

"We both froze. Cindi dropped the mop handle. It slid down the wall and smacked the floor with a crack. Cindi said we should go out together."

"Damn! Then what?"

"I grabbed her hand, staying as close to each other as possible, we headed out to confront whatever the hell was happening. I held the swinging door, being as quiet as possible. When we reached the counter, the damn bell rang again. Cindi let out a small scream."

"Holy shit, Debbi!"

"I know, Mitch, but wait." Debbi looked pale now.

"Cindi wondered if I saw the door close, which I had, so I told

126

her I had. She shook her head and whispered, "No, Mom that's not what I mean. Did you see someone go out the door?"

Mitch finished off his tequila-laced lemonade, wiped his mouth, and tried to relax.

"I asked her to tell me exactly what she saw. She said it was like a man. But not a man. She described something part Indian and part bird. I don't know how to explain the whole incident, but I saw the same thing. I thought for a second of an eagle walking on a man's legs. The thing also seemed to blend into the surroundings."

"Jesus?"

Debbi laughed nervously.

"Well, I thought about calling the Sheriff, and then Cindi said I should try you. Strange thing is Mitch, the more I replay the event, and talk about what happened, the presence seemed calming or reassuring in a way. As if I shouldn't have been scared. Something, besides the obvious, seemed off."

"Well, I'm impressed how you both handled the situation."

"Thanks, Mitch, because at the time I wasn't sure what to do. We stared at each other, and then I called you. Cindi kept talking while I dialed, asking me what was going on. I told her I didn't know, so we locked up and got out of there. The cleaning could wait."

Mitch paused in thought, and Debbi stared at him not knowing what to say next. Mitch held up his glass.

"Wow Debbi. You did the right thing and I'm going to need a refill now."

Chapter 32

Do Kachinas Like Espresso?

When Debbi described what she and Cindi had seen, the hair on the back of his neck straightened. Her description took Mitch back to what he and Mabey saw on the road the other night. There had to be a connection. His sub-conscious had been working nonstop trying to make sense out of what they'd seen. Mitch couldn't put his finger on exactly what it was. Hearing Debbi talk about their incident guided Mitch's thoughts into focus: Kachina dolls. A real in-the-flesh Kachina. At least real in Mitch's mind.

"Debbi, you remember the other night—the flower club fundraiser?"

"Yeah Mitch, please tell Mabey I'm sorry I wasn't able to stay. I had to close the Shack myself that night and was just too tired."

"Sure, I'll let her know. She knows how hard you work. Besides, after the way things went, she wishes she hadn't gone, either."

"Oh, do tell."

"Oh, nothing really. Just Mayor Jenkins' being his typical charming self. He had several of the flower clubwomen feeling as if they were failures for not raising more money. He's an ass most of the time. That night was no exception."

"No argument from me."

"Okay, anyway, Mabey and I left about ten or so. She drove and took Riverside Drive home. Near Deadman's Bend she hit the brakes hard, and I slammed my head into the dash. After greeting her with a couple of properly chosen expletives, I saw why she had stopped. Smack dab in the middle of the road was what appeared to be an Indian on a magnificent white horse."

"Seriously, Mitch? What did you guys do? What happened?"

"Well, you know me. I had to have a photo, so I fumbled for the camera on my phone. I took the shot, but no images recorded but night sky and a dark road. The Indian disappeared as quick as he arrived."

"Geezus. Have you guys told anyone?"

"I told Old Man Jasper and now you. I don't think Mabey has mentioned it to anyone. We considered calling Gunther." Debbi and Mitch paused, looked at each other and let out a simultaneous laugh.

"Yep, we certainly know how that would've turned out," Debbi replied.

"So, what did you and Cindi see?"

"I have no idea. It was startling and looked real. Hell, the whole atmosphere in the Shack felt odd. You could tell a presence lingered. But, as I said earlier, it was more startling and unexpected than frightening. I have been wondering why the coffee shop though?"

"It's strange that something like that would go in there, unless it had heard good things about your espresso. You do make an outstanding espresso, Debbi."

"Very funny. Geezus, how does Mabey put up with your shit? Want another lemonade?"

"I do, but better not. I need to get home soon. This does put clarity on what Mabey and I saw."

"Clarity?"

"What I'm trying to say is your description gave me a clearer understanding. I'm surprised I didn't think of it earlier."

"Really, do tell. I'm all ears."

"Have you ever heard of kachina dolls?"

"No, I can't say I have."

"Well, I don't know much about them, but I do know that they derive primarily from Hopi Indians. From what I read, the Navajo had them as well. Anyway, brief research online showed the Indians used the dolls to teach their young about their spiritual beliefs."

"No joke? Literal dolls?" Debbi asked.

"Yeah, next time you're over, look in my office. I have a few of them. I always thought they are fascinating. Mabey and I got a couple last year when we were vacationing in Sedona. Anyway, the thing you and Cindi saw,"

Mitch looked around as if he were telling a secret and didn't want anyone to hear before he finished with, "made me think Mabey and I saw a Kachina spirit... being... whatever."

"Like a ghost or something?"

"I guess. We didn't see a ghost. It looked real. It just happened to disappear quickly, almost as if it were coming in and out of this world somehow. Now I sound like a conspiracy nut."

"Not to me, you don't."

Mitch checked his watch. 9:10. He needed leave so he could beat Mabey home and give himself time to hit the internet to look up Kachinas. He needed to talk with Jasper as soon as possible; these events had to fit in with what he'd been explaining. The arrows were too much of a coincidence.

"Shit!"

"What, Mitch?"

"I forgot. Remember at our barbecue when Jack got shot by an arrow?"

"Oh my God! That's right. Do you think..."

Mitch handed Debbi his empty glass. "There has to be a connection. I need to get going. Will you be okay? You and Cindi are welcome to stay with us if you'd like."

"Thanks, Mitch, but Cindi won't be home until midnight, and we have Delilah. She can keep an eye on things."

"Okay, but you're welcome any time: you know that." Mitch turned and stepped off the porch heading toward Black Steel. "Come on, General! Let's go, boy!"

General and Delilah had settled down at the far end of the porch after wearing each other out with all their lawn-chasing. General got to his feet, licked Delilah's head, and jogged to Mitch at the foot of the steps.

"Get in the Jeep, boy. Okay, Debbi, thanks for the lemonade. Remember, if you want to come over, just give us a call. It really is no problem."

"Thanks, Mitch. Tell Mabey hello and not to be such a stranger at the Shack. Let her know I have a new smoothie she'll want to try."

"Will do."

Mitch buckled General in the harness. He climbed in, fired up the Jeep, and backed Black Steel out of the driveway. He'd be home in fifteen minutes and could get online. Mitch had research to do, and he also had to prep for the Crater Lake shoot.

"Shit, what the hell is going on, General? Are Aliens looking to take over Rogue River?"

"Woof, woof, woof."

"I couldn't have said it better myself, boy."

Chapter 33

Phone Etiquette

The drive home proved uneventful. Mitch had the camera ready and the Go-Pro video-cam rolling on the front of the Jeep, the likelihood of seeing anything unusual dropped precipitously; his cynical mind reminded him. Damn Murphy and his laws. General got a face full of fresh air and used every opportunity to try and stink Mitch out of the vehicle. Mitch wondered if his buddy needed a trip to the Vet because no animal's insides, if alive, should smell so awful. He chuckled, and damn if General, in typical Labrador fashion, didn't smile.

"No walk for you tonight, you ungrateful little turd." Mitch reached over and gave General a quick shoulder rub and felt hair slide off the dog and stick to his hand as the Jeep reached home.

It was nine-thirty at night, and Jack's pickup wasn't in the driveway. Mitch pulled into his own driveway pressing the button on the visor. The garage door opened; Mabey wasn't home yet.

He hesitated a moment, wondering where Jack might be. Mitch hadn't talked to him recently, which was unusual. He wanted – hell, needed – to check on him soon.

"General, come on, you fart machine. Straight to the backyard for you tonight, boy."

Mitch's respect for Mabey was too strong to put her through one of General's bowel symphonies. General went to the door leading into the house and barked.

"Nope, not tonight boy. You get your system cleared out, and then

132

we'll talk, okay? For now, you're going straight out back."

Mitch grabbed his collar as the garage door was closing and led him to the side door. Once inside the house, Mitch turned on the lights, opened a few windows to let in the nice river breeze, and then headed up to his desk. Before he sat down, his cell buzzed. Mitch checked the screen.

Leaving now, dropping Michelle off, and home by 10:15. Love U, M.

He texted back, *B safe, I'll hv wine ready when u get home. WM*

Mitch, relieved Mabey was okay, calculated about forty minutes before she arrived. Mitch sat and pressed the computer's

power button. While the laptop booted up, he dialed Jasper. His leathery neighbor picked up after the first ring, and Mitch at once recognized Jasper's distressed voice on the other end.

"Mitch, they got me! Please, help. I'm scared."

Silence followed before Mitch asked. "Jasper, is that you? Are you okay? Jasper… Jasper…"

Now a faint whisper, "It's a pack of rodeo clowns. Hurry, Mitch, hurry!"

A second or two of silence, and then Jasper laughed loudly on the other end.

"You son-of-a-bitch, I should have known better."

"Oh, Wilde, you are so gullible. Paybacks are a bitch, aren't they?"

"Paybacks? For what?"

"Never mind. Why are you calling me so late, fancy pants?"

"A couple of things happened today, and I want to talk with you about them. Outside of Mabey, you're the only person I can confide in with this shit. I wanted to tell you earlier when you showed me the arrow, but we ran out of time. Anyway, I'm hoping you might have answers. If you have a few minutes, I'd appreciate your perspective. How about nine tomorrow morning if you're available?"

"Sure thing. See you then. Gotta go." Click.

"Unbelievable. Why in the hell are people hanging up on me lately?" Mitch said.

The home page stared back at him, providing no answers on phone etiquette.

Chapter 34

A Full House

Mitch made his way back to the kitchen during his phone conversation with Jasper. After hanging up, he grabbed one of his favorite old-fashioned whiskey glasses—thick crystal with heavy scrolled etching, a wedding gift. Only three of the set of four remained, thanks to a rambunctious General. Mitch collected ice, found the Jameson's in the liquor cabinet, and poured himself three fingers' worth. He pocketed his cell phone and went back upstairs.

Mitch set his glass on a coaster, took a seat in his desk chair, and let out a nice sigh. It felt good to sit down at home, safe and now secure. Mitch pulled up to the desk, opened his journal application, and started writing.

M.W. June 13, 2145 hours

Too much has happened the last couple of days to adequately jot it all down. Suffice to say a lot of weird shit going on in Rogue River. Is it a regional issue or more widespread? I've been isolated the last day or so and have paid little attention to outside events except the mention of the Indians' disappearance in the newspaper. I forgot to mention it at Jasper's place. Mabey and I saw a live kachina, (still need to Google that), on Gandalf's horse. Jack was shot by a magical arrow which apparently, but not surprisingly, has had a negative effect on him. Health-wise he seems better than ever, but something is off with him. The local barista and her daughter have seen chameleon-like kachina beings in their coffee shop. General found an arrow in the river during one of our walks that matches an arrow Jasper found a couple weeks ago, and, oh yeah, he tells me, and starts to prove to me, that something is apparently toying with the planet. That about sums it up for the night. Over and out.

Since the office clock read 10:05, Mitch realized he had a few minutes to do research on kachinas, Aliens, and anything else that came to mind. He skipped steps down to the kitchen and poured himself another Irish whiskey with fresh ice and a little seltzer this time. Mitch wanted to be fresh when Mabey got home and prepped for any potential carnival ride she might give him. This, of course, depended on Mabey's mood and energy. Tonight, he selfishly hoped she had a stress-free and productive day. He was feeling a little backed up and was in no mood to take care of the pressure himself.

Mitch went back upstairs and launched a web browser. There was no shortage of links to kachinas. He found instances primarily of Hopi and Navajo tribes with plenty of references across the board. Mitch specifically searched chameleons and Aliens, and again there was no shortage of information on either. While reading information on one particular site, the hair stood up on the back of his neck.

"What in the hell is going on?" Mitch copied the link, opened his email, and sent a quick note to Debbi.

Subject line: *Hope all is well, here's something interesting...*

Debbi,

Look at this link http://en.wikipedia.org/wiki/Shapeshifting tomorrow and let me know what you think. You may not want to open it tonight if you want to sleep. It has to do with what you and Cindi saw down at the Shack. By the way, see you in the morning. I have to pick up coffee and bagels for a meeting with Old Man Jasper.

Later, M.W.

Mitch sent the email and then realized he should have waited until tomorrow. Debbi might be freaked out if she checked her email tonight. It was too late now. It was 10:17. Mabey should be here by now. He grabbed his cell and found no messages. He started to dial when the garage door signaled its opening.

Mitch walked downstairs and poured his wife a glass of Merlot. He had half a mind to strip down to his shorts with no shirt and stand in the kitchen leaning against the counter like a Greek god waiting for his special lady. Fortunately for him, enough whiskey hadn't cleared his lips to be courageous enough to follow through.

Mabey was talking with someone; the door opened, and in walked Mabey and Michelle. Oh, special day, this should be an interesting night.

"Hey, Mitch, Michelle is here."

"How's life treating you these days, Michelle?" Stupid question he thought, wishing he could reel it back in.

"Hey, Mitch," Michelle said in a sadder-than-normal voice.

"Michelle, could you take this out to General? He loves his treats, especially when I get home. I'm sure he's already at the sliding door. Flip on the light, and you should see him."

Michelle grabbed the box of dog bones and went to the slider. General greeted her with his typical enthusiasm.

Mitch would try not being too hard on her since she was his sister-in-law. She wasn't a bad person, just prone to making bad choices. She was fond of General, and the canine got amped up when she came around. Must be worth something. He turned his attention to his beautiful wife.

"I'm so sorry, but Michelle had a rough day. Her boyfriend not only left her, but he also left with a bunch of her stuff from the apartment. Looked as if he ransacked the place."

"Did she call the police?"

"No. I tried to get her to, but she just wants to put it behind her."

"Well, I have a ton of stuff I need to tell you, but we can't talk in front of her."

"Why not?" Mabey shot back.

"We just can't. What's your schedule like tomorrow? Can we do dinner?"

"I have a light load tomorrow in Grants Pass. The shorter drive and dinner would be great. How about we try the new restaurant on the river? What's it called? The Rogue Urban Eatery? I think it's the Rogue Urban Eatery. Anyway, it's supposed to be good. Why don't you Google it and make sure?"

"Okay, how about six? We'll pretend we're seniors for a night. I don't want to eat late because I need to be in bed early with the Crater Lake photo shoot the following day."

Michelle walked back in, and General followed. She tried holding him back, but he was determined to join the group.

"I have to warn you both that he had bad gas earlier tonight. So if it smells in here, it's him, not me."

"Mitch!" Mabey said.

"Well, I'm just saying."

Michelle let out a little laugh which made Mitch feel better for her. No one should have to put up with the shit that this girl seems to find. Bad choices or not, she needed a break, or three.

At 10:45, Mitch decided to go to bed. Mabey and Michelle opted for another glass of wine. Mitch rinsed his glass, set it in the sink, and excused himself.

"Good night, you two. Good to see you, Michelle."

"I'll be up in a few minutes. Michelle and I are going to decompress a bit more."

The doorbell rang. "Who could it be at this hour?" Mabey said. "Be careful, check through the peephole first."

"Yes, dear. Little Mitchey will be really careful," he said in his best smart-ass voice.

Michelle laughed a little louder, making Mitch smile. General barked and joined him at the door. Mitch looked through the peephole and yanked open the door. Standing on the threshold were Debbi and Cindi. Both looked scared out of their minds.

"Mitch, I'm so sorry, but can we come in?"

"Of course, get in here," Mitch stepped aside, and they rushed in. General jumped on Cindi and greeted her. Mitch closed the door behind them. Cindi had short breath as she nudged General aside and peeked out the side window.

"Is it still out there? Can you see it? Please tell me you don't see anything."

Mabey yelled from the kitchen, "Debbi, is that you?"

"Yeah, I'm so sorry, but it's been a strange day. Cindi and I were hoping we could hang out here for the night."

Mabey entered the foyer. "Of course. What's wrong?"

"Hasn't Mitch told you?"

"I haven't had a chance yet."

Mitch cut his eyes to Mabey, so she'd know this was part of what he wanted to talk with her about.

"Cindi, how are you doing? God, you look great. You look more like a model every time I see you." Mabey was like an aunt to her.

Michelle entered the foyer, told her sad hellos while trying to smile.

Cindi turned to Mitch. "Mitch, would you please go out to the car and get Delilah? I hope you and Mabey are okay with it, but Mom brought Delilah, as well."

"Sorry, but it didn't seem right leaving her behind," Debbi added.

General had stopped and tilted his head; both ears raised a little, forming bends at the tips. He clearly heard a word he recognized and let out a happy bark.

"Of course, we don't mind. General will love it. I'll get her, then take them around the side and come in through the kitchen. Be right back."

Debbi grabbed Mitch by the wrist before he could reach for the doorknob. "Mitch, you have a gun, don't you?"

"Why, what's wrong?" Mabey said.

"Yeah, I have several," Mitch replied. "What's going on? Is there something I should know before I go out there?"

"Remember the thing Cindi and I saw in the coffee shop?"

"Sure. Why? Did you see it again?"

"Yes, at least something similar."

"What the hell is going on, Mitch?" Mabey asked, more than a little irritated that she wasn't in the know. She put her arms around the visibly shaken Debbi, took Cindi's hand, and led them into the kitchen.

"Come on; let's get you something to drink. You're okay now. Mitch will go out and get Delilah."

Mitch hesitated a second before opening the door, contemplating whether to get his gun or camera. He passed on both, and General burst out the door as soon as Mitch pushed it open.

There was a strange feeling in the air for sure. He figured he must be a little unnerved by the women's reactions. Mitch opened the car door, and Delilah burst out, growling and barking. She came to a dead stop at the back of the car. General joined her; the hair on both dogs stood straight up on their backs. They looked like pointers—both perfectly still.

Mitch closed the car door, then pivoted, trying to see why the dogs were growling. His first thought was a raccoon. They always seem to come out on clear nights with a full moon. Mitch walked next to them. General sidestepped to block him from advancing further. Ahead, he saw something walking toward Jack's house. Mitch couldn't make out the figure, but it appeared to be grey, without clothing; it moved fluidly. Mitch called, "Hey, Jack, is that you?"

It, stopped, turned in a creepy, unnatural way, and stared at Mitch. It frightened him. Mitch took a step back; the dogs backed up too, but kept their eyes glued to the thing. He squinted to focus on the figure. It quickly changed and appeared to become Jack. It was dark out, yes, but Mitch knew it had to be Jack. General stopped barking; Delilah sensed a difference as well, changing her bark into a low whimper. The thing, whatever it was, turned, walked into the house, and closed the door. General and Delilah looked at each other, then up at Mitch. They were ready to go into the backyard, and Mitch had no problem with this. He should go over and see if Jack was okay, or perhaps not, at least not right now. He had ladies inside the house to take care of.

"Yeah, I'm with you two. No damn way I'm going over there right now. Jack can wait until tomorrow. He obviously can more than take care of himself. If he's in trouble, he'll call. Yeah, he'll call if he needs us. Come on, you two; let's go."

Chapter 35

Lock the Doors

This was going to be one interesting, and potentially long, night. When Mitch walked back into the house, he half expected to see the entourage sitting cross-legged on the floor with glasses of wine and an Ouija board between them. Either that or they'd be huddled at the top of the stairs, each with a gun pointed at the door or, quite possibly, a panty-pillow fight. Mitch shook the teenage thought out of his brain.

To Mitch's adolescent disappointment, none of them held a pillow. They were in the kitchen, and Debbi was telling Mabey and Michelle what had happened at the Coffee Shack.

"Mitch is that you?" Mabey yelled.

Mitch walked into the kitchen. "Sorry to interrupt, but I'm going up and get the spare rooms ready. Then I'm coming back down, and I want to hear just what the hell is going on."

"Mitch, you can do that later. Stay here, please."

"I'll be right back, I promise. I have to get something." Mitch hurried away, knowing Mabey would object. He felt her eye-daggers piercing his back, deciding it best to go without explanation; and he didn't want to have any discussions about why at the moment. Nor did he want them feeling any more uneasy than they already were.

Mitch turned on the light in the spare bedroom. All looked good, so, he went across the hall to the den, pulled out the hide-a-bed for Michelle, got sheets from the hall closet, and tossed them on the bed. Mabey and Michelle could throw them on when they were ready.

Mitch stepped into the politically correct owner's suite, retrieving the Smith & Wesson .38 from the safe. Shoving the gun in the back of his pants behind the belt, he yanked his shirt over the top and walked back downstairs.

"Sorry about the quick exit, everyone. Debbi, the spare bedroom is ready for you and Cindi. Michelle, I pulled out the hide-a-bed in the den. You and Mabey will need to put the sheets on it. You know the routine, Sis."

Michelle nodded and gave Mitch a nice smile. Mitch knew she liked him, and he worked to dissuade her guilty feelings of imposition. She struggled too much with guilt.

Mabey looked a little more than perturbed at Mitch. He hoped her facial expressions had more to do with the stress her friends were under than something he did. He was certain she'd understand once she got the full picture.

"Thanks, Mitch," Debbi said. "Cindi and I will get out of here first thing in the morning."

Mabey commented, while looking at Mitch, "Nonsense, you can stay as long as you need."

"Mom, can we stay a couple of days? I don't want to go back home until we know what's going on."

Mitch grabbed the bottle of Irish whiskey, got a clean glass, ice, and poured himself a short one.

"I just finished telling Mabey and Michelle what happened this afternoon," Debbi said.

"Mitch, can you believe it?" Mabey chimed in. "What in the world…"

Debbi cut her off before she could finish her sentence. "You all ready to hear why we're here now?"

"Absolutely," Mitch said.

"Jack was walking around in our house. At least I think it was Jack."

"Jack Jenson?"

"Yes, but it may not have been him. I'm not sure. He didn't speak; he was acting sneaky, and frankly, I felt a desperate need to get out of the house. It was strange. I'd already called Cindi and told her I was picking her up at Shontey's. I was calling for Delilah, so we could get her in the backseat. I couldn't find her, so I went up the steps thinking I must have closed her in the house somehow."

"Was she in the house?" Michelle asked, anxious.

"No, she was hiding behind a chair on the front porch. She looked as if she had seen a ghost. I thought she was dead; she was so still. I tried pulling her out, but she wouldn't budge. I finally got her out and had hold of her collar. I was talking to her to calm her. Then there was another sound in the house. Delilah growled. I crouched and looked through the front door. Walking around the living room was this thing. It was grayish green, had large scary-as-hell eyes, and scaly looking skin. It was staring straight at me."

Michelle squealed, and Mabey squeezed Mitch's arm so damn hard his man-jewels flexed.

"What the hell, Mom?" Cindi let out.

Debbi continued with her tale, "I took off for the car. Thankfully, Delilah was right on my heels. We got in. Of course, I fumbled with my keys. All I could think was this is just like in the movies. I might get Alien probed and then brutally murdered. Is there a difference between Alien rape and a good old-fashioned alien probing?" She gave a tiny, nervous grin. "I didn't want to find out."

"Damn, Debbi, I can understand why. I would have dropped them a dozen times."

Mitch's mind told him that in the same situation, he would have been calm and cool, no problem with the keys whatsoever. He didn't have the heart to share it with Debbi though.

By now, the meeting in the kitchen was a close-knit group of scared-shitless friends. Any closer and Mitch realized they would all be touching. He thought it was interesting how fear drove people together.

Fortunately, he was unable to think of a better group to be close with: four beautiful women. Mitch brought his brain back to the present and listened closely as Debbi continued.

"I finally got the car started and looked at the house one more time before backing out. Staring back at me through the front door," she shivered, "was the intruder. It had its eyes locked on me as if it were going to kill me. Here's the kicker. Are you ready for it?"

"Spit it out, Mom, seriously!"

"It was Jack Jenson. Sort of, anyway. I'm sure of it. Shit, I can't think straight."

Mitch swallowed the last bit of Jameson's and prepared his ears for what he thought was about to happen. Mitch couldn't wait though. He had to tell everyone he just saw the same creature go into Jack's house. No, it wouldn't serve any real purpose but to ratchet everyone's fear even higher. As freaked out as he was with the dogs in the driveway a short time ago, Mitch didn't get the sense that the Jack-creature was looking to harm anyone.

Mitch broke the silence. "Okay, everyone, I'm going to lock all the doors and set the alarm. If anyone needs to leave for any reason, please wake one of us. General and Delilah will be fine outside together. You okay with this plan?"

Cindi and Debbi nodded. Michelle said a quiet "yes," and Mabey replied, "You think they'll be okay out there?"

Mitch wanted to say that he thought they would be safer out there than they would be inside, but fortunately his mind was a few seconds ahead of his mouth for once, and instead he replied, "They're both smart and know when to be heroes and when not to be. They'll sleep under the porch and be glad for the companionship. If you'd rather, we could put them in with us..."

Mabey looked a little startled. "You think they're okay?"

"Yeah, they're fine. I'll check on them, and then I'm heading up to bed. My agenda's packed tomorrow, and I want to get to bed."

Mitch set his glass in the sink and got the last word out as he exited the kitchen closing the patio door behind him. He paused on the porch and looked skyward through the towering pines. Mitch gazed into the night sky with a new curiosity. He felt that all the stars were somehow brighter tonight. General and Delilah raced over to greet him.

Chapter 36

Mercy of the Fallen

Smiling, enjoying the carefree attitude of the dogs, Mitch watched them run energetically around the backyard for a couple of minutes. Impressed with the canine ability to shake things off so effortlessly, Mitch made sure they had plenty of food and water, patted them both on their backs, and told them good night. He walked around the side of the house to the front; he wanted to see if there was anything else going on at Jack's house.

It was a perfect star-filled night with a familiar faint whisper high atop the majestic pines. Inside was another matter. Mitch quietly opened his front door, popped his head into the kitchen, and told everyone good night. Mabey followed him to the bottom of the stairs.

"The dogs are fine. They're having fun out there," he said.

"Okay. What are your plans for tomorrow?"

"I'm getting up early and snooping around Jack's. Then I'm hanging out with Jasper. Perhaps he knows what the hell is happening."

"Is that it?" Mabey asked.

"No, I also need to get the taillight fixed on my Jeep. It's broken. I'll explain later."

"What about our dinner plans? Don't you remember?"

"Oh, of course, I'm sorry. A lot of crazy shit has been going on, and I'm having a hard time keeping track of everything. Would you mind if we ate around five? I need to leave early for Crater Lake, and I want to

144

be in bed early. Looks like Jasper's going with me, after all. He seemed excited."

"So, senior time already, huh?"

"I know, just this once. I need to get a good night's sleep. Haven't had much success with it lately."

"Okay, where are we going for dinner?"

"You'll be in Grants Pass, right?"

The women in the kitchen were now giggling and laughing, a good sign. Debbi called to Mabey, "You're out of Bailey's."

"I'll be right there; just give me thirty seconds," Mabey shot back.

"I hope you can sleep tonight, babe. They sound pretty amped up."

"Oh, it'll die out pretty quickly, usually does. Anyway, yes, I'm in Grants Pass tomorrow."

"Let's try the new restaurant downtown on the river. It is the one next to the Peacock Hotel: Rogue's Urban Eatery. They apparently brew their own beer, and I hear it's pretty good."

"Okay, sounds good. Text the address tomorrow, and I'll see you there at five. Go get some sleep. We'll try to be quiet. Will I see you in the morning?"

"No, we'll head out pretty early."

"Okay, love you, and see you for dinner."

Mabey kissed Mitch on the cheek, then went back in to the kitchen to hang with her entourage. Mitch got himself up the stairs. He removed the gun from behind his shirt, grimacing as the steel stuck to his skin. He laid the gun on the nightstand and strode to the bathroom. A couple minutes of washing and brushing, then he dropped his dirty clothes into the hamper and headed for the bed. Mitch put his usual, Dar Williams' *Mercy of the Fallen* on the clock radio, turned on the sleep timer, turned off his lamp, and was out before Dar got to the second chorus.

Chapter 37

Magazine of Choice

Gunther tossed and turned; sweat trickled down his forehead. His feet fought with an unneeded cover at the foot of the bed. He'd turned in a little earlier than normal tonight. Gunther wanted to be on patrol early in the morning, cruising town looking for anyone with taillight issues. The small-town Sheriff wanted his bonus money this year; the revenue quota for tickets was a lagging. He wasn't too worried as a few heavy days of ticketing could easily get the funds back on track.

Tomorrow he had plans to spend time looking for a particularly well-known black Jeep rumored to have a busted taillight. Should be fun, he chuckled.

A call interrupted his thoughts. "Sheriff, sorry to bother you at home, but we've had a lot of calls coming in from scared townspeople."

"About what?" Gunther sat up on the edge of his bed rubbing his eyes.

"They're seeing Indians on horseback."

Gunther laughed in disbelief, rolled his eyes, and then condescendingly questioned his dispatcher. "What a load of shit. How many calls are we talking about?"

"At least a dozen calls so far, Sheriff, from different people. That's why I called. We don't have the manpower to check out all these reports. What do you want me to do?"

"Who's on standby?"

"Brubaker."

"Call him in. I'll be there as well. Dispatch the calls in the order they came in. Make sure to get a statement from each person. If the people who already called didn't leave their contact information, then have the deputies do drive-bys and report anything unusual. Then move on to the next call. Do you understand?"

"Absolutely, Sheriff."

"Okay, I'll be ready in fifteen minutes. Over and out."

"Dammit!" Gunther slammed the phone onto the nightstand and headed for the bathroom. This would put a delay on his hunt for that prima donna with the cracked taillight.

Not to worry, he thought with a sly smile; he would get Wilde's sorry ass and make the ticket the largest fine allowable. Gunther started to giggle as he pulled down his Green Lantern pajama bottoms.

Chapter 38

Starting to Get Weird

Lying in bed, Mitch thrust his body upward—something wasn't right. Rubbing his eyes, he looked at the clock: 3:35 a.m... Beside him, Mabey lay sound asleep. The house seemed eerily quiet considering it was full of guests. He shuffled to the window, peering into the backyard. The dogs were asleep by the shed.

Mitch walked out the bedroom door and down the hall. He noted the guest room door was closed. The den door was slightly open; he peeked in seeing Michelle sound asleep on the hide-a-bed. Wondering if she would ever find a respectable guy and settle down, he groggily made his way to the kitchen for a glass of water. Everything appeared normal. Remembering there was juice in the refrigerator he shut the water faucet off and shuffled sideways a few steps. He opened the refrig door, grabbed the O.J. carton, and took a swig. It was the good stuff from Harry and David's. Mitch hated the watered-down Sunny Dee crap and Mabey only made the mistake of buying it once.

On his way back to bed, Mitch looked out the side window by the front door. Everything looked okay... at first. He had started to walk back upstairs when something caught his eye. Something was happening above Jack's house. It was as if the wind were dancing around in one spot, changing the shapes of things. Mitch rubbed his eyes. No change; he still saw the same damn thing. It wasn't the wind: it was a type of aircraft hovering over the roof.

The thing looked big, twice the size of the house, and it appeared to be cloaked, almost invisible. Mitch could barely make out a vague outline;

it seemed to flicker, or shimmer with subtle variations of motion or movement. All this shit as getting really upsetting. Mitch was more than content where Mabey and he were in life right now. This Indian wizard, horse-riding, Alien-appearing, Kachina-disappearing shit was putting a big crimp in their lives. And he had a sinking feeling that things were only starting to get weird.

Mitch hurried down the hall to the studio for a camera. At the front door, he set the camera to shoot video, and ever so slowly, he opened the door. He stuck the camera out through the opening and then peered through the side window for a better view. The stuff above the house was still going on, which was good. As he gently pressed the shutter release button to start recording, he wondered if Jasper was getting an eyeful too.

Chapter 39

Jasper's "Son"

The eastern sky, fading from the night, broadcast a purplish hue mixed with gold. Admiring it, Mitch knocked on Jasper's black-ops garage door at 6:14. He adjusted the camera strap pinching his shoulder. Jasper showed up after the second knock which meant he was awake, or he was sleeping on a cot in the garage.

"Geezus, Mitch, you show up this early, you better have coffee."

"Sorry, I don't, but since you're up, let's go down to the Coffee Shack and grab a cup. I have something I want to show you."

"Okay. I'll drive since you have a busted taillight."

"Damn, that's right. I completely forgot."

"Don't worry, pansy, your replacement should show up today, and you can get it swapped in time for the Crater Lake trip tomorrow. We're still going, right? I have something I want to check out up there."

"As of right now, yeah, I'm still going. So much is happening, though, taking a few photos is low on the list of priorities."

Jasper grabbed his keys from the wall, closed the door, and brushed past Mitch. "Let's go, Wilde. You need to let your boss know that little Mitchey is going for a ride and won't be home for a while."

"Bite me, old man!" was all Mitch could think to say. It was still early, and he hadn't gotten much sleep. Mitch wasn't yet up to his usual smart-ass self. The old guy was far ahead.

Jasper let out a nice laugh, went to the other side of his house, and pressed a button on his key fob. A ten-foot-wide steel gate swung outward. Poised behind it was an impressive looking four-door metallic grey Jeep

Rubicon. Mitch later described the vehicle as decked to the hilt without being obnoxious.

"Hang right here. Let me back out first, and then you can get in. Not much room on the passenger side, and I don't want you scratching up my paint."

"Sounds good, old man."

A few seconds later, Jasper rolled down the window and called over the engine noise with a huge grin. Mitch noticed for the first time the geezer had nice white teeth. "Get in and buckle up. You can see what a real man drives."

"This beauty comes standard with a V-10 that Ford's been making for a while now. Since Ford bought Jeep, they've done a great job of redesigning the entire line with state-of-the-art technology."

Mitch had to admit, the thing growled and purred at the same time. He could feel the power under the hood. The engine noise was a growl. The type of noise appreciated by a car lover. "Nice ride, Jasper."

"You done drooling now, pretty boy? There's nothing to be ashamed of with your vehicle. In fact, if I didn't own this, I'd have bought your model. One shortfall is the turning radius on this baby. So far though I've been okay with it. Your Jeep is nimbler and can get in and out of tighter spots."

"Why in the hell haven't I noticed it before?"

"When I take it out, it's mostly at night. As a matter of fact, this is the first time I've taken it outside during the day since I bought it."

Jasper closed the gate with a button on the visor and headed into town.

"Where did you buy it? I haven't seen a model like this on a dealer's lot around here."

"Got it off Amazon," Jasper replied.

"No shit? Amazon?"

"Yep, I buy almost everything online. I didn't have to put up with all the salesperson bullshit process they all act out. What a crock it is."

Mitch chuckled. "No doubt about that. Can you believe they still pull that crap? I guess there are still people buying cars who think the sales guy's really going to bat for them in working a deal. So, how did they ship this?"

"I picked it up at the dealership in Grants Pass. We going to talk about shopping all morning, or are you going to tell me about what you saw at Jack's last night, why you had guests show up in the early morning hours, and why you were sticking a camera out your front door at a quarter of four this morning? Let me know because if we're going to talk shopping; Mentally, I need to shift gears."

Son-of-a-bitch, how in the hell did he know all this? Mitch hadn't said shit about anything. Mitch swallowed and gathered his thoughts.

"Well, since you already know it all, why don't you turn around and take me back home?"

Jasper slammed on the brakes and brought the Rubicon to a full stop in the middle of the highway. Mitch lurched forward hard, this time with a seat belt on, fortunately. He wasn't sure his forehead could take another slam so soon.

"Jesus, what the hell? I've about had it with people slamming on their brakes lately." Mitch turned forward, half expecting to see something in the middle of the road. The asphalt revealed nothing.

Jasper looked straight at Mitch. "Listen, Wilde, let's get one thing straight. This is serious shit, and you need to understand something. I brought you on board with what I know because I thought I could count on you. If you can't handle it, or if you want to go back to living in denial-ville, say so now, and I'll take you back to your protected life."

Mitch, more than a little surprised, willed himself to grab hold of his composure.

"Screw you, Jasper. I came to you because I trust you. If I wanted to hide out in my goddamned house pretending none of this was happening, I wouldn't be sitting here right now. If you want to play games, then kiss my ass. I'll figure this shit out on my own. Might take me longer, but at least I won't have to put up with your bullshit."

The two sat there for another ten or fifteen seconds staring at each other. A car eased around them, honking. Jasper let off the brake,

152

accelerating toward the Coffee Shack. "Wilde, if I had been fortunate enough to have a son, I would have wanted him to be just like you."

Mitch said nothing though his stiffened back relaxed. He looked straight ahead following the winding road with his eyes. Mitch tried not to let Jasper see him clear the lump in his throat.

Chapter 40

A Small Round of Applause

Jasper pulled up across from the Coffee Shack. He slapped Mitch on the leg. "Let's go, I'm buying."

Mitch got out, grabbing his camera backpack.

"I'm parking across the street, so your Sheriff buddy won't go after my taillights. He does, and I'm going to his car and take out his headlight. Man, will he be surprised when I present a video to the judge of his breaking my light."

Mitch chuckled. He shouldn't be surprised Jasper had equipped his vehicle with cameras.

"Don't tell me. You got them from Amazon, right?"

The old-guy laughed heartily but didn't reply. The duo crossed the street and stepped through the front door under the familiar cling, cling, cling of the bell. The obnoxious sound comforted Mitch every time he heard it. The hustle and bustle of a crowded place made him feel connected.

He didn't see Debbi or Cindi behind the counter and until now hadn't really thought about it. Their car was still in the driveway when he headed to Jasper's. Debbi's assistant manager, and another employee were holding things together nicely. The place was busy, but not packed. It wouldn't get crowded until eight or so.

"Mitch, go grab us one of those tables in the back where we'll have a little privacy, will you? I'll bring our stuff over as soon as it's ready."

"Okay, sounds good." Mitch, moving toward the back of the

154

establishment nodded a few hellos while searching for a booth. Fortunately, today, he didn't know anyone in the place. This was a weekday, so it was only a matter of time before regulars showed up. For now, though, he and Jasper would have privacy.

Mitch found a booth and briefly admired the atmosphere of the Shack: dark with lots of wood. The previous sandwich shop had left behind, old, well-used, tables and booths. When she took over the place, Debbi made few changes, except adding an expensive espresso machine and new front windows to let in more light. The back section was bathed in a low-level soothing light and privacy wasn't a problem.

Jasper showed up a few minutes later with coffee and an egg and cheese sandwich with bacon. Mitch's stomach growled slightly in anticipation of the Tillamook cheddar Debbi used. Mitch hoped like hell the sandwich was his and not Jasper's.

"I didn't figure you for much of a sweet tooth this early in the morning, so I went with the egg sandwich instead of a muffin or donut. You okay with that?"

Mitch smiled as his stomach murmured a thank you. "Perfect and thanks. Have you been recording what I eat, too?"

Jasper slid into the booth across from Mitch. He had a bagel with generously spread cream cheese.

"No, I don't have any cameras down here. The young guy behind the counter said you usually get the egg sandwich."

"Well, thanks again. Listen, Jasper, I filmed hot footage last night, but I get the feeling you've already seen what I have."

"If you're talking about your buddy Jack's place, yeah, I saw the activity going on. I was recording myself, but my cameras are set up around the garage for an overall perimeter view, so it isn't very clear. I want to see what you have."

Jasper took a healthy bite of his bagel and chased it with sweet smelling black Kona coffee, a Shack staple.

"Besides, you're the pro, what you have has to be better than what I captured with my security cameras."

"Here you go then. I have almost fifty minutes, but it's pretty much the same thing. So, after a few minutes, if you get bored, I'll fast forward it to the last twenty seconds."

"Okay, sounds good. Let me finish this bagel. I'll need to wipe my hands; I don't want to get your camera all greased up."

"Good point. I hate it when my equipment gets all greased up."

Jasper got a big shit-eating grin on his face. "Oh, Wilde… there's a thousand comebacks I'd love to use after a statement like that. Several are rolling around in my fertile brain, but I'll leave it alone for now."

Mitch chuckled and pushed the sandwich into his mouth. It was still warm. When the cheddar hit the back of his tongue, he suddenly realized he was starving. And, of course, the hot black coffee tasted great. A minute later, Jasper polished off the bagel and downed most of his coffee.

"Let me know when you're ready to play this thing and I'll start it for—"

Jasper grabbed the camera, positioned the pivoting screen to the best viewing angle, and pressed Play. Mitch continued to be impressed by Jasper's grasp of current technology.

"I prefer Nikon myself, always loved the F3 High Point," Jasper said, "but Canon makes a good product. While I'm watching this, would you mind getting me a refill on the coffee? If they don't remember, it's the house Kona."

Mitch finished his sandwich and wiped the corners of his mouth. He took a swig of his coffee, then grabbed Jasper's cup, and went to the coffee bar.

Cling, cling, cling. Mitch recognized Sheriff Gunther as he pushed in through the door.

"Dammit," Mitch muttered. "Why do I let this guy get under my skin so much?" He looked around to make certain no one heard him. He knew he shouldn't give Gunther any part of his thought process – ever. Until now, he wasn't able to suppress the feelings, something he knew he had to think about and figure out the reason why. The reasons why the bastard irritated him so much weren't a mystery, he simply hadn't had any success putting a stop to the feelings.

Mitch paid the Sheriff no attention, beat him to the bar, and asked for refills on both mugs. The young tattoo-laced kid—his name placard read James—greeted Mitch. "You want a refill, buddy?"

"Yes, please, Kona on both, and the name is Mitch, Mr. Wilde, Wilde, hey you, anything but 'buddy' please. I'm not eight years old." Mitch knew his snappiness was more of a reflection of his anger toward Gunther.

The kid, with his ink-covered arms, was clearly embarrassed. Mitch wished he hadn't said anything.

"I'm sorry, Mr. Wilde, I didn't mean anything by it. I say buddy to everyone out of habit. Debbi keeps telling me to stop."

Mitch made a mental note to say something nice to Debbi about the kid. He dropped his chin and closed his eyes briefly, a reflexive habit when he was disappointed in himself.

The kid returned with Mitch's coffee, handed him both cups. He wouldn't make direct eye contact. "Sorry, I didn't mean to come across so harsh, James. I know you're just being personable. I have a negative connotation being called buddy. I must have been bullied by someone as a kid."

Gunther was now behind Mitch in line as Mitch turned with the refills.

"You hassling the hired help, Wilde? God, you can be such an ass. You can't go a full day without trying to make someone feel bad about himself, can you? Just like high school. You haven't changed a bit."

Mitch clenched down on his lower lip and started to move away, but then he pivoted and stood within inches of Gunther's face. The Sheriff drew back, clearly startled by Mitch's atypical reaction. Mitch looked him square in the eyes and said in a very low voice so only the
Sheriff could hear, "I know you broke my taillight, Gunther, and if you want to keep fucking with me, I'll gladly spend a night or two in jail as a consequence."

Mitch backed up a bit, clearing space. He looked around to see if anyone, other than the barista, was watching.

"Consequence for what?" Gunther said in a meek voice.

"For my beating the hell out of you; that's what. I'm tired of your shit, and just as in high school, I'll shut you up again if you keep pressing me. Now back off, you thinly veiled wannabe sheriff. If anything else mysteriously happens to my Jeep, I'll figure out a way to press charges. Go cry on your favorite Mayor's shoulder and leave me the hell alone."

Mitch deliberately turned and walked away. Long forgotten was the tension between Mitch and the kid behind the counter. A new strain of stress now filled the air. Mitch half expected a wood shampoo from Gunther as he back went toward his booth. He listened as the Sheriff stepped up to the counter. The kid greeted him. "Morning, buddy, what can I get you this morning?"

Mitch smiled at that one. He knew damn well the kid was sticking it to the Sheriff. Mitch slowed so he could hear Gunther's reply. His high school nemesis replied to the barista with a cracking voice. "Give me a double decaf soy vanilla latte with extra foam to go, and don't call me buddy, you little shit."

Mitch looked back at the counter and the kid making the latte. Hidden from Gunther's view behind the espresso machine, James had a wide smile on his face. Now Mitch really felt bad for jumping down the kid's throat.

"So, what the hell was all that about up there? Gunther afraid you're going to take his sheriff job away in the same way you took his quarterback position?"

Mitch laughed. "Yeah, probably. I told him to back off, that I knew he broke my taillight, and that I would gladly spend time behind bars for kicking his ass. Again."

Jasper threw his head back and laughed aloud. Mitch noticed small scars under his chin and made a mental note to ask him what caused them. Jasper put the brakes on his laugh. "You'll have to tell me what 'again' means later on."

The front door of the Shack slammed hard, and the glass rattled as Gunther left the coffee shop. Mitch smiled at the small round of applause throughout the diner.

Chapter 41

I Am Done With You

Gunther exited the Shack and slid into the city's white Crown Vic cruiser. He pounded the dashboard and cursed. He looked in the rearview mirror and was ashamed at what he saw. Gunther hated Wilde. He allowed the anger to flow because it kept potential tears at bay. Putting the key in the ignition, he steadied his shaking hand. The Sheriff pounded the dashboard one more time for final release.

He started the engine and backed out the cruiser. There was a screech as a car skidded to a stop inches from his rear bumper. He shot a hateful stare at the driver in his rearview even though he was one at fault. Gunther peeled his teary eyes from the mirror, placed the car in drive, and pressed the accelerator.

He rubbed his forehead with the back of a still-shaking hand while looking up and down the street. He didn't see Wilde's Jeep, so he flipped on the car's blue and red emergency lights and aimed toward the Mayor's office.

Gunther plowed the police car into his private parking spot in front of City Hall. Rogue River's Sheriff cleared the security scanners and made a beeline for Mayor Jenkins' office on the second floor.

When he surged through the outer office door, Jenkins' secretary, Trudy, greeted him. "Good morning, Sheriff. Mayor Jenkins is on the phone. Please wait a moment, and I'll let him know you're here."

Gunther grunted an utterance of disrespect and disdain, brushed past the elderly woman, barking, "He's expecting me, Trudy; he won't mind."

The secretary jumped up from her seat and followed, close on the sheriff's heels. She normally just rolled her eyes when he passed, but this time she was letting Gunther know this was her domain. He didn't pause. Gunther pushed his way into the Mayor's office. He felt the damn secretary's breath on the back of his neck where the hair still stood in shame and anger over Mitch Wilde.

Jenkins was, indeed, on the phone. He was hanging up as Gunther entered. "Mayor Jenkins, I'm so sorry, I tried to tell the Sheriff that you were on the phone, but he barged right in."

"It's okay, Trudy; I'm done. Put my calls on hold for the next few minutes and please close the door behind you."

"Yes, Mayor." Trudy gave the door a satisfactory slam behind her.

"Geezus, Bob, you can't barge in here like that. The sky had better be falling. What the hell is happening?"

Gunther paced back and forth in front of Jenkins's desk. Jenkins walked around the desk and sat on the edge. "Sit down, Gunther, and talk to me."

Gunther swigged his foamy latte and sat in one of the chairs facing Jenkins. "That goddamn Wilde is pissing me off again. I want to make the asshole pay."

"For high school still? I told you, it's time to get over whatever happened. It was what, twenty-five years ago? Move on already, Robert. Jesus!"

"Yeah, whatever. He is just so damn arrogant. He threatened me at the Coffee Shack a few minutes ago."

"Threatened you?"

"Got up in my face and told me he was going to kick my ass if I didn't back off."

"Back off. Why would he say that?"

"He accused me of busting the taillight on his Jeep. Said he'd gladly spend time in jail for kicking my ass. Something along those lines." Gunther took another drink of his latte with a steadier hand. Being in Jenkins' presence had a soothing effect on him. He seemed to be the only one who understood him and cared about him. Truth of the matter, Gunther knew deep down the Mayor didn't really care that much about him. He knew the relationship was more convenience for the Mayor and staying on the Sheriff's good side made sense. One time the Mayor had admitted the uniform turned him on. Gunther set those thoughts aside, hoping someday the Mayor would have a change of heart and embrace him fully, the way he needed.

"If he really threatened you, go arrest him. You can't let people get away with that."

"Oh, he'd be out in less than an hour. There weren't any witnesses."

"If it's that bad, make it inconvenient for him for a couple of hours. Perhaps he'll get the picture and back off as you put it. First, tell me something before you go down this road. Did you break his light? Does this have anything to do with your shouting at him at the Shack the other day?"

Gunther stared out the window and didn't respond.

"Bob." Jenkins snapped his fingers. "Did you break his light?"

"Yes, I broke the goddamned thing!" Gunther yelled. "He deserved it, and I would do it again."

"As Mayor, I didn't just hear that, and unless you're 100% sure that no one saw you, you'd better stay away from Mitch. Last thing we need is for someone to come forward with a video showing what you did."

Gunther shot from his chair, spun, and headed for the door. "Oh, the hell with you, then, Jenkins. I'm done with you."

"As you see fit but take a little advice from a friend. You are one of the least liked persons in town, and it's not because you're Sheriff. It's because you can be a vindictive asshole."

161

Gunther arched his back and stuck out his chest. He walked back toward Jenkins placing his empty cup on the corner of the desk in a small act of defiance. He stared at Jenkins for a moment as he fought back tears of hurt and desperation. God, how he wished Jenkins would hold him right now.

"Friend, huh? Is that all I am, a friend?"

The Mayor stared back with blank eyes. Gunther lowered his gaze, stifling his hurt and anger, realizing he wouldn't get what he thought he wanted and needed. Dejected, he straightened his slumping shoulders and back before walking away. Feeling as if his own body had rejected him, Sheriff Gunther slammed the door as he walked out.

Chapter 42

Clear Out

Mayor Jenkins picked up his phone and pressed zero. Trudy answered before the first ring finished, "Yes, Mayor, what can I do for you?"

"Find me Mitch Wilde's cell phone number if you can and quickly. If you can't find it, let me know right away, please."

"Excuse me, Mayor, but don't you already have it saved on your cell phone in case you need to get ahold of his wife for your training?"

"Shit, that's right. Thanks."

The Mayor hung up the desk phone and grabbed his cell phone. He zipped through his contacts, located Mabey Wilde, and then found a note tagged 'Mitch.' Mabey had given it to him as a backup in case she was with a client and couldn't answer.

The Mayor dialed Mitch's number, hoping like hell he picked up. If he didn't, he would have to call the Coffee Shack directly.

"Hello, this is Mitch Wilde. Can I help you?"

"Wilde, it's the Mayor. Are you by any chance at the Coffee Shack right now?"

"Mayor, how did you get this number?"

"Mabey gave it to me as a backup in case I ever had to cancel an appointment and couldn't get hold of her. Listen, we don't have time to chat. You should get out of there as soon as possible. The Sheriff is heading your way looking to arrest you."

"Oh, really? This should be interesting. Why?"

"I have a feeling you know what for, and whether it's justified or not, he's looking to prove a point. Just do me—hell, do yourself a favor, and clear out." The Mayor hung up. He hoped like hell that Wilde got out of there before the Sheriff arrived. The town couldn't afford for the Sheriff to come unglued on one of the town's favorite citizens.

He leaned forward and put his elbows on the desk. The Mayor lowered his head in the palms of both hands pushing the palms inward creasing his forehead. He did not know how else to get the Sheriff to let go of his anger toward Wilde. He grabbed a pen and started making notes on potential replacements for the Sheriff.

Chapter 43

The Clown Always Shows Up

Mitch stared at his cell phone as if it would somehow explain the strange and unexpected call.

"The Mayor, huh? Was he looking for you to campaign for him?" Jasper smiled and took a long drink of Kona.

"No, but nice guess, smart-ass. Let's go before things get ugly." Mitch took the camera from Jasper, slid it into the camera bag, and walked toward the door. He stopped at the counter and addressed the kid he had berated earlier. "It's James, right?"

"Yes, Mr. Wilde, and again, I'm sorry for calling you buddy."

"Listen, I'm sorry for being an ass. I know you didn't mean anything by it. Please call me Mitch from now on, and I promise not to act like a jerk." Mitch dropped a twenty into the tip jar. "Thanks for the good service. Next time I see Debbi I'll let her know how professional you are."

James face lit up. "Thanks, Mitch, and sounds good!"

Mitch and Jasper hurried across the street to Jasper's Jeep.

As they were pulling away, sure as shit, Gunther stopped his cruiser in front of the Coffee Shack. He exited his police car with a purpose.

"Good thing you got a heads-up. The way he pulled in there, he might have gone in there and shot you."

Mitch felt uneasy, realizing he'd gone too far with Gunther. The thought about a cornered animal popped into his head. He looked down at his left knee, jerking up and down, and he put his hand on his leg to slow the movement. Mitch lowered the window and let cool air hit his face.

"Okay, Wilde. Does Gunther hate you simply because you took over as starting quarterback in high school? Seems to me, it goes deeper."

Mitch, enjoying the breeze on his face, rode along in Jasper's Jeep considering his response. "Gunther has had a lot to overcome in his life. He had a drunk for a father, and his mother could not get out of her own way. I believe I'm nothing more than a sad reminder to him of a messed-up childhood."

"No shit?"

Mitch pinched the bridge of his nose; he always thought this action helped clarify his thoughts. After a while, Mitch lowered his hand and glanced over at Jasper. "I went to his house a couple of times between our sophomore and junior years. The first year I was in Rogue River, he invited me over to throw the football around. At first, I thought he was sizing me up, seeing what his competition would be. But I realized, listening to him talk, he had no friends and was lonely."

"What brought you to this conclusion?"

"Well, he wasn't used to having anyone over. He didn't know what to do or how to act. He didn't invite me inside and kept looking around as if people in the neighborhood would see us. He was nervous and uncomfortable, clearly in uncharted territory. When I asked about different players on the team, classes coming up, and teachers, he never talked about other people or school. The third and final time I went over, I got to meet his father."

Jasper came to a stop at a four-way. "Keep going."

Mitch paused; his memory did a fast rewind, taking him precisely to the moment in time when he could feel the heat off the pavement and the rough leather of the football. He took his time transitioning back into conversation mode with Jasper.

"Gunther and I were out in the street throwing the football. We were laughing and joking around, having a good time. A pickup comes to a screeching stop in the driveway, and someone jumps out. Gunther had the ball in his hand and just froze. He got pale and turned to me. "Get the hell out of here, Wilde. I'll call you later.""

Jasper kept his eyes on the road ahead. He nodded slowly, waiting for Mitch to continue.

"The guy who jumped out of the pickup ran inside Gunther's house. Gunther dropped the football in the street and repeated, "Get the hell out of here, Wilde.""

"I just stood there, curious. I wanted to see what would happen. The tension scared and intrigued me. You know when you slow down to look at the accident on the other side of the street? It's not that you wish bad things for anyone or that you're happy there's an accident to start at, it's nothing more than your mind looking to size up a bad situation, I suppose."

Jasper let out a nervous cough, covering his mouth with the inside of his right elbow. "I know exactly what you mean. So, you hung around?"

"Well, it happened so fast, I would have had to take off running like a schoolgirl." Mitch paused for a few seconds, the memory wrestling in his mind. Every time he ran it in his head, he felt bad for Gunther.

"Anyway, Gunther was about twenty feet or so from his front door when his dad busts out carrying a bunch of magazines. He starts screaming at Gunther calling him a 'goddamned faggot' and throws the magazines at him."

"Magazines?"

"Yeah, near as I could tell they looked like male skin magazines."

"No shit. That explains a lot," Jasper replied. "I always thought he was a homo. Frankly, it's none of my business, but you can see it in his eyes the way he looks at Jenkins sometimes."

Mitch cringed over the "homo" comment but chalked it up as nothing more than a generational word, leaving it alone for now.

"Yeah, it's hard not to notice."

Mitch rolled up his window a bit as the air blowing across his ear and the road noise made it hard for him to hear.

"So, while Gunther was scrambling around picking up the magazines, his dad was whaling on him. His mom came out of the house, drink in hand, and stood on the front porch looking dazed and not saying a thing."

"She must have felt sorry for Gunther, but glad she wasn't the one taking the beating," Jasper replied.

"I'm sure you're right. By now, I had somehow ended up with the football in my hand. I had started to go home as he'd asked, but the pavement pulled me, Jasper. It was as if I was stuck in mud and could barely move." Mitch looked out his window and took a deep breath allowing the Oregon air to calm him.

"I couldn't stand to see Gunther's father whaling on him, and Gunther bawling and frantically picking up the magazines."

Jasper brought the Jeep to a stop and signaled for a left turn. "You leave then?"

"I should have, but I still had his football."

"So, you walked away? Not like you could have done anything."

"I often wonder how things would be now if I'd just walked away."

"Look forward, Wilde. Never look back. Doesn't matter, the clown always shows up."

Mitch, bewildered, let Jasper's odd statement slide by. Mitch thought it might be a reference to Jasper's wife leaving him. Obvious pain lingered with Jasper, and who could blame him? It didn't quite fit his look-forward motto, though.

Jasper continued, "Well, standing there seeing a friend get whaled on by his dad isn't pleasant, but it isn't the worst thing either. You know how many thousands of friends see that shit happen?"

"Yeah, I'm sure. But it gets worse."

168

Jasper tapped the dashboard lightly with his open palm to get Mitch's attention. "Seriously, come on, spit it out; we're almost home."

"So, I stood there; Gunther's dad at one point stopped, looked at me, and said, 'You a faggot, too, boy?'"

"Holy shit, Mitch, did he come after you?"

"For a minute, it appeared he would. You could see the thought occur in his eyes, but he was so mad at Gunther, he turned his wrath back on him. So, I gripped the football as hard as I could and..."

"You didn't."

"Yep, one of the best passes I've ever thrown. I called to get his attention. At the same time, I let fly as hard as I could from 15 to 20 yards. I threw a perfect spiral. Hit him square in the face— knocked him down. The bleeding started, and he was surprised and dazed."

"He'd never had anyone stand up to him."

"Here's the kicker." Mitch paused, drying both palms on his jeans. The motion was deliberate as if rubbing hard enough would wipe the memory clean.

"Gunther jumped up and started yelling at me. Calling me a motherfucker an asshole and who knows what else. He and his mother raced to that prick's side and asked him if he was okay. Gunther and I never really spoke after that, except when he taunted me, trying to provoke me. He has always been afraid I'll tell people what happened."

"You never did, I bet. You also mentioned something about beating him up. Was that the same day?"

"No, that was at a football practice one day later in the fall. The air was cold; our pads were like rocks while we were scrimmaging, and we were all exhausted. Just then, the little shit came in on a weak-side blitz and blindsided me with an obvious late hit. I even had on the red jersey and was off limits for hits."

"Pansy-ass quarterbacks." Jasper slapped Mitch on the chest with the back of his right hand. "Did the coach jump in?"

"Yeah, but a little late. I picked myself off the ground. By then Gunther was laughing his way back to the defense's huddle. I took off for him, body-slammed him to the ground, and started pounding on him.

"By the time the coach got there, a few other players had pulled me off. He was crying like a baby. He couldn't wipe his face very well because of the helmet. Coach threw him out of the scrimmage and sent me to the sidelines for the rest of the practice."

"Damn, Wilde, I can't believe you haven't been put into jail since he became Sheriff."

"The only person I've told other than you is Mabey. I haven't even told Jack. Just didn't seem right."

"You're a good humanitarian, for sure. Most people would have told as many people as possible. Says an awful lot about you, I might even shed a tear or two." Jasper looked at Mitch and smiled.

The simple smile made Mitch feel good. He could tell Jasper was trying to hide his true feelings behind humor.

"I guess I always felt Gunther owed me something, not so much for plastering his dad, but for not spouting off and telling everyone. It should've earned me a certain level of gratitude, but he's been after me ever since."

"Shit, Mitch. I can certainly see why you replay that one repeatedly and at the same time trying to forget about it altogether.
Damn humans. Why do certain people have to be so cruel? And Gunther's own father: certain people shouldn't be allowed to have kids."

Jasper pulled in his driveway and pressed the side gate button; the gate swung open, and Jasper brought his Jeep to a stop.

"Hop out, Mitch, so I can put this beast away"

Mitch opened the door and eased his way out.

"Hey, I hope the next time I piss you off no football is lying around." Jasper smiled.

"Now close the damn door before you let the flies in, you pansy-ass QB."

Chapter 44

I'll Be Right Back

Mitch stood there thinking about all those years ago. A wave of regret washed over him. A common occurrence, for a time, after rehashing his high school events with Gunther. Mitch agreed with Jasper how certain people shouldn't be parents, and he knew what happened at Gunther's was one of the main reasons he never wanted to have kids. There was no way to tell if you're going to be a good parent or not, he always told Mabey. She usually said. "Not like the kids have a say in the matter."

Mitch often wondered how differently Gunther might have turned out if his dad had loved him for who he was, and not what he thought he should be, and if his mom wasn't a walking-dead drunk. The kid never stood a healthy chance under their roof. Mitch had thought for years that he should sit down and talk with Gunther. They shouldn't let it drag out. They were adults now and had the maturity and experience to rectify this, right? Any come-to-Jesus meeting would have to wait a while longer, though. There were a few more pressing issues happening in Rogue River now.

Jasper closed the door to the Jeep as the gate closed.

"Dammit, I'm a little depressed now, Jasper."

Jasper didn't respond. Smart, Mitch thought. If you don't know what to say, it's usually best not to say anything. He had to hand it to him; it wasn't a good time for a smart-ass comment, a skill still eluding Mitch's own inner voice.

Jasper patted Mitch's shoulder on the way by. "Hey, I wonder if your taillights are here yet."

"I doubt it. It's a little early."

"They could be, Mitch."

Mitch kicked stones in the driveway, still thinking about Gunther. "Jasper, I can't thank you enough for ordering the taillight for me. I appreciate it. Gunther will drive all over town today hoping to give me a ticket. The busted light would give him his excuse."

"Damned straight he'll be looking for you. Other than my disdain for a certain rodeo clown, I have never seen anyone dislike someone as much as Gunther does you. At least now, I have a better understanding why. Not a valid reason, but it does make more sense."

Let's go see if we can break down that video a bit more. Want anything to drink?"

"I'm fine, but thanks. By the way, I'm going to go over to Jack's in a few minutes and see if he's home. I want to see if I can figure out what's going on over there. I'm a little concerned how he's been acting. Not sure how he'll react, but I need to know."

"Okay, sounds good."

Mitch followed Jasper through the side door to the garage. Jasper flipped on the lights and pulled up a couple of chairs. He grabbed the backpack, took out the camera, removed the memory card, and placed it into one of his laptops.

"Focus, Mitch. Let's look at this video again. Press Play, will you?"

"Jasper, before you start the video, give me a minute. I'll be right back."

Chapter 45

Okay, Whatever

Mitch needed a minute alone and using the bathroom was a good excuse. He turned the cold water on at the sink and bent over, letting the water run gently into his cupped palms. He lowered his face and splashed the water over it. He grabbed a hand towel and dried himself. He looked into the mirror.

"You are not a bad guy, Mitch. You're not a bad guy." Mitch exited the bathroom feeling better.

Jasper jumped back into discussion mode. "This is good footage you have here. The end is a little shaky, but I got to figure your arm was getting tired."

"Yeah there were several times I wanted to stop. But I couldn't."

"What can you tell me about the last thirty seconds or so?"

"I see you fast forwarded already."

"Yeah, I did that back at the Shack while you were getting ready to spend a night in jail. Good thing the place wasn't packed, or Gunther might have arrested you in front of everyone to make a show."

"You're right. I pushed it a little too far. You know he's already thinking of a way to get back at me. If he can get himself out from under the mayor's desk long enough."

Jasper laughed.

Mitch liked his neighbor; he wished he'd spent more time with him over the last few years. He missed having a trusted mentor like his dad around. Jasper, Mitch saw, was like his dad in many ways.

"Okay, so what about the last thirty seconds—notice anything in particular?"

"I was hoping you could tell me. It looks like something climbs into the thing, and it takes off. Straight upwards and without any noise other than what sounds like wind."

"Yeah, I saw all that, Mitch, but did you notice the front door of the house before that?

"No. What about it?"

"Here, look for yourself." Jasper pointed to a spot on the monitor. He gave Mitch the mouse to the PC. "Here, you control when to start and stop."

Mitch clicked Play on the screen. He realized he needed to rewind. He backed up about fifty seconds and pressed Play again.

"Pay particular attention to the door."

"Got it." Mitch kept his gaze locked on the front of the house. "Holy shit are you kidding me! How'd I miss that?"

"The eye is drawn to the roof for obvious reasons. You would've seen it, eventually. Over the last ten years or so, I've developed an ability to look at whatever I'm not supposed to be looking at. Try watching your favorite movie, something you've seen several times, and look everywhere but where the camera wants you to look. You'll be amazed how much more you notice."

"Damn, how many are there, and, more important, what are they?"

"I counted at least sixteen…" Jasper's words tapered off. "What's your opinion, Mitch?"

A quiet Jasper watched as Mitch pressed Rewind and watched the last thirty seconds again. When he got to the end, he pressed Stop, and looked at Jasper. "Not sure, but if you put a gun to my head wanting an answer, I would say two separate parties are having a gathering or meeting of sorts."

"My feeling exactly."

All this shit was giving Mitch a stress headache. He brushed the hair off his forehead and rubbed his scalp before continuing. "It looks like Indians, and an Alien race—being, entity, whatever the hell I'm supposed to call them—coming out of a big powwow."

"A potentially proper term considering one of the parties appears to have ties to Indians," Jasper stated.

"They look like my kachina dolls come to life. This is nuts. What do we do, Jasper?" Mitch thought his tone sounded more like a plea than a simple question. He didn't care right now. He was more than a bit worried.

"Well, Mr. Wilde, if you believe in God, you might want to crank up your prayer time. If you don't believe, then what the hell do you care? Let's enjoy the ride and go out fighting. Perhaps your buddy Jack can put in a good word for us, and they'll lock us in special cages with extra creature comforts at their petting zoo."

"Shit, Jasper, don't be so depressing. I gotta go. I want to track down Jack. Are you still going to Crater Lake with me tomorrow?"

"Yeah, if the invite is still open; there are a few things there I'd like to check out myself."

"Okay, sounds good. Let's leave at four a.m. There's a place on the east rim with a great view where I've taken nice photos in the past. That should give me plenty of time to get what I need, and then you can poke around all you want."

"It's settled then. I'll be out front at four. Let me know if anything changes. Can I keep the memory card and play around with the footage?"

"Sure, keep it. I have plenty. I already sent a copy to my Cloud drive while we were driving back, so we're good."

"Cloud drive?"

"Yeah, it's secure. I have it password protected," Mitch stated with trepidation as he tried to get out the door.

Jasper shook his head. "I have a lot to teach you, but so little time. There's nothing secure about the Cloud. You know the government created the Cloud, so they could have easier access to their population's data. Every time any of us plugs into the web, we are fair game. Just depends if someone is hunting us."

"You know, Jasper, a few years ago I would have thought you were paranoid. Right now, I have a few bigger things to worry about than whether our government is viewing my photos in the Cloud."

"Incrementalism and lax attitudes like yours are what have led America down the path to socialism the last couple of decades, my friend. And it isn't your neighbor you should worry about," Jasper shot back with a smile.

"Okay, whatever. I need to get going. We can talk about it tomorrow." Mitch, now feeling more uneasy than any other time in his life that he could remember, closed Jasper's door behind him and walked to Jack's place.

Chapter 46

Night Fishing

Mitch left Jasper's garage lost in his thoughts. The warm, pine-scented breeze comforted his lungs. The air in Rogue River made Mitch thankful his father chose to live here long ago.

Jack and Mitch had been inseparable since that first day at Rogue River High School. How certain individuals clicked in life fascinated him. It was as if they had the same blood flowing through their veins and the same neurons popping in their brains. Mitch felt close to Mabey and the two Jacks, and he didn't share an ounce of so-called family blood with any of them. Was life more about being part of a collective conscious than singled out, alone, connected only by family genes? "The force be with you," he often joked to Mabey. Mitch held fast to the belief that everyone was connected in some way.

A large box sat on Mitch's doorstep. He figured his taillights had arrived; he'd check in a few minutes. First things first though. The smell of the air led him to a memory with Jack during the summer before their senior year. Wondering how and why his mind would pick this memory at this time Mitch recalled how he and Jack snuck onto Mitch's old girlfriend's property to go night-fishing. Once at the small pond, Jack hooked a big fish within minutes after they had trudged through the woods. Excited, he yelled out and woke up everyone in the house. The now-awake residents let loose their dog, so Mitch and Jack had to make a quick escape. Jack had to throw his fishing pole into the pond. That was a great source of entertainment for Mitch. To this day Jack got upset with Mitch over the loss of his pole. Mitch always reminded Jack that his screaming like an excited little schoolgirl is what got the dog set loose on them.

Mitch found himself on the front step outside Jack's place. He wondered how he was able to walk from Jasper's place to Jack's and not remember anything but fishing at Mary's Pond so many long years ago.

Mitch laced his hands behind his head and yawned, then stretched his arms towards the sky. Nervous, he reached for the doorbell reminding himself he would do just about anything for Jack and he hoped his friend knew it. He made a mental note to make sure he told Jack as much as he rang the doorbell.

Chapter 47

An Unexpected Jack

The doorbell rang with no immediate response. Mitch did not expect one since Jack's pickup wasn't there. Mitch started to walk away when the door opened. His heart jumped as he turned back toward the door.

Standing in the doorway was Jack Junior.

"Junior, what the hell are you doing home? Why aren't you playing baseball?"

"Hey, Mitch, good to see you! Remember how I got stuck in Portland? Well, the team told me to wait four days and then fly to Seattle. They'll be on a road trip there. Anyway, I've been worried about my dad and, a good thing too, because something isn't right. I've been knocking on your door and calling your phone for over an hour."

"Shit, sorry. I've been over at Jasper's. He has a strange men-in-black rule about no cell phones being on in his place."

"What are you talking about?"

"I can explain later. I've been a little worried about your pops myself, and that's why I'm here now. I've hardly seen him since you left."

"He left for work. He said he'd come home early, so we could go eat and catch up. But not sure I believe him."

"Why is that?"

"That's just it. I don't know. Body language, the tone in his voice: it just didn't feel right. I know this will sound strange, but it's almost as if

179

my dad is someone else."

"Junior, with what's been going on here the last few days, it doesn't sound strange at all. What do you say we take a ride to his office and see if we can talk him in to an impromptu lunch?"

"That sounds great. Thanks, Mitch."

"No problem. Give me about twenty minutes and come over. I have a busted taillight I need to switch out on my Jeep first."

"Okay, see you in twenty." Junior stepped back in the house.

As Mitch walked home, he couldn't stop thinking about what Junior had said: an impostor. He debated telling Junior about what had been going on. He certainly didn't want to scare the kid; Junior was already upset, but he did have a right to know. Once he told Junior, the kid might not go back to baseball, probably disastrous to his career and certainly devastating to his father. Mitch knew him well enough to understand if it came down to a decision of either a career or his dad, Junior wouldn't hesitate. But if they all became Alien pets, baseball wouldn't matter, unless the Aliens enjoyed watching it. Mitch smiled.

At the house, Mitch made sure General and Delilah had plenty of food and water, took a quick leak, washed his hands, threw on a clean tee-shirt; 'Black Against Me' from their 2014 "Black Me Out" tour. He retrieved the carton with the taillights and opened the box. He grabbed a screwdriver from the toolbox, removed the old light... The doorbell rang.

"Junior, I'm in the garage."

Junior trotted over. "Can I help with anything, Mitch?"

"No, I just about got it, a couple of screws, and we're good to go."

"What'll you do with the old light?"

"Throw it in the recycle bin, if you don't mind."

"You got it."

Mitch tightened down the last screw. "Okay, good to go. Let me put this screwdriver away, and we'll get going."

Junior jumped into the passenger side of Mitch's Jeep.

"You like coffee, Junior?"

"Sure, why?"

"We have a bit of drive to your dad's office, and I could use a pick-me-up." Mitch had already had his cup-for-the-day at Jasper's, but one more wouldn't kill him. He had another motive for the stop: Cindi should be working by now. Stopping in with Junior would be a nice, covert, and strategic move to get the two together.

"What happened to the light?" Junior asked

"That, my friend, is a good question. Ever hear of a prick named Gunther?"

"Sheriff Gunther? Why?"

"Never once accused of being an honorable civic example and leader for our youth, he busted it."

"No shit?" Junior asked.

"No shit. I can't prove it, but I know he did it."

"How can he get away with that?" Junior added.

"I couldn't have said it better myself." Mitch walked to the workbench, put the screwdriver away, grabbed water from the refrigerator and tossed one to Junior. "Okay, let's go track down your old man."

Mitch climbed in and buckled up. "Hey, do me a favor and check to be sure the new light works, will you?" Junior went to the rear of the Jeep. Mitch stepped on the brake and then turned on the signal.

"Looks good, Mitch."

Mitch accelerated out of the cul-de-sac. "So Junior, you must be dying to join the new squad and start throwing heat?"

"I guess."

"Really, kid? Man, I would have thought you'd be ready to roll."

"I'm afraid I won't be good enough. Moving up to the next level is no guarantee. Pros get much better each step along the way. Coach seems to think I have what it takes, though, so we'll see."

"Remember, the managers at the lower levels, most of them anyway, want to get a shot at making it to the big leagues themselves. It makes sense for the organization to bring somebody in who can help them win. They wouldn't think about calling you up if they didn't think you were ready."

"I guess, but it's still hard to believe sometimes. It's happening so fast. Coach did say I'll be starting shortly after the all-star break, so we'll see."

"Well, Junior, the only failure is not giving it 100 percent. Trust me. If you can't cut it, go down with a fight every time."

The radio broadcast a top-of-the-hour news jingle, and the announcer led with, "And in national headlines, the all-too-strange disappearance of Native Americans continues. Let's go to Jessica Sample in Klamath Falls, Oregon."

Thanks, Jim. Here at the Klamath and Modoc Indian Casino just outside Klamath Falls, local patrons, as well as tourists, are at a loss for the sudden closure of the popular tourist attraction on the upper end of Klamath Lake. The casinos simply don't have enough employees to open. Over the past thirty days, more than fifty Native American employees have stopped showing up for work. The casino prides itself on having more than 75 percent Native American staff made up of locals from Klamath, Modoc, and other area tribes. There's no known sickness or clear foul play at work here, but when the executive board is pressed, they admit they do not know where the people are.

Many other Native American casinos across the country are also reporting sudden employee losses. Speculation runs rampant as to what is going on: the end of the world, Native Americans' reclaiming their love of nature and heading for the wild, a mass rapture of some kind. The remaining few Native Americans showing up for work will not talk with us. For now, the slots are not spinning, the crap tables are empty, and the doors are quiet.

This is Jessica Sample reporting. Back to you, Jim.

"God, this is crazy, Mitch. You think this has anything to do with my dad getting pierced by that arrow?"

Mitch turned down the volume, so he and Junior could hear each other more easily. "With all the strange shit that's been going on here lately, I agree with you. As for the radio broadcast, I vote for the part about the 'end of the world' like the reporter said."

"Well, it had better hold off for a while; I haven't even gotten a chance to pitch at Chattanooga."

Mitch smiled nervously. He himself wanted more time on this planet with Mabey. They had a lot left to do.

Another minute of silence and boring squawks from the radio passed before Junior asked, "Mitch, you knew my mom pretty well, didn't you?"

"Yeah, I went on a double date with her one time in high school. Your dad has probably told you the story."

"No shit! Are you serious? What happened?"

Mitch pulled up to the Coffee Shack, aggressively parking right in front as he thought of Gunther. "Let's grab our drinks and then head to your father's office. I'll tell you all about it on the way." The two climbed out of the Jeep.

"Junior, come around to the back here for a second, will you?"

"Sure thing, what's up?"

"Okay, you see both my taillights, right? Neither one of them is broken, chipped, cracked?"

"No, they look fine to me. Just like when we left your house. Why?"

"Never mind, if it comes up I want to make sure I have a credible witness to back me up."

Before entering the Shack, Mitch looked up and down the street: no sheriff cars in sight.

Cling, cling, cling. That sound made many disparate thoughts run through Mitch's mind. He half expected to see Gunther getting his boy-toy a cup of coffee. It seemed that every time he was at the Shack, the asshole showed up. Mitch wanted to get in and out fast this time. He wasn't in a mood for any more bullshit from Gunther. His patience with the town's Sheriff was growing increasingly thin.

"Mitch, good to see you," Debbi said from behind the counter.

Mitch glanced around and didn't see Cindi. Dammit, she was the main reason he stopped in here.

"Thanks again for letting Cindi and me crash with you and Mabey last night. We were both more than a little freaked out."

"You're both welcome anytime. Where's Cindi? I brought a baseball star with me and thought she might want to get an autograph."

Debbi smiled. Junior looked at Mitch in bewilderment.

"She's in back prepping for the lunch crowd. I'll get her."

Just then, the kitchen door swung open, and Cindi popped out wearing an apron, her hair disheveled, and a generous streak of flour across her forehead.

"Cindi, Mitch brought someone in to say hi. You remember Jack Junior, don't you?"

Cindi looked at Mitch, and without a word let him know her thought, "You bastard, how about advanced warning next time?"

Then she let out a surprised little squeal, spun around, and disappeared back in the kitchen.

Mitch gave Junior a little elbow. The kid smiled from ear to ear. "Told you she liked you."

"I'm sorry, you two; I'm not sure what's gotten into her. Give me a second, and I'll go get her."

"Not necessary, Debbi, I have a feeling she'll be right back."

"So, what can I get you guys this morning?"

"I'll have an iced chai latte."

"What about you, Junior; what's your beverage of choice?"

"I'll try one of the summer lattes. Make mine iced, too, please."

"Small, medium, or large, gentlemen?"

"Medium for me, please, ma'am," Junior replied.

"Same for me."

The kitchen door swung back open. This time out popped a fresh and put-together Cindi.

"Hello, Mitch, thanks for letting my mom and me stay with you last night. How's Delilah?"

"I just left the house. Delilah and General were tearing around the backyard having a great time. You know those two; every time they get together, they can hardly stay in one spot."

Mitch was halfway through his response when Cindi's eyes left his and zeroed in on Junior.

"Mission accomplished." Mitch thought and grabbed a newspaper to look at the headlines.

Junior wore a sly little smile on his face. Mitch thought Cindi might climb over the counter, grab Junior's hand, drag him in the back, and attack him. Damn, the girl had a major crush. Mitch smiled thinking about his own youth.

"Hey Cindi, how are you? You look great. This is your senior year, right?"

Mitch left the two lovebirds, went to the espresso and told Debbi he'd be right back. He went out the front door, stopped on the sidewalk, looked left and then right. Sure, as shit, here came a sheriff's car down Main Street. Unbelievable! Mitch thought for a second about ducking behind a car, but he couldn't. He had no legitimate reason to hide other than avoidance or a way to watch the Sheriff bash in his taillight again. For a moment, Mitch contemplated doing just that. Then he thought the best thing right now would be to hash it out with Gunther once and for all.

The car pulled up a couple of spots from his Jeep, and out jumped one of Gunther's deputies. Real young kid looked as if he hadn't even started shaving yet. The way he walked made Mitch think of Barney Fife. Mitch was relieved it wasn't Gunther. As much as he knew their relationship issues needed to be resolved, he simply did not have the time or desire right now.

The deputy carried a ticket pad. He walked to the rear of the cars lined up in front of the Coffee Shack and stopped behind Mitch's Jeep. He walked around to the front, then back around to the rear. He reached up on his shoulder for his two-way and said something. Mitch made out a returned, "Shit" from the deputy's radio.

Mitch casually walked over to his Jeep. "Anything I can help you with, officer?"

"No, sir, Mr. Wilde, we'd received complaints about a Jeep passing through town with a busted taillight. We were afraid it could cause an accident."

"Who is 'we,' might I ask?"

He shrugged. "The Sheriff's office."

Mitch smiled and told Deputy Bob, "Make sure to let the 'we' know I'm watching. If he messes with me in any way, he'll be making a big mistake." He started to turn away but stopped. "Oh and have a nice day." Then Mitch stepped back into the coffee shop.

Junior was coming outside with drinks in hand. Debbi stayed behind the espresso machine and gave a slight wave to Mitch. Cindi stood close to the register in a statuesque pose as if she had just won the lottery.

"Hey, Junior, I didn't pay for those. How much do I owe you?"

"Cindi's mom said they were on the house."

"Thanks, Cindi. Will Mabey and I be seeing you guys again tonight?"

"Yeah, if you don't mind. We're thinking one more night, if it's okay with you guys."

"Sure thing. See you later."

Junior handed Mitch a drink, opened the door, and casually looked over his shoulder in a very cool and collected way. "Thanks, Cindi. I'll text you."

With that, Mitch joined Junior as the Shack door closed. Mitch laughed because he knew damn good and well that Cindi had just had herself a private moment.

"Damn, you're smooth, kid!"

"Helps when you already know someone likes you. Thanks for the tip."

The two climbed into Black Steel, and as Mitch backed out, he realized the kid was right; people will generally act differently when they know there's little chance for rejection. Mitch wondered if this was the reason Gunther consistently harassed him. Making a mental note to explore this line of thinking further, he put on the turn signal, stuck the straw in his mouth and took a nice big swig. It tasted good all the way down his throat. He turned onto the on-ramp to the freeway.

'Now here's a golden oldie from Huey Lewis and the News," the radio said.

"Dad loves Huey, Mitch."

"So, do I, kid. Good stuff."

Mitch turned up the volume. He had to agree with Huey. It is "Hip to be Square."

Chapter 48

Twists of Fate

Mitch daydreamed as he and Junior continued the journey down Interstate 5. Junior fidgeted in his seat.

"So, Mitch, what's this about your dating my mom? I'm dying to know. Dad never said anything. I guess I was too young for Mom to bring it up."

Mitch cleared his throat and checked the rearview and then his speedometer. He chuckled and then paused.

"It was only one time, a blind date, and not a very good one at that."

Mitch confirmed the cruise control was set on 65 mph. Junior popped the knuckles in both hands in anticipation of the story.

"Your dad had his eye on a girl in algebra class for quite a while. He finally got up enough courage to ask her out. She agreed, but only if he'd set up her friend on a double date with me. The girl was your mom-to-be. Your dad told her no problem: 'How about Friday night?' He knew I'd be up for it – all, of course, before asking me."

"Sounds like Dad."

"So anyway, he developed this grand plan where we'd double date at the drive-in and take his pickup and throw a couple of lawn chairs in the back. He could off-load me and Ginny on the lawn chairs, and he and his date would be alone in the pickup. I had no interest in going out whatsoever. I was trying to stay focused on my athletics and studies."

"You went to Portland State, right?" Junior asked.

"Yep, the home of the Vikings. Your dad and I wanted to go there, both to play football if possible and stay relatively close, but not too close, to home. For me, the school had good photography and history programs, and I really liked Portland. Football would have been great, but I was more interested in getting in with a scholarship – football, baseball, or academic. Portland was hip and a fun place to be for young adults. Anyway, on that date, I mainly wanted to have fun, drink a few beers, and call it a night. Not too many teen girls in this town thought as I did. It was always about promise rings, the next formal dance, and being seen around town with a letterman jacket on."

"Not much has changed."

Mitch gazed out the window staring at the rows and rows of apple trees. Some of the best in the country, he thought. He loved the symmetry and orderliness an orchard provided. He longed for the order in his personal life right now.

"You know, it's funny, Junior, but not much ever really changes outside of technology. Anyway, your dad had everything planned out and picked me up in his old F-150."

"The old red one he has out back?"

"Yep, I don't think he'll ever get rid of it. The first time he met your mom was in that pickup."

"Damn, I didn't know that. I always wondered why he wanted to keep that thing; it's horrible on gas. He always said he needed it to haul stuff, which makes no sense since he has a new one he drives every day."

"Well, your dad worshiped your mother, as you know. I can't imagine what it was like for him to lose her the way he did."

"That damn garbage truck."

Mitch gave Junior a moment of silence.

"Then what, Mitch?"

"Then your dad picked me up, and we drove over to your mom's

189

friend's house. Her name was Sondra. Your dad had the lawn chairs and a couple of blankets in back, a cooler full of soda on top and beer on the bottom. He was so damn excited because of his crush, or a lust, I should say, on Sondra. We went over this grand strategy. Once we arrived and got a good viewing spot, I was supposed to ask your mom to go get snacks. Your dad was going to stay back and get the chairs set up and make plans with Sondra."

"Plans?"

"Yes, plans to camp out in the truck because of his hay fever. He was going to claim he didn't want to sneeze all night. If he stayed in the pickup, the pollen wouldn't affect him."

"Dad has hay fever? I didn't know that."

Mitch laughed. "He didn't have hay fever. He was a strategy guy, always has been. He was angling for his best opportunity to get alone with Sondra."

Junior chuckled. "Dad is too funny."

Mitch figured another ten minutes before the exit. Traffic flowed smoothly as always in the Rogue Valley.

"We stopped and picked up the girls. They were waiting on the curb which was awesome. No parent meetings... always hated that shit. Felt like the parents were waiting for me to take the first opportunity to soil their precious little girl, but I digress. Your dad pulled to the curb, and the girls all but sprint to the truck. Your dad didn't even have the key out of the ignition yet."

"No shit. Why were they so anxious?"

"Well, they definitely had their own strategy. As I got out, Sondra pushed your mother into the pickup first, so she'd be sitting next to your dad. Sondra slid in next to your mom, and I was standing on the sidewalk knowing your dad was going to blame me for this less-than- perfect start to his night. Your mom was looking straight ahead, clearly uncomfortable; Sondra was looking at me with this horny mischievous grin. We couldn't see each other, but your dad stared straight through both of them with a look I can only describe as our friendship ending and a Wilde-I-am-going-to-kill-you."

"That's hilarious. So, this Sondra girl all along wanted a shot at you and wasn't interested in Dad at all?"

"Yeah, that became clear pretty quickly."

"That sucks for Dad, but I'm glad it happened. Why didn't you just go around and let Dad get in the passenger seat?"

Mitch laughed then reached up and rubbed an eye. "Damn, Junior, I didn't even think of it. Clearly, the girls outfoxed us. Son of a bitch, I can't believe we never thought of it."

"So, what happened the rest of the night?"

"Well, it went downhill from there. Sondra talked to me during the whole twenty-minute ride to the drive-in. Your dad and Ginny just sat there and barely spoke. It sounded to me as if she tried to engage him. I got the impression she liked him. However, your dad couldn't see it and said perhaps five words. I still had a chance to right things the way he planned. I figured as soon as he parked, I could jump out, ask your mom if she would get popcorn with me, leaving your dad alone with Sondra. Well, Sondra had evidently been planning this for a while. So, right after your dad paid for tickets, and just before we parked, Sondra blurted out something like, 'I'm paying for popcorn and nachos. Will you help me get them, Mitch, while Jack and Ginny set up the chairs and blankets?' Nail in my coffin. I felt bad for your dad. He had been planning this for a long time."

"How long did he stay mad at you?" Junior asked.

"That's what a weird night it turned out to be. He ended up thanking me. To make a long story short, and since we're near our exit, Sondra ended up giving me a tonsillectomy, among other things. Your Dad and Mom were inseparable after that. We all became great friends, all ended up at Portland State together. The rest, as they say, is history."

"What ever happened to Sondra?"

"I made healthy use of her medical skills and let her make sure my tonsils and other parts of my body were functioning correctly. Her father was a pastor, by the way. Stay away from pastors' daughters, Junior, unless all you want is outrageous partying."

"Man, if that ain't the truth. I knew a couple of sisters in school whose dad was into the church big-time. Anyhow those two loved to party."

Mitch put the turn signal on and exited the freeway. "Sondra and her family moved about a month after that night. I will admit she was a lot of fun, but, man, am I glad she moved. I couldn't hydrate quickly enough, and my grades were slipping. Your dad and I laugh about it now."

As Mitch exited the freeway, he thought how strange life can be. In an alternate universe, perhaps Ginny and Mitch marry, and Junior is his son. Mitch liked it much better the way it turned out.

"Strange how twists of fate work out, Junior."

Chapter 49

Snake Eyes

Junior said little after Mitch's story about blind dating his mother, Ginny. He had a smile on his face, so Mitch hoped the story added to Junior's fond recollections of his mother.

Jack's business, an outdoor sporting-goods store, kept a good part of the local community of Medford supplied with everything: backpacking gear, bikes, climbing gear, and skis. It was a small store, but surprisingly well stocked. He'd been able to keep up with the chain stores by having outstanding customer loyalty and great service. Jack had low overhead and owned the building outright; plus, there were several apartments upstairs.

Mitch guided Black Steel around back.

"Dad's pickup isn't here, Mitch. That's weird."

"I noticed that. Think he already left for lunch?"

"I doubt it. You know Dad; he usually doesn't go out for lunch. If he does, he usually goes across the street to the deli."

"Well, let's go check and see if anyone knows where he is."

In a dejected tone, Junior replied, "Okay, sounds good."

Junior jumped out of the Jeep and made his way to the employees' entrance in back. He punched in the code on the keypad and let himself in. The door closed before Mitch could grab it.

Mitch punched in the code and followed Junior who was looking around Jack's office, which didn't hold his father. Junior made his way to the front and stood at the counter talking with one of the register clerks when Mitch finally caught up with him.

"I don't know where your dad is, little Jack," said the clerk.

"Who else is here now—is Johnson around?" Johnson was Jack's right-hand assistant and usually ran the place when Jack was out of town.

"Yeah, check over in the fishing section. Pretty sure he was helping a customer pick out a rod and reel."

"Thanks," Junior responded.

Mitch followed Junior to the fishing section where Johnson was watching a customer walk away wearing a smile.

"Jack, what are you doing here? I thought you went south to play ball."

"I'm home for a few days on a bit of a break, Dad didn't tell you?"

"I haven't seen much of him. Truth be told, he hasn't been in the store much the last couple of days. Frankly, I'm not sure where he's been spending his time. He used to keep me in the loop. I figured he was having a tough time of it with you out of the house now, and his being alone and all."

Junior was getting more and more worried. "Do you know if he came into the store today at all?"

"Hey, Mitch, good to see you, and no I'm not sure. He usually leaves an office light on, so we know he's been here, but they were all off. Is everything okay?"

"Thanks, Johnson. If he does show up, could you let him know we're here and want to meet him for lunch? Just have him call one of us. We'll hang around in town for a while."

"Sure thing, Mitch, and good seeing you, Junior. Let us know how things are in Chattanooga, will you?"

Junior tried to eke out a smile, gave Johnson a little shrug, and then headed for the back of the store.

"Thanks again, see you later." Mitch followed Junior to the parking lot.

Junior placed both his hands on the hood of the Jeep and dropped his chin. Mitch could tell the kid was becoming very concerned.

He put a firm hand on Junior's shoulder. "Listen, Junior, I know a few places your dad sometimes hangs out. Perhaps he's at the health club."

Junior stood up and, arching his back, just like Jack Senior, gathered newfound confidence. Mitch smiled, recognizing the mannerism.

"Okay, Mitch, I must admit I'm getting worried. What I'm hearing isn't like Dad at all."

As the two hopped into the Jeep, Mitch decided to roll the dice and come clean with Junior. He hoped like hell that he didn't throw snake eyes.

Chapter 50

Someone Else's Heartbreak

They drove to Jack's favorite gym, a short fifteen-minute ride back through town. Mitch laid out pretty much everything going on in Rogue River the last few days.

"Geezus, Mitch, and you weren't going to tell me? What the hell?"

Black Steel lurched into the Fitness World parking lot, and Mitch circled looking for Jack's pickup.

"Well, if you can, try to see it from my perspective. What do I do pick up the phone, give you a ring and say, 'Yeah, Junior, everything's going good. Mabey and I saw Gandalf's horse with an Indian warrior. Debbi and Cindi have an Alien ghost in their house and are staying with us. Our neighbor Jasper is convinced that every major natural disaster the last hundred years or so hasn't been so random and natural, and, oh, yeah, your Dad had a spaceship land on his house, and I've barely seen him.' How do you think you would have responded to all that?"

Junior made a show of looking for his dad's pickup. Mitch hoped the kid was processing what to do and not steaming with anger at him.

Mitch became aware of his white knuckles on the steering wheel. He relaxed, looked out his window, and took a deep breath. After winding through the parking lot without seeing the truck, Mitch pulled in front of the club and parked in a visitor slot. He got out of the Jeep.

"Junior, why don't you stay here in case your dad pulls up? I'll go in and find out if anyone's seen him this morning. I'll be right back."

"Okay, I'm not going anywhere." Junior's tone was gruff and distant as he jumped out of Black Steel and paced around, watching cars pass on the street.

Mitch ran into the club, checked with the front counter and returned.

Junior was where Mitch had left him. "Well?"

"He hasn't been here today. They checked the sign-in sheets and said he hasn't been in all week."

"You know my dad. If he goes more than a couple of days without working out, he gets all uptight and cranky. What the heck is going on?"

"You saw him yesterday, so you know he's okay. We'll find him, figure this out, and…"

"Hey Mitch, I know what. Let's go over to Ashland Ford. Perhaps he took his truck in for an oil change or something."

Dammit, Ashland was another thirty minutes away. It was almost one o'clock. He had plans with Mabey at five for dinner. There was still enough time, but clock-watching was becoming more important than ever. Mitch looked forward to a micro-brew. More importantly, he wanted to spend time with his better half—much better half – he would say. If something happened time-wise, ultimately, he'd be okay. Mabey would be disappointed he missed dinner but pissed with him if he left Junior alone looking for his dad.

"Good idea, Junior."

Mitch got Black Steel back onto Interstate 5 south towards Ashland. The two didn't say a single word to each other on the trip. Mitch wondered if all this scenic grandeur was about to change. He was finding a completely new appreciation for every tree back-dropping Southern Oregon and even the schleps he passed on the freeway.

"Mitch, mind if I turn on the radio?"

Mitch rubbed the back of his neck and pivoted his head in a circular motion to relieve pressure.

"Junior, see if you can find a good country song, will you? Let's listen to someone else's heartbreak for a few minutes."

Chapter 51

Can't Find Jack

Mitch stared at the mountains and the rain-threatening clouds hovering over them. A little precipitation would be nice. Perhaps the Alien things would melt. Hell, it happened in the movies all the time, right? Mitch thought they would grow stronger. He wiggled his toes and flexed his lower legs trying to keep the blood flowing.

"Which exit is the Ford dealer? Do you know, Junior?"

"Yeah, it's in the north end of town. It's called Valley View. I'll recognize it when we get to it."

"Oh, yeah, I remember now. Mabey did PT work for a therapist not too far from there."

Mitch pulled Steel off I-5 onto the South Valley View exit. They drove south on Highway 99 and parked in front of the service department at the dealership. They went inside.

Jack wasn't in the waiting area. "Junior, why don't you check the coffee area and the restroom? I'll ask at the service counter."

"Okay, I'll meet you back here." Junior walked around the corner and out of sight.

"How can I help you, sir?" asked the clerk at the counter.

"I'm supposed to pick up a friend while his vehicle is being serviced. Can you tell me if he's here? His name is Jack Jenson."
The clerk checked the service slips lying on the counter.

"Yeah, he dropped off his pickup at eight this morning. We said we'd have it ready between two and three. Hope that helps."

"Yes, and no. Thanks."

Mitch made a beeline for the waiting area and met Junior there.

"He isn't in the bathroom or getting coffee."

"The good news is he dropped off his truck this morning." Mitch saw the first bit of a relief on Junior's face. "At least we're getting close." Mitch's watch said it was a little after two. Still okay on time. His drop-dead time to leave and meet Mabey was three-thirty for safe driving, four o'clock for idiot driving.

"Yeah. He doesn't like sitting around for anything more than a half hour. He says it's a waste of time."

"Where else could he have gone?"

"I can't think of a single place and I still can't get him on his cell."

They went out to check the new truck lot hoping to see Jack looking at new vehicles. No such luck.

"This is a long shot, but I have an idea. Come on."

Mitch guided his Jeep down Highway 99 into Ashland towards the University. One of the things he's known about Jack over the years is when he doesn't understand something, he gets almost to the point of obsession until he figures it out. Mitch was relying on the fact that he wanted a better understanding of things going on inside him.

He hoped like hell the idea panned out. Since someone has seen Jack, Mitch felt better, but not completely. He desperately needed to find Jack.

Chapter 52

Just Like Now

Junior knuckled his eyes, squeezed his head with both hands, and rubbed his face while yawning. The kid was uptight, and Mitch understood why.

"Where are we going?"

"You know when your dad doesn't understand something and becomes consumed with whatever it is until he can resolve it? What does he do?"

"Spends hours online. Why?"

"He didn't take his laptop; I saw it on his desk at the store. What if he's at the university library? That would be a good place to begin if he's trying to figure out what's going on."

"Good call. I hope, anyway."

Mitch heard longing in Junior's voice. He parked Black Steel in one of the campus lots. They got out and checked the campus directory board.

"Okay, it says we're here. Good to know since I thought we might be over there." Junior chuckled, which pleased Mitch since he could only imagine how the kid felt.

"Looks as if the library is down this path and over behind that building." He pointed on the sign for Junior to see.

Wow, two-thirty already: it was getting close to the time he'd need to text or call Mabey. A quick-paced five-minute walk got them to the library. It was summer, so the campus seemed like a ghost town. The library had better be open because he'd run out of ideas. The door opened, and they walked in.

"Excuse me, ma'am, where are the computers?" Junior asked the cute young girl at the counter.

She blushed a bit. Damn, this kid could date any girl he wanted.

"Go up one floor. The stairs are over there. Do you need to use one of the computer stations?"

"No, just looking for someone. Thanks, though." Junior didn't give the girl a second glance. In fact, he barely looked at her at all. Worry over his Dad had really clouded the kid's concentration. One would think a hot young woman clearly interested in him would snap him out of it. Apparently not.

"C'mon, Mitch, let's go."

At the top of the stairs, a sign pointed left to the computer room. Junior pushed through the finger-smudged glass door, and sure as shit there was Jack.

"Dad, damn, it's good to see you." Junior put a bear hug on his father before he could even stand up.

A couple of other people in the room stopped what they were doing to look up.

"What are you guys doing here?" Jack asked.

"We came to surprise you for lunch, but you weren't at the store. Johnson didn't know where you were; you haven't answer texts or calls so we started searching the places we thought you might be."

"Yeah, sorry, Ace, (one of Jack's affectionate names that developed when Junior started pitching), the dealer let me use a loaner. I turned my phone on silent mode when I came into the library. Didn't even think to look at it; I've been killing time online."

Mitch didn't ask what about. There was a dozen or so books next to the monitor plastered with Aliens, Indians, and Southwestern folklore, natural disasters, and more. One glance at the titles and anyone would have a good idea what he was looking into. Junior looked at Mitch and silently nodded.

"I'm pretty much done. My pickup might be ready now too. I suppose I should go outside and give the dealer a call. If it's done, you guys want to grab something to eat?"

"Thanks, but I can't. I'm meeting Mabey in Grants Pass for dinner about five. I really need to get going. Glad you're okay, douche bag. Perhaps next time you can let someone know where you are."

"Butt out, Wilde! You aren't my mother!"

"No, nice observation but I am not your mother. I couldn't care less what happens to your sorry ass, but perhaps you could think about your son. Ass-face."

The back-and-forth garnered a nasty look from an older woman sitting at a nearby table. Mitch smiled and mouthed, "Sorry." She rolled her eyes, returned her glasses to their resting place on her nose, and buried her face back in her book.

"Simmer down, you two. Let's go," Junior said.

Jack set the computer screen back to the library's main page, stood, and pushed in his chair.

"Dad, don't you want your books?" Junior asked.

"Those aren't mine. They were there when I sat down. Let's go."

Junior shrugged at Mitch, hoping they could talk about it tomorrow. They tromped downstairs.

Less than a minute later, with a very flirtatious, "Goodbye, hope to see you again soon," from the young woman to Junior, they were all out front.

Jack dialed the dealer and learned his truck was ready.

"I'm heading up to Crater Lake tomorrow for a sunrise photo, so Mabey and I are dining early. You and Junior want to meet us?" Mitch knew Mabey wouldn't mind, and it would be interesting to see what Jack would talk about if anything at all.

"I can't. I have to be at the store. I haven't been there much lately, and Johnson needs to leave early. Thanks, though."

"Junior, you want me to drop you off at home, or the coffee shop?" Mitch added the last part with a smile.

"No, thanks, I am going to hang with Dad."

"Okay, boys, later. Let's get together for dinner before you head back to Chattanooga, Junior. Mabey would love to see you."

Jack replied with, "My schedule is pretty crazy right now, but I'm sure Junior could."

Mitch laughed. "Your schedule? What the hell are you so busy with?"

Jack didn't reply but instead looked at Junior with a straight face. "Let's go, Junior. I need to get back to the store." Jack climbed in, aggressively swinging the door shut behind him.

Junior walked around to get in the passenger side, but spoke over the car before getting in. "Thanks again, Mitch. I appreciate your help today. Just let me know when you and Mabey want us over for dinner. I'll get Dad there."

"Sounds good. See you later," Mitch replied knowing that Jack wouldn't be coming to dinner, no matter what Junior did to him. Something was going on, and his best friend didn't want to talk about it. Jack screeched the tires out of the lot. He couldn't get away from Mitch fast enough. It reminded Mitch of the time in college when Jack thought he saw Mabey two-timing him with someone on the football team. For a couple of weeks Mitch hardly saw him, which was bizarre. Mitch finally cornered Jack one day on campus and forced it out of him. He looked as if he were going to burst when he blurted out, "I saw Mabey with Nate Josephs a couple of weeks ago. They were holding hands. She's cheating on you."

The whole incident ended up being nothing. On top of that, Mabey was pissed at Jack for thinking she would cheat. She was attentive to him over the next couple of weeks, which was nice, but Mitch felt bad for her because she hadn't done anything wrong. Mabey was often accused of cheating because of her involvement in physical therapy. Still went on to this day—miserable people looking for ways to make others around them miserable. Anyway, Jack should have known better at the time. He was so afraid it was true, he couldn't face the thought of telling Mitch something was up. So, he avoided Mitch.

Just like now, Mitch thought.

Chapter 53

Kind of Like Jell-O

Mitch headed towards his date with Mabey. He shook his left wrist freeing the watch loose from his sticky skin. He had ninety minutes to get to the restaurant. Plenty of time, enough that he took the back way to Grants Pass and the restaurant. Memories of his youth flooded his mind as he steered through the winding country roads.

Mitch had a keen interest in memories and the random way they entered his mind. Why on earth, he said to Mabey at times, would a song from high school pop into his head while taking photographs at Crater Lake? Why would a smell take him backwards to moments during his youth? These thoughts had no known discernible connection, as far as he could tell, but the frequency they occurred was fascinating to him.

It was 4:15. Plenty of time, so he peeled off Highway 238 and drove down Upper Applegate Road for a quick peek at the lake. About a mile farther and around a bend, a local sheriff, a state cop, and what appeared to be a Fish & Game vehicle blocked the road.

Mitch pulled close to the blockade and rolled down the window. The sheriff walked over to the door. "Hey, Sheriff, what's up? I was hoping to get a look at the lake today, take a few pictures." "No photos today, sir. Someone reported something hitting the lake, a meteor or something. So, as you can understand, we're keeping everyone out, even the residents."

"A meteor?"

"I know, sounds crazy, doesn't it? Funny thing is we got a dozen or so phone calls within minutes, all reporting basically the same thing."

"No kidding?"

"Yep, everyone claimed something from the sky crashed into the lake close to the dam. For obvious reasons, we have to check it out. The folks from the U.S. Army Corps of Engineers are on the way. They have to give the all clear before we can open the road again. It'll be several hours I am sure."

"So that's all you know for now?"

"Yep, all I know. I get a call from dispatch to set up a roadblock, and here I am. Chatter on the police band is all speculation at this point."

"Okay, no worries. Thanks and let me get out of your way."

"Be careful turning around."

Mitch closed the window and brushed the sweat from his forehead. He made a sharp spin of the wheel and headed toward dinner. It was 4:45. He had little time to dilly dally. He put the pedal down and hit search on the AM dial.

The local station blared a news flash:

Dave Dillson, KAJO. 1270 on your AM dial. Again, reports are coming in from all over the Pacific Northwest of what are being called, for now at least, meteor strikes. Most of the events appear to be in or near lakes, and from my estimation, man-made lakes, which may or may not mean anything. The state police have notified KAJO that travel to both Deep Creek Lake and Applegate Lake has been restricted to everyone. I repeat, no one, not even those who live around Deep Creek and Applegate lakes will be allowed entrance to the lake area until the Army Corps of Engineers gives the all-clear. Please stay tuned to KAJO for your up-to-the-minute news. Now we take you back to regular programming.

Mitch's phone buzzed. He figured it was a text from Mabey. The radio muted, and the sexy Irish voice Mitch selected for his text-reading spoke.

Mitch, I'm going to be a bit late. There is crazy traffic in town right now.

207

Should make it by a quarter of six. Mabey :-)

Mitch loved the way the Irish lass referred to the smiley face in the text as "I am happy."

"Too funny," he said to the radio. Mabey's name still made Mitch chuckle at times.

Now he had a little over an hour before needing to be at the restaurant. If Mabey said 5:45, it might be more than a few minutes later. For all she got on Mitch about being on time, she always seemed to be a few minutes late.

Mitch braked and whipped the wheel. He had plenty of time for a quick look at the lake. Mitch knew a back way he didn't think would be blocked. It was four-wheel access and usually impassable during the winter.

He pressed and held the main phone button, and the voice activation popped up. Reply to Mabey. *No problem, Mabey, I will see you soon. B Safe - M.* End reply.

A half mile from the roadblock, around a corner out of view of the sheriff, Mitch guided the Jeep off the road. An eighth of a mile in, he stopped and engaged the four-wheel drive. He started up the steep and slow climb of what looked like nothing more than a deer trail but was an old fire access road. Jack and Mitch used to come up this way in high school to go fishing and hang out with girls. Not many people knew about it. The two never advertised it in hopes of keeping it private.

The trail ended at an isolated section of the lake surrounded by maples and tall pines, not too far from the dam. The only other way to get to this spot was walking the bank or boating in. Mitch found this comforting since he wasn't supposed to be here. He would get in and out before anyone noticed. Ten slow minutes later with nothing new on the radio, Mitch parked out of view from anyone at the dam or on the lake and grabbed his camera pack from the backseat. He had about ten minutes before needing to leave for the restaurant. After a quick jog to the tree line at the edge of the lake, he stopped near their old rope swing—tattered and very weather-beaten dangling from a sturdy and weathered white oak. Anyone dumb enough to swing on the rope in its current condition would surely be sorry. Mitch half expected to see a new rope, thinking new kids were using the area.

Mitch leaned against a tree and got his camera into viewing position. The LCD screen was a battery hog, but it gave Mitch the advantage of having both eyes open. He liked to let his camera worry about the target, so he could pay attention to the surroundings. Mitch angled the 70-300mm zoom toward the dam. A helicopter was flying around at a deliberate angle and pace, probably examining the dam structure. On top of the dam, police vehicles guarded each end, keeping everyone off. Nothing spectacular to look at there, Mitch realized.

He eyeballed the perimeter of the lake. There were no boats, odd for this time of the year, but under the current circumstances, it made sense. If there had been any boats, Fish & Game patrol moved them ashore. Mitch did see a boat at the far end of the lake: A Fish & Game craft skirting the perimeter. He made a mental note to keep track of it.

Mitch's eye caught a movement on the distant shoreline, not too far from the eastern edge of the dam. It was a large ripple in the water. The helicopter was still hovering around the dam—out of view of this ripple. As Mitch brought the camera back to a shooting position, another large ripple appeared. The movement reminded Mitch of a massive gator lurking in the shallows. No gators in this part of the country though. He rubbed his eyes. He brought the camera to his face, found the rippling area, and pressed Record. A minute or two went by with nothing happening. Then, as if Moses himself were on-site, the water folded back on two sides, and a bright metallic object slid out of the lake and slithered up the bank. Mitch wondered if there were anyone else around to see what he witnessed. The helicopter, still near the dam, would not have a vantage point allowing anyone on board to see the cove Mitch stared at in disbelief.

The thing appeared to be about the size of a small car, but not as wide. It looked like liquid more than a solid form, but held its shape, like Jell-O pulled from a refrigerator. The movement of the object wasn't like any natural earth motion he'd ever seen.

About thirty feet up the bank and just inside the tree line, the thing stopped. Jiggling a bit, as if it was shaking itself free from water, it moved again. The outer lining—Mitch couldn't think of anything else to call it—started to dissolve and dissipate into the air. Mitch flinched as the camera revealed what was inside: two bodies. The outer shell completely disappeared, and the bodies, apparently in a fetal position, started to untangle and expand.

Mitch glanced from the camera's LCD, knowing he was still recording, to locate the Fish & Game boat. He couldn't see it, so he returned his eyes to the camera.

The things—two of them—stood and stretched, then, and very deliberately, looked around their surroundings. Mitch assumed they were checking to see if anyone had spotted them, but then he realized it was more likely they were looking for something themselves. Their actions made him duck behind the tree as if they were looking for him. The camera never moved from its intended target though. Mitch fought off a college memory by a crusty old college professor who repeatedly said, "You never take your camera away from the action, Wilde, never."

Sage advice, he repeated to himself as he had done countless times over the years. The lake creatures moved again, this time trekking up the hill toward the dam.

Then, more quickly than they appeared, they were gone, simply vanished. No amount of eye rubbing or shaking his head brought them back.

"What the hell?" Mitch whispered. He hoped with all that was in him that the recording was clean.

Mitch pushed the camera into the pack; the coarseness of the heavy fabric scraped his hand. He started a light jog; his feet felt heavy as if he were in mud. He made sure the coast was clear and headed for the Jeep. After dinner, he'd get this footage to Jasper, who most certainly would have an explanation.

A bead of sweat broke his hairline and ran down his cheek. It wasn't hot enough to be sweating. Plus, the dense white oaks and Douglas fir were all but hiding him from the sun. Fear slowly began to edge its way into Mitch's psyche.

Chapter 54

The Sandwich Was in Trouble

Junior leaned against the doorframe of his dad's office at the sporting goods store. The edge of the wood pressed hard into his left shoulder. It felt good in a way — made him feel connected to something. Right now, he needed it. His father was in a different place mentally, and he wasn't sure what to do.

"So, Dad, how've things been the last few days?"

"Oh, you know same old stuff, different days, and different weather patterns." Jack made no eye contact with Junior. Junior shifted his weight and repositioned his shoulder against the doorjamb. "Johnson says you've hardly been at the store lately. I was just wondering what you've been up to? Have you been to the doctor for a check-up as you promised?"

"Son, I'm fine. I've just had a lot of business stuff to take care of and haven't had time to be here as much as I'd like."

The automatic response didn't contain any emotion whatsoever. It was as if someone were putting quarters in a slot on his Dad's back. Once enough money was inserted, he'd blurt out an answer.

"Anything I need to be concerned about, or anything I can help you with while I'm home? Thanks to the weather and the airlines, you have me for a few more days."

"No son, everything's okay, and you don't need to worry. I have everything under control and should be back to regular hours in the store very soon. Did I tell you I'm toying with expanding the place by knocking out the wall between the vacant insurance office and us? I might increase the bicycle lines and build a new mechanic work area. With the high gas prices, bikes continue to sell well. I can make more money adding another line or two. Then you can run the store and have security the rest of your life, in case your baseball career doesn't pan out, or in case something should unexpectedly happen to me."

"What in the hell are you talking about, Dad? Unexpectedly happening? Are you taking up skydiving or hang-gliding? Something I need to worry about?"

"No, but things seem to happen in life when you least expect them, and I want you to be prepared in case you wake up one day and I'm not here. Especially if something happens to me before you have a chance to have your own family."

"Geez, Dad, you're depressing the hell out of me. I'm beginning to wish I hadn't come back home. Why in the hell do you keep calling me 'son'? You never call me that."

A long pause stretched out before Jack replied. "Sorry, son – I mean Junior – things happen in life when you least expect them, and I just want you to be prepared." Jack repeated the last statement again without any inflection or emotion.

"If I didn't know any better, the way you treated Mitch at the library and the way you're acting now, I'd swear your somebody else."

Junior pushed his body upright and off the doorframe. He felt his brow furrow and the edges of his lips turn down as he turned away in frustration. "I'm going to the deli to get a sandwich. I'm starving."

Junior started out of the office. He stopped suddenly and pivoted to face his father. A chill ran up his back and tingled as it crawled to the base of his head. Junior took a half step backwards. His Dad stared straight at him with cold steel eyes, not moving a muscle. No part of his body looked as if it had any life, except the eyes. They locked in as if they were lasers about to eviscerate him from existence.

"Uhhh, Dad," Junior stammered as he shook off the chill and regained his composure. "Do you want anything from the deli?"

As quickly as the look occurred, it was gone. Junior felt that someone had thrown a switch and brought back his real dad. He wondered for a moment if his father was struggling inside himself, fighting to break free of something.

"No, I'm good. Thanks, though, Ace. Let's try to leave by seven; I'd like to get some quality sleep tonight. I'm exhausted. You okay with that, or did you want to do something?"

Junior stuttered, still caught off guard. "Uh, what… oh, no, I'm good. I was thinking about going out with a friend tonight if that's okay with you."

"Sure, who're you going to see, and what are your plans? If I can ask? Oh, never mind. Go get your sandwich. We can chat about it on the ride home. Of course, it's all right with me. You're a grown man; you don't need to ask."

Junior forced a smile as he left the store. He stopped at the crosswalk, pressed the Walk button, closed his eyes, and replayed what had just happened with his dad. He'd talk to Mitch about it, and he wanted to make sure to get it right. He opened his eyes and shook his head as the light changed from yellow to red. He walked to the deli banking on hope that food would comfort him.

The smell of warm baked bread and deli meats eased the tension in his brain.

"Ace, is that you? I thought you were back East working your way up to the majors." The man behind the counter, owner of Anthony's New York Deli, was a business friend of Jack's. He was a baseball fan and went too many of Junior's local games. He'd seen him grow up, and Junior had been coming in for lunch as long as he could remember. Junior loved it when he was little and got to come to work with his dad. At lunchtime, they'd walk to the deli hand-in-hand through the crosswalk, after his Dad let him push the magic light button telling them it was safe to go. Junior would forever remember holding his father's calloused hands and feeling there wasn't a thing in the world capable of harming him.

"Hey, Mr. Dantonio, good to see you; I had an unexpected break and came home for a few days. I needed to grab a few things I forgot to pack," Junior lied. He didn't want anyone other than Mitch and Mabey to know he was home because he was worried about his dad. He told Mitch it was because of a plane delay, which was partly true, but he could have stayed one more day in Portland and met up with the team. Baseball could wait, and the flight delays were a blessing in disguise.

"Make sure your dad keeps us posted on your progress. I want to make certain to watch the first time you pitch in the show."

"Will do, Mr. D."

"The usual, Ace? Salami and turkey on whole wheat, extra mustard, black pepper, and light lettuce?"

"Sounds good, and thanks, but only half a sub, please. It's late, and I don't want to spoil my dinner appetite." Junior lingered near the register looking at his phone. He searched for the newly added contact. He tapped for messaging and sent a text: *Cindi, want to hang out tonight? Jack*

Junior watched the sandwich being made and slid his phone into his back pocket. The phone vibrated before his hand could leave the pocket.

Sure, what time? C :-)

Junior smiled and texted a reply: *How about 8? I can pick you up. What is your address?*

Five seconds later: *Perfect. Mom and I are staying at the Wilde's house tonight. Pick me up there. C U at 8! C :-)*

"Ace, here you go. Want a soda with that?"

"No, thanks, Mr. D; how about a small iced tea? How much do I owe you?"

"Ace, here's a cup for the tea, and it's on the house. Your money is no good in here. How about you promise me tickets to one of your games when you're in the Bigs. Deal?"

"Sounds good, Mr. D, and thanks."

"Tell your dad hi and not to be such a stranger. I haven't seen him in a while."

Neither have I, thought Junior. "Will do, and thanks, again."

Junior snuck a ten-dollar bill into the tip jar and got his tea. With a lid and straw in place, he left the store, waving goodbye to Mr. D. Junior was looking forward to his date with Cindi. First things first though; this sandwich was in trouble.

Chapter 55

The End of the World Can Wait

Mitch wasn't one to get overly excited about too many things, but this latest event took his heart up a beat. He laid the camera pack inside Black Steel and hopped in for the ride to town.

Pushing the Jeep a little harder than normal, Mitch drove down the fire path. First, he was stunned and felt in his gut something was wrong; and second, he wanted to get the hell away from the lake. Mitch felt strange eyes home-in on him. Probably paranoia, but all the same, the needed-to-be-shaved hair on his neck was at full attention. What came out of the lake would rattle nearly anyone—outside of Fox Mulder. As much as Mitch liked to think he was a rational, calm, and collected individual, his Canon gave him a legitimate reason to be on edge.

His gut urged him to get to Jasper's place at once, but his heart and mind encouraged him to meet Mabey. He gripped the steering wheel with both hands and twisted back and forth as if he was wringing out a towel. The choice was easy; he smiled thinking of Mabey. The world was coming to an end, and he couldn't think of anyone he'd rather be with than his best friend. Dinner it is. The end of the world can wait.

Chapter 56

A Nervous Tic

Jasper lowered the volume on the AM station and turned it up on the shortwave.

Radio Free Idaho here. More secret events appear to be happening at some of Idaho's biggest lakes. Highway 2, 200, and 95 going into and around Lake Pend Oreille are reportedly all shut down. Numerous reports of an object or objects hitting the lake near Sandpoint have, as of yet, not been confirmed. Speculation is rampant, from a small meteor strike to a crash of a military craft to the more popular heavily rumored airplane-sub the U.S. Government is building with Alien technology. There are also unsubstantiated—and this reporter repeats, unsubstantiated—reports of something coming out of the lake not far from where the supposed object entered. This reporter is currently reaching out to all locals with short-wave radios trying to get actual, on-scene reports, for further clarification and confirmation.

Again, all locals and travelers… Highways 2, 200, and 95 are shut down in and around the Lake Pend Oreille area of Idaho. Locals are not permitted to return to their homes until further notice. There has been a shelter and information center set up at the Sandpoint high school.

Jasper touched the pause button on his recording system. He pressed rewind and listened to it several more times. "Holy shit, this is happening." He went to the other side of his workstation, grabbed a mouse, and started an automated search for object strikes in North American lakes. He limited the focus to the Pacific Northwest for now.

All ten monitors lit up with dozens of events over the last sixty minutes. He recorded everything, but one screen caught his eye: the one showing Crater Lake, an unmistakable image like no other because Wizard Island stuck out plain as day. Jasper had been at the lake enough times over the years to know it when he saw it.

He turned down the volume on all the monitors, except the one showing Crater Lake. He took notes. "This could come in useful tomorrow." Jasper spoke aloud to the monitors hoping for a response that he knew would never come. He wished like heaven that Wilde was here.

This was the first time in decades that he remembered wishing someone other than his ex-wife sat with him. He didn't have time to contemplate whether the feeling was a good one to have. The Rewind button called to him.

Chapter 57

Don't Be an Ass

Mitch listened to the radio, hoping for new information. Nothing: the radio jocks, DJs, newspersons stated the same thing repeatedly. He scanned the dial, but nothing provided further insight. Mitch checked the phone signal. Two bars, good for out here.

Mitch rubbed his thumb and forefinger together clearing them of dirt then pressed and held the call switch on the steering wheel. "Call Jasper." The radio muted and dialed Jasper's number.

One ring later, Jasper picked up. "Hey, Ansel, how're you doing? Have you had the radio or a TV on by chance?"

"I have. We still on for tomorrow morning and a quick trip to Crater Lake? We'll be leaving early, okay?"

"Nothing's changed on my part. Why?"

"We'll talk later tonight or early tomorrow morning. My cell reception isn't too good…" *Crackle, pop.* "Breaking up."

Jasper chuckled. "You must be in the mountains, huh?"

He got it, good, no talking on an open line. He'd taught Mitch well. Mitch pressed End on the steering wheel. He made it to the restaurant by 5:40, plenty of time to park and occupy a table before Mabey arrived. They had to compete only with the over fifty-five crowd, so they should be fine. The restaurant wasn't a typical hangout for seniors, so he didn't need to make a reservation. Mitch grabbed the camera pack and headed in. He got a table and ordered a Rogue River Porter. Mabey showed up seven minutes later when Mitch was two swigs into the dark beer. He thought the Porter was good, not great by his standards, but very drinkable.

Mitch stood, pulled out Mabey's chair, and kissed her warm cheek. Mitch still got a tinge of excitement kissing her.

"Thanks, babe, you been waiting long?"

"No, only about five minutes. Want a drink?"

Mabey got a nice big smile on her face and blew a kiss to Mitch, one of the favorite things she did.

"God, do I! What are you having?"

"The Rogue River Porter, which is good so far. They apparently, according to the menu, have an Oregon Blackberry Hefeweizen I thought I'd try next."

The waiter walked up, greeted Mabey, and asked if she wanted something to drink.

"Yes please, I hear you have a blackberry Hefeweizen?"

The young, awkwardly handsome waiter smiled. "Sure, but can I see your I.D. first, please?"

What a flirt! Did he not see Mitch sitting there? A few years ago, Mitch would have felt the urge to push up his shirtsleeves and show his biceps. Now he just sat back and smiled. Maturity has its benefits. People hitting on his wife and flirting with her made her even more attractive. He knew damn good and well he didn't have to worry about Mabey's stepping out.

If she ever did cheat, he had Black Steel, his Canon, a faithful dog, and a map to all his favorite fishing holes. He would be fine. Mitch stifled further laughter by putting his mouth on the Porter's rim. The poor kid was in for a treat. Mitch couldn't wait.

Mabey shot back with a deliberately condescending giggle as if she were eighteen. "Oh, aren't you so sweet. Are you old enough to serve alcohol?"

Zing, snap, shut him down! God, Mitch loved this woman. The

expression on the waiter's face was priceless. His face turned red. "I'll be right back with the beer, ma'am."

Mabey halfheartedly dug through her purse. "Oh here, let me get out my I.D." Mitch could see the definition in her arms, enough to be taut but still feminine.

"No, I trust you." The waiter spun away and damn near ran from the table.

Mabey looked at Mitch. "I don't have time for that shit any more. God, I am glad we aren't on the dating scene. Don't you ever cheat on me or leave my sweet ass, Mitch. I don't have the patience to put up with that pretentious shit. Can you believe he was flirting with me?"

"First – ditto. You are hot, don't look a day over thirty-two, do have a 'sweet ass,' and frankly, if I were single, I'd hit on you as often as possible."

Mabey smiled one of her love-filled smiles reserved only for Mitch: a deep, genuine smile that made her eyes twinkle.

"I'm glad you don't make a big deal of it and get all jealous, but sometimes I wish I could watch you roll up your sleeves and take out these schmucks."

"Just say the word next time, babe, and I'll launch these babies." Mitch smiled, winked, and massaged his biceps.

A few seconds later, a female server showed up at the table with Mabey's beer.

"Here you are, ma'am; I believe this is yours."

"Yes, it is. Where's our waiter?"

"His dinner break, ma'am, I'll be your server the rest of the evening. Are you ready to order?"

Mitch stuffed the beer to his face to hold back another chuckle.

Mabey rolled her eyes and asked the young woman, "Can you give us five minutes, please? I haven't even seen the menu yet. If you have a chicken wing appetizer, please bring that for starters."

"Yes, ma'am, I'll bring them right away."

Mitch sat back in his chair, enjoying Mabey's presence and confidence, the great view of the river, and the carefully crafted, and quite satisfactory, micro-brew.

"Let's hope the Mabey-soiled waiter isn't in the kitchen adding a few extra things to our order."

"He doesn't have the guts, Mitch. He's all flash."

"Well, I hope so. How was your day?"

"Fine, typical stuff, I got a new gig at the racquet club in town. They apparently want to add a personal training instructor to their staff. Do you remember Sally Gerome from Portland State? She was in several of my classes. I hung out with her from time to time at the gym: redhead, pretty hot."

"The one with the really nice…" Mitch paused for effect.

"Yes, she has really nice boobs." Mabey smirked.

"I was going to say smile, but if you insist on boobs, okay."

Mabey laughed. "You are so full of shit, Mitch."

He took another drink of beer and wiped his mouth with the napkin from his lap. "Yes, I remember, sweetie. Why?"

"She's managing the racquet club now, the one over on Main. It's under new ownership. I met a client there today, and we started chatting.

"Sally got out of personal training, but wanted to stay in the fitness industry, so she convinced the owners to give her a shot at managing. She wants a new personal trainer and is looking for someone, like me, to be on staff. I would still be independent but under a contract with them for six months. It's worth looking into, and there's great money, which we could use since you aren't bothering to take photos anymore."

"Hey, I sold a dozen shots to *USA Today* online just last week. We should see the check in another week. I also have the Crater Lake shoot tomorrow, and, if I play things correctly…" Mitch looked around as if someone might be listening. "What I captured today could make us extremely wealthy in a short amount of time."

Mitch dug the camera from his pack.

"What on earth are you talking about?"

Mitch powered up the camera and handed it to Mabey. The waitress was heading toward the table with their appetizer.

"Play this as soon as she leaves."

The server dropped off the wings with celery and blue cheese. "I'll be right back to take your order and please enjoy."

He leaned forward, used his small plate, laid the napkin on his lap, snatched a wing, and dug in.

Mabey set the camera on the table, took a healthy swig of her beer, nibbled on a wing, wiped her hands, and then picked up the camera. "What is this, Mitch, a dam and a helicopter? Is it Applegate and what's the point?"

"You haven't heard the radio, have you?

"No, why?"

"Just watch until the end. Man, these are tasty wings, grilled just right. Don't worry, sweetie; I won't eat them all."

Mitch enjoyed the appetizer, watching patrons out of the corner of his eye, as if at any time he expected black-ops thugs to crash into the restaurant and grab the camera from Mabey. He didn't know if he was more worried about losing the camera, or that Jasper would be pissed at his failure to secure the footage. Mitch thought for a moment he'd uploading it to the Cloud and then call Jasper, but he knew the shit storm and lecture he would face from the old sage, so he decided to wait.

Mitch set down his napkin, heavily covered in a very good wing sauce, and grabbed for his beer.

Mabey's skin had turned pale.

"Mitch is this a camera anomaly or a prank?"

"No. What do you think?"

"How do I rewind?"

"Hi, are you ready to order?" The server had appeared out of nowhere. Mitch had to pay better attention.

"Mabey, do you know what you want?"

"I'll have the grilled chicken salad, with the house dressing and another beer, please." Mabey took a nice long pull off her Heffewiezen.

"And you, sir?"

"I'll have the pork chops with the grilled garlic mashed potatoes, broccoli, a house salad, and a side of applesauce please, oh, and one of the Hefeweizens."

"How would you like your pork chops done, sir?"

"I want them to be done really good, please."

"Mitch don't be an ass," Mabey replied as the waitress laughed.

"Medium well, please."

The server with noticeable exuberance repeated the order and headed back to the kitchen.

"Okay. How do I rewind this, and can I pause it?"

Chapter 58

The Magic Light Button

Junior sat outside the deli at one of the tables, worried now more than ever about his dad. He didn't know what to make of it. Did his behavior have anything to do with his leaving the house? It had to be a shock for parents when their child left home. He took a bite of the sandwich and felt the roughness of the bread on his lips, a welcome, but temporary, distraction.

His dad was more than capable of taking care of himself, and Junior knew it. A flood of memories flowed through his head of his childhood and all the time he'd spent with his parents.

Road trips to Yosemite, the Grand Canyon, and countless weekend camping trips trying out new vendor gear for the store. Most of their trips took them down the Rogue River, deep into the woods toward the Oregon Coast in sections rarely visited by humans. One time they flew to Alaska when his dad was thinking of buying a store in Anchorage. Thank God, they went during the dead of winter. His mom hated it. Had they moved, he might never have played pro baseball. He wondered how many major league players had ever come from Alaska.

Junior's favorite memory was the time when the three of them drove to Mount Bachelor and spent a week hanging out at a river, visiting local eateries, riding bikes, doing a little fishing, and rafting. His mom learned to play golf. She was a natural with a short, compact swing.

She wasn't concerned about how far she hit. She kept her right elbow tightly hinged to her hip and focused on hitting the ball correctly beating both of them on the first nine holes. Unbelievable he thought as he wiped a mustard trail from the corner of his mouth. The Mount Bachelor trip was not his favorite because something spectacular or particularly memorable happened, but because a garbage truck mowed down his mom two weeks later.

Junior pushed back a tear and finished the last bite of sandwich, took a final swig of ice tea, collected his garbage and tossed it in the trashcan. At the crosswalk, he realized what he was so worried about: not that his Dad couldn't take care of himself, but whether he could manage without his Dad. He was all he had left. Then, a small tight smile emerged from his lips.

Junior stopped and pressed the magic light button.

Chapter 59

Survival Instincts

Mitch mentally faded from the restaurant as his thoughts took him back to a childhood memory. One pierced into his brain with precision. It was a weekend, with a two-hour trek in a stuffy and cramped car to spend time with "friends" of the family. It was supposed to be fun. Often, the weekends ended in an embarrassing moment for one of the families. There were drunken outspoken moments of truth that generally stopped all present in their tracks.

Being only nine, Mitch was along for the ride. This was life, and options were limited to the environment, with no way to escape until he was old enough to survive on his own. Or, he was old enough to understand compartmentalization and the burying of feelings. If he got good enough at it, these events simply never happened. "Survival," Mitch said to Mabey.

With each of these depressing "fun" weekends, he got a little better at burying feelings, learning to keep his mouth shut, and gaining more of an understanding how much his parents were clueless at life. Was it possible for a nine-year-old to realize his parents were helpless, insignificant actors on life's stage? Mitch understood this early on. His grandma always told him he was an old soul, wise beyond his years.

"Mitch, hello; are you with me? Mitch?" Mabey said.

"Oh sorry, babe, what's up?"

"What in the hell's going on? Where were you?"

"I was thinking about that time that my dad punched me in the stomach in front of all their friends at a barbecue. With everything that's going on right now, I guess my 'survival' instincts are kicking in."

"Was that the time you were helping him with the fish he'd caught?"

"Yep, not really sure why it stuck with me so much, and why I would think of it now."

"Your dad was an awful parent. He had no clue how to raise a kid. As much as I hate to say it, your mom's departure was the best thing that could have happened. Your dad became a completely different person after that. You're under unusual stress right now, and your survival instincts are emerging."

"Yeah. So, what d'you think of the video?" Mitch stopped his beer bottle from reaching his mouth, frustrated at her for not answering more quickly.

"Looks like a moving is being made and they don't want anyone to know about it. Looks like something out of a high-budget sci-fi thriller."

"Well, dear, it isn't. Did you see any film crews around anywhere?"

"What about in the helicopter?" she replied.

"Why are they going back and forth around the dam, and not around the corner of the cove filming the thing coming out of the water?"

The server showed up with their food. "Grilled chicken salad for you ma'am, and good pork chops for you, sir."

"Can I get either of you anything else right now?"

"I'll take a glass of ice water, please."

Mabey added, "I'd like water as well, no ice. Thanks."

"Okay, I'll be right back."

"Where were we?" Mitch stated.

"You were asking about the helicopter and why it wasn't filming the cove which is a good point, by the way. Then what are those things, and what are they doing?"

"The billion-dollar question, babe."

Mabey handed Mitch the camera; he put it back in the case next to his chair.

"As soon as we get home, I'm going to Jasper's, so he can see what I shot. I won't stay long because I have to leave early for Crater Lake."

Mabey put both her elbows on the table and crossed her hands. This forced her fork towards Mitch as if she were intentionally pointing it to get his attention. She tilted her head slightly as she spoke. "You're still going to Crater Lake?"

Mitch recognized the irritation in her posture and speech. "I have to get out and do something, babe. It'll also give me a chance to talk with Jasper about all this."

"I don't think you should go. I have only one early appointment tomorrow in town. Why not go with me, and then we can spend the afternoon on the river or something?"

"Thanks for the offer, but I want to go, and you keep telling me I'm not earning enough money."

"Not fair, Mitch." Mabey smiled slightly, closed her eyes, and gently shook her head.

Mitch smiled knowing he got a point in without really pissing her off. "Babe, I'm not really sure why, but something tells me I gotta go. Cancel your appointment and ride up with Jasper and me."

"I can't. The appointment is with the Mayor; he always gives me a good tip, and I don't want him taking his business elsewhere. He's finally getting back into good shape, and I don't want him to lose momentum. I owe it to him."

Mitch tilted his head back closing his eyelids as he laughed.

"No wonder Gunther likes you so much. You're getting his sugar daddy into great shape and increasing his stamina if you know what I mean."

"Mitch, you're so bad."

Mitch smiled. "Yes, I am, and you love it when I am bad."

Mitch chuckled, reached across the table squeezing Mabey's hand with as much deliberate love as he could push through his skin onto hers before finishing with, "Pass the pepper, please."

Chapter 60

Give 'em Hell

Junior crossed the street with a full belly and walked into his dad's store. Johnson said, "Hey, Ace, your dad said to wait for him here. He went next door to talk with the tenants and said he'd be right back."

"Thanks. I'm going to wait in his office. Let me know if you need any help out here, okay?"

"Sure thing, Ace, if I don't get to say goodbye to you, give 'em hell in Double-A, and remember, that damn plate is yours." Johnson grinned, patted Junior on the shoulder, and returned to the fishing section.

Junior laughed, said, "Yes sir," went into his father's office and sat at his desk.

He moved the mouse for the PC to disable the screen saver. The web browser was on the main page of *Wolf News*. Plastered all over the site were images of lakes across the U.S. One of the headlines asked, "Is America Under Attack?"

Junior almost clicked on it, but he didn't feel like delving into something that was depressing at best. Something told him to click on the down arrow and look at browsing history. It was a long list of everything from Aliens to Indians, end of the world, Indian mythology, ancient astronauts, but one link caught his eye: "Alien Infection."

Junior went to the page. The site had a long list of entries with victims, supposedly infected by aliens dating back about twenty years. The date range itself wasn't what caught Junior's eye. What did catch his attention was puzzling. Junior nervously tapped his right forefinger on the mouse. Most of the dates formed a pattern. A couple a year, it looked like. Sometimes there were gaps for several years—until the last month, that is. It looked as if the entries from the last month would be more than the total sum of the previous twenty years.

The back door of the store opened. He quickly typed in movies and the Rogue River zip code. His dad walked into the office.

"What're you doing, Ace?"

"Hope you don't mind, Dad; I wanted to see what movies are playing tonight at the theater. I might want to go if there's anything decent."

"*Switch Hitter* with Tim Krooze is playing. It's supposed to be pretty good. You don't feel like watching a movie about baseball though. Do you?"

"If it's good, I don't have a problem with it. I might not be watching much of the movie, anyway." Junior lifted his chin with a nodding motion and grinned.

"Oh really, who're you going with?"

"Cindi Howard. Mitch got us together at the Coffee Shack this morning. He said he wanted to stop and get coffee, but it was pretty obvious the real reason was for Cindi and me to see each other."

"Are you sorry you stopped in?"

"No, I've liked her for a while now. Never thought she would go out with me, so I didn't ask. Anyway, Mitch said she liked me, so what the heck. If she said no, I'd be gone in a few days, so no biggie. I could always tell her I was joking if she said no, right?"

"Why would anyone say no to you unless she had a boyfriend already? Damn, Junior, you're handsome, polite, smart, fun to be around, and a pro athlete. Women will beat down doors for a shot at you. Get used to it. Cindi's a nice young woman. Her mother has done a great job raising her on her own and at the same time running the Shack. You'll have a good time."

"What are you doing tonight?" Junior asked.

"I'm hoping to catch up on some sleep. I've been having a rough time sleeping lately. I keep waking up. Strange thing is I don't know why I'm waking up. I'm not really tired, but restless and strained ever since I got pegged with that damn arrow."

Junior was sure his eyes betrayed his surprise that his father brought up the arrow incident. "You ever get to the doctor?"

"Yes, I finally went. I should have told you, but I guess I didn't want you to think I was worried."

"I would have worried less if you'd told me."

"You're right. I'm sorry."

"Thanks," Junior replied. "So, what did the doc say?"

"When I explained what had happened, he acted as if I were a psycho or something. All my blood work was normal, my blood pressure was outstanding, and I looked ten years younger than my actual age. Then he recommended I go to a psychologist. Something about dealing with your mom's death and that I haven't moved on."

"What did you say?"

"AT first, I laughed because I couldn't believe he'd bring up her death that way. Once I gathered myself, I told the doc he had the bedside manner of prison staff, to kiss my ass—and yes, I said kiss my ass—and that I would be going somewhere else from now on. The jerk barely looked my way. With the new health-care bill in place, thanks to our wonderful federal government, doctors no longer seem to care. They're going to get the same amount of money each month whether I use them or not. The whole disgusting plan frightens me."

Junior smiled, stood up, powered down his father's PC out of habit, and put his hands up in a boxer's pose as if he wanted to go a round or two.

"Well, other than being a nut-job, Dad, at least you're in good shape."

Jack raised his hands in a reciprocal pose, and the two pretended to box, throwing a few air-punches.

"Pound sand, you prima donna; let's close up and get out of here. We need to get you home, so you won't be late and disappoint your beautiful lady friend," Jack said with a smirk on his face.

Junior made for the back door and headed for his dad's pickup while his dad was shutting down and locking up. It was good to see him acting himself.

Would it last though? Junior wasn't sure.

Chapter 61

Impending Danger

Mitch left a nice tip. She put up with his smart-ass attitude and gave excellent service after Mabey's boy-toy bailed. The food was good, and the beer was more than adequate. The Wildes added the establishment to their list of preferential dinner spots.

As they left the restaurant, Mabey placed her hand on his forearm. "Mitch are you really worried about what you saw at the lake today?"

"I was, but now that you bring it up, I feel calmer. Must be your soothing presence, babe."

Mabey grinned and kissed Mitch lightly on his cheek.

"Perhaps I should be worried, but I don't get the sense that there's any danger. I might change my mind after I speak with Jasper. Could be missing something important in the video or be a bit naïve about everything going down. You okay?"

"If you're okay, then I'm good, too. You must promise you won't take any stupid risks or chances tomorrow. I want you home all in one piece. Do you understand? I hate the thought of facing any time without you."

"I hear you. I don't plan on climbing any trees or hanging from any cliffs."

"That's not what I'm talking about, Mitch."

"I know; I just don't feel like talking about it right now. Later, okay?"

"Okay. I'm going to stop at the grocery store on the way home and pick up wine and a few other things. Do you want anything?"

"I thought we had plenty of wine."

"We did, but it looks as though Debbi and Cindi will be staying over again. I want to make sure."

As they walked in the parking lot, Mitch shot back, "Will Michelle be there also?"

"Not sure. She might. She's trying to get back together with her boyfriend. Not sure why you get so irritated over her, Mitch."

"You could tell I was irritated?" Mitch furrowed his brow.

"Yes, pretty obvious."

"I'm sorry. You know I can't stand to see her let people take advantage of her. At times, you feed into it. Just frustrates me, and I don't know what to do about it."

"I'm a big girl and can take care of myself. If I don't want to do something for her, you'll be the second to know."

Mitch smiled, squeezed Mabey's hands, and kissed her lightly on the lips.

"Hey, can you pick up granola bars for me, a couple packs of turkey jerky, a couple of low-sugar energy drinks, and a bag or two of tortilla chips? Tomorrow will be a long day."

"Sure, should I get anything for Jasper?"

Mitch thought for a second. "Thanks, but I couldn't even guess what to get him. Knowing Jasper, he'll have a cooler and a backpack as if the world were going to end tomorrow."

"Okay, I should be about thirty minutes behind you, that is, if you're going straight home."

"Yep, I'll check on the dogs, then stop in and see Jasper for a few minutes after, but that's it."

"What time is it?"

"Twenty of seven." Dinner had been quick, which worked great for both.

"So, you should be home by seven-thirty then, right?"

"Yeah, give or take. If you think of anything else we need, text me, okay?"

Mitch opened Mabey's door and kissed her again, this time very lightly on the cheek—one of her favorites. He stood tall, arched his shoulders not wanting to slouch if she were looking in the rear view, and watched her drive out of the parking lot. Mitch headed for Black Steel with a heaviness weighing on his shoulders as he thought about tomorrow thinking it would be a long day.

Chapter 62

Have Fun Tonight

Interstate 5, Southern Oregon, heading north to Rogue River…

"Mind if I turn on the radio, Dad?"

"Go ahead, Ace. It's probably on the talk and news station. I haven't been listening to any music lately."

Junior turned on the radio.

Repeat, the announcer said. *We have no new developments in the past thirty minutes for the events at Applegate, Deep Creek, and Crater Lake. Numerous people have confirmed the impact sightings, but, again, we have no confirmation of what exactly, if anything, hit the lakes.*

Junior stared at his father who was looking straight ahead as if he'd heard nothing.

"Dad, you hearing this?"

"Yeah, probably a hoax; I wouldn't worry about it too much."

"I'm not worried yet. You have to admit it sounds a little freaky."

There was no reply from Jack.

Coming to us live is Jane Tunuda, KAJO news reporter. Jane, what do you have for us now that you're on the scene?

Yes, Jim, I'm just outside of Applegate Lake, about three miles from the dam. The State Police have Upper Applegate Road blocked off at the Little Applegate

Road intersections from the north and just over the Oregon/California border to the south. They are not letting anyone travel on these roads, for reasons they will not disclose. All they are saying on the scene is that the U.S. Corps of Army Engineers is examining the dam for structural integrity. I've talked to several local residents. They're making a wide variety of claims, from meteors, to failed test rockets, to – and this is my favorite—an Alien vessel carrying a couple of Aliens who disappeared right after they escaped their pod when it hit the lake. So, as you can hear, Jim, we have a hot one out here. This is Jane Tunuda, live on Applegate Road just south of Applegate Dam. Back to you, Jim.

Jack turned off the radio without saying anything.

"Damn, Dad, what do you think?"

Junior watched carefully as his father did nothing. He gave no reply, no cough, no blink, just straight-ahead driving.

"Dad?"

"Um, oh, uh, it's probably a hoax. Nothing exciting ever happens around here, you know that."

"Why don't I believe you for a minute?"

Jack turned the radio back on and selected 94.7 on the FM dial. Junior had to sit there and listen to Swift croon about another man-lover who didn't turn out to be what she'd hoped. It irritated Junior that he found her so damn appealing. Since his father clearly wasn't in a talkative mood, Junior drifted into childhood thoughts about his parents together, and individually, as he grappled with the local events and his dad's behavior. He stopped daydreaming when his mind reached the Wilde's party and the arrow pierced his father's shoulder. Junior had been worried from right after the event and into the evening, begging his Dad to go to the hospital, but he wouldn't.

He kept saying, "I'm fine, Junior; don't worry about it."

Junior thought differently. Many things had changed: his dad's mannerisms and the way he spoke. His voice inflection had become too perfect. Junior's real dad had a drawl at times. Physically, he seemed more energetic and youthful, stood a little straighter, and moved more fluid than Junior was used to. Subtle differences, but perceptible. Junior cupped his forehead between both palms and rubbed away the tension. He looked forward in going out with Cindi knowing she'd be a pleasant distraction, if only for a few hours.

The pickup lurched to a stop next to Junior's Fastback. "Have fun tonight. I'll leave the front light on for you. Tell Cindi I said hi. I'm going to shower and go to bed. Perhaps I will see you in the morning."

"Uh, okay, and hope you get some rest. Love you."

His dad walked inside closing the door, leaving him as if he weren't even there. Junior sat in the pickup with his mouth slightly open; he was growing nervous again. He wanted to talk to Mitch.

Chapter 63

Mitch and His Big Mouth

Junior didn't know if he should go out tonight. If he did, he'd need to block out current events as best as he could. It wouldn't be fair to Cindi if he were disengaged. He paced around the front yard, picked up a rake, and leaned it inside the garage. As he stood there, Cindi and her mom drove up and parked in front of the Wilde's house. Cindi jumped out, slammed the door, and hurried to the front door. As she fumbled with her handbag, she yelled back to her mom who was just now closing her door, "I'm going straight for the shower, Mom. If Junior comes by, tell him I'll be ready in twenty minutes."

The door slammed, and she was gone.

"Okay, dear," Debbi said, too late but with a smile on her face. Debbi headed for the front door and abruptly stopped. She looked over her shoulder. Junior edged back, hoping to be out of view.

Debbi pivoted and hurried in his direction.

"Shit," he said under his breath. He didn't feel like talking right now. Junior hoped she was coming over to see his dad.

Junior stayed out of view as Debbi strode up the front walkway. The doorbell rang. He hoped his dad would come to the door. Debbi rang it again. His dad did not open the door.

Another "shit" under Junior's breath. He left the garage.

"Hey, Mrs. Howard, how are you doing? Can I help you?"

"Yeeep!" Debbi let out a slight screech and hopped back a bit.

"Oh, Junior, you startled me."

"Sorry, ma'am, I was in the garage. I thought my dad would answer. He must be in the shower or something."

"Well, it was you I wanted to talk with, anyway."

"Really, what about?" Junior hoped the lame question covered the blank look he felt on his face. He had a good idea what was about to come out of her mouth. Junior had heard the 'parent' speech more than a few times.

"We all know about your reputation in high school. I don't know whether it's fair or not, but just the same, Cindi is excited about going out with you."

Junior jammed his hands in his pockets hoping there were coins or something he could use to occupy his mind. The lint his fingers found was a disappointment.

"Uh, Mrs. Howard, I don't know what you've heard, but most of it wasn't true. I never tried to stamp the talk down because it was, um… a badge of honor in a way. You know, high school bravado?"

"Well, I appreciate your saying as much. Cindi really looks up to you. Not having a father around has been tough for her. As her mother,

I wasn't able to do certain things for her. Like show her how a man should properly treat a woman. I can talk all I want about it, but there's nothing like seeing it firsthand."

"Mrs. Howard, I have nothing but respect for you and Cindi. I wouldn't be disrespectful to her in any way. Mitch says she's special. And I know what the Wildes think about the two of you."

She nodded. "Mabey's been like her aunt, and Mitch has been like a father to her in many ways, and I'm so grateful." Awkward silence stretched a moment. "Junior, I didn't mean to ambush you. I appreciate your being frank. I want the two of you to have a good time tonight. Have any specific plans?"

"Does Cindi like the movies? I always feel a movie is a good first date. Kills a couple of hours, and you don't have to talk much. You can settle in and get used to being around each other. Then perhaps head over to the Roadhouse Biker Saloon and get hammered. You okay with that?" Junior smiled during his attempt to lighten the mood.

Debbi smiled too. "You smart-ass. You've been around Mitch way too much." She patted him on the shoulder almost exactly the way his mother used to. Junior unconsciously leaned into the moment hoping to make it last.

"Cindi's wanted to see that new Tim Krooze movie, but you probably don't want to see a movie about baseball."

"Hey, I'm game as long as it isn't a boring romance."

Debbi turned and walked away. She yelled over her shoulder, "Don't you hurt my daughter, Junior! You hear me?"

"Yes ma'am, I hear you." Shit, Mitch and his big mouth. Junior wondered what Mitch had gotten him into.

Junior went into the house to clean up. Was he going to regret this? Why in the hell did his flight get canceled?

Chapter 64

WTF

Mitch pulled his Jeep into the garage seventeen minutes later. Wanting to be in place at the lake for a five-thirty sunrise meant in bed by 9:30 in hopes of getting his requisite hours of sleep.

Reflecting on his invite to the old-man, he contemplated if it were a mistake to do so, Mitch wondered if Jasper would ask him to slow down while driving. Too bad if he did: Mitch knew the road well as he'd been up to the hole left by an erupting Mt Mazama more than twenty times. Mitch extended the invitation which meant Jasper would have to get in step with him: Man's rule.

As Mitch was about to exit toward Jasper's place, the door opened behind him. Startled, he wheeled to see who it was. "Debbi, I didn't even notice your car out front. You and Cindi are crashing here again tonight?"

"Yeah, I hope it's okay. I should go home, but with what I'm hearing on the radio and all the talk at the Shack, I am a bit skittish."

"It's nice having you here. You and Cindi are like family. No, check that – good friends – if you were family, I wouldn't want you around as much."

Debbi laughed. "I know what you mean, and thanks, Mitch. Could we talk a minute?"

"Uh, sure, what's on your mind?" Mitch met Debbi about halfway in the garage on Mabey's side.

"What do you think about Junior? He's taking Cindi out tonight.

I'm told that you all but set it up."

"Hey, whoa, now." Mitch rubbed the back of his neck, a nervous reaction, and he knew it.

"I told Junior what a sweet young lady Cindi was, and that I thought she liked him. Those two did all the heavy lifting and panting." Mitch smiled hoping to get a return smile, but apparently his humor was lost on Debbi.

"Funny. Should I be worried at all? I know he had quite a reputation in high school like his father's. I wouldn't have let Cindi go out with Jack when he was in high school; that's for damn sure."

"High school rumors and total bullshit. Junior's a classy kid. His parents raised him to be a gentleman. Debbi, if I had a daughter, I'd let her go out with Junior. As I said, he's a great kid; all the crap you heard about him in school was just that: crap! I hope he and Cindi hit it off. I know both well enough to know they will. Not saying they'll end up getting married, but they will have fun. Junior will do right by her. Trust me."

"Okay, I hope so. I figured you might be behind their going out. I know how much Cindi flirts with you. Made you uncomfortable at times, didn't it?"

"Uh, you could say that."

"I am sorry, Mitch. I've talked to her several times about it. You're a father figure in a way, but she never really learned how to act around her father. She went too far the other way at times, and I cannot begin to tell you how much I appreciate you being such a good man and friend. Truth be told, I'm more worried about how Cindi will behave tonight with Junior."

Mitch cleared his throat as if he had something stuck in it. "Again, Junior is completely trustworthy. You can count on it."

"Thanks. I feel better. I hope to God Junior can handle her."

Mitch rubbed his neck again and wondered if he would regret encouraging the two kids.

"Where's Mabey?"

"She stopped by the market. She should be back by seven-thirty. If you or Cindi need anything, send her a text."

"Okay, and thanks again, Mitch."

"Sure. I'm going to go see Jasper for a few minutes. I'll be back by the time Mabey gets home."

Debbi went into the house. Mitch had forgotten the SD card in the camera. He went out to the Jeep, grabbed the camera out of the bag, and ejected the card. The whole time, he worried a little more about Junior and Cindi. If Cindi overtly flirted with Junior, the young man would be in for a very long and agonizing night. Cindi had a body that made it very difficult for many young men to think clearly. Mitch couldn't help but remember his raging hormones as a teenager and the distorted thinking, or lack thereof, that went on in his brain.

Mitch, in his entire smart-ass splendor, knew the kid was in for a tough hormonal ride for sure and was anxious to see how the night played out. The superstar had better be ready to take a long cold shower when he got home. Mitch had the feeling Cindi might try to stake her claim tonight. God, Mitch hoped not. There was too much other shit going on: a lovestruck Cindi and worried-sick Junior were two things he didn't feel like dealing with right now. WTF had he done, stopping off for coffee?

Mitch stopped short of Jasper's door and grabbed for his cell phone buried in his back pocket.

Chapter 65

Plastic or Paper?

Mabey's phone buzzed in her handbag. She reached for her shoulder bag and snagged the phone from the side pocket. Debbi's picture was flashing on the screen with the message: *you have an incoming video chat.*

Mabey slid her cart to the side of the produce aisle and pressed the Accept button.

"Hey, Debbi, what's up?"

"Thanks for answering. Mitch said you might be at the market. Are you still there?"

"Yes, why?"

"I was wondering if you could buy a bottle or two of Merlot and Cabernet. I'd love to have a glass when you get home."

"One step ahead of you. I already have it in the cart. Robert Mondavi okay?"

Mabey swiped down on the screen engaging both the front and back cameras, so Debbi could see inside the cart as well as her face. "See, Deb? These okay?"

"Thanks so much, Mabey."

Mabey swiped the phone again, turning off the split screen. "Of course, Deb, anything else?"

"How about cheese and crackers? Cindi is going out with Junior tonight; I'm feeling a bit nervous. The wine and food will help me settle."

"Oh really, tonight? Mitch said he was going to try to get them together. You have nothing to worry about in any way. I would trust my own daughter with Junior. If anyone should be worried, it should be Junior," Mabey said with a nervous smile.

"I know. I want to act as if I am worried about Junior, but it's really Cindi I'm concerned about. I'm afraid she's going to be overly aggressive and put him in a tough spot. She's so damn attractive, I can't imagine being a twenty-year-old guy going out with her and not wanting to give her a good spanking, if you know what I mean."

Mabey looked around the market to see if anyone was close enough to overhear the last comment. She turned the volume lower and felt her cheeks flush a little. "Damn, Deb, that's frank, but of course I know what you mean. Want me to call Mitch and have him talk with Junior?"

"No, I already did. I most likely scared the crap out of the kid. I'm making a big deal out of nothing."

"Who knows? You may be looking at a future son, Deb."

"Oh god, don't talk about that yet. I want her to go to college. All right, thanks for listening. I can't tell you how much I appreciate what you and Mitch keep doing for us. Love ya, sis, over and out."

"See you in about twenty minutes." Mabey ended the call. She had just placed the phone back into her bag when it buzzed again. It was a text from Mitch saying he was on his way to Jasper's and would see her when she got back.

Mabey replied, *OK,* put her phone back in the bag, and moved forward with the cart. She needed to go to the dairy section for cheese. Coming down the aisle toward her was Mr. Delightful, Sheriff Gunther.

Mabey didn't have time for what she knew would be his typical boorish behavior. She grabbed the handles of the cart a little more firmly, felt the tendons in her forearms flex tightly around the plastic, and headed straight for him. She figured she might as well get the unwelcome encounter out of the way. Gunther had a smile on his face as he sucked his gut. He also moved his hand against his forehead and brushed back his hair as if that could magically make it look wonderful.

"God could a person be any vainer?" Mabey whispered to herself.

"Well, good evening, Mabey; how're you doing this evening? Nice running in to you," Gunther said condescendingly.

"Hello, Sheriff. Arrested anyone for a mysteriously broken taillight lately?" Mabey looked him straight in the eye. She passed by and smiled without slowing. Mission accomplished. Gunther had clearly tried not to flinch, but his facial expression was one of guilt, shame, and defeat.

"Asshole," Mabey said under her breath. She was tired of his flirting with her; she knew it had nothing to do with him liking her. It was all about his distorted want for competition. God, the man needed to wake up and get on with his life. Mabey almost felt sorry for him – almost!

At the dairy section, she grabbed Irish cheddar, Asiago, and sharp Tillamook cheddar. She hurried over to grab crackers. Gunther had paid and was leaving as she arrived at the cashier. Good. Part of her wanted to yell out, "Have a nice evening, Sheriff Gunther," but that would be cruel. As much as the man pissed her off, it wasn't her style to be deliberately mean. A little ornery at times, as she proved a few minutes ago, but never over-the-top mean.

Mabey wanted to get home. She was tired and looked forward to time with Debbi. She pushed the cart forward, took a quick glance at the tabloids, thought about picking one up, but instead looked away and started placing items from the cart on the conveyor belt.

"Good evening, Mrs. Wilde, plastic or paper?"

Chapter 66

They Are All Clowns

Mitch sent Mabey a quick text.

Going to Jasper's for a few, turning phone off. Back home in 15-20. Debbi &
Cindi there now. Luv M.

Mitch pressed the send button. Not waiting for Mabey's reply, he
turned off the phone.

"Come in, Wilde."

Mitch twisted the handle and let himself in. "I have something you
have to see Jasper."

All the monitors in the room were on, and sound emanated from
several of the speakers. Plus, several radios were making noise. Jasper wore
a bulky pair of headphones, angled so one ear was covered and the other
not. He apparently was listening to his shortwave.

"Hey, Wilde, are you aware of what's been happening while you've
been screwing around all day?"

"Nice to see you, too, Jasper. Oh, and kiss my ass." Nothing like a
little playful banter to get things rolling.

"Don't get your panties in a bunch. What? You want me to run over
and hug you? That's what Mabey's for."

"Okay, old man, I hear ya. But, I have something you need to see
now."

"More important than what's going on at the three lakes in our neck
of the woods?"

"It's footage from Applegate Lake. I worked my way around a

roadblock this afternoon. It's near the dam. You won't believe what I have."

Jasper yanked off the headphones, stepped down from his stool, and grabbed the SD card Mitch was dangling in front of his eyes.

"So that explains your cryptic phone call and pretend disconnect earlier. What is it, a few college girls skinny-dipping?"

"Don't you wish? Just get it in one of your PCs. It's the only file on the card. And it's the only copy."

Jasper turned down volume on the radios and monitors.

"Do us both a favor, and copy the video to a hard drive, ASAP. I don't want that thing getting damaged."

Jasper popped the SD card into the side of a laptop and copied it onto what appeared to be two separate hard drives. He then opened the file and watched the entire three-minute video keeping a concerned look at Mitch out of the corner of his eye. Pressing Play again, this time he paused the video at the point before the things appeared out of the water. Jasper back-tracked the video file one frame at a time. He stopped, rewound, started, stopped, rewound, started, and stopped again.

"You noticed this, didn't you?" Jasper asked.

"What, the water ripples just before they make their exit?"

"No, up on the hill behind the trees."

Mitch's heart seemed to flutter before resuming its normal rhythm. "What are you talking about?" He inched closer to Jasper and the screen.

Jasper pointed. "Watch here the entire time. Don't look at the lake or the things coming out of the water. Look here and only here."

"Okay, I got it."

Jasper pressed Play and slowly pulled his finger from the screen. Swallowing hard, the hair on Mitch's arms stood up.

"Holy shit, I was so busy looking at the things coming out of the water, I forgot about what you said."

"Yep, you gotta pay attention to what's going on away from the so-called action. Takes practice, boy, but you'll get it."

Jasper patted Mitch on the back and then squeezed his arm. Mitch, focusing on the screen, felt reassured as he was sure Jasper intended. Behind the trees, about forty yards up the bank, stood two horses. Sitting on their backs were what appeared to be Indians in full authentic garb, looking like they rode right out of the 1830s.

"I'm going to play it again, Wilde."

Jasper pressed the button and let it run. When the video got to where the things were coming out of the water, Jasper spoke again.

"Notice how the Indians ride up and stop behind the tree line just after the things emerge from the lake."

"Yeah, so what?"

"Well, I am no *Ancient Alien* scholar, but it looks as if they knew exactly when and where those things would be coming on land. I can't help but think they're communicating."

Mitch nodded and replied.

"Isn't the bigger question why they are communicating?"

"That, my good friend, is the question. I've been following the stories about the casinos in the state, how so many of their Indian employees have just stopped coming to work. Now we have all these sightings of Indians, in towns, cities, and highways, like ghosts scaring the shit out of people."

"Like Mabey and me."

"If I had to bet on it, the Indians are talking with the Alien entities and making plans for an invasion. Perhaps small-scale test runs in Oregon and the Pacific Northwest to see how things go before they plan a bigger all-out attack."

"Are you serious, Jasper?"

"Well, think about it; it's almost as if they are probing to see how we react to their presence. With so many Indians presently unaccounted for, they may be planning a ground war or invasion. You test shit out with the locals first rather than risk your own forces. The Aliens can use the Indians for the initial attack to see how things go. It will lessen their losses and give them a good idea of how we respond. Is it possible the Indians and the Aliens come from the same place? You ever watch *Ancient Aliens Internet Edition?*"

"Didn't know there was an internet edition."

Jasper, clearly in deep thought, paused. Mitch roused him by responding a little louder than normal.

"Huhum, well so far, it doesn't appear that we've responded at all as if we have no clue what's going on or how to respond."

"Don't be so sure. I've seen several classified videos this evening from my source in the government. There's satellite footage of pods affecting Crater Lake, Applegate, Deep Creek, and Klamath Lakes, all within several hundred miles of each other, and all here in Southern Oregon. There's only one other report I can find of anything outside this area, somewhere in Idaho, which in the larger scale is close. We appear to be in the middle of an invasion zone."

"Great. As if I didn't have enough going on, now I have to worry about saving this little town. It never ends, I tell you." Jasper let out a big laugh.

"You're enjoying this, aren't you?"

"Damn straight, I am. I've been living most of my life in preparation for something like this."

"They're Aliens and Indians, Jasper, not clowns."

Mitch couldn't believe he just made that comment. Why in hell was he taking a passive-aggressive shot at his friend? Mabey always told him he tended to push people away when they got a little too close. Mitch knew it was a defensive mechanism used to decrease the fear of rejection. He regretted his words towards Jasper.

The old-guy looked surprised and hurt. In an unusual soft-spoken voice, he said, "Well, it doesn't really matter now, does it? They're all clowns to me."

Chapter 67

Turn and Embrace It

After a moment of awkward silence, Mitch looked at his watch. Shit, 7:45 already. He hadn't intended to be at Jasper's this long. "I have to get going, Jasper, so I can prep for Crater Lake tomorrow. You still game on coming?"

"Yeah, I was planning on it, asshole. What time are you leaving?"

"I want to be on the road by 0345 so I can be in position for sunrise. I'll pull up outside your driveway at 3:46 at the latest."

"Okay, see you in the morning." Jasper handed Wilde the SD card from the computer.

Mitch took it, stepped outside, turned on his cell phone, and headed home. The closed garage doors meant Mabey was most likely home, a good thing. He needed to see a smiling face.

Knowing he'd taken things too far with the clown comment, Mitch kicked a rock on Jasper's driveway. He was trying to figure out how to apologize so they could move on. This wasn't a strength of Mitch's, according to Mabey. Apologizing, that is. It wasn't that he didn't care and didn't realize when he'd hurt someone; Mitch simply wasn't skilled at making the other person realize he regretted the hurt.

Mitch stopped at the edge of his driveway and picked up a rock. He hurled it as far as he could down the street. He wondered if he should return to Jasper's and say something now. He mumbled "dumb-ass" to himself and walked up his driveway. He'd better make a genuine apology in the morning.

He entered the side fence to feed the dogs. Both were already face-planted in food bowls on the back deck. Mabey and Debbi were in the kitchen, and Mabey spotted Mitch in the backyard. She waved for him to come inside. Mitch mouthed, "I'll be right there."

Mitch hurried to the shed to deposit the SD card in the safe and make sure the guns were in place. He hustled back toward the house, stopping for a couple of seconds to pet both dogs. General was happy as could be now that he had his sister around. They barely acknowledged Mitch and kept right on eating.

He let himself into the kitchen. Mabey at once engaged him in conversation. "Hey, honey, how are things going? Any news on what the hell is happening at the lakes?"

"Hey, babe, and hi to you as well, Mabey. How're you guys doing?"

Debbi was standing next to Mabey. She blushed. Mabey gave Mitch her loving you-will-pay-later look and then smiled.

Mitch realized he just dug another hole. He reached up and rubbed his forehead.

Mabey responded while topping off Debbi's wineglass. "What was that, Debbi? Did you hear him say that he wants to sleep with the dogs tonight?"

"Okay, I hear you, Mabey. I'm just trying to lighten the mood. It's been a pretty weird and stressful day."

Mitch approached Mabey to peck her on the cheek. She let him kiss her, but only because Debbi was standing there. Dammit, how could he go from hero to zero so fast? He headed to the bar, grabbed a glass, and poured two fingers of Irish whiskey. Debbi and Mabey continued with haven't-seen-you-in-a-while banter; something about events at the coffee shop as Mitch re-entered the kitchen.

"Nothing new that I can get on the radio. You guys ready for Jasper's theory?"

"Why? Is it bad?" Debbi asked.

"May as well hear it now," Mabey said. "Not sure if I want to, but let's go."

The doorbell rang. All three looked at one another as if they'd never heard the sound.

Debbi talked first. "Oh, it must be Junior. I'll let Cindi know he's here."

Mitch took a drink, letting the whiskey warm his tongue and evaporate down the back of his throat. "That's right; the big date is tonight. I'm glad those two are going out. They'll be a great fit. Can you imagine what it'll be like for Cindi during her senior year to tell all the schmucks she goes to school with that she's dating Junior, the pro baseball player? Upside for Cindi, you too, Debbi, and perhaps even more, is that she won't get caught up in all that drama of boy-chasing this year. She can focus more on her studies and less on who to take to what dance."

Debbi smiled; that possibility hadn't occurred to her.

"You have this all figured out, don't you, Mitch?" Mabey said.

"No dear, but men are always trying to figure how to work things out with women. And we aren't always good at it as you well know."

He chuckled and headed for the door. Debbi was scooting up the stairs. Mabey busied herself in the kitchen, restocking the crackers and cheese on the plate.

Mitch opened the door. "Hey, Junior, long time, no see. Come on in."

"Thanks, is Cindi a, a, here?"

Mitch chuckled. He'd never seen Junior nervous or stammering before.

"No, she isn't here. What are you talking about? Come on in. It's always good to see you."

Mabey practically sprinted into the foyer from the kitchen.

"Mitch, you jerk. Hey, Junior, great to see you; Cindi will be right down."

Junior gave Mitch another look reminiscent of both Jasper and Mabey's stares, all in the last forty-five minutes. He realized he was in full-fledged smart-ass mode and was having a hard time stopping. He made a mental note to scale back the weak attempts at humor the rest of the night. He chuckled, only this time he realized he was as nervous as Junior. Everyone was on edge, and his clever quips appeared to be making things worse.

Debbi came downstairs. "Cindi will be right down Junior. Where did you decide to take my daughter?"

"Thanks, Mrs. Howard. Um, if Cindi's up for it, I thought we'd go to the movie we talked about. It starts at 9:15 and runs about two hours. We should be back between eleven-thirty and midnight, if that's okay, ma'am."

Mitch smiled at Debbi. She had nothing to worry about with Junior. Mabey disappeared briefly from the entryway, then returned to hand Debbi her wineglass.

"Thanks, Mabey," Debbi said. "That sounds great, Junior, and thank you. A warning, though: I'm sure Cindi will press me for a later time, but I want her home after the movie, okay?"

"Sure thing, Mrs. Howard."

"Press you for what, Mother?" Cindi came down the stairs.

Mitch couldn't help but notice her deliberately model-like walk. The way she threw her head gently back, shaking her dark blonde hair, and the way her eyes had a laser-like focus on Junior. Mitch smiled and thought, "You poor bastard."

"For a later at-home time tonight, dear."

Cindi's last step onto the entryway was a ballerina-like landing, made with precise ease. Mitch had to hand it to her, the young-lady exuded confidence and class.

"We'll be home by one, Mother. Not a problem."

All the adults peered at each other and smiled. Junior just stood there with a look of, "What have I gotten myself into?" Mitch thought Junior's response was smooth like his fastball.

"Cindi, sorry, but if it's okay, I need to be back by midnight at the latest. I promised my dad I'd have breakfast with him. It's a tradition with us."

"Well played, Junior, well played," Mitch thought.

"You look nice, Cindi." Mabey referred to Cindi's very tight-fitting blue jeans, and a tank top covered with a Daisy Duke style flannel shirt. Mitch agreed; she did look nice.

"Thanks, Mabey."

"Oh, and, Cindi, we have to open the Shack at five in the morning. Another reason you need to be home early. We can't flake on opening tomorrow, okay?"

"No problem at all, Mother. Let's get going then, Junior, away from all the stuffy, manipulating parents." Cindi grabbed Junior's hand and tugged at him all in one motion, somehow. Junior grunted and looked puzzled. The poor kid probably thought a small tornado was after him, and he didn't know if he should run away or turn and embrace it.

"Text me when you get to the theater, and on your way home, please, Cindi," Debbi yelled as the door closed.

A muffled voice came through the door, "We will, Mrs. Howard."

The three of them just stood there for a few long seconds and then went back into the kitchen to refuel.

"Cindi looked really nice, Debbi. She's so gorgeous."

"You should have seen what she had on when I went upstairs. She was in tight neoprene black pants with a white skin-tight top and no bra. She looked as if she were on the way to a raunchy hook-up at a bar. I made her change. It's why she's mad at me."

Mitch again, regretfully, opened his mouth one more time, "Hey, if you got it, flaunt it, right?"

"Mitch, don't you have to get ready for your photo shoot?" Mabey replied, exasperated.

Debbi laughed. "You know, Mabey, Mitch is right. Our society blasts these kids every day with images all over social media with women hardly dressed. Magazine covers are plastered with headlines like, "How to Get Your Man," "Fifty New Positions," "Take It Out on the Town Tonight." It's shocking there aren't more teen pregnancies."

'Thanks Debbi," Mitch thought.

"Nevertheless, Mitch needs to learn to keep his mouth shut sometimes, hell, most of the time."

"One of the things I've always appreciated about the two of you is that you speak your minds. I never have to guess where you're coming from. Mitch has been a great influence on Cindi, and I know how much she respects and looks up to him."

Debbi raised her glass to Mabey and Mitch. "So, thanks. I don't know how I'd have managed without you both after dick-head left."

They clinked glasses. A warm rush of positive energy flowed through Mitch's body. He and Mabey never wanted kids. Both realized they were too selfish and too driven. If Mitch's current pleasant feeling came from being a parent, though, he wondered if they'd made the right decision.

"Thanks, Debbi. As Mabey and I have always said, you're a dear friend, and we consider you and Cindi better than family."
Mitch set his glass in the sink, gave Mabey an affectionate kiss on the cheek—this one warmly accepted—and embraced Debbi with a hug.

It was 8:47. He was doing okay on time, but he wanted to get to sleep. "Okay, ladies, I have to pack, and then I have to get to bed; I'm getting up at 3:20. Where is my stuff from the market, Mabey?"

"On the counter in the garage."

"Thanks, babe, I'll see you late tomorrow evening." Mitch walked up the stairs where he hoped to fall asleep quickly.

Chapter 68

Let's Go, Ladies

Junior opened the passenger door to his '66 Mustang Fastback—a hand-me-down gift from his dad. Cindi slid in. He looked back at the Wilde's house to see if there were any gawkers. Relieved there weren't, at least that he could see, he started the car.

"I was thinking we could go see the new Tim Krooze movie."

"Or we could go down to the river and just park, watch the stars, talk, and get to know each other." Cindi said with a smile.

Junior wasn't sure, but he thought he felt a bead of sweat hanging on the left side of his face.

"I'm just kidding, JJ. Can I call you JJ, or you do you want me to call you Junior like everyone else? Or should I call you Jack?"

"Whatever you feel most comfortable with, Cindi. Any of them are fine. No one has ever called me JJ. A few people have called me Jens, and Jenson, but never JJ."

"Well, I don't like being like everyone else, so JJ it is. Would you mind if my friend Shontey joined us at the movie? She'd love to meet you. She's a big baseball fan."

Junior thought, "A friend would be nice." His hormones were already standing on a cliff ledge. Having a friend of hers around should help.

"No, I don't mind at all. I would like to meet her. Is she a senior as well?"

"Yeah, we've been best friends since eighth grade. She's an actor or at least wants to be one. She hopes to go to NYU, but she's looking at other schools with strong drama departments."

Cindi grabbed her cell phone and started texting. Junior didn't know exactly what she was saying, but figured it had to be to Shontey.

"NYU, huh? Do they have a good theater program?"

"According to Shontey, it's the best in the country. It is a long shot and expensive, but with any luck, she hopes to get in there. You'll like her. She's prettier than me, really smart, and really funny."

"Shit! Prettier than Cindi? My hormones are damned," Junior's mental response.

Junior turned down Main toward their destination. They'd be early, but they could go across to the burger stand for a shake or something. Time always flies by on first dates with someone you really like, so he wasn't worried. His problem, he knew, was that time would go by too fast, and he'd be back in Chattanooga in a couple of days and wouldn't see Cindi again for a while.

"So, what's it like playing pro baseball, JJ? Do you get nervous when you pitch? Will the players be a lot better in Chattanooga than they are here?"

Junior couldn't believe how fast Cindi talked. He chalked it up to nerves. He glanced at her and smiled, taking his eye off the road for just a second.

Cindi screamed, "JJ! Look out!"

Junior faced forward. The rear end of a horse was just leaving the road into the thick woods. He slammed on his brakes, wrenching the wheel right; the back end of the Fastback fishtailed before Junior gained control. The car came to a shuddering stop on the shoulder, angled a bit off the pavement.

Junior's right leg flexed as he put enormous pressure on the brake pedal. His heart raced. "Cindi are you okay?"

Junior noticed her hand on her knee pushing it down to keep it from shaking.

In a quieter and softer tone, Cindi replied, "I'm fine, JJ. Nice driving. Man, that was close."

"Did I see what I thought I saw?"

"If you mean a horse with an Indian on the back, then yeah, we saw the same thing."

"I saw it was a horse with something on it, but I couldn't tell what it was. It happened too fast. I took my eye off the road for a second. I'm so sorry. I should have been paying better attention."

Junior gently touched Cindi on her shoulder. "You sure you're okay? Perhaps we should call it a night and go back to the Wilde's."

"No, I'm fine, but thanks. Just a little scared. It happened so fast. Please, let's still go to the movie. I need a break from all the old people. I'm fine, really."

Junior removed his hand from her shoulder. He felt her energy, and it made him feel alive. He loved it. They both turned and looked out the left side of Junior's car gazing deep into the woods, wondering if they could see the horse and rider again.

"It's long gone, Cindi. Shit, that was sudden. My adrenaline redlined."

Junior found Cindi's nervous laugh cute.

"Can we go? I want to get to the movies and relax."

"Okay, let's go, as long as you're sure you're all right. I'm hungry, and I've been looking forward to spending time with you all day."

Junior glanced up at his rearview mirror and caught a glimpse of Cindi's face. She was beaming. He took his foot off the brake and eased the car back onto the road toward dinner and a movie.

"Cindi, did you say it was an Indian on the horse?"

"Yes, like the ones you see in the old westerns. I don't know though; it happened so fast. I don't get it. Why would an Indian be on a horse crossing the road like that? I tried to look after we stopped, but I couldn't see anything in the woods. It was freaky."

"The way things have been going around here the last few days, it doesn't surprise me at all."

About ten minutes later, Junior pulled the Fastback into the side parking lot at the theater. It was ten minutes after eight. The show started at 9:10, so they had forty-five minutes to kill. The movie had been out a couple of weeks, so he didn't think there'd be a crowd.

"Hey, how about we go get a burger and fries? Or would you like to wait and eat popcorn during the movie?"

"Oh, yeah, a burger is fine, if you want. I like popcorn during the movie, if that's okay, but you get a burger. I'll grab a Diet Coke or something."

Cindi grabbed her phone and texted again while Junior walked around to open her door. Cindi sat there for another second or two. "I'm sorry; Shontey wanted to let me know she'll be right here. Her mom is dropping her off. Thanks so much for letting her meet you."

"No problem, as long as she doesn't ask for my autograph," Junior said with a smile.

Cindi got out of the car and Junior locked the door. "I really like your car, JJ It's old, but cool. And the brakes work really well."

Junior smiled and put his hand on the small of her back gently guiding her across the street. "Cindi, you sure you're okay? You feel as if you're shaking."

"You're so sweet. I'm not used to guys, besides Mr. Wilde, being so nice. I'm just a little startled, I guess. My mom and I saw something in the coffee shop that scared us. It's why we're staying at the Wilde's house."

"I know. Ever since their barbecue, my dad has been acting strangely. I'm not sure what to make of it. Perhaps we should share notes. Cindi, if you don't mind, I'm going to try to call my dad. It shouldn't take long. Something about that horse has me thinking I should talk to him."

"Go ahead, Junior; I'll keep texting Shontey."

Junior pressed the speed dial for his dad on his phone. It rang several times and then went to his dad's voice mail. Junior hung up without leaving a message.

"He didn't pick up."

"Why didn't you leave a message?"

"And tell him what? That I almost totaled the car hitting a horse with an Indian on its back? This type of discussion is better in person."

"I'm sure you're right."

"How is Shontey? Is she on her way?"

"She should be here any minute and she can't wait to meet you. She doesn't believe I'm going out with you and thinks I'm making up this whole date. I hope you like her."

"If she's anything at all like you, I'm going to like her a lot."

Cindi smiled as she reached for Junior's hand.

Chapter 69

Anyone Need a Refill?

"So, Debbi, how're you feeling about Cindi now?" Mabey asked as they gathered around the kitchen table with Michelle, who was apparently staying for another night. "Damn boyfriend of hers," Mabey thought. She should sic Mitch on his sorry ass.

"Well, I'm thankful she isn't double-dating with her friend, Shontey."

"Why is that?"

"For some reason, when they get around men, they feel a need to challenge each other and get more aggressive than normal. Cindi acts completely different when I see her around men by herself."

"Shontey and Cindi probably feel more confident around each other. You know, they have each other's backs," Michelle chimed in.

"Yeah, that makes sense. I trust Cindi, but I don't want her making a mistake and getting pregnant. She thinks she's ready for the world because she's eighteen."

"Junior will be bursting in his jeans; I'm sure – the poor kid. But he won't try anything," Mabey added. They all laughed. Mabey stood up from the leather couch and started for the kitchen. "Want more wine, Debbi? I'm going to top off my glass."

"Thanks, and sure."

"I hope they go to the movie and not down to the river where everyone hangs out and parties," Michelle added as Mabey reached for Debbi's glass.

"Thanks, Michelle, much appreciated," Debbi threw in.

"God, Michelle, why don't you think sometimes before you speak? You remind me of Mitch with that big mouth of yours." Mabey said as she went to the kitchen.

"Oh, you know they're going to the movie. Junior would never say they were going to one place and then go somewhere else."

"No?" Debbi added.

Mabey yelled in from the kitchen, "No, Michelle is absolutely right. You have nothing to worry about."

"Well, I hope you're not just saying it to make me feel better."

"Mabey wouldn't do that, Debbi. She doesn't believe in trying to make people feel better," Michelle added.

"I heard that, sis, and what the hell is that supposed to mean?" Michelle didn't respond, and Mabey knew there was more to the comment. She returned from the kitchen. "So, Michelle, what was the jab for? If I know my little sister, something's on your mind other than me, and you're being passive-aggressive. What's up?"

Michelle said nothing, nervously took a sip of her wine, and looked at the photos on the fireplace mantel.

"Okay sis, now I know for a fact something's up. Are you upset about your latest boyfriend and his trashing your place? Is work going okay?"

"Work is fine, Mabey."

"Where do you work, Michelle? I don't know if I ever heard."

"Oh, no, just a second, Debbi, let's not change the subject so fast, okay? She's a dental hygienist by the way, and a very good one."

"Damn Mabey, why don't you lay off?"

"Michelle, I know you want to talk about something, so spill it. Come on; you're in good company, and you know it. No one's saying another word until you tell us what's going on."

Mabey knew that Michelle wanted to talk, and it was why she kept pushing. She grabbed a cracker and cheese off the tray on the coffee table and settled back on the sofa, next to Michelle sipping her wine.

"You have to promise me, Mabey, you won't get mad, okay?"

"You know I can't make that promise. You also know that I'm not one to overreact, so it would have to be something pretty awful for me to get mad."

Michelle blurted out, "My boyfriend didn't ransack my place."

"What? Who did then?"

"Until tonight I thought I was going crazy, but after listening to Debbi and Cindi, I know I'm not."

"What are you talking about?" Mabey set her wineglass down on the coffee table, then leaned forward.

Michelle didn't say anything.

Mabey started to say something when Debbi interrupted. "You saw something like I described in my house, didn't you, Michelle?"

"How did you know?" Michelle was genuinely surprised.

"Are you serious? You said it was your boyfriend."

"I didn't want you to think I was going crazy."

"Shit, sis, with all the stuff that's happening the last couple of days, it doesn't surprise me at all. I don't get it, but it doesn't surprise me."

"I was in the apartment, and I knew that James, my ex-boyfriend, wanted to come over. I told him he could but to bring the key and be prepared to pick up his stuff.

Anyway, I was on the bed reading when I heard the door jiggling. I thought it was James, so I got up. When I got to the bedroom door, I looked down the hall, and there was this thing. It looked human, kind of, but also disguised as if it were camouflaged or something."

"That's exactly the same type of thing we saw, Michelle." Debbi leaned forward and moved closer to the sisters on the couch.

"What did you do, sis?" Mabey asked.

"I didn't know what to do, really. A voice in my head, Mitch's actually, told me not to panic and not to scream. So, I got under the bed. I have a baseball bat under there, so I wrapped my hand around it and then tried to breathe normally. I knew that if the thing pulled me out, I would stand up swinging."

"Geezus, sis, I'm so sorry. I wish you'd told me. You must have been terrified."

"That's what's strange, Mabey. I was, but I wasn't. I don't know how to explain it. The thing was rummaging around in the family room for a couple minutes, knocking shit over and breaking stuff. That's why it looked like a break-in. Anyway, the thing came to the bedroom door and glanced in... well, near as I could tell, because I could see only its feet. No shoes on, by the way, and the feet looked scaly, like a lizard's skin."

"That's what was in my house too! I wasn't really sure, but, yes, scaly like a lizard."

Michelle nodded at Debbi who continued, "I grabbed the bat and prepared for the worst, but it turned and went into the kitchen. Another minute or so of ransacking the kitchen, and it left."

Chapter 70

Heavy Eyelids

Mitch tossed, turned, and grew increasingly agitated. Dar's music, normally a soothing elixir that helped Mitch fall asleep quickly, wasn't working tonight. The seventeen minutes he'd set on his phone's sleep timer flew by, and Mitch heard all four and a half songs tonight with no possibility of sleep.

He couldn't shut down mentally: he thought about Jack and his strange behavior. When those thoughts settled, his brain replayed his clown comment to Jasper. Occasionally he heard the women's voices downstairs, and he was glad they were there.

Mitch rolled over and stared at the clock and his cell phone docked on top, charging. Both projected 10:49 p.m. as if they were on a rocky shore keeping vessels from crashing against the jagged rocks. Mitch pushed the covers from his chest in frustration and threw his feet to the floor. He sat up and rubbed his face with both hands.

He turned on the nightstand lamp then walked to the bathroom. He relieved himself, lowered the lid out of respect for Mabey, and washed his hands. The warm water felt soothing. Mitch leaned with both hands on the edge of the counter, staring at the mirror, deep in thought. So many questions: Why did he and Mabey see the mysterious horse and rider? Was it a coincidence or meant for them to see? How could Jack get shot by an arrow and not only live but also show no wound and no loss of blood? What in the hell hit the lake, and what exactly did he see? What caused the cut on his shoulder, and how in the hell did it disappear? Why was the government not providing information about the lakes and all the disappearing Native Americans?

Perhaps they didn't know what exactly was going on. On the other hand, perhaps they did. Why did the Sheriff have it in for him and was there any way to stop it? Mitch hoped he'd be able to stay awake on the drive to Crater Lake. Did he really need to go? Most of all, should he apologize to Jasper, or should he pretend his clown statement didn't mean that much? So many damn questions, and no solid answers.

After pondering the many issues, Mitch's went back to bed: 11:13. He turned off the light, lowered his head on the pillow, and pulled the blanket and sheet tight to his chin. He yawned, finally realizing what he needed to say to Jasper. He closed his now-heavy eyelids and faded into a deep sleep.

Chapter 71

Tired and Ragged

Mabey settled down with her sister and best friend in the living room. The next few hours passed quickly. On her last visit to the kitchen, she returned with more wine and cheese. She was becoming tired.

Debbi continually checked the time. The latest check of the clock showed 11:43 p.m. The front door opened. Mitch was asleep, so it had to be Cindi or a very confident burglar. Debbi jumped off the couch and moved toward the front door as Cindi walked into the living room looking as lovely as ever. Debbi sat back down.

"I heard you talking in here, so I thought I'd say good night."

"How'd it go? You're home early," Debbi replied.

"It went great," Cindi added.

"That's it? Went great?"

Mabey and Michelle chuckled. Debbi rolled her eyes. "Yep, I know we have to go in early, so can you make sure I'm up in plenty of time? JJ is coming in for breakfast. I told him I would make it for him."

Cindi started to turn to go upstairs when she pivoted and walked slowly to the edge of the family room. Mabey noticed she looked a little pale as she directed carefully chosen words toward her mother.

"Is there something you need to say, honey? Are you okay?"

"I'm fine, Mom, but on the way to the movie, not long after JJ and I left here, we almost hit a horse on the road. No one got hurt, and JJ's car is fine, but it shook both of us a little."

"A horse, dear? Are you sure?"

"Yes, Mother, I know what a horse looks like. The horse isn't the strange part. What was strange? There appeared to be an Indian in costume on the horse. Not sure why I'm telling you, but I thought, you should know with all the crap going on. Good night, Mabey and Michelle. See you in the morning, Mother." Cindi turned and headed up the stairs.

Mabey looked at Michelle briefly, then Cindi. Both had blank stares on their faces. Mabey wasn't sure how she looked, but she felt exactly like the other two looked: surprised, tired and a little ragged.

Chapter 72

Half a Cup Sounds Good

Mitch woke to a clock displaying 3:18 a.m., two minutes before the alarm was set to ring. It seemed as if it had been only fifteen minutes after he got into bed. He wasn't sure if the quick-passing time meant he slept really well, once he finally fell asleep, or he needed more. He'd know soon enough on the drive up to the lake.

Mitch sat up and made sure the phone's alarm was off and not just 'snoozed.' He touched Mabey's arm and adjusted the blanket over her shoulders. She barely moved. Good, he hated waking her when he was leaving early.

He showered, dressed, and went into the walk-in closet. Mitch knelt and opened the gun safe to grab the Beretta 92FS.

He checked Mabey one last time. She was fine, snoring ever so slightly. Mitch always said it was more of a purr than a snore. He sent her a quick text she would get when she woke.

Love you, babe. Sorry I was an ass last night with my comments. Reminder, at Crater Lake today shooting; plan to be home by nine. Jasper is going with me. Have a good day. Tell Mayor I said Hi - Not. :-) Love, M.

Both guest room doors were closed, so he assumed everyone was asleep and okay. He walked downstairs and out to the Jeep. Mitch had prepped Black Steel the night before. He needed only to get the food

Mabey had picked up for him. He checked to make sure the shotgun was still under the seat where he'd placed it last night. Mitch set the 9mm in its holster between the seats, and his pack of food behind the driver's seat. He let the Jeep idle its way out, so he wouldn't wake anyone. It was 3:35. Good, he was a few minutes early. He hesitated briefly, wondering if Jasper would be ready; he'd most likely be waiting. Mitch remembered his clown comment to Jasper; he got nervous, wishing he were heading to the lake alone.

He backed out of the driveway, spun the wheel, and his lights at once shined on Jasper standing on the edge of his driveway. He pulled up next to him and stopped. "Morning, Jasper, all ready to go?"

"I'm not standing here for my health, Wilde."

Jasper carried a backpack; it had an internal frame capable of handling up to seventy pounds. Mitch wouldn't be surprised to learn it had forty pounds in it, a lot for a day trip. He also had a thermos, and what looked like a cool walking stick. Jasper was wearing nice-looking hiking pants and boots, a light jacket and vest, and a solid black baseball cap.

"Damn, you look as if you've done this before," Mitch replied as Jasper threw his pack into the backseat and then hopped in front.

"Yeah, you could say I've been to a rodeo or two in my day," Jasper said with a big smile.

Mitch grimaced a bit. The rodeo comment took him back to his last foot-eating episode. Mitch hoped that Jasper's smile meant things would be okay. He eased Black Steel into gear and accelerated down the street toward town and their destination.

There was a minute or two of dead air. Mitch pushed his left palm against his leg, wiping sweat that wasn't there. He nervously blurted, "Jasper, about my clown comment yesterday, I'm sorry. I didn't mean anything by it. I don't think sometimes before I say things. I shouldn't have said it."

Jasper said nothing, not a single word. The silence and lack of response made Mitch feel awkward. Was it a mistake taking him to the lake this morning? He felt better getting it out, but now wondered if the words had left his mouth.

Finally, Mitch's neighbor spoke. "Don't sweat it, Wilde. We're all under a lot of stress right now. I must admit it hurt a little though. Then I got to thinking why a few poorly chosen words would hurt. They were intended to be funny in a sick, demented, way."

"Okay, I get it," Mitch interrupted.

"All these years later, I clearly haven't gotten over being left for a damn rodeo clown. An issue I need to deal with. After you left, I focused on the ordeal, and I've been able to let it go. Best I've felt in years. Now let's put it behind us, go take a few photos, and spy on Aliens and Indians, okay?"

"Fair enough, and thanks, Jasper. Your friendship is important to me."

"Okay, already, Wilde. Loosen your lady-pants a notch or two, and come back down to man-earth, will you, or this is going to be a long day.

You want coffee?" Mitch smiled while Jasper held up his thermos.

"Sure, I have a mug right here." Mitch pointed to the mug between the seats. "Half a cup sounds good, and thanks."

"Don't mention it, kid. All is good."

Mitch put his left hand back on the steering wheel. Black Steel made its way down the empty street. A wave of relief flashed through him, and once again he looked forward to the day.

Chapter 73

No, Just Saying

"What's the gun for?" Jasper asked as he poured Mitch's coffee.

"I have a carry permit. I take it on all my shoots. Never know what might come up, right?"

"I absolutely hear you."

"I usually carry the 9mm and stash a shotgun under the backseat. I made a custom storage place with the help of a survivalist website. It can hold a couple of guns, my re-curve bow, extra ammunition, food and water supplies, and a heavy-duty first aid kit. I can put more in the back of the Jeep, but I have to cover it with a blanket. Anyone looking in through the back would know something was there. If they wanted it, they could get it as I am sure you already know."

"I have a similar setup in my rig but went a step further and built a custom space, a false bottom where the spare tire used to be. I can pack a shit-load of stuff in there. A thief peeking in the back window, if they can get through the window tint, sees nothing more than a regular seat. I could help you do the conversion to this rig if you want."

"When things settle down, I'd like that, thanks."

The clock on Black Steel's radio read 3:51 as they pulled onto the interstate. There were only a few exits before the state highway going most of the way to Crater Lake.

"Shit," Mitch said.

"What, Wilde?"

"I don't know what I was thinking, or not thinking, but we have to drive around Deep Creek Lake this morning. The roads are blocked. Dammit!" Mitch turned on the radio.

"No worries. I had the radio and news on all night. Reports coming in now are saying that all the roadblocks have been lifted, and nothing was found to have impacted any of the lakes."

"Really? Nothing found? What a surprise," Wilde said in his best smart-ass voice.

"Yeah, so we should have smooth sailing travel-wise."

"Good, 'cause we should be there in less than sixty minutes."

Mitch steered Black Steel off the freeway at Gold Hill and got onto State Route 234 that would take them around Deep Creek Lake and most of the way to Crater Lake.

"Listen, I studied your film another thirty minutes or so after you left."

"Find anything else?"

"No, I wished you could have stayed there longer and seen if the Indians were meeting up with the Aliens or were tracking them. I assume they were there to meet them. The more I thought about it, though, what if they wanted to track them? What if the Indians aren't working with them at all, or what if they're negotiating?"

"That makes sense, I suppose. Why, though? What's your theory?"

"Remember the footage from on top of Jack's house? What if they weren't there in cahoots, but in a negotiation or peace talk?"

A chill ran down Mitch's spine, stopped and headed back up tickling the back of his head.

"Well, shit."

"Exactly what I was thinking. Makes a fella wonder which side he should be on. An Alien force that we don't seem to know anything about: they could want us for slave labor to strip the planet of its resources, or perhaps they need the planet for a docking-station on their way to another galaxy. On the other hand, there's the side of the Indians, excuse me, Native Americans. We, being white Europeans, systematically pushed them out until they were damn near extinct. I'm not one to cry over survival of the fittest, but in hindsight, there had to be a better way. This is a huge country, and there must have been a way we could have coexisted. Well, it doesn't matter now. If they're still pissed—and I am guessing they are—this may be a good time to think about moving."

Mitch brought Black Steel to a stop and turned left on Highway 62. They were making good time and should be at the lake in plenty of time for sunrise. Mitch wondered if the photos would matter in the end. Would the paper even want them? With everything going on, would a few beautiful images of a national landmark matter to anyone?

"Wilde, you listening?"

Jasper brought Mitch back to focus. "Perhaps if the Indians win, but what if the Aliens win? You think they're targeting only Oregon?"

"Hell, no! I don't think so any more. There's internet chatter worldwide about similar sightings in the Soviet Union, Australia, Africa, the Middle East, and more. There aren't too many places left on the planet where indigenous peoples thrive. They've been all but wiped out or dislocated in one way or another."

"Well, hell, I had nothing to do with it. How many years ago was that, anyway? Why now?"

"My theory is that the Aliens need resources and are here bargaining for them."

"Which begs the question, why the Indians, and why not the Pentagon?"

"I haven't come up with an answer yet. But I've been thinking about it."

"Of course you have, Jasper, and I'm glad, by the way."

The two rode in silence for several minutes. Mitch wrestled with Jasper's recent theories, trying to make a modicum of sense out of them.

He broke the silence.

"Jasper, when we get to the lake, the plan is for me to set up near Danger Bay, so the sun is at my back. There's a turnout not far from there where I hike a couple hundred yards to a rocky outcrop that gives me a vantage point and unique access. Not a lot of people know about it."

Jasper fiddled with the radio buttons hunting for legible noise. "How were you able to find this spot?"

"Mabey and I used to come here often. One day we stumbled onto it. We were rock climbing, and it dropped down, obscuring our view of the lake. A few more feet up, a steep angle in the rock reveals nice ledges. The payoff waits at the top where there's a flat spot large enough for three or four people or for two and a tripod. You're coming with me, right?"

"Well, if you don't mind, Ansel, I was hoping you'd let me off at the lodge. I thought I'd poke around there a while."

"It doesn't open until nine this time of the year. The park is open, but you won't be able to get into the lodge."

"That's fine. I have no desire to go inside. I want to hike over near Eagle Cove and perhaps farther on up for a good view of Wizard's Island. I've been seeing images from there on the net lately and they have my curiosity piqued. I have my binoculars and my G15 camera in my pack. I want to find out what I can see firsthand."

"I thought you preferred Nikon?"

"I do for an SLR, but for a compact, the Canon G-Series is pretty hard to beat."

"I agree. My backup is an old G11."

"Anyway, I can drop you off at the lodge. Not far from where you'll be is Watchman Tower with an awesome view. If you haven't visited it before, I highly recommend it. You have food in the pack, I imagine. If not, there's plenty of jerky, granola bars, energy gels, and water in back. Help yourself."

"Thanks, Wilde, but I'm good." Jasper pressed the power button on the radio turning it off.

Black Steel glided from the highway onto Munson Valley Road for access to Crater Lake and Rim Drive. The clock read 4:57. Record time.

"Mitch, if anything should happen to either one of us today, it's been really nice getting to know you."

"Whoa, partner, got plans that I should know about?"

"No, just saying…"

Chapter 74

They Should Hold Up Great

Mitch eased the Jeep to a stop. "Okay, Jasper let's meet back here at noon. We can figure out what to do next. Do you have a cell number I can have just in case? Not like the signal is reliable up here, but may be worth a shot, if necessary."

"Do I look like somebody who carries a cell phone?"

"Yeah, I hear you, dumb question. Halfway out of my mouth, I realized it was stupid."

Jasper opened his backpack and tossed Mitch a very fancy looking two-way radio.

"These are top-of-the-line Garmin Rino radios, Wilde. You lose it, you owe me five hundred bucks," Jasper said with a smile. "They're pretty straightforward to use, read the screen icons and you can figure it out. I use channel ten almost exclusively. If for some reason I get interference, I switch to channel nine on odd hours of the day, and then back to ten on even hours. Make sense?"

"Yes Jasper. As you say, primary is channel ten, but if I can't reach you, I'll try channel nine on odd hours and back to channel ten on even hours until contact is made. Okay, my entry point is around the north end of Danger Bay. A natural rock tower of sorts is over there. It isn't visible from the road, but anyone at the lodge is familiar with where it is. I usually park just off the east side of the road far enough, so the Jeep isn't visible. I then hike it or ride my mountain bike. I'll bike today to save time."

"Sounds good, Wilde, see you at noon." Jasper slammed the door.

Mitch eased Black Steel into gear at 5:02, driving toward the tower. This gave him roughly twenty minutes to get to his target area and to set up; he could do it, but it'd be tight. He pulled off Rim Drive and parked along the fire access road behind a rock formation: 5:11. If he hustled, he could make it in about five minutes, a couple of minutes up the rock tower and a few more to set up. Sunrise was at 5:37.

Mitch grabbed the pack with the camera equipment, the 9mm with clips, and his basic food supplies, sliding it over both shoulders to lie squarely on his back. Mitch put a little used steering bar on Black Steel, locked up, and took the bike off the rack. Normally he'd wear a helmet, but on these camera shoots, it was too much of a pain. He wasn't doing anything except riding a short distance on a flat trail. There were no crazy climbs or downhills, so he always guessed he'd be fine hoping the odds never caught him.

Fighting a little as he always did with the tripod hanging from the side of his pack and hitting his leg, Mitch pedaled away. Minutes later, he arrived at the base of a large boulder. The sun was making an effort to crest over the landscape and splash onto the lake. He needed to hurry. Mitch leaned the bike against his usual tree and wrapped the cable lock around the bike, wheels, and tree. If anyone wanted to steal it while he was taking photos, they would have to be motivated and have an ax.

"Shit, the radio." Mitch couldn't believe he left it sitting on the passenger seat. Jasper would have his ass.

Too late to go back so Mitch jogged up the trail. The still dark lake waited for the sun's call to start her daily warming cycle. Mitch mounted his camera on the tripod and put on the wide-angle lens, pointed it toward the rising sun, and selected panoramic mode. He rotated the camera 360 degrees from the north end of the lake toward the east and around to the south end, then west until he came full circle facing the north end again where he started from. As he swept across the lake, the sun painted its golden beams of life over the lake's surface. Mitch was ecstatic that the shot he'd planned had come to fruition. To be safe, he put on the normal lens, and took shots of the lake with the early sun dancing off the water and crashing onto the western slopes. Never hurts to have more stock images. This lake brought in more money for him over the years than any other single thing he photographed.

Mitch finished with several telephoto shots of interesting points around the lake as well as a couple dozen shots of Wizard Island zooming in and out to change perspective. The polarizing filter would add intriguing depth to the clouds floating above the western slope. The new 70-300mm lens was nice. It should be for what it cost. Thirty minutes later, he finished. Mitch confident he had a new and unique perspective that would bring in needed revenue over the coming months, smiled.

He grabbed his pack and took a seat next to the tripod to enjoy the cool morning air and million-dollar view of one of the deepest and most mysterious lakes in the world. The cold from the rock penetrated his pants sending a slight chill up his back. He looked around for something to put between the rock and his butt, briefly thought about his hat but decided against it. He found an almond granola bar in the pack – thank you, Mabey – and bottled water. Mitch spent the next thirty minutes trying hard not to think of all that had happened in the last several days. It wasn't easy, but the majestic view helped.

What a beautiful place. He did think about the Indians and their deliberate avoidance of this place. Numerous legends claim too many bad incidents in their mythological history of spirits have occurred. Supposedly, the Indians, when guiding settlers around this area, avoided Crater Lake altogether. They thought it was bad luck even to talk about it. Mitch decided he needed to read more about Native American history in Southern Oregon and in particular their relation to the mesmerizing lake.

He remembered something about a couple of battling spirits but couldn't remember the specifics. Jasper had also mentioned a potential connection with recent events and the lake, even more intriguing.

Mitch put the empty granola wrapper in a side pocket of the pack, took a swig of water, and then removed the camera from the tripod. He wanted to see what he had photographed now before he packed up and left.

Mitch positioned the camera and LCD screen for better viewing and pressed Play. He stepped his way through the images one by one. The exposure was perfect, and the images looked sharp and fantastic.

No longer keeping track of time, Mitch was only worried about noon, which wasn't a problem.

Mitch set his watch alarm for eleven-thirty, giving him more than enough time to get to the lodge. He thought of the radio back in the Jeep, hoping like hell that Jasper wasn't trying to get hold of him for anything. He didn't want to catch any shit for forgetting it. Mitch decided he'd try to contact him as soon as he got back to the Jeep so Jasper would know he had the damn thing and could figure out how to use it.

For the next ten minutes, Mitch worked his way through the images he'd just shot. He slowed down on the Wizard Island frames. He wanted to see the sharpness of his new, expensive lens. The photos looked amazing. Mitch couldn't wait to see a few of the premiere shots printed.

From the first glimpse, he thought the images would be sharp and make excellent media images and perhaps a potential print for his office. He could never tell for certain on the small viewing screen of the camera and would need his laptop and Photoshop to know for sure. Taking another swig of water, he realized his ass wasn't only cold, but had entered into the realm of numbness.

Mitch set his water down and placed the camera and lens back in their respective spots in the pack. He stood, brushed off his pants, and then lifted both hands towards the sky, stretching out the kinks. Yawning,

Mitch realized for the first time since he left home this morning how tired he was. Jasper had helped him stay alert on the drive.

He looked around; it felt as if someone were behind him, but he saw nothing other than dirt, trees, and rocks. There were no birds or squirrels: odd, but he gave their absence no deliberate thought. Mitch twisted his body from the waist up, stretching further, hearing a few small pops in his back. The sun warmed his face and efforted heating the rock beneath him. He sat down again, realizing the sun hadn't had enough time to do her job on the rock. Mitch grabbed the camera from the pack for another look at his morning images. He chuckled to himself thinking about Jasper calling him "Ansel" this morning. He flipped on the camera and rubbed his sleeve across the camera LCD screen to get rid of any settling dust. Mitch wondered what Jasper was doing at this very moment.

Chapter 75

It's Mayor Jerkins

Rogue River's Sheriff struggled to enjoy the morning. The air was warming with the appearance of the sun, and the breeze coming through the driver's window felt nice, but like always he couldn't relax and simply be in the moment. His cell phone rang. Looking at the screen on the BlackBerry, he recognized it was the Mayor. The contact image on the phone was one of Gunther's favorites, a badge-pinning ceremony when the townspeople elected him Sheriff. Perfect timing, he thought, since he planned to call him in about thirty minutes. He'd take advantage of the opportunity.

"Good morning, Jenkins. Glad you called. I can't take it anymore. Mitch Wilde acts as if he owns this town. He can't talk to me the way he does in front of people. Something has to give, and it isn't going to be me."

"Listen, Bob, calm down and back off. I'm sick of telling you this. A man in your position must have a calmer approach. Even if you're panicked, keep it inside; you can't let the public see you lose your shit."

"Blah, blah, blah. I'm tired of hearing it, Jenkins."

"It is Mayor Jenkins, Bob, and I'm sick and tired of telling you. We're finished. From here on out, you'll absolutely address me as Mayor Jenkins. Do you understand?"

"Yes, Mayor JERKins. I understand." Gunther, hurt and more than a little stunned, did his best to annunciate Jerk in a childish attempt at striking back at his lover.

"Excuse me, Sheriff, what did you say?"

There was a long and awkward pause.

"Gunther are you there?"

"Yes, sir, Mayor Jenkins, I am here, and it's Sheriff Gunther from here on out. I was elected Sheriff by the lousy people of this shitty town, and I should be addressed properly."

Mayor Jenkins chuckled on the other end of the line. It made Gunther hurt even more.

"Okay, Sheriff, I have something for you. Now listen and don't interrupt because this is important. I don't have time for you to go off again about your petty issues with a private citizen. You hear me?"

Gunther rubbed his near-to-tearing eyes with his left hand. He took a deep breath, focusing on each exhale as he fought to hold back his emotions. He wanted to hang up, but at the same time, he didn't want to lose any remaining hope at a connection with the Mayor.

"Okay, Mayor I hear you. What do you have for me then?"

"My office has received a number of phone calls the past forty-eight hours, most especially from the State Police and the Department of Homeland Security regarding unexplained sightings of different entities around town."

"What kind of sightings and entities?"

"They were vague at best, Gunther. I got the impression they weren't sure themselves. Anyway, I need you and your deputies to be on alert for anything out of the ordinary and document any such events."

"We've received a bunch of calls already. I've been up all night investigating the so-called sightings and disturbances – none of them verified. People keep telling us they are taking videos of Indians on horseback and Aliens that look like chameleons snooping around, but no one has brought in anything specific yet. The deputies are already on alert for anything out of the ordinary as we always are."

"Elections are coming up, as you know, and neither of us wants anything negative to happen. At least not in situations we can control. Call my office with updates. My staff needs to be kept aware of what's going on, so we can be involved in the decision-making process."

The radio in Sheriff Gunther's patrol car squawked.

"Sheriff Gunther, this is dispatch. Are you available? Over."

"Gotta go, Mr. Mayor Jenkins, have a lovely day." Gunther pressed the End button of his cell phone.

On the edge of town, Gunther spoke into his two-way. "I'm here, Wendy. What's going on?"

"There's a report of a disturbance at the Coffee Shack. The caller sounded panicked and wants someone over there ASAP. Over."

"Is that it, a loud disturbance? Dogs messing with garbage cans in the alley, perhaps. Anything more specific? Over."

"They didn't say, sir, only that they needed help. They sounded scared. Didn't sound like it had anything to do with dogs in the alley. Something about Indians again. Over."

"You say Indians, Wendy? Over."

"Yes, sir, they said Indians, sir. Over."

"Okay, ETA is three minutes. I'm on my way. Over." Gunther set the two-way mic back in its cradle and flipped on his flashing red and blue lights. He left the siren off thinking a more silent approach would be best. He'd turn the lights off a block or two from the coffee shop. His chest still ached from the Mayor's comments, but the distraction helped. Hell, he welcomed distraction at this moment.

Two and a half minutes later, Gunther approached the Shack. He turned off his lights and slowed. One more right turn, and the Coffee Shack would be in sight. He rolled through the intersection and took the turn onto Main Street. Something was wrong. He hadn't noticed until now, but all the traffic lights were out. Gunther slowed the car a little more. The Shack was now in plain sight. Gunther stopped, put the car in Park and slid down behind the wheel. He wondered if his painfully red eyes deceived him. "What the fuck?" Gunther mumbled.

Lying across the front bench seat, he reached over and turned off the car. His gut told him he needed to be as quiet as possible. Sliding the locking mechanism of his shotgun into the release position he pulled it out of the holder with his left hand and brought it to his chest, so it was parallel with his body. He moved his head up a few inches at a time until he was able to see over the dashboard.

There were five, perhaps six, what appeared to be 1800s Indians on horseback sitting in front of the coffee shop's entrance. They had it blocked. He lifted his head a bit more just in time for Chief Don't-Look-This-Way to turn his head and look directly at Gunther.

"Shit!" Gunther whined. He thought, "What a baby I am! How in the hell did I get this job?"

One of the majestic and very powerful-looking Indians on an equally impressive paint horse turned and trotted toward his patrol car. Peeking again, the sheriff thought he had about fifteen seconds, give or take, to do something.

Gunther grabbed the mic. "Wendy don't interrupt. Send backup downtown now. Tell all cars to meet me in the parking lot of Parson's Hardware and to leave sirens and lights off. Repeat, sirens and lights off. Over."

"*10-4, Chief,*" Wendy replied.

Gunther dropped the mic and let go of the death grip he had on the shotgun lying on the passenger seat next to him. Sitting up, he started the car and slammed it into reverse. Scared, his instincts took over as he turned the wheel around so he was now perpendicular with the Indian and horse which now had broken into a run toward his car. Gunther struggled to maintain speed with the car in Reverse and contemplated braking and spinning to get the car in a forward-facing position. He didn't think he had the time, as the Indian, which appeared to be holding a bow, reached over his shoulder in a smooth fluid motion. Gunther guessed what he was reaching for and an instant later an arrow flew by him slamming into the passenger window with a loud crack. The tip burst open and a silver substance exploded out of the arrow tip dripping down the door's interior. He should have rolled up the driver's window: basic police training he'd forgotten. On the other hand, perhaps he was supposed to leave the window down. Hell, he couldn't remember. Gunther screamed, "Shit!" His foot stayed planted on the accelerator as the car jumped over the curb and the rear end slammed into a building. His head lurched forward hitting the steering wheel.

The magnificent horse with the powerful-looking Indian now stood next to his car. Dismounting, the Indian walked with erect confidence and reached for the door handle. Gunther felt something warm spreading through his pants while his mind faded into still darkness.

Chapter 76

Sure-Footed as a Mountain Goat

Mitch made it through most of the images on his camera when something unexpected caught his eye. What he thought was an anomaly on the screen near Wizard Island's shoreline turned out to be much more. He grabbed a screen cloth from the pack and cleaned the LCD. The anomaly was still there. Backing up a couple of images, the anomaly disappeared. Mitch worked his way forward one image at a time until it reappeared. He zoomed in on the spot, a couple of clicks at a time, re-centering the image after every click. As the spot grew larger, he felt himself grow pale; his neck and arm hair bristled.

Mitch centered the anomaly and zoomed in tight. In the middle of the Canon's screen was a type of spacecraft. More than one it looked like. They appeared to be crashing into the side of the island. Hoping to see a live view, he brought the camera up to his eye and zoomed in as close as he could near the spot of the island in the images. He saw nothing but a few trees and rocks all the way down to the water's edge. Mitch packed up; he wanted to find Jasper.

Mitch put everything away in less than thirty seconds. He slung on the camera pack, grabbed the tripod, working his way back to the bike. He must have been moving too quickly because he slipped and fell about halfway down the boulder toward the base of the tree guarding his bike.

It couldn't have taken long to fall, but it seemed like an eternity. His first thought was how much he loved Mabey and how smart she was. Man, was he lucky. Then, for obvious reasons, he thought about the first aid kit in Black Steel. He thought about the camera pack: was it padded enough, and would the new, very expensive, lens survive his fall? Mitch's next-to-final thought as he bounced down the twenty feet of rock towards his bike: he hadn't stumbled or tripped on anything. He was as surefooted as a mountain goat. Something between his shoulder blades gave him a nice, firm, how-do-you-do, and enjoy-the-fall push. As Mitch fell, his final thought besides the unknown fear: why hadn't he put on his helmet, and the rocks near his bike were lining up perfectly with his head.

This is going to….

Thud.

Chapter 77

Thank the Stars

"Mitch, this is Jasper, you there? Come in, Mitch. Don't screw around. I need to talk with you and fast."

There was intermittent crackling, silence, more crackling and not much more.

"Okay, Mitch, if you can hear me, change to channel nine in ten minutes just past seven o'clock."

Jasper kept his binoculars locked in on Wizard Island near where he'd seen the activity almost an hour ago. He thought he heard voices not far from the trail around the upper rim of the lake. Occasionally it sounded as if a car drove by on Rim Drive, but he wasn't sure. Noise, or lack of noise, was strange. Jasper realized the outdoors was eerily quiet. He hadn't seen or heard any chipmunks or squirrels. There didn't appear to be any birds chirping or whooshing about. It was as if the entire lake and surrounding park was on Pause.

Picking himself up from his prone position, Jasper brushed himself off and threw on his backpack. The binoculars stayed out and around his neck. He picked up his walking stick and tried Wilde on the radio one more time. Jasper shook his shoulders a bit and wiggled his knees trying to generate a little body heat. "Mitch, you there? Come in, Wilde. Press Talk when you're speaking, dumb-ass."

Jasper continued walking north on the trail for a different, and hopefully better, angle of the island. Perhaps he could make it over to Watchman Tower that Mitch had mentioned.

"Okay, Wilde, come on." Jasper hoped Mitch remembered the Channel 9 and 10 drill on the hour. He switched over to 9. "Okay, Mitch, Channel 9, now. Come in. You there, Wilde?"

Nothing, shit! Jasper had the Tower in sight. He spent the next fifteen minutes making his way toward it. At least he had now heard a car go by on Rim Drive; a glimpse of it said it was a Fish & Game vehicle, mint green, probably heading to the Tower.

Jasper caught up with a young couple on the trail ahead of him. He figured they must be hiking to the tower as well. One of them stopped to tie a shoe.

As Jasper approached, and before he was right on top of them, he barked out, so he wouldn't spook them.

"Hey, there, how're you two doing this morning? Beautiful out here, isn't it?" Jasper hoped his tone came across as friendly and non-threatening.

They simultaneously wheeled around, and the young woman spoke.

"Good morning to you, sir. It's awesome out here. I can't wait to get to the Tower for an even better view. How're you doing?"

Jasper quickly reached the two and worked his way around them so he would be ahead on the trail. The young man finished tying his shoe and stood up. He wasn't smiling or frowning; it was more of an alert look as he sized up Jasper.

Jasper reached out his hand to the young man first. "Hello, my name is Jasper, and you might be?"

"I might be John, or I might be someone else." The young man timidly shook Jasper's calloused lumberjack grip.

"John, stop it, you jerk." The young woman slapped him across the shoulder.

"My name is Sadee, and this is my boyfriend, John."

"Well 'Might-Be-John', it's nice to meet your girlfriend, Sadee." Jasper let go of John's hand and shot Sadee a wink and a smile.

Sadee giggled, turning her face toward John. "That'll teach you, Mr. Friendly. I can't take you anywhere."

"Well, it's early still, Sadee. Perhaps Might-Be-John hasn't fully awakened yet. Again, nice to meet you, I hope the both of you have a nice day." Jasper turned and quickly worked his way ahead on the trail, his final push to the Tower.

Jasper glanced repeatedly over his right shoulder, half expecting the island to erupt.

He continued trying to reach Mitch on the two-way with no luck. He wasn't too worried. He figured Mitch had the volume turned down and had buried his radio in his pack somewhere. He would dig it out eventually, or, worst-case scenario, they would meet at noon at the lodge as planned.

Jasper worked his way up the Tower. A Park Ranger appeared around one corner of the tower. "Good morning, sir, how're you doing?"

"Good, and you?"

The Ranger looked all of twenty-five, a kid really. "I'm doing well, thanks. Come up here often?"

"First time on this Tower. A friend said it was worth the hike, and I have to agree with him. There is an outstanding view."

"It sure is. I'm fortunate to have this job. Can't think of any other place I'd rather be."

"Hey, listen…" Jasper paused for a second. "You see anything strange around Wizard Island just before or just after sunrise?"

"Can't say I did; I was at the fuel depot filling up my pickup and grabbing coffee. I have to fill up a couple of times a week since I spend so much time in the truck. Take today, for example. I'll work my way around the entire rim twice. It's only about thirty-five miles, but when you figure I stop at many spots around the lake, usually stop for lunch at the lodge, aid a hiker or two from time to time, stop and annotate certain forest and weather conditions at reporting stations, it can go by quickly. Anyway, I use a lot of gas. The old pickup is heavy and doesn't get the best mileage. Only seven to ten miles a gallon, I would think…"

The kid wouldn't stop talking. Jasper pressed the radio up to his mouth to block out wind noise. "Wilde, come in, you out there? I need to talk with you. Come in, Wilde."

"You lose someone, mister?" the kid asked.

"No. My friend is on the other side of the lake, and we're just testing out these new two-way radios I bought."

"What kind are they? Perhaps I can help?"

"Dear God, this kid might talk me to death if I'm not careful," Jasper thought.

Before Jasper could put his walking stick across the back of this kid's head to silence him for a few minutes, John and Sadee came hoofing up the stairs. "Thank the gods." Jasper whispered to himself thinking this kid and Might-Be-John should hit it off splendidly.

The ranger-kid spun around to greet the trail couple. "How're you all doing? Enjoying the day so far?"

Sadee smiled, and Might-Be-John gave a frown that looked priceless to Jasper. Jasper laughed, took advantage of the gap in conversation, and made his way past the young couple, nodding as he passed.

"Have a nice day, everyone. I'm going to catch up with my friend."

"You still want me to look at that two-way for you, mister?" the kid yelled.

"No. How about you shut the hell up for thirty seconds and enjoy the silence," Jasper said under his breath. Not loud enough for anyone to hear, he hoped.

"No, I'm fine, thank you," Jasper said loud enough for all as he continued down the stairs and away from the future talk show host, and now current Park Ranger. Thank the stars for John and Sadee, Jasper thought as he fiddled with the two-way one more time.

Chapter 78

Koyaanisqatsi, a Hopi Indian word that means "World out of balance... a state of life that calls for another way."

A Familiar Voice

Mitch, groggy from the fall, was unsure of his current condition. His head throbbed. His face tingled from the cool breeze, longing for the warmth of the fading sun. He couldn't be sure of his location as he willed his heavy eyelids to stay open. They kept reflexively closing from the sudden penetration of light. After a few effort-filled seconds, the lids stayed open, and the light brought more recognition to his current situation.

Mitch's less-than-graceful tumble down the boulder replayed in his head. He wasn't completely sure what had happened. Each replay brought forth a slight variation of events. Man did his head feel awful. He couldn't remember pain like this before. Ever! Mitch became aware enough to realize he was bobbing up and down in water, probably a lake. Tied to something, his arms were drawn behind him and bound extending the pain from his stretched shoulders; the constant throbbing reminded Mitch of his predicament. The smooth texture touching his back was cold and hard like a pole, or perhaps a tree. The bindings on his wrists cut into his skin; it felt as if his wrists were oozing blood. He was too unaware and dizzy to know for sure.

With care, Mitch moved his head back and forth. He wished he could shake it and get out all the cobwebs, but the pain would be excruciating. Mitch could make out the shoreline, and as he rotated, a small island came into view. It looked familiar, but he couldn't identify it. He looked down, straining his eyes; his chest was bare. The water felt so cold that he had little feeling below his neck. Mentally, he wiggled his feet, which seemed free, but numbness kept him from being sure. Mitch wondered about Mabey. He would love to see her right now. Desperate and scared, he wondered if he would see her again. He was slowly bobbing in circles, and he lost sight of the island. The approaching shoreline soothed him in a strange way. It appeared as though they would never reach it. Like a dream where you can't reach the end of a hallway.

A bird screeched in the distance. Mitch lowered his chin to his chest; his neck was stiff, and it took a lot of concentration and effort to keep his head upright. He had to close his mouth as the water lapped up and down against his face. Concentrating, he lifted his head again and saw the shoreline come back into view as he continued to rotate.

"Crater Lake, I'm in Crater Lake," Mitch mumbled the words aloud. The recognition gave him courage in the form of familiarity. His memory's betrayal faded as he threw-up. Numb insides gave no advanced warning. Chunks of what looked like granola swirled around his face in the ebb and flow of the water. Mitch thought of his grandmother and the journal she gave him as a young boy. This would be an interesting entry. Mitch laughed as he spit up something else.

"That looks like turkey jerky." He tilted his head to tell a falcon he thought was sitting on top of a stump, Mitch's life support.

Mitch's feet were free as his mind wrestled with a scan of his body and all its parts. A rope wrapped around him at least twice under his armpits held him upright. The water level rose and lowered as he bobbed with the tree. He tried desperately to keep the water out of his mouth by keeping his chin raised. His hallucinations deepened. "Listen, Mr. Falcon, could you please fly somewhere and get me some help? I would be forever grateful."

Mitch, saddened over the bird's lack of reciprocal dialogue and seemingly uninterested behavior, wished a moth would fly by so he could whisper in one of its little ears. If Gandalf could do it why couldn't he?

Mitch gingerly shook his hurting head trying to clear his thoughts. His mind spun up to full speed. The floating tree or stump, his best guess, was the Old Man of the Lake. Mitch remembered that legend said the tree had floated around the lake since the late 1890s. He'd photographed it countless times over the years. As he continued bobbing, Wizard Island came in and out of view every so often.

Mitch couldn't remember how he got here. His hands repeatedly tried to come to the aid of his head wanting to hold it between his palms as if the pressure would lessen the pain. He wasn't sure how long he'd been in the water and had no idea how events would play out. When the sun went down, he'd be on borrowed time. Mitch felt naked, and not metaphorically. He hoped like hell he wasn't, but there were bigger problems right now.

Mitch remained patient with his uncommunicative guest. He tried to understand the bird's point of view and see where things went. Fifteen minutes or so passed, and Mitch ran out of bird jokes when he heard something in the distance. "Perry,..." he now called the bird by name as if it were a pet. "Are you real Perry or is this a bad dream?"

His imaginary feathered friend took off. Something, other than Mitch's jokes, had spooked him. Mitch thought the last joke weak, but he didn't think it weak enough to chase Perry, away. He couldn't understand how the bird could disappear so quickly, but the way his head felt, he didn't make an effort to figure it out. Mitch guessed he had about an hour or so of sunlight left. As he bobbed around once again, Wizard Island came back into view.

Something was approaching. From this distance, it appeared to be a boat. Whatever… it was coming directly at him, and fast. Mitch wondered if the whole thing was a hallucination. A tear fell from his face and made a noisy entry into the lake.

As the object grew closer, it looked as if it held a single person, perhaps two. No, he saw one, but his tired eyes weren't able to make out male, female—or falcon. The vehicle appeared to be a type of hovercraft because it was more above the water than in it. It slowed just before getting to the Old Man and Mitch. Peering over the side wearing a strange look on his face was Jack.

"Jack is that you?" was all Mitch could think to say. He remembered being a little cautious of his best friend these days. Besides, he wasn't sure if what he was witnessing was real. He lowered his head, finding new energy, he picked it slowly back up with as much strength as he could muster. Taking a deep breath, he hoped like hell Jack could help him. Man, did he miss Mabey.

"Yeah, Mitch, it's me. Let me cut you loose. You'll have to get up on this thing fast. We may have only a minute or two before they're on us. If they catch us, we'll probably die."

Jack took out his pocketknife and sawed away at the rope.

"Thanks, Jack. My head hurts so badly, and I can't feel my legs or my jewels." Mitch panted trying to catch his breath after the last sentence. He focused on each breath. Mabey would be proud of his vinyasa at this moment in time.

"Jack, are you okay? I'm so tired and sore."

Jack cut the strange rope-like material around Mitch's chest.

"Shit, your hands are tied as well. I have to stick my head under water and feel around to get you free. I hope your feet aren't tied. I'm afraid we don't have much time. Are your feet tied?"

"I can't tell. Jack, I'm so cold."

"Your lips are swollen and blue. I almost have you." Jack re-gripped the knife. "Here goes, bud; I'll be right back." Jack leveraged his feet against the edge of the craft and then stretched over the side as far as he could, dunking in the water, extending both hands. He felt with his fingers and found the rope around Mitch's hands. There was a gap which was good. He sawed, making quick work of the rope. Out of breath, Jack lifted and looked around. So did Mitch—no one was coming. Yet.

"Damn, the water is cold; how're you holding up?"

"All good, my brotha, now that you're here." Mitch did his best to sound strong.

"Good. One more dunk and I should have you free. That's if your feet are free. If not, you might be on your own, bud."

Jack smiled and then ducked under one more time. Mitch replied, but to deaf ears as Jack was under the water already. "How is Mabey? Don't suppose you've seen or heard from her, have you?"

Thirty seconds later Jack reappeared and shook his head. "Dammit, the water is cold. How long you been in here? Come on, help me out." Jack grabbed Mitch's shoulder, pulling him towards the craft. Mitch started toward the side straining as he lifted both hands upwards.

"My feet feel free Jack." His lips smacked into each other, and his teeth chattered.

"You better hope they are, bud, 'cause I ain't diving in to cut them free. I love you, man, but not that much."

Mitch forced a smile, then extended his bleeding wrists and shriveled-up hands.

"Come on, bro. I'm going to pull. I'll try not to hurt you, but I might scrape you up a bit."

"Before who is on us, Jack?"

"Seriously, Mitch, help me get your fat ass in here." Jack pulled, and Mitch spun around so his back was against the edge of the craft.

Jack finally got Mitch over the side and into the boat. Other than his wrists, there didn't appear to be any external damage. Mitch stumbled to his feet and immediately fell back down. He rallied, wiping crusted blood from his forehead, stood again, albeit wobbly, as he took the sweatshirt Jack handed him, wrapping it around his waist before sagging.

"Don't try to stand just yet. Your legs are too weak. Geezus, Mitch, I didn't realize the water was that cold." He stared at Mitch's lower half.

Mitch replied with chattering teeth, "Very funny."

"Hang on, little man; we gotta go." Jack laughed.

"What is going on? Why are you here, and where is Jasper?"

"We don't have any time to chat right now. Trust me. I'll explain everything as soon as we're safe on dry land."

Mitch was so relieved to see Jack. He grabbed something to steady himself. He wasn't sure what. A seat handle or something. Jack pressed a button, and they were quickly zipping towards the shoreline.

Jack looked over his shoulder and spoke to Mitch. "I have something to tell you, and it's serious."

Mitch couldn't stop shivering as his body temperature tried to acclimate to the warmer air. "Now what?"

Mitch looked around as they accelerated away from the Old Man of the Lake. He hoped he never saw that damn floating tree again. Mitch watched Jack push his hair back realizing how handsome his friend was and what a welcome sight. There was silence between the two as the cooling breeze tingled the tip of his head. A bit of strength came back to his body. Looking forward, he wondered where they were going. He carefully touched his mouth and ran a finger over lips that felt huge and puffy. They were cold and starting to itch and hurt. His head still pounded, but his body was bouncing back. He became increasingly aware of the benefits of being healthy, thankful he was in good shape as the shoreline was getting much closer. Whatever boat they were in was smooth and fast.

Jack touched something—controls Mitch surmised—in the craft, and it slowed. The shore was close. Mitch could feel his toes and see them wiggle. He stood, gathering his legs under him as he steadied himself, grabbing the console for support.

A voice came from what sounded like Jack's ass. Jack reached into his back pocket and pulled out a walkie-talkie. He recalled how he'd left Jasper's in the seat of his Jeep and wondered how much hell he'd receive on his little oversight.

"Here, Mitch, sounds like someone wants to talk with you." Jack reached back and placed the walkie-talkie onto Mitch's open palm. "Press down on the button, and just say hi."

Mitch put the device close to his swollen lips, which rubbed against the device. He pressed the button down gently and said, "Hello."

"Well, I'll be a son of a gun, you piece of shit. It's about god-damned time you responded."

The voice on the other end was obvious, and Mitch could tell from the inflection that it was a relieved one. He smiled but didn't respond. He and Jack coasted the last few feet into shore. Mitch wanted to ask what was going on, but it was all he could do to stay upright. He figured there'd be time enough for Q & A.

Mitch handed the walkie-talkie to Jack who slid it into his pocket as he got hold of Mitch's shoulder. Jack's voice showed concern. This was the friend he remembered, not the stranger of the last couple of days. Mitch kept his balance, body shaking, and held the side of the craft. Jack's hair was a crazy mess from the wind, but he had a confident, comforting air about him. Mitch needed his supportive friend now more than ever.

As the boat slid its final few feet to the bank, Mitch looked past Jack toward the shore where a familiar face waited on a deer trail. Jasper was a welcome face for sure, but the one face Mitch really wanted to see, and the person he wanted holding him, was missing. Mitch had a flash that perhaps Mabey was at the top of the ridge waiting for him, but his heart knew this wasn't the case as Jack reached for him. His best friend uttered the words, "Mitch, let's go. We need to get back to Rogue River—and now."

304

To Be Continued...

In

The

Rogue River

Incident

Case XI

Book II

Chapter 1 available
in the following pages.

Author's Remarks

Don't miss Mitch and his entourage as they return in book II of *The Rogue River Incident.* The stakes are raised as the quest continues to figure out what is going on in their little Pacific Northwest town of Rogue River.

I would like to thank Katherine Mayfield for her creative suggestions early in the editing process, Jennifer Dessert for line editing, Cindy Davis - The Fiction Doctor, for story editing, Jill Foltz for proof and copyediting, and finally, Dan Van Ross for the awesome book cover.

Thanks to the Native Americans, specifically the Klamath Tribes, for pointing me in the right direction for using some of their language in this novel. Any Native American words and phrases are those from the Klamath Tribes and were taken directly from their website:

http://www.klamathtribes.org/mobile/sentences.html
https://www.facebook.com/KlamathTribes
San'aaWawli ʔan ʔambo - I want some water.

Moo ʔan dic hoslta - I feel great, I am feeling very fine.

If you enjoyed this novel, please take a moment and write a review on Amazon, Goodreads, or the platform on which you purchased it. An independent author's best friend are thoughtful reviews. Thank you.

Notes

1. Maccabee, Bruce 1949 "The Rogue River Incident", Nicap.org
   http://www.nicap.org/reports/490524rogue.htm

Drawing from PBBSR #14, page 86

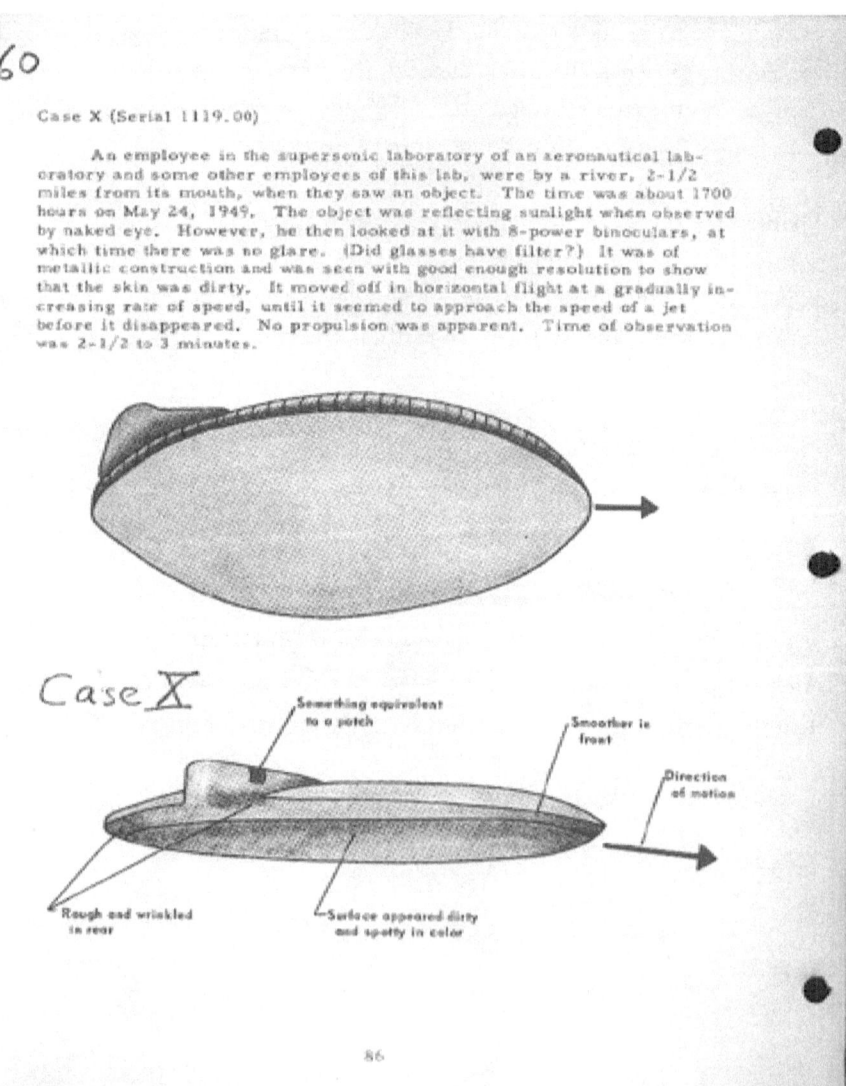

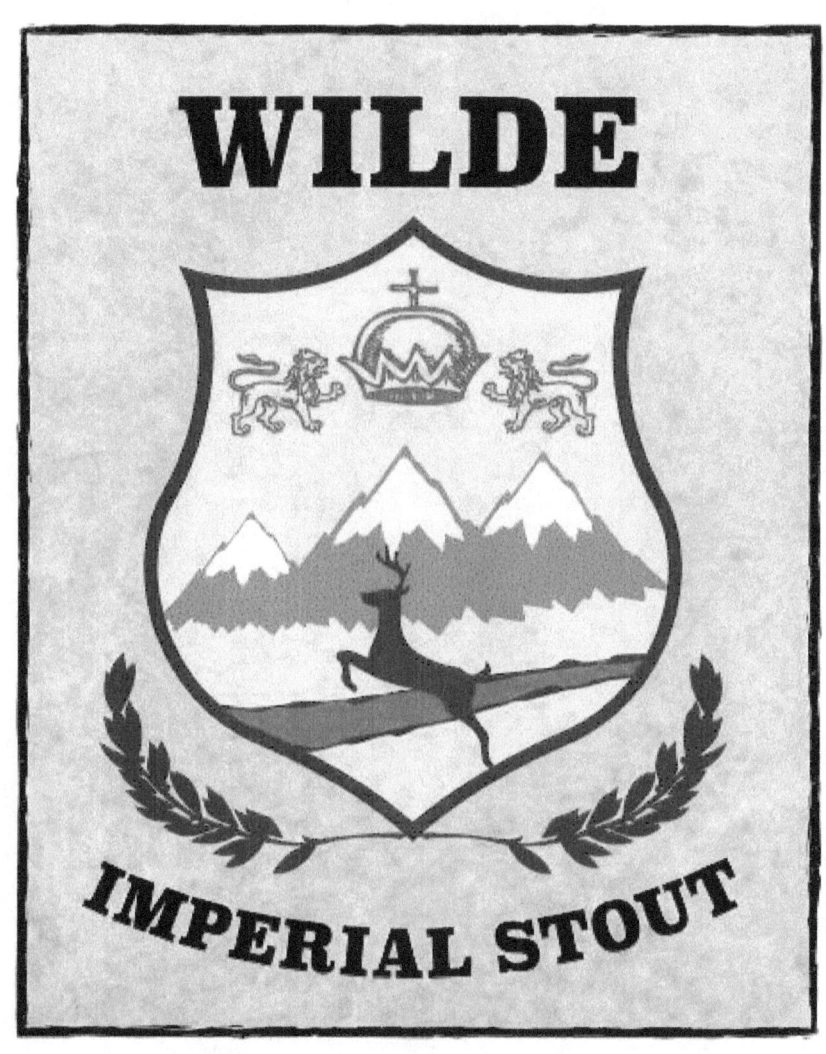

Mike's Social Media Presence

Web Site: MikeWaltersNovels.com

Facebook: https://www.facebook.com/MikeWalters24

Twitter: https://twitter.com/MikeAWalters

Instagram: https://www.instagram.com/mike_walters_novelist/

Pinterest: https://www.pinterest.com/MikeAWalters24/

The Rogue River Incident - Book II

Chapter 1

Let's Go Hunt Some Clowns

Nauseated, Mitch struggled to keep his balance as intense pain ricocheted back and forth against his skull. His best friend and rescuer, Jack Jenson, piloted the alien-looking watercraft toward the bank. Focusing on Jack kept Mitch from vomiting as he wondered how Jack knew how to drive the damn thing. Trying to speak, unable to muster the energy, the pain overwhelmed him, so he tried shifting his thoughts to his wife Mabey. With quiet desperation, he wished she were here, knowing her presence alone would be a comforting salve. Tingling lips felt massive as if he had rubbed mango rind all over them and they'd swelled in an allergic reaction. An accident that once happened to Mabey. She liked the result on her lips so much; she started thinking about lip injections. Mitch encouraged her to refrain; her lips were perfect as they were.

Mitch watched as Jack turned and looked directly into his eyes. Reassurance soothed Mitch because Jack seemed familiar again. The last few days, ever since Jack had been shot with an arrow filled with a mysterious silver liquid, Mitch had been hoping to see his friend in a normal, and expected, state. It was comforting to see the familiar glint in Jack's eyes again, and he hoped his friend was back for good. At this very moment, Mitch may not have Mabey's warmth and loving touch, but he did have Jack back. Or so it appeared.

Jack starting to speak, stopped abruptly. Mitch could see he was struggling with what to say. What came out of Jack's mouth roused Mitch with a new intensity; his head pain and swollen mouth forgotten in an instant.

"Mitch, I don't know how to say what I am about to say without coming right out with it."

"Sp, Sp, Spit it out, Jack. I'm, not, in, the, mood, for, games."

The words struggled to get out of Mitch's mouth, tumbling over his lips like a five year old trying to read for the first time.

"I'm sorry, my brother, but the town of Rogue River is under attack, and people are in hiding. We need to get back at once."

"Sure, Jack, but why so quick?"

As Mitch continued to warm up, the swelling in his lips subsided and his speech began to sound normal again. At least to him.

"Mabey is missing, Mitch."

As if the cold water hadn't done enough temporary damage to Mitch's manhood, Jack's last comment about Mabey took shrinkage to a new level. Mitch slumped over and fell onto the floor of the craft. He grabbed his head with both hands and carefully squeezed, trying to push the pain away and focus on what he had just heard. He moved his lips back and forth, opening and closing his mouth forcing the movement to quicken the blood and hasten his skin's return to normal. He dropped his hands, rose to one knee, and raised his head in a newfound birth of energy and resilience. He could hurt later; right now, it was time to focus.

Jack roused Mitch from his thoughts with encouraging words.

"Mitch, come on we'll find her."

Mitch listening intently to Jack, in a rare instance, had no idea what to say. He was trapped in defeatist thoughts.

Jack looking forward again, toward the bank, pointed and said, "Mitch, your backpack, and clothes are over by that large outcrop of rocks next to the tree."

"Is that Jasper?"

"Yes, it is. He's the reason I found you. As soon as we get you ashore, get dressed. I don't know how much time we have to get out of here unnoticed. I'm thinking minutes, so the quicker we get in your Jeep and on the road, the better."

Jack, concerned with the fading daylight didn't voice the thought since he wasn't sure Mitch heard much of what he was saying right now.

"My Jeep is around the other side of the lake, Jack."

"No, Jasper brought it around. It's at the top of the rim, so we need to hustle and get up there as quick as you can manage. So, suck it up, mister. Your wife needs you. You'll have time to hurt later. Okay?"

"Shit, Jack, I can hardly feel the lower half of my body. I'm so cold, I think my balls are completely sucked up inside my stomach."

Jack smiled. "They'll drop, bud; don't worry. If not, then I'm sure Mabey can help you with them."

Jack decided he would mention Mabey as often as possible right now to motivate Mitch. Not that his friend – hell, his brother – needed extra incentive, but Jack had read somewhere that adrenaline can be a wonderful elixir. He knew Mitch wouldn't have any issue in cranking out adrenaline now that Mabey needed him.

Mitch replied in what Jack thought was an eerily calm voice.

"You said Mabey is missing, Jack. How do you know she's missing?"

Jack eased the craft the final few feet to shore; Mitch felt it settle and stabilize. Jasper stood on the bank ready to help if needed.

"Mitch, let's get off this thing. Get your clothes on, and we'll hike up to your Jeep. We'll have plenty of time to talk about Mabey on the ride back to Rogue River."

Mitch grabbed Jack by the arm and steadied himself, finding new strength and stubborn determination in his legs. The sweatshirt Jack had given him to tie around his waist fell off leaving him naked again. He didn't care.

Mitch grabbed Jack with as much force and strength that he could muster.

"Damn it, Jack, tell me what the hell is going on?"

A familiar voice came from the bank.

"Geezus, Wilde, the water was pretty cold, huh?"

Mitch ignored Jasper. "Jack, I mean it. Where is Mabey?"

"We don't know, Mitch, and let go of my arm. We're on the same side. Remember?"

"Are we, Jack? I've seen a lot of weird shit surrounding you the last couple of days. Ever since that fucking arrow dissolved in your shoulder, you haven't been the same person. Am I right, Jasper?"

Jasper kicked the ground. Mitch knew the old guy was searching for words.

"Let's get going, you two nannies. You can verbally cage-fight in the Jeep. We need to get back to Rogue River. We're running out of daylight."

Jack jumped off the craft and headed up the trail. As he walked away, he heard Mitch try to yell, with a hint of desperation in a tired voice.

"Don't you dare walk away from me. How do you know Mabey is missing, Jack?"

Jack stopped and pivoted to face both Jasper and Mitch.

"I found her car in the middle of town with the door open and the keys in the ignition. That's all I know. Now get him dressed, Jasper, and you two meet me at the Jeep. And, hurry, damn it! We'll be lucky to get out of here as it is."

Jasper reached out and took Mitch's hand, helping him off the craft. Mitch watched as Jack moved up the deer trail toward the rim of Crater Lake.

"Come on, Wilde. We need to get you dressed and gone from here. We can talk more on the ride."

As Mitch stepped off the craft, it lifted with a low hum, then spun and started moving away from the lakeshore under its own power. It was as if someone was pulling it.

"Do you see that, Jasper?"

"Yes, Mitch, a lot of strange shit is going on right now. This Alien boat can be added to the list."

Mitch tried to smile. He remembered he was naked when he felt a mosquito bite his ass. He swatted at the damn thing.

Jasper guided Mitch toward the rocks and his backpack. He picked it up and handed it to Mitch.

"Sorry, Mitch, I couldn't find your underwear. You'll have to free-ball it. I think most everything else is here, even your shoes. Now hurry and get dressed. You can tell me about it later if you remember. Shit, Wilde, were you sun bathing or taking photos? Your clothes were scattered all over the place. Amazing I found everything but your shorts."

Mitch stood and reached for his pack. He searched his clouded memory. The last image it returned: packing his camera gear to reach Jasper as fast as possible and show him the photos of Wizard Island with a ship flying into it.

Mitch struggled to button his Levis. He slid on his shirt, then plopped on the ground to pull on his socks and shoes. His feet were swollen and tender. Mitch stood as best he could, sensing Jasper's impatience.

"Jasper, should we trust him? We both know something has been going on with him."

Jasper patted Mitch on the shoulder, and Mitch soaked up the reassuring gesture.

"Mitch?"

"Yeah, old man?"

"I'm going to be honest with you; you know I'm like that. So, no, right now I don't trust Jack. We don't have much choice, though, Mitch. If it weren't for his showing up and taking that strange Alien boat out to you, tonight would have been your last night on earth. That damn Old Man of the Lake had hold of you and wasn't going to let go. So let's get up to your Jeep, get back into town, and find that wife of yours. For now, we have to trust him."

"Jasper?"

"Geezus, Wilde. Hurry up, will you?"

Jasper stopped and turned. Mitch saw the concern in his face as the old man's eyes pleaded for him to hurry.

Mitch made a weak try at running in place. His feet were mushy, and his legs felt like rubber. His entire body itched and felt like dagger tips pricking him from his chest on down. He adjusted his backpack, and as he reached Jasper, he grabbed his shoulder to catch his breath and steady himself.

"Jasper, I'm glad you're here. I don't know how I'd be handling this if you weren't with me."

"Good, Wilde. Now, man up, and let's go hunt some clowns."

Mitch smiled at Jasper's reference to clowns. It seemed like so long ago when Jasper told Mitch the story of how his first, and only wife left him for a rodeo clown.

Jasper grabbed Mitch and started pulling him up the trail.

"I can tell you're laughing a little inside, Wilde, and don't worry, I'm not going to get pissed at you. I feel better now knowing your brain is functioning. Good to see you have your memory working."

Mitch slipped on a rock turning his ankle. He wondered why he didn't register pain but his cold body was still numb masking potential damage. Sighing, he breathed in, shook his leg gently, and almost fell over.

The daylight continued to fade, and he wanted – hell, needed – the warmth of the sun. Mitch felt his shoes flex against the gravel trail. As he struggled to maintain Jasper's pace, he wondered when the last time he'd turned on the heater in his Jeep.

The rest of the story will be available 9/28/2018.

To finish the story, please go to my website and click on any number of links on the "buy" page for your eBook or print copy of The Rogue River Incident --- Case XI, Book II.

If you enjoyed this novel, please take a moment and write a review on Amazon, Goodreads, or the platform on which you purchased it. Thank you for purchasing and reading.

Please follow Mike on Facebook: MikeWaltersNovelist, Twitter: @MikeAWalters, Instagram: Mike_Walters_Novelist, Goodreads: Mike_Walters, and for more information in general including photography, media kits, bio, author writings, and more, please go to my website: MikeWaltersNovels.com.

For more Oregon independent authors, please keep an eye on SelfReliantPress.com in the coming months.

Self Reliant Press

Featuring Indie Authors

www.ingramcontent.com/pod-product-compliance
Lightning Source LLC
Chambersburg PA
CBHW030624110726
47901CB00002B/303